the Comeback Cowboy

NEW YORK TIMES BESTSELLING AUTHOR

MAISEY YATES

USA TODAY BESTSELLING AUTHOR

CAITLIN CREWS

JACKIE ASHENDEN • NICOLE HELM

Maisey Yates is a *New York Times* bestselling author of over one hundred romance novels. Whether she's writing strong, hardworking cowboys; dissolute princes; or multigenerational family stories, she loves getting lost in fictional worlds. An avid knitter with a dangerous yarn addiction and an aversion to housework, Maisey lives with her husband and three kids in rural Oregon. Check out her website, maiseyyates.com, or find her on Facebook.

USA TODAY bestselling, RITA® Award–nominated and critically acclaimed author **Caitlin Crews** has written more than one hundred books and counting. She has a master's degree and PhD in English literature, thinks everyone should read more category romance, and is always available to discuss her beloved alpha heroes. Just ask. She lives in the Pacific Northwest with her comic book–artist husband, is always planning her next trip and will never, ever, read all the books in her to-be-read pile. Thank goodness.

Jackie Ashenden writes dark, emotional stories with alpha heroes who've just got the world to their liking only to have it blown wide apart by their kick-ass heroines. She lives in Auckland, New Zealand, with her husband and two kids. When she's not torturing alpha males and their gutsy heroines, she can be found drinking chocolate martinis, reading anything she can lay her hands on, wasting time on social media or being forced to go mountain biking with her husband.

Nicole Helm writes down-to-earth contemporary romance and fast-paced romantic suspense. She lives with her husband and two sons in Missouri. Visit her website: www.nicolehelm.com.

the Comeback Cowboy

MAISEY YATES
CAITLIN CREWS
JACKIE ASHENDEN · NICOLE HELM

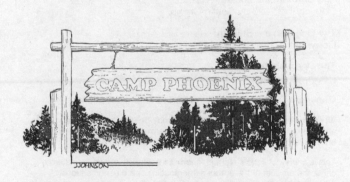

ISBN-13: 978-1-335-50818-8

The Comeback Cowboy

Copyright © 2023 by Harlequin Enterprises ULC

The One with the Hat
Copyright © 2023 by Jackie Ashenden

The One with the Locket
Copyright © 2023 by Caitlin Crews

The One with the Bullhorn
Copyright © 2023 by Nicole Helm

The One with the Trophy
Copyright © 2023 by Maisey Yates

Copyright © 2023 by Jeff Johnson, interior illustrations

Recycling programs
for this product may
not exist in your area.

For questions and comments about the quality of this book, please contact us at CustomerService@Harlequin.com.

HQN
22 Adelaide St. West, 41st Floor
Toronto, Ontario M5H 4E3, Canada
www.Harlequin.com

Printed in Lithuania

Contents

The One with the Hat

Jackie Ashenden

Voltron FTW!

PROLOGUE

SHERIFF BILL MCCLAIN had grown up playing cops and robbers in the rural ranches of Southern Oregon, always the cop. He'd been a cop his entire adult life, and even now, as a middle-aged man, he got a simple thrill from putting the *bad guy* behind bars. Even on days when *bad guys* and *bars* weren't so simple.

On those complicated days, he had Camp Phoenix. His baby. The highlight of his life. Because as a young man, he'd seen the sad fact that the ones who suffered most from crime and bad behavior were the children of the perpetrators.

So, for almost fifteen years, he'd built Camp Phoenix from a small program of tents in the Oregon wilderness, to the fully functioning, funded and scholarship-offering summer camp it was today.

Tonight was their opening evening services. The campers had had a few days to get acquainted with the layout, the rules, and now they were all hiking up to the chapel where they'd have their official camp opening ceremony.

Bill led the group walking under the madrone trees until he reached the end of the aisle. The campers filed in, counselors spaced between them to keep watch on the newly formed friendships, alliances and bitter feuds. But as the teens settled, a few of his counselors came to the front, as they did every year.

These four bright men had been his personal projects. He'd seen something in them. They'd become closer than campers; they were like his sons, though he'd never had a biological son of his own.

They were also *examples*, of everything Camp Phoenix could be to a young kid finding himself—or herself—in deep trouble.

"Welcome to Camp Phoenix," Bill said, and he didn't need a microphone. His voice boomed across the rough-hewn pews made from trees. "This summer can be just about anything you make of it. And you're a very lucky group because we have some of the best counselors around. I know you don't want to hear about an old fart like me." This got the usual smattering of surprised laughs out of the desperate-to-be-bored crowd of teens.

Desperate to find something or someone to change their lives.

"But I want to introduce you to our counselors, who came right from where you're sitting. Flint Decker, who's now a sheriff's deputy right here in Jasper Creek, Lincoln Traeger—US Marshal Traeger to you lot, Jackson Hart, who's just finished the rigorous application process to become a DEA agent, and Duke Cody." He slapped the young man on the shoulder as he came to stand beside him. "Another sheriff's deputy here."

Bill continued with his usual welcoming notes. That he expected respect and responsibility. That there could be fun...once the work was done. Then, as he always did, he handed off the spotlight to Gale Lawson, the social worker and art therapist he let run the female side of things.

He personally wasn't any good at that. Even if he did have a daughter of his own. Who was currently scrambling toward him. She came up next to him, pushing up to her tiptoes to whisper in his ear.

"Dad! Those girls are talking about fighting. Like, actually punching fighting," Clementine said, pointing to a cluster of girls in the back.

Bill sighed. He'd prefer Gale deal with the girls, but she was still talking to the crowd, so Bill got up and moved around the crowd to the little commotion now happening in the back corner.

Two girls were facing off, angry looks on both their faces. Mrs. Zee, the godsend who kept the dining hall running, was standing between them while her little helper for the summer stood off to the corner, her glasses sliding down her nose.

"Now, what's going on here?" Bill demanded, keeping his voice low so he didn't interrupt Gale.

"Nothing," the girls both hissed, glaring at each other. Not him.

"Now, the first thing about Camp Phoenix you two are going to have to learn is that y'all don't have to be friends. But you've got to learn to work together."

They were both dark-haired and angry, small and full of vinegar.

"Why?" the girl with hot eyes and a belligerent expression asked.

"Because I said so."

"That's a *terrible* reason."

Bill wanted to smile, but he kept his stern expression in place. There was a lot of potential in all that backbone, if Gale could get through that angry shell.

The other girl had her chin up. She was glaring over at Flint, and Bill remembered Flint had arrested the girl himself just a few months back, for stealing. "I'm more than happy to work together," she said loftily, then smirked at the other girl.

"I'll be in charge of this one," Mrs. Zee offered, putting a hand on the girl closest to her.

"Then you'll come with me," he said to the argumentative one. He didn't wait, didn't look back; he simply walked away, expecting her to follow.

She did.

They concluded the welcome ceremony, then began the hike back down the hill to the main camp area. Bill let the counselors take the lead, let Clementine bound off with the other girls, and he stayed behind as he often did during the welcome ceremony.

His boys stayed with him.

They hiked in the quiet, long after everyone else had made it back to the camp, and when he got to the space where the trees thinned out, he could see all of Camp Phoenix laid out before him.

Everything he'd built. All the good he'd done, as evidenced at the very least by the four men he'd introduced tonight.

"I'm proud of you boys. I hope you know that."

There was the uncomfortable silence of men who'd learned how to be responsible, good, upstanding men...but were still a little bit those lost boys at heart. "Go on now. Get to your bunks," he ordered them, as he stayed behind.

All the lights but a few were out. The bright Oregon stars shone above.

He was not a perfect man, Lord knew, but he had built this place, and because of the quality of people it attracted, something...magical happened here. Healing. Happiness.

Hope.

And his hope was that it always would.

THE ONE WITH THE HAT

CHAPTER ONE

BREE WHITE WALKED quickly over the gravel of the parking area and she didn't look back. Time was of the essence.

She'd arrived at Camp Phoenix, the summer camp for juvenile delinquents that had changed her life back when she'd been fourteen, a full thirty minutes before she was supposed to, mainly so she could claim the best cabin before everyone else arrived—and she wasn't ashamed to admit it.

It was a little surprising that Jackson Hart, the former DEA agent who'd bought the run-down camp and sent out the call for volunteers to help get it ready for a new season of campers, wasn't here to greet her. He was apparently living in the shabby house near the camp entrance, but she hadn't seen hide nor hair of him.

Then again, she *was* early. And she didn't mind not seeing Jackson. He'd been his usual drill-sergeant self, harassing her relentlessly to volunteer to help, and while she was all about helping, she wasn't a fan of being told what to do. Never had been.

Even ten years ago, when she'd been sent to Camp Phoenix by Sheriff Bill McClain, the man who'd started the camp, she'd hated all the rules and regulations, and had chafed against them. Yet those same rules and regulations had given her a structure and routine that her chaotic childhood never had. They'd changed her life.

Camp Phoenix had basically been the best thing to ever

happen to her. That's why she was here. And it wasn't anything to do with Jackson Hart, so much as it was her, wanting to give back. Perhaps help change a few lives the way hers had been changed, and for the better. She was looking forward to it.

Bree paused in front of the small cluster of buildings surrounded by a green lawn and bordered by tall pines. Everything looked…smaller than she remembered, not to mention a lot more neglected. There were a few dilapidated cabins that were the bunk rooms, and the big dining hall where Mrs. Zee, the cook, used to reign supreme. The showers and bathrooms were in their own building, and then there was the administration cabin. And over there by the dining hall, the art hall that was once run by Gale Lawson.

And…ugh. There was Hollyhock Hill, which all the campers had to climb at 6:00 a.m. every morning to raise the flag, and where the day's chores were handed out.

She'd never been much of a morning person, but that, in particular, had felt like torture. Well, they were all adults now, and presumably, there would be no 6:00 a.m. wake-up calls this time around.

The camp looked deserted, which was good, so Bree headed over to the least-run-down-looking of the cabins, where the counselors used to sleep. Jackson had said at least one of the cabins was better than the others, so she was assuming it was this one, and that she could claim it for herself.

She assumed no one would be sharing like they once had, when it was ten to a room. At least, *she* wouldn't be sharing; not these days. She'd come a long way from her past and her family of low-level criminals who expected her to follow the same path they had. Now she had her own place in Jasper Creek and a great job as a real estate agent. She didn't have to steal for a living like her folks had.

And all thanks to Camp Phoenix.

Nothing at all to do with Flint Decker.

Bree scowled as she headed toward the old counselors cabin, trying to shove off the irritating reminder that Flint Decker had been her arresting officer back when she'd been fourteen. He'd caught her shoplifting from the local 7-Eleven, which was something she did not like to remember, if she could help it.

A bit difficult *not* to be reminded, though, when Jasper Creek had been virtually wallpapered with his handsome, arrogant face thanks to the sheriff's elections a couple of months back. She hadn't been able to get away from it. Even more annoying that he'd won the election. By a depressing margin.

She had nothing to do with him these days, determinedly ignoring him whenever they passed each other on the street. And she definitely didn't look behind her as he went by, noting the breadth of his shoulders, his narrow hips, long, powerful legs, and—

Bree nearly tripped over a piece of wood that seemed to be lying randomly in the grass, and only just stopped herself from an ignominious face-plant.

Damn new sneakers. Nothing to do with thinking about stupid Flint. She'd bought them especially for tramping about the camp and they were already giving her blisters.

She took a quick look around to see if anyone else had turned up to witness her embarrassing stumble, but the place was still deserted.

Just as well.

Bree examined her brand-new, spotless blue jeans for any suspicion of dirt, but they seemed to have escaped. She brushed them off just in case, since she wasn't a fan of dirt. She wasn't a fan of jeans either, but the little business skirts she usually wore weren't very practical, so she'd gone on a bit of a shopping spree.

She wasn't that sullen, angry teen who had turned up at camp with nothing, not even a sleeping bag.

She'd come prepared this time.

She approached the cabin and cautiously pushed open the door.

It was one room with a wooden floor and three sturdy wooden bunk beds pushed up against the unlined walls. The floor looked clean, at least, but one of the bunk beds had no mattresses, which left four beds to choose from. It smelled a bit musty but nothing an open window wouldn't fix.

Bree gave herself a moment to frown at the spiderwebs in the ceiling between the rafters, then directed her attention to which bunk to choose. One of the top bunks, of course, since those had always been the most prized. Back in the day, there used to be battles. There was one girl, Violet Cook, who Bree had taken an instant dislike to, and one day, she'd hung Violet's sleeping bag from a tree before stealing her bunk. That had earned her toilet cleaning for a week, but it had been worth it.

Of course, she'd never do anything like that now. Now she loved her life and was no longer angry at the entire world.

Moving over to the bunk beside the window, she carefully examined the mattress on the top bed, since that seemed to be the least lumpy, and decided it would do.

She didn't like being uncomfortable, but camp—as Sheriff McClain had always said—wasn't about being comfortable, so she'd resigned herself to a bit of discomfort. Not that she had a choice, since her house was having its plumbing upgraded and she couldn't be there anyway. Really, coming to camp was excellent timing in many ways.

Bree put her little suitcase onto the bottom bunk in preparation for unpacking.

Other people would be arriving, she assumed. Given Jackson's insistence on the importance of getting the camp up and running before the end of June, and given how he was a bossy asshole, he'd probably called every single person who'd ever stayed here and guilt-tripped them into helping.

She hoped they would be nice people, not—

"Please don't tell me we have to share. Goddamn Jackson."

Bree froze. She recognized that voice. No. Did it have to be? Not Violet Cook, whose sleeping bag she'd stolen. Not Violet Cook, who'd treated every day at camp like she was auditioning for *Survivor* and had basically lorded it over everyone, trying to prove she was the baddest.

Surely, she wasn't here. Surely not.

Yet the door was already opening and in came a small, stunningly pretty woman with long, wavy black hair, black eyes, and wearing the most ridiculously feminine and flouncy maxidress Bree had ever seen. She tottered in on sky-high wedges, towing behind her a huge bright pink suitcase, and the moment she spotted Bree, she stopped dead.

The world's most awkward silence fell as ten years vanished in the blink of an eye.

"Great," Violet said, scowling. "Bree White. What the hell are you doing here?"

Bree had an urge to scowl back, but she forced it aside. She wasn't fourteen and feral anymore. She was twenty-four and a professional, with a reputation for being the nicest Realtor at her agency. Violet might not have changed, but Bree certainly had.

"Hi, Violet," she said, smiling determinedly. "Nice to see you. We should definitely catch up later, after you've found your own cabin. I think the one next door is still free—"

"Unfortunately, we're sharing," Violet interrupted, obviously unimpressed. "None of the other cabins are habitable."

Bree blinked. That was *not* what Jackson had said. "Sharing? What? But I thought…" She trailed off as Violet, ignoring her, eyed the bunk bed Bree was standing next to before moving over to the bunk pushed up against the opposite wall.

Bree opened her mouth to try to make the silence more pleasant, when the cabin door opened again, and two more women came in.

This time she barely stifled a groan. Kinley Parker and Clementine McClain? Seriously? She hadn't known Kinley that well. She'd been so shy and quiet she'd virtually blended into the wallpaper, but apparently lived in Jasper Creek, not that Bree had ever seen her around. Clementine, on the other hand, was Sheriff McClain's daughter, and Bree remembered her as being the biggest tattletale ever at camp, treating every rule like it was handed down by God himself. No wonder she'd ended up as the sheriff's deputy, or so Bree had heard.

Anyway, this was great. Just great. So, what? She had to share her cabin with all three of them? Unacceptable. She was going to need a word with Jackson.

Keeping her smile pasted on, Bree directed it to Kinley and Clementine. "Oh, wow, you guys are here as well? How great is this?"

Kinley clearly did not think this was great. Her brown

eyes were woeful behind her large glasses as she looked at the bunk situation, and Bree found herself putting a possessive hand on the top bed of the bunk she'd chosen. "Sorry, this one's mine."

"And don't even think about the top bunk here," Violet said without turning around. "It'll have my pillow on it in approximately two seconds." She'd opened her giant pink suitcase on the bottom bunk, and had pulled out a soft-looking pillow in a pillowcase embroidered all over with wildflowers, and... Were those fairy lights?

Kinley sighed, glanced at the third mattress-less bunk and sighed again. "I guess I'm here, then," she said and shuffled over to the bunk where Bree stood. "Do you mind if I take the bottom?"

Bree gave her the biggest smile she could manage. "No, not at all."

"Uh, hi." Clementine gave a nervous-looking wave, an equally nervous-looking smile on her face. Her hair was still as red as Bree remembered, and she still had as many freckles.

She glanced with some trepidation at Violet's bunk and the only other habitable bed. "Um, well, I suppose I'll take this one."

Violet had now put her pillow on the top bunk and was in the process of hauling out what appeared to be bed linens, along with what were definitely fairy lights.

"I don't think we're allowed those in here," Clementine said as she stared at the bed currently taken up by Violet's giant case. "The fairy lights, I mean. At least, I don't think you can?"

"Too bad," Violet said. "I'm not doing lights-out at nine. Especially not when I want to read. Plus—" she sent a chal-

lenging look to the room in general "—they're pretty." Her
gaze settled on Bree. "This bed stays mine, okay?"

Bree's smile became fixed. Dammit. It appeared Violet
hadn't forgotten the whole sleeping bag/bunk stealing incident. "No problem," she said brightly.

Kinley, meanwhile, had sat down on the bunk underneath Bree's, squeezing herself awkwardly between Bree's
case and the end of the bed.

And suddenly, it was too much. The room felt tiny and
there were too many people in it, people she didn't like
and didn't know, and none of this was anything like what
she'd expected.

There had to be somewhere else she could stay. In fact,
she'd take it up with Jackson right now.

Her smile felt fake and forced, but if she didn't smile,
she was going to end up growling, and she didn't want to
growl. She wasn't a feral beast.

"I'm just going to…um…" She went over to the door
and paused. "No one touch my stuff."

It wasn't until she'd gone through it that she realized
what she'd said. As if she were fourteen again, hating the
camp, and Sheriff McClain, and basically everyone who'd
forced her here.

Ugh. She had to make sure she didn't fall back into old
patterns. That meant no growling or getting angry, or being
generally unpleasant. She was Bree White, the friendliest,
most professional, most successful Realtor in her agency,
and sharing a cabin with three of her enemies from a particularly dark time in her life wasn't *that* bad.

Still. It was worth checking other options, just to be sure.

Bree stopped outside the cabin, looking around at the
rest of the camp. Where the hell could Jackson be?

Then, from around the corner of the dining hall, came

a man wearing a very familiar hat. A battered black cowboy hat.

And her heart sank all the way into her brand-new sneakers.

So. Not only was she bunking with her three sworn enemies, but he was here too?

Please not him. Anyone but him.

But the man striding over the grass toward her didn't miraculously turn into someone else. He was tall, but then, he always had been. Even at twenty, his shoulders had been broad and his chest wide. The black cotton of the T-shirt he wore was stretched lovingly over a chest and shoulders that seemed even wider and more muscular ten years later. On the T-shirt there was a picture of a cabin in gold with a phoenix above it, wings outswept, and the words *Camp Phoenix* above, while underneath the cabin was the camp motto. Rise Up. Her brain had barely registered the T-shirt before it got distracted by the way the worn denim of his jeans clung to his narrow hips and powerful thighs.

Not that she was noticing his thighs. Not when eyes greener than the grass beneath her feet were focused on hers with magnetic intensity.

Flint Decker. Sheriff Flint Decker and his stupid hat.

Okay, if Jackson wasn't around, then she'd have a few words about sleeping arrangements with the sheriff himself.

Bree lifted her chin and prepared to do battle.

CHAPTER TWO

FLINT DECKER HAD been meaning to have a word with Bree White for months now, so when he'd seen her car go past Jackson's house, where he was staying while he was working on the camp, a full half hour before anyone was supposed to arrive, he'd immediately volunteered to go see if she needed anything.

He'd only just gotten to camp himself and, since he'd also noticed his deputy Clementine had arrived and that Jackson was busy grimacing over his welcome speech, he'd thought it the perfect time to greet the ladies.

Or rather, one particular lady.

A lady he still couldn't reconcile with the feral wildcat he'd arrested ten years ago for shoplifting.The wildcat who'd hissed and spit and kicked the front seat of his patrol car as soon as he'd put her in it.

Then she'd been at camp back when he'd been a camp counselor, though he hadn't had anything to do with her, preferring to keep his distance. After that, though, she'd disappeared off his radar, and then, two years ago, a gorgeous woman had walked into one of Jasper Creek's cafés where he'd been waiting for his usual coffee. She had long inky black hair and big dark eyes, and she'd been in a blue pencil skirt that had fitted her curves to perfection, a discreetly feminine white blouse with a couple of the top buttons undone and sexy blue pumps. Drop-dead gorgeous. He hadn't been able to stop staring.

It was only in the days afterward, when he noticed her photo popping up on for-sale signs in various yards, with her name attached, that he'd realized that Bree White, Realtor, was the same Bree White he'd arrested all those years ago.

The wildcat was all grown up. And she was hot.

Uncomfortably so.

To make matters worse, she'd been determinedly ignoring him whenever they happened to pass each other on the street or in a store or café. Treating him as if he was a complete stranger to her.

Initially he'd thought it was because she didn't remember him, but then it became clear there was a degree of intent in the way she looked past him as if he wasn't there. And he didn't think it was because she didn't remember him. It was because she did. After all, you didn't ignore someone that aggressively if you didn't know them from a bar of soap.

At first he'd been amused. Then, as the ignoring went on, he became less amused. People liked and respected him. They definitely did *not* ignore him, and especially not women. He wasn't one to blow his own horn, but he generally couldn't move for women. They were all over him. So it shouldn't have mattered that Bree White cut him dead every single time. Yet it did.

Flint had never been a man who sat back and let things come to him. He went out and got them himself. And he'd been thinking that maybe it was time to ask her what exactly her problem was and that maybe they could go for a drink to talk about it.

Then again, perhaps he shouldn't be thinking about asking the woman he'd arrested back when she was fourteen out on a date. He wasn't a rookie cop anymore or even the fledgling bad boy he'd been back in the day. He was the sheriff, and a good one, and he had a reputation to uphold.

Flint came to a stop in front of her and gave her his sheriff's smile, the one that normally inspired trust and respect in everyone he bestowed it on. And he couldn't help feeling pleased that she was actually looking at him now, her luminous dark eyes full of those sparks he remembered from years ago.

Seemed like you could take the woman out of the wildcat, but you couldn't take the wildcat out of the woman.

"Bree," he began.

"Sheriff Decker," she said, before he could go on. "I need to talk to either you or preferably Jackson about the accommodations."

Flint did not like the "preferably Jackson" part of that sentence at all. Jackson was a former DEA agent and his friend, whom he'd met right here at camp back when he'd been a teenager too, along with Lincoln Traeger and Duke Cody. And sure, Jackson could answer her question. But so could he.

He kept his gaze very firmly on hers, taking care not to let it drift down over the tight-fitting, new-looking jeans that showed off her luscious hips and thighs, or over the white casual shirt that had one of the top buttons undone, revealing an expanse of pale cleavage. He couldn't stop from noticing her hair, though, which was black and glossy and neat as a pin in a little ponytail, making him kind of want to pull out the elastic band that held it back and watch it fall all over her shoulders.

"Of course you can talk to me," he said pleasantly, smiling at her and forcing away thoughts about her hair since now was not the time. "What's the issue?"

She didn't smile back, a distinct coolness in her expression, not to mention the tiniest touch of ice in her voice. "I was under the assumption that we'd have our own cabins. That's what Jackson led me to believe."

A small prickle of irritation crept under Flint's skin. She wasn't responding to his smile at all, and she didn't seem to find his perfectly pleasant tone compelling. But most of all, there was absolutely zero acknowledgment of the fact that they had met before.

He didn't rile people up on purpose. That wasn't his job. His job was the law and the upholding of it, but he wasn't at Camp Phoenix in his role as sheriff. He was here as a favor to Jackson, to help out with getting the camp up and running again, and it was a cause he believed in. He used to come here himself as a teenager, and Sheriff Bill Mc-Clain, who used to run the camp, had been a mentor of his. Flint had gotten a lot out of camp then, so after Bill died and Jackson had bought it with the intention of reviving it, Flint had been first in line to help.

Except he *really* didn't like that after determinedly ignoring his existence for two years, Bree White had finally acknowledged him only so she could complain.

"Pretty sure Jackson said that at least one of the cabins would be ready for the volunteers." He kept his tone level despite his irritation because there was no point starting things off on the wrong foot.

She lifted her chin, as if she was looking down at him, even though she was a full head shorter than he was. "He said 'at least.' Which indicates that one cabin was the least of the cabins that would be ready. The implication, I can't help feeling, is that there would be more than one."

Flint's irritation prickled a little more. Seriously? No "Hi, how are you?" No "Long time, no see"? No "Sorry for ignoring you completely for two years"? Only disdain and an iciness that he couldn't understand. Was she really still pissed that he'd arrested her? Because if so, that was nuts. It had been ten years ago, and he hadn't so much as arrested her as taken her from a bad situation and brought her back to the station so Bill could help her.

"Well," he said, slightly less pleasantly than a few seconds earlier, though he kept on smiling, "I'm sure it did imply that. But implications are not facts, and the facts are that there is only one cabin ready."

For some reason, Bree glared at him. "That's ridiculous. I can't sleep there tonight. What about if I move the mattress to another cabin, then? They can't all be completely uninhabitable."

Flint's irritation deepened into annoyance. Getting this camp up and running was the important thing, not her being difficult about sleeping arrangements. Besides, complaining about having to share a room with other people at summer camp was stupid. She wasn't here on a vacation. She was here to help renovate the camp.

"This isn't a hotel, Miss White," he said, adding a hint of warning to the words. "You can't change rooms just because you don't like the one you're in."

People listened when he spoke in that tone of voice and then they did exactly what he said. But not, apparently, Bree White.

Her mouth compressed and her whole body stiffened as if he'd personally insulted her and not simply given her a light reprimand. "It's 'Ms.,' thank you very much."

"My point stands, *Ms.* White."

"I know it's not a hotel. You needn't be quite so patronizing. But if one of the other—"

"Which one would you like, then?" he interrupted, both

his temper and his patience running thin. "The one with the leaking roof or the one with the rotten floor? Or maybe you'd prefer the one that doesn't have any glass in the windows or doors? Or perhaps the one full of black widows that we're going to have to get pest control in to get rid of?"

Bree's jaw had gone rigid, sparks of anger glittering in her lovely eyes.

"And while we're on the subject," he went on, because he might as well keep going, "it's nice to see you again, *Ms.* White. What has it been? Ten years since I last saw you? Oh, but no, it's eight, isn't it? Since you've been in Jasper Creek for two years and never once bothered to acknowledge my presence."

A tiny flicker of shock moved in her gaze and then it was gone. "I'm sorry, but what did you expect?" she said coolly, not even bothering to deny it. "'Gee, thanks for arresting me back when I was fourteen and stupid'?"

"I didn't actually arrest you, if you recall," he said. "I told you off and then took you back to the station so Bill could deal with you, but yes," he said. "That might have been nice."

For a second, their gazes locked and held, and there was an instant where he could feel electricity crackle in the space between them.

Then she sniffed and glanced away, smoothing the nonexistent creases on her jeans.

The pulse at the base of her throat was beating fast, and he was aware of a very specific kind of satisfaction settling inside him. The satisfaction of a man who knew that a woman he wanted wasn't entirely unaffected by him.

Stupid to feel so pleased with himself, especially when it wasn't as if he'd ever had trouble getting a woman before. If she wanted to ignore him, then who cared?

He certainly didn't. He didn't need any extra complications in his life, and Bree White had *complicated* written all over her. Besides, they were both here for the camp and he might very well end up working with her, so it probably wasn't a great decision to start arguing with her right away.

"Would you like me to tell Jackson about your issue?" he offered, deciding to extend an olive branch. "He might be open to getting one of the other cabins ready sooner rather than later."

"No, thank you," she said stiffly, still not looking at him. "I'll stay where I am. It's fine."

It clearly wasn't fine, but he wasn't going to push her about why. It was better if they didn't linger on the subject. Or, indeed, any subject.

"Good," he said briskly. "So, is there anything else you need? Perhaps I could show you around the—"

But Bree had already turned and, without a word, headed back to her cabin, leaving him standing there like a fool staring after her.

CHAPTER THREE

NOISE CRASHED INTO Bree's dream like a freight train, and for a second, she lay in complete darkness, disoriented and groggy, wondering why on earth reveille was being played at earsplitting volume in the middle of the night in her neighborhood.

Then she remembered she wasn't in her neighborhood.

She was in Camp Phoenix.

"What is that *noise*?" Violet demanded from across the room.

"Reveille," Clementine said, already leaping from the bunk underneath Violet's, as if she got up at middle-of-the-night o'clock regularly.

"No," Bree groaned, reaching for her pillow to pull it over her head, memories of being dragged from a warm sleeping bag to go on various hikes and other early-morning activities replaying in her head. "Not the 6:00 a.m. wake-up—please, not that."

As the notes of reveille died away, there came another earsplitting sound, this time the shriek of a bullhorn.

"Rise and shine, campers." Jackson's voice boomed from somewhere outside. "Up and at 'em."

Kinley was muttering from the bottom bunk and Bree was certain she heard her say, "I'm going to kill that man." She could only wholeheartedly agree. Did Jackson really expect them to get up at six like they were young teenagers again? Unbelievable.

Violet had festooned her bunk with fairy lights the night before, which she'd refused to turn off because she didn't like the dark—or at least that's what she'd said when everyone had complained about them. Bree suspected that she kept them on *because* everyone had complained, and so, she'd already resolved to ignore the lights the next night.

It had taken her ages to get to sleep and not only because of the lights, but because of stupid Flint Decker.

She'd been so determined not to let her temper get the better of her, and yet she'd nearly lost it the day before. He'd just been so damn…condescending, with that patronizing smile curving his mouth as he'd informed her about the cabins. It had been a pleasure to wipe it off his face, to see irritation glitter in his green eyes.

But she hadn't expected him to call her out on how she'd ignored him for the past two years. She hadn't thought he'd even noticed, and yet it seemed he had. And if she wasn't much mistaken, he was annoyed about it.

Something warm flickered deep inside her at that thought, but she ignored it. Just as she ignored the memory of that charged moment between them, irritation and something more, something hotter, making the air crackle around them.

Ugh. A man shouldn't be allowed to be that sexy, especially not him.

She very much wanted to keep lying like a slug in bed, but since everyone else was getting up, she hauled herself out of her sleeping bag, muttering a calming mantra under her breath.

Today, she'd keep that temper of hers under wraps. She'd handled sharing a room the night before, and now she'd handle getting up at 6:00 a.m. No, she hadn't been expecting any of this, but she wasn't going to let Flint Decker turn her into a moaner. She wasn't going to complain again. She'd handle anything that was thrown at her, and she'd ace this just like she'd aced it back when she'd been fourteen.

Besides, apart from anything else, there were the future campers to think about. The kids who needed someone to give them order and boundaries and, most of all, to care. That's what they needed. Just one person to care, and she did. After all, she'd been one of them.

Ten minutes later, Bree staggered out into the darkness to the lawn in front of the admin cabin. Clementine strode beside her, all bright-eyed, with Kinley trailing silently behind them. Violet was still in the cabin doing something with her makeup, which Bree found ridiculous. What was the point of makeup at camp?

She'd almost made a snarky comment, then had bitten it back at the last moment, because she'd sworn to herself she wasn't going to be snarky today. Today was for positive vibes only.

Four men stood on the porch of the admin cabin.

Jackson in the middle, gray eyes steely, holding his bullhorn in an iron grip. He was handsome for a tyrant, as was the man standing to the left of him, a lazy smile on his face. Lincoln Traeger, one of Jackson's friends and a US marshal. He had eyes the color of dark bourbon, and they were currently fixed on the counselors cabin as if he was looking for someone. Duke Cody, Sheriff Decker's sergeant, stood beside Lincoln. He had the bluest eyes Bree had ever seen and he was grinning too, though at Clementine, and she was grinning back as if the two of them were sharing some private joke.

Bree found it much easier to look at the other men—they were all very easy on the eyes—than it was to focus on the tall, broad figure of Flint Decker, standing at Jackson's right. He was in his camp T-shirt and jeans, and he had his hat on, because of course he had his hat on. She was also conscious that he was staring at her, which made something she didn't like flutter uncomfortably in her stomach, reminding her of that first day of camp years ago, when he'd been introduced by Bill as a counselor and she'd realized that he was the cop who'd arrested her.

But she wasn't going to think about that. It was positive vibes only today, and that meant being especially positive and pleasant around Flint, since he was the one who bugged her the most. Also, she'd already complained to him once; there would not be a second time.

Keeping a smile on her face, she directed the full force of it at him. His eyes widened slightly, then narrowed into thin, suspicious slits of emerald, as if he found her smile insulting in some way.

"Get on with it, Jackson," Kinley growled unexpectedly from behind her.

Bree forgot about Flint and almost turned to look at the other woman. Kinley had been silent all last evening in the cabin and during the incredibly awkward meal in the dining hall, and she hadn't said a single thing this morning either, apart from muttering about killing Jackson. Bree had just about forgotten she was there.

Then Jackson raised his bullhorn. "Attention, everyone," he barked through it, though he was scowling at Kinley. "Lateness will not be tolerated. You are to be here at 6:00 a.m. sharp every morning for the climb up Hollyhock Hill. The flag will be raised, then daily chores will be distributed."

"Relax, Jackson." Violet, who had finally come out of the cabin, sauntered over to where everyone stood. She was made up perfectly, her hair glossy, and she wore another flouncy, pretty maxidress. There was a slight smile on her face. "I'm not that late. And we're not campers, remember? We're here to get the camp ready for the actual campers."

"You're staying here, which means you're campers," Jackson said flatly, still through the bullhorn. "Lateness involves a penalty. You're on latrine duty today, Violet."

Violet's eyes widened and she opened her mouth, but Jackson rolled on like a freight train. "Since it's the first day and you're the first ones here, we'll do the chore distribution now. By the way, other volunteers will be arriving in the next couple of weeks, so don't worry—you won't be renovating the entire camp yourselves. Okay, so today, Lincoln will assist Violet with looking at what we need to do with the art hall. Clementine, you and Duke can check out the other cabins and get a list of materials we're going to need in order to get them habitable."

A sudden tension gripped Bree. Lincoln was with Violet; Clementine was with Duke. That meant...

"Bree, you're with Flint. You two have a special job and he'll give you more info about it after breakfast. Kinley, you're going to be in charge of the cooking. Come with me and I'll show you around the kitchen."

There was an audible growl from Kinley, while Bree very much wanted to growl too, positive vibes be damned. Of course she was with Flint. Why was she with Flint? Perhaps if Kinley didn't want to be with Jackson, she could be with Jackson instead.

"I could go with you instead, Jackson," Bree said, totally forgetting she wasn't going to complain. "Kinley might prefer to be with Flint—"

"There's a reason you're with Flint," Jackson interrupted, frowning at her. "And like I said, he'll tell you about it later. After we've gone up the hill for the flag raising and some exercise."

Flint's handsome face gave absolutely nothing away, but she was sure she could see something that looked like satisfaction in it. As if he knew something she didn't.

Wonderful. This day was off to a *great* start.

"Exercise?" Violet muttered, frowning down at her maxidress. "No one said anything about exercise."

"It's camp," Clementine said perkily, already starting toward the hill as if she couldn't wait to get up it. "There's always exercise at camp."

Violet muttered something unrepeatable, while Kinley was stomping angrily in Clementine's wake. Bree couldn't help glancing again to where Flint stood, arms folded across his broad chest, his eyes still narrow slits.

She had no idea what the hell his problem was, but she didn't like it.

It was tempting to return his challenging stare with one of her own, but she resisted, giving him another of her perfectly pleasant, professional smiles before turning around and heading determinedly up the hill after the others.

She could remember doing this, tramping sulkily up the pine-covered slope and loathing every second. Not wanting to take part in any of the activities and isolating herself from everyone. At least, she had at first. Before Bill had taken her personally under his wing, pairing her with a girl from another cabin and giving them the job of preparing all the canoes that were used for water activities on Crow Lake. She hadn't wanted to do it and had protested mightily, but then she'd discovered that doing a task with someone else made it easier, not to mention more pleasant. Especially if you and that someone were friends.

She'd learned a good life lesson that day, about how to

put her anger aside and work effectively with others. About how to make friends, ask for help when she needed it, and how to be polite and respectful, and not an animal.

Lessons that had proved vital to her finishing school and getting a good job, and not ending up in jail like the rest of her family. Which had always been her goal.

She wasn't going to be a typical member of the White family, a small-time career criminal.

She wanted more than that, and so she'd gone out and gotten it, all thanks to Camp Phoenix.

An hour or so later, exercised, showered and breakfasted, everyone scattered to do their assigned chores. Violet and Kinley muttered imprecations about theirs and, quite frankly, Bree related.

She wanted to drag her heels, but that would be letting Flint get to her, and she was not, under any circumstances, going to let Flint get to her.

He was waiting for her just outside the dining hall as she came out, his arms still folded, dumb hat firmly on his head. "Ready to go?"

Bree gave him her Realtor smile again. "Oh, absolutely. But first, you're going to have to tell me where it is we're going and what it is we're doing."

Amusement glittered in Flint's green eyes, and though she wasn't sure why, she had a feeling it was at her expense. "Jackson wants to get some sponsorship from some of the business owners in Jasper Creek to help fund the purchase of materials. Plus, he needs someone to allay fears about a bunch of young criminals being in the vicinity."

Instantly, Bree stiffened, feeling a flicker of defensiveness since she'd been one of those young criminals herself. "They're *not* criminals. Not at that age."

"Hey, I know that," Flint said. "Nevertheless, we've had

a few protests. So I thought we could kill two birds with one stone. You can help with the sponsorship, since you know a lot of the business owners, and I'll help allay fears, since that's kind of my wheelhouse." He paused a moment, then added, "You're a camp graduate too, and if anyone can get them on board with the camp, you can."

The fluttering feeling in her gut fluttered harder, but she shoved it away. She wasn't going to find Flint Decker sexy as hell, and she certainly wasn't going to let her head get turned with his subtle compliment either.

"Fine," she said coolly. "I'd better get changed, then. I didn't think I'd be going into town to talk to people and—"

"You don't need to change." Flint's gaze dropped to her legs, which were currently bare due to the jean shorts she'd put on earlier in anticipation of hiking up Hollyhock Hill. "You're fine as you are."

It was silly to blush because he was looking at her legs, yet she blushed all the same. "Nevertheless—"

"Leave the shorts," he interrupted again, and he unfolded his arms, thrusting out a small bundle of black material at her. "But you could put this on."

Bree took it and shook it out. It was a Camp Phoenix T-shirt exactly like the one he was wearing. Normally she would have loved it—it was a pretty cool T-shirt—but the real issue was that if she put it on, then they would be wearing the same thing.

Twinsies. Ugh.

Positive vibes only, remember?

Bree could feel her smile become wooden. "Okay, not a problem." Then, in a bid to stay in control of the situation, she added, "We can take my car if we're going into Jasper Creek. It's electric. Save on gas."

Flint's gaze slid from her legs over to the parking area.

"Sure. Unless you forgot to plug it in, and since I didn't see any cord running from it last night, I'm pretty sure you did." His gaze gleamed. "Which means we'll be taking my truck."

Bree bit back a curse. She couldn't believe she'd forgotten. She'd been planning to organize some power after dinner the night before, but she'd gotten distracted by Violet arranging her fairy lights around her top bunk, then laying down a rug, of all things, and then pillows, and after that performance, having to charge her car had completely slipped her mind.

She didn't want to drive in Flint's truck. She didn't want him being in charge of getting her to and from camp. She didn't want to spend the whole day in his company, with his stupid sexy T-shirt, and his stupid sexy green eyes, and his stupid, *stupid* hat.

And she definitely did not want her stupid heart to beat the way it was beating now, far too fast and far too hard.

What she wanted was to be far away from him and all the memories he brought back. Of feeling his heavy hand on her shoulder at the 7-Eleven that night as she'd walked out with her stolen food. Of feeling her stomach plummet into her sneakers as she'd turned and seen his green eyes first, then his badge.

He'd been patient with her but firm, making her return what she'd stolen. Then he'd put her in the back of his patrol car. She'd been furious because she'd only stolen the food because she was hungry. Her mother had spent the family's grocery money for the week bailing Bree's father out of jail yet again, and she hadn't eaten. And she'd hated the pity in Deputy Decker's green eyes, the way there was always pity in all the eyes of the adults she came into contact with. And she'd kind of hated herself too.

Because she'd always been determined she wouldn't be like her family. She wouldn't take the easy way out. She'd get away from them one day and make something of herself, and her success would definitely be on her own merit. It would have *nothing* to do with breaking the law.

But not that night. That night, she'd slipped up, and she hated remembering it. Especially when it wasn't her now. She was Bree White, Realtor. Not Bree White, petty shoplifter.

Flint raised one dark brow. "Well? My truck? Or would you like to walk instead?"

Bree couldn't find her pleasant smile or her positive vibes; they'd all vanished. All she had left was a scowl, so that's what she gave him. "Fine. We'll take your stupid truck."

CHAPTER FOUR

FLINT HAD EXPECTED much more firecracker and much less frost on the drive to Jasper Creek, and he had to admit he was disappointed.

Bree sat in the truck next to him, her hands clasped tightly in her lap, her black hair in its neat, shining ponytail. She was very contained today, the same cool expression on her face as there had been the day before, and he would've thought she'd put the wildcat on ice if it hadn't been for the rigid way she was sitting. As if she had to keep herself very still in case she flew apart.

Getting them to partner up today might have been a mistake, but he'd discussed it with the guys the night before and they'd all agreed it was logical that he and Bree be the ones to do the sponsorship drive.

She had the business connections, while he had the respect of his office, plus the experience to put people's doubts about the camp to rest. And there had been a few rumbles about "juvenile delinquents" and "young criminals" being near town and how there was the potential to cause trouble.

Flint understood people's worries. He'd been one of those delinquents himself once, stealing cars and racing them on backcountry roads, drinking far too much beer and heading toward dropping out of school. Until his mom had started dating the sheriff. He'd hated Bill at first, and then Bill took an interest in him. Flint's dad had never been in the picture and Flint didn't realize he needed a father figure until Bill turned up. The relationship with Flint's mother didn't last, but Bill continued to take an interest in him. And eventually he stopped stealing cars and started studying. Then he joined the police force as soon as he graduated and never looked back.

Bree clearly didn't want to look back either. So much so that she barely seemed to tolerate being in his vicinity. Perhaps, to save them a whole bunch of trouble, he should have waited to do this with her until she'd gotten used to the whole camp thing again. Then again, maybe it was better to tackle their past now. Take the bull by the horns, so to speak.

"So, are you going to answer my question?" he asked after the silence had sat there way too long and it was clear she wasn't going to break it.

She'd turned her head, looking pointedly out the window. "What question?"

"Why you've been ignoring me for the past two years."

"I was not ignoring you." The breeze blowing through his open window toyed with the ends of her hair. 'I simply didn't remember who you were."

Flint gave a short bark of laughter because that was ridiculous. "I see. So that's why you mentioned the whole 'gee, Officer, thanks for arresting me' thing yesterday. Because you 'simply didn't remember' who I was."

The flush in Bree's pretty cheeks deepened. "Okay, fine," she said, her voice on the edge of a snap. "I did remember you. I just…" She let out an annoyed breath. "What do you care anyway?"

Good question. Why *did* he care? It was uncomfortable to think that it might simply be stung masculine pride over the lack of acknowledgment from a pretty woman. He hadn't thought his pride was that fragile. If a woman wasn't into him, he moved on; it wasn't a big deal.

It's this woman, though. That's the issue. She's different.

Flint did not like that thought one bit. Bree was beautiful and he'd admit to that flicker of attraction, but she wasn't different. And he wasn't going to get into thinking about how she was different either. His brain could shut the hell up.

"I don't care," he said flatly. "I was only making conversation."

Another tense silence fell, one that lasted all the way into Jasper Creek, and he kept his mouth shut, because he'd be damned if he broke it first.

Jasper Creek had a pretty main street, with flags hanging from lampposts and porches, hanging baskets of flowers, and rows of historic old stores.

Flint parked the truck and got out. Bree did the same and he tried not to pay any attention to how the black cotton of the T-shirt pulled tightly across the curves of her full breasts. The black cotton suited her, the gold lettering somehow drawing gold fire from her dark eyes.

He wasn't going to look at her legs in those little shorts again. Nope. That wasn't happening.

She shut the truck door and came around to where he stood, all cool and calm and collected. That overly pleasant, saccharine sweet smile she'd given him back at camp as they'd assembled for morning chores was long gone and thank God. It didn't suit her and it wasn't convincing.

He preferred her riled the way she had been the day before by the cabins, when she was all glowing cheeks and glittering dark eyes, reminding him of that girl scowling at him from the back seat of his patrol car years ago. To this day, he didn't know why she'd stood out to him back then, made his heart feel tight behind his ribs. He'd still been angry himself, a sullen burn he'd kept locked away, and perhaps it was that he'd admired the way she was so open and honest with hers.

Whatever. She was all grown up now and downright beautiful when she was angry, and it kind of made him want to get her angry again.

Why don't you pull her pigtails into the bargain, you petty dick? You're not ten anymore—get a grip.

Flint gritted his teeth and forced the thought away. "Right," he said. "Let's start at the feedstore and make our way down the street."

"Why the feedstore?" Bree asked. "We could start at the diner and make our way up."

Flint eyed her. That T-shirt-and-shorts combo was sexy as hell and he did not like one bit his body's interest in it. Really, it felt like he'd been having a sexual dry spell, and nothing could be further from the truth. Maybe he hadn't had time in the past couple of weeks to visit Medford, where he usually found his hookups because he didn't like screwing around in Jasper Creek. He was the sheriff, after all.

Maybe he needed to make some time for a visit. Find some pretty woman in a bar and work out any…issues with her.

Of course, one day he was going to find himself a wife and settle down, but that day hadn't yet come. He had too much to do, what with his job and his ranch, so until then, it was hookups all the way.

You could hook up with her.

Yeah, that wasn't happening. He wasn't going to have a brief affair with a woman who lived here. Besides, she didn't seem the brief-affair type anyway. Whatever she might be on the outside now, she was still a wildcat inside, he'd lay money on it, and while he might like the idea of tangling with her, it probably wasn't in his interests to do so. Especially not with the damn camp to get up and running.

"You'd tell me it was raining if the sky was nothing but blue, wouldn't you?" he said, irritated and frowning and quite unable to do anything else. "We'll start at the damn feedstore."

"It's not raining," she said calmly. "And how about *you* start at the feedstore and *I'll* start at the diner."

She didn't want him around, that was clear, and he was annoyed enough about that to be a dick and call her on it.

"Looks like you got a problem with me, *Ms.* White." Flint folded his arms and looked down at her. She was small, the top of her head just reaching his shoulders. "Come on—out with it. Are you afraid of me? Is that the issue?"

Bree's eyes narrowed, little dark flames leaping in them. "Afraid of you? Please, Sheriff Decker. Why on earth would I be afraid of you?"

And he couldn't resist; he just couldn't. She was gorgeous and he remembered the moment between them the day before, when attraction had simmered in the air, and so he took a slight step forward, getting in her space. "I can think of a reason, Ms. White. Can you?"

This time her eyes widened and the flush in her cheeks deepened, though she didn't make any attempt to move away. Then her gaze dropped to his mouth, as if she couldn't help herself, and Flint felt a growl of satisfaction start to form in his throat.

Because of course that was the problem, wasn't it? He affected her.

"Something about my mouth interesting to you?" he

murmured. "Or maybe you're just curious to see what I could do with it."

Bree jerked her gaze back up to his again, fury in her dark eyes, her blush gone from a delicate rose to fire red. "I couldn't be less interested in your stupid mouth," she snapped, lying through her teeth, he was sure of it. "And while we're on the subject of how stupid you are, your hat is dumb too."

"My hat?" Flint repeated blankly. "What about my hat?"

But Bree had turned on her heel and stormed off toward the feedstore.

Damn woman. First she was arguing that black was white, then she was looking at his mouth, and now the comment about his hat? What the hell?

He went after her, her short strides no match for his long legs. "And what, pray, is wrong with my hat?" he asked when he'd caught up. Because he honestly couldn't fathom. She'd been ignoring him for years, so why, of all the things, was his *hat* a problem?

She strode on, not looking at him. "It's stupid. That's what's wrong with it."

And just like that, Flint's irritation drained away. She looked so cross and so completely adorable with her flushed cheeks and glowing dark eyes. Cross that she was attracted to him and didn't like it. In fact, perhaps that's why she'd been ignoring him all this time. Because she wanted him. Now, wasn't that a pleasant thought?

Completely forgetting he wasn't supposed to be tangling with her, he smiled. "Alright, wildcat, I'll bite. What's stupid about my hat?"

Bree stopped, bringing him up short, then turned to look at him. "I am *not* a wildcat."

"Sure you are," he said, enjoying her fury, which was

probably wrong of him but too bad. "Spitting and hissing and scratching at me."

This time, it was her who took a step forward, glaring up at him as if she wasn't five-foot-nothing and he six-four. "If I'm a wildcat, then you're…you're…" She shook a finger under his nose. "You're just a…a dick. And while we're on the subject, that hat is dumb because you're a sheriff, not a cowboy. And if you're going to call me 'wildcat,' I'm going to call you 'Sheriff Dicker,' because that's what you are. A dick!"

Then, her tirade clearly finished, she turned once again and continued to storm onward toward the feedstore.

CHAPTER FIVE

FURY BOILED IN Bree's veins and she was aware she had her fists clenched at her sides.

Well, that was childish.

She clenched her teeth. Yes, it was, as was losing her temper on the main street and calling Flint "Sheriff Dicker," as if she were fourteen again.

What had she been thinking? She was supposed to be keeping hold of her temper, not losing it.

It was only that the whole trip had been a nightmare, sitting in his truck with his long, muscular body stretched out beside her, the cab full of the scent of his aftershave, like pine and something warm and earthy and masculine. It had been delicious.

She hated it. Just as she hated him.

You don't hate him. Don't be ridiculous.

Okay, no, she didn't hate him. But when he'd taken that step toward her by the truck, and she'd looked up into his green eyes and seen heat there, felt the crackle of attraction between them, she'd certainly *wanted* to hate him.

It was either hate him, or step even closer and pull his mouth down on hers.

But she wasn't going to. He'd been witness to her lowest moment, when after swearing to herself she was going to be different from her family, he'd caught her stealing, making her no better than them. She didn't want to be reminded of that moment every time she saw him.

Doesn't the camp remind you of those things, though?

Maybe. But camp also had good memories associated with it—well, mainly good memories, if you didn't count the enemies and getting up at six thing. Of those, small achievements such as making a new friend, keeping her bunk spotless or being the first to get to the top of Hollyhock Hill. Earning an extra cookie from Mrs. Zee for helping clean up without being asked, or a word of praise from Gale in the art hall for actually putting effort into a drawing. And knowing the people at camp were there to build you up, realize your potential, not to tear you down so you were as small and petty as everyone else.

Anyway, her positive vibes determination might have only lasted until she'd gotten into his truck, but she was going to find it again. She couldn't allow him to get under her skin.

Um, I think he's already there.

Bree growled in frustration.

"Definitely a wildcat," Flint murmured, catching up with her again.

She didn't dignify that with a response.

"Also," he went on, "I'm totally entitled to this hat because I have a ranch."

A flicker of surprise went through her. She hadn't known that. Fighting a curiosity she didn't want to feel, she studied the display of A Simple Thread, the knitting store that had opened last year, as they went past. "Do you?"

"Yes, I do. I bought it last year. Off Jim Carew."

Bree felt like growling again. So, he was the one who'd bought Jim's ranch. She'd heard about the sale, but it had been done through Karl Jenner, her competition. "I could have got you a better price," she said, even though she knew she shouldn't.

"Could you?" Flint asked idly. "Or would you have ignored every single one of my calls?"

Bree decided she wasn't going to answer that and she wasn't going to ask him a question about his dumb ranch either. Instead, she headed straight into Riley Feed and Gardening Supply, Flint following at her heels.

Chatting to Pru Riley, who owned the feedstore, about sponsorship was a piece of cake. Bree liked Pru a lot and Pru was very encouraging about the camp. Ten minutes later, Bree had an agreement from Pru for her store to donate any plant supplies the camp might need. She hadn't even needed Flint for that. He'd stood there beside her, looming silently, and she hadn't let him get a word in edgewise.

"That was the easy one," Flint muttered as they left. "Just wait until we hit Frank's."

Frank Anderson owned a hunting and fishing store and he was a crusty old man with a crusty old personality to match. Bree had dealt with him before and he was difficult, but she was sure she could get him on board, if that was what Flint was worried about.

"We'll see," she said and headed into the next store.

The whole block, which included A Simple Thread, Happy Ever After Books and The Sugar Shack, proved to be easy ones too. Charity, Kit and Hope, the owners of said stores, were all fully supportive and wanted to help out. Charity with knitting and craft kits for the art hall, Kit with enough books to start a little library, and Hope with supplies for the dining hall kitchen.

All three women smiled at Flint as he greeted them, but

when Bree launched into her spiel about the camp, they ignored him and chatted with her instead.

It would have been more satisfying if he'd been annoyed at trailing along behind her and being ignored, but she had a horrible feeling that he wasn't. In fact, she had a horrible feeling that he was more than happy to stand back while she talked, and it made her want to know why.

So annoying to be curious about him. What did she care? She didn't. Not at all.

The next few stores offered cash donations, which were greatly appreciated, and Bree was feeling pretty good about what they'd managed to get so far, and so she was confident as they entered Frank's store.

At least, until he gave Bree a disdainful up-and-down look from behind the counter, before directing his attention to Flint. "Sheriff," he said shortly. "What can I do you for?"

"Hey, Frank." Flint took no notice of the older man's unfriendly manner, smiling easily, his broad shoulders relaxed. "How's the next season shaping up?"

After five minutes of a hunting discussion, Flint then somehow segued into talking about the camp with no discernible change of tone, keeping things easy and casual and friendly.

Sure enough, Frank soon relaxed too, then started into a rant about how he didn't want any "delinquents" hanging around, which instantly got Bree's back up. She wanted to say a few choice things to Frank, but that wasn't going to get them any sponsorship and could even end up making things worse if the townspeople put their protests into action.

It annoyed her that Flint didn't shut him up and in fact seemed intent on letting him have his say, and she almost interjected a few times. But Flint only nodded, asked Frank a few questions, and then, when his rant was done, said,

"All good points, Frank. I hear you. But you see Bree here? She's a graduate of that camp, and she's no delinquent, as you very well know. She's a Realtor, owns her own home, contributes to the town and is incredibly successful. A real inspiration. That's the point of the camp. To get these kids off the streets and turn their lives around, and Bree is proof that it works. And you know Jackson. He'll keep everyone in line, and so will I. We were former campers too, remember?"

Bree felt that flutter again, deep inside. An inspiration, he'd said. Did he really think that about her? Not that she cared about his opinion. Nope, not one single iota.

Frank gave her another look up and down, but it wasn't as disdainful this time, more considering. "Huh," he muttered. "Guess I'll think about it."

Flint didn't insist. All he said was "Appreciate it, Frank." Then he glanced at Bree and the two of them went out.

She didn't want to ask, but she couldn't stop herself. "Why did you let him say all that stuff? About the kids being criminals? That's not what they are."

"I know," Flint said calmly. "But sometimes you got to let someone have their say. Some people just want to be heard, and once they feel they've been listened to, they're much more open to having their minds changed."

Bree didn't want the grudging respect that gathered inside her, but it was there all the same. As was the startling realization that she could almost understand why people had voted for him for sheriff in such numbers.

Based off what? One interaction?

Yeah, but she'd seen him around town carrying out his duties. She'd heard him being talked about. People respected him, and if she was honest with herself, she could see why.

As if he could read her mind, Flint smiled, a slightly wicked glitter in his green eyes. "What say we get a coffee and continue our discussion about my dumb hat?"

Actually sit down and talk to him? Spend more time that was just them? Absolutely not.

"I have no interest in your hat." Bree turned away, hoping like hell that she wasn't blushing as intensely as she thought she was. "Let's just talk to as many businesses as we can today and then get back to camp."

Flint didn't push and she wasn't sure if she was further annoyed by that or relieved, but by early afternoon, they'd finished talking to as many of the business owners as they could, at least down one side of the street.

There were some holdouts and some doubters, but Flint had handled them deftly and had gotten if not wholehearted approval, then at least a grudging agreement to at least see how the first year went.

Bree would have called it successful if she hadn't started to feel antsier and antsier as the day went on. It was all this standing around watching Flint charm the pants off various people, and if she was the one doing the talking, then it was standing around feeling his gaze on her. Feeling that fluttering get more and more intense.

By the time lunchtime came around and he once again mentioned grabbing a bite to eat, all she wanted was to be out of his vicinity.

"I need to get back to camp," she said shortly. "I have some…stuff to do this afternoon."

"Stuff?" He raised a dark brow. "What stuff?"

"Just…you know, stuff." She turned and started to head back to where he'd parked the truck. "Feel free to stay here if you want. I can take your truck."

Annoyingly, Flint followed her, saying nothing. He unlocked the truck, then insisted on holding the door open for her. "Am I getting to you, wildcat?" he murmured as she got in, his deep voice sending the most delicious chills right down her spine.

And she almost changed her mind. Almost decided to get that bite to eat and then spend the rest of the afternoon proving to him how little he got to her. But she suspected that would only end in disaster, so she ignored him instead.

The drive back was as silent as the drive there. Or at least it would have been if Flint hadn't been whistling the entire way, as if he hadn't a care in the world.

But it wasn't until she was tucked up in her bunk that night, the glow of Violet's fairy lights illuminating the rafters above, that Bree realized she was going to have to do something about him.

"Do what about who?" Violet asked from her bunk in the semidarkness.

Oh. Had she said that aloud? How embarrassing.

"You mean Flint, right?" Clementine said unexpectedly.

Okay, great. Had her annoyance with him somehow been that obvious?

Bree stared at the ceiling, feeling her cheeks heat. Yet the darkness made it easier to talk, and if anyone understood how annoying a smug man could be, she had a feeling it would be these women. She had a few friends in town, no one close, though, and no one who knew where she'd come from. But Violet, Clementine and Kinley did, and there was something…freeing about that. She didn't have to pretend she'd never been in trouble with the law and she hadn't come from a crappy background. They knew, because you didn't attend Camp Phoenix as a kid if everything in your life was going right.

"Yes," she said into the darkness, not even minding that

Clementine had somehow guessed correctly. "He's a smug asshole."

"So is Lincoln," Violet muttered. "I always hated him. Asshole with a capital *A*."

"Jackson," snarled Kinley from the bunk beneath.

Bree grinned at the waves of agreement that radiated through the cabin. "They need to be taken down," she said. "Somehow."

"Amen," Violet said. "Got any ideas?"

And that's when it came to her, the most beautiful idea. Glorious in its audacity and guaranteed to wipe that smug-ass smile off Sheriff Dicker's handsome face.

"I do," Bree said. "I'm going to steal his hat."

CHAPTER SIX

FLINT DIDN'T KNOW what to do about Bree White.

Over the next couple of days, after their initial day in town, they went again to visit the remaining businesses on Main Street, and on each day, Bree was as nice as pie. Giving him that cool yet pleasant smile and talking about mundane things. The weather. Violet's annoying fairy lights. House prices. Jackson's irritating bullhorn. The new plumbing that was being installed in her house.

In fact, he'd heard a lot about her house. And it wasn't that he had problems with it per se—it did sound very nice—it was only that what he wanted, perversely, was her getting irritated with him and fighting with him the way she had that first day, not chatting easily about which wallpaper she'd chosen and what paint, the best flooring in the kitchen, and the color of the tiles in the bathroom.

Except, she seemed determined not to fight. In fact, he got the distinct impression that all the small talk she was directing at him was a bit of a smoke screen, a distraction. He wasn't sure what she was trying to distract him from or why, but it was annoying as hell.

The little shorts she persisted in wearing with her Camp Phoenix T-shirt were also annoying as hell. He wanted to tell her to change, but of course that would have given away how affected he was by her long, bare legs, and there was no way that was happening.

No point making the situation any worse. But still, he couldn't deny that part of him wanted her to call him Sheriff Dicker again, just so they could have another fight.

You want the wildcat.

Hell, yeah, he did. But, as he'd already told himself, that would be adding a complication he didn't need right now. Plus, he was pretty sure all the people who'd voted for him for sheriff would be horrified at the idea that he was dating the woman he'd arrested when she was fourteen. They deserved better from him than that.

It was late in the dilapidated house Jackson lived in at camp, and since they all had to get up early the next morning, they'd decided that the round of poker they were currently playing would be the last. Poker passed the time nicely since it gave them all an opportunity to have a beer, complain about gas prices, reminisce about old operations and talk about women.

Flint leaned his elbows on the rickety Formica table that Jackson had found when he'd moved in. As usual when they played, Jackson was looking at his cards like he wanted to set fire to them, while Lincoln played casually, as if he didn't give a shit whether he won or lost. Duke, meanwhile, kept up a running commentary that was clearly a distraction.

Flint just played to win, like he always did, and he was winning now, which was satisfying, a nice little pile of quarters building up at his elbow.

"So," Duke said, tossing out a card. "Are we going to talk about what's up with you and Bree?"

Flint was so intent on his cards that for a moment he didn't quite process what Duke had said. Then he did and couldn't stop himself from scowling. "Nothing is up with me and Bree. Also, asking questions is a tell, so your hand is obviously shit."

Duke only grinned. He enjoyed teasing Flint and Flint mostly let him get away with it. Mostly. "My hand is none of your business. Come on. There's some tension going on there—don't deny it."

Chatting about Bree was the last thing Flint wanted to do, since for the past couple of days, he'd been actively trying *not* to think of her. Which hadn't worked out too well, if he was honest with himself.

"You're mistaken," he said. "There is zero tension going on there. Linc?"

"I'll raise you," Lincoln replied, since it was his turn, flicking in another quarter. "Maybe I'll ask her out on a date," he added with a lazy grin. "She's pretty."

"Do that and I'll punch your face in," Flint said automatically. Then realized what he'd said. Shit, why should he care whether Lincoln asked her out? Because God knew he wasn't going to. Right?

Lincoln's grin turned even lazier. "Is that a fact?"

Flint debated punching the asshole in the face anyway, since it was an obvious windup and he'd fallen for it. It was extra aggravating that he had no idea where the possessive urge had come from, only that it had been strong and instinctive.

He did not want another man asking Bree out on a date or anything dating related—or even dating adjacent.

Because she's yours.

"If you tear those cards, you'll owe me another pack," Duke murmured, making Flint aware that he was clutching his cards a little too tightly for their own good.

He forced himself to relax.

No, he couldn't start thinking she was his. She wasn't.

He was attracted to her, sure, he'd admit that, but he wasn't going to do anything about it for all the reasons he'd already told himself. Maybe tomorrow night he'd go and hit a bar in Medford. Find himself a woman for the night. That would get rid of any inappropriate thoughts concerning pretty Bree White.

He wondered why that thought didn't seem as appealing as it might have even a week ago.

"Look," he said flatly to the table at large, "regardless of what attraction there is between Bree and me, it isn't happening."

"Why not?" Duke asked.

Flint fixed him with a direct look. "You mean apart from the whole me-arresting-her-when-she-was-fourteen thing?"

"Correct me if I'm wrong, but she wasn't fourteen the last time I checked," Lincoln pointed out. "Which was this morning. And in fact, she's—"

"None of your damn business," Flint interrupted, trying not to sound pissy and failing. "Besides, she's six years younger than I am, and I'm the sheriff. I'm supposed to set an example."

"An example of what?" Lincoln asked.

"An example of decent and proper behavior, asshole," Flint said, glaring. "And proper and decent behavior does not include dating the much younger woman I happened to arrest years ago."

He was annoyed that he had to even mention it, since his friends all knew his reasons for running for sheriff. It was a chance to do Bill proud and repay the faith he'd put in Flint. Sheriff McClain had taken an angry teenager heading down a destructive path and put him on a better one. Showed him that there was more to life than stealing cars, running drag races and vandalizing public property. If not for Bill, who knew where he would have ended up?

"You do realize that nobody would care if you started dating a well-respected Realtor, right?" Duke apparently didn't care that he'd taken his life into his own hands by not decently dropping the subject. "In fact, I bet nobody in Jasper Creek even knows you arrested her."

"That's not the point," Flint argued.

"Then what is the point?"

Flint opened his mouth to deliver a lecture on behavior and examples and the debt he owed to Bill when Jackson suddenly growled, "Shut up, for Chrissakes." He was staring at the cards in his hand as if they'd offended him personally. "We're here to play poker, not talk about women."

"Speak for yourself," Duke said. "I would very much like to talk about women."

Jackson bit off a curse and threw his cards down on the table. "I'm out anyway."

Flint put down his hand—a full house—making Duke groan and Lincoln shrug negligently. Then he gathered his winnings.

The rest of them were rising from the table and making noises about getting some shut-eye when Flint caught an odd sound coming from outside. He lifted a hand, his head tilting sharply to one side. "Did you hear that?"

Instantly all four men stilled, listening.

"I can't hear anything," Lincoln said.

"Me neither," Duke added.

Jackson's gray eyes were sharp. "Nothing except that damn owl."

Huh. Flint listened hard again, yet there was nothing but silence. "Thought I heard someone…giggling," he muttered.

"Giggling?" Jackson said the word like he'd never heard it before. "Are you sure?"

Flint frowned. It had been faint, but he was sure that was what the sound had been. "Yeah, I'm sure."

Jackson reached for the cane that was by his chair. He didn't use it all the time, but the injuries he'd sustained in an operation that had gone wrong years ago gave him a bit of trouble in the evenings. "I'll go and check outside."

"No, let me go," Flint offered, knowing his friend was in a bit of pain tonight, and since the guy hated people doing things for him, he added, "My sleeping bag's in the back of the truck, so I might as well go and get it now."

Jackson grunted an assent, so Flint went out through the hallway to the front door, pushing it open and stepping outside.

The night air was fresh and cool, and smelled of pine, the stars clear and bright, glittering in the black sky. All around the house were the dark forms of trees standing guard.

Flint took a deep breath, allowing the little knots of tension that had gathered inside him over the past couple of days to relax.

Damn, he loved it here. Being in the great outdoors and doing hard but satisfying physical labor. Remembering the lost, angry boy he'd once been when he'd first come here, and how he'd found determination and a future under Bill's tutelage.

Yes, that's what he was going to think about, and definitely not Bree White. Bree White and her little shorts and her tight T-shirt. Her cool smiles and the small talk that drove him crazy, and her absolute refusal to be anything but professional with him.

This was going to end up being a long few weeks.

He moved over to his truck and hauled out his sleeping

bag, pausing for a moment to listen for that giggle again, but there was nothing but the rustle of the trees and an owl calling.

Clearly he'd been hearing things.

Flint tossed the sleeping bag over his shoulder and went back inside.

"OH MY GOD, VIOLET," Bree hissed once Flint had disappeared back inside the run-down homestead. "You nearly gave us away."

Violet, who had giggled far too loudly over something Kinley had muttered under her breath, only shrugged. "Sorry," she said, sounding not sorry at all.

"We shouldn't be doing this," Clementine said worriedly. "It's dark. Someone will fall over and break their neck. Also, I'm a cop. I shouldn't be aiding and abetting."

The four of them were standing in the darkness among the trees close to the house, having spent a couple of delightful hours planning the "hat heist," as Violet gleefully termed it.

Delightful since, even though it was a difficult operation, everyone had been thoroughly on board and excited about doing something that wasn't chores or flag raising or cooking or cleaning. Something that was a bit illicit, a bit forbidden, because, after all, at least three of them had been in Camp Phoenix for a reason the first time round. And it wasn't because they'd been angels.

Stealing Flint's hat was wrong and Bree knew it. She'd sworn to herself all those years ago that she wasn't going to break the law again. But really, he was asking for it. And it wasn't as if she was going to keep it, or sell it, or profit from it in any way. Or hurt him. It was only some minor thievery that any sane woman would be driven to after the last few days she'd spent in his company.

However, she'd been forced to wait until she was sure Flint was staying at Jackson's, since the only time she could secure the hat was when he took it off. Which was almost never. She'd briefly thought of driving to Flint's house and sneaking in, but given the run-down state of Jackson's, she thought it would be easier to get into.

Clementine had been in charge of getting intel from Duke, and she'd hit pay dirt after a conversation about how the boys played poker most nights, and that sometimes Flint stayed, especially if he'd had a couple of beers.

Which made it a simple issue of waiting until she was sure Flint was staying there. In the meantime, she kept him at a distance with small talk and a cool manner, privately enjoying how much that seemed to annoy him.

Clementine had found out that morning that tonight was poker night, and Flint was planning on staying, which made tonight the perfect night for the heist.

The biggest problem was the fact that all four men were lawmen, which meant they'd be much more likely than the average man to spot someone breaking into the house. So Bree had decided that a distraction was required.

It reminded her uncomfortably of some of the planning discussions that had gone on in her own family years ago, when they were organizing a burglary, but she'd shoved that aside. She was only stealing one idiot man's hat, that's all.

Violet had entered into the whole planning thing enthusiastically and had volunteered to mastermind the distraction. She also volunteered both Kinley and Clementine to help, Clementine looking half thrilled at the thought as well as half terrified. While Kinley, her eyes big behind her glasses, just looked terrified.

But as the front door shut behind Flint's tall figure, Bree felt a familiar adrenaline rush. Because no matter how much she'd told herself she never wanted to follow in her family's footsteps, she couldn't deny she got a thrill out of doing something illicit.

She shouldn't enjoy it, she knew, and her life had all been about putting that behind her and not making more mistakes, yet this felt different. No one stood to get hurt. She was only taking a smug man down a peg or two and, well, having a little fun while doing it.

She hadn't had any fun in so long.

"Okay," she whispered to the others after some time had elapsed. "Go do your thing."

Instantly, Violet, Kinley and Clementine moved off through the trees, getting close to the front door of the house. Then Violet started singing. Loudly.

That was Bree's cue.

She ran off in the opposite direction, moving quickly around the side of the house. Clementine had gotten the layout of the inside after questioning Duke discreetly, so she knew which room Flint took when he stayed over. She'd already done a mini reconnaissance earlier in the day, and it seemed that the window of Flint's room had a broken latch that was easy enough to open.

She crept up to the window now and peered into the room.

There was no one in it, but his hat was sitting on the bed.

Bree grinned, a thrill running through her.

Quickly, she managed to get the window open and then wriggled inside.

The loud singing from the others had started to move away from the house now, and she could hear the low rumble of irritated male voices. Hopefully all four men would be drawn outside to investigate, leaving her free to grab the hat and go.

The wallpaper in the room was peeling and the paint on the ceiling cracking, but the floorboards were smooth enough as she crept over to the bed. It was a fairly rustic affair, but there was a mattress and a sheet, though Flint had unrolled his sleeping bag on top of them. His hat sat on top of the sleeping bag.

Bree leaned over to grab it, just as a heavy hand suddenly gripped her shoulder.

She froze, her heart racing, a dreadful suspicion forming inside her.

Then Flint's deep, rough voice said, "What the hell do you think you're doing?"

CHAPTER SEVEN

As soon as Flint's hand gripped her, Bree felt a rush of an old, remembered shame. Of trying to furtively stuff chip packets and candy under her sweatshirt and then walking out, thinking she was home free. Only for that heavy hand to descend on her shoulder, freezing her in place.

Just the way it was doing now, ten years later.

Instinct almost had her shrugging it off and running for the door, but as she turned, she realized his muscular figure was blocking her exit. Then she actually looked and all thoughts of running vanished from her head.

Flint wore nothing but a towel wrapped around his lean hips, leaving the rest of him very, very bare. Water droplets gleamed on the broad expanse of his chest, outlining every hard muscle of his torso. His black hair was damp and his green eyes gleamed as they met hers, obviously taking note of the fiery blush that she could feel sweeping across her face.

She shouldn't be looking at him, she really shouldn't. Except she couldn't tear her gaze away.

"You want to tell me exactly what you're doing in my room?" Flint asked.

What to tell him? She didn't have any excuses prepared, no handy lies presenting themselves. All her thinking had been completely obliterated by his impressive chest, and now she couldn't get her brain to work.

"Uh…I…um," she said intelligently.

"Go on." He raised a black brow. "I'm all ears."

"I…uh…" She stopped, unable to think of a single thing to give him except the truth. "Okay, fine. I'm stealing your hat."

Surprise flickered across his handsome face. "You're what?"

"Your hat." She tried to keep her gaze away from his chest. "I was going to steal it."

"Why the hell would you want to do that?"

Again, Bree racked her brain to think of a decent reason that wasn't the actual reason and came up with nothing. "Because you're a dick," she said at last. "Because you're annoying and smug, and I don't like you."

Flint surveyed her for a long moment, and much to her irritation, one corner of his beautiful mouth curved. Amusement glittered in his eyes. "You don't like me, so you decided to steal my hat."

"Yes." She faced him squarely, drawing back her shoulders and lifting her chin. It was very, very aggravating that he was so tall. "That's what I said."

"And I presume all that shrieking outside was—"

"It was singing, Flint," Bree interrupted, feeling protective of the other women. "Loud singing."

"Okay, the *singing* outside was what? A distraction?"

She was blushing again, dammit. Why did he have to make her feel so…antsy? Like she wanted to crawl out of her skin? She *hated* it.

"Yes," she said. "And you were supposed to go outside with all the guys."

His mouth curved a little more. "I was in the shower. I thought they could handle it themselves."

"Don't you dare laugh, Sheriff *Dicker*," Bree snapped,

furious for reasons she couldn't have articulated. "It's not funny."

But that fascinating mouth of his was curving into a smile that was all glory and his green eyes were alight, and all Bree could think of was how she could wipe that smile off his face, get under his skin the way he got under hers, put him off-balance, make him sweat.

So she did the first thing she could think of.

She took a step toward him, getting right up close. Then she put her hands on his powerful chest, the shocking heat of his bare skin against her palms stealing her breath.

His eyes widened, the laughter draining away. "What are you doing—"

But he never got to finish, because then she rose up on her toes and pressed her mouth to his, silencing him.

For a second, he was still, obviously frozen in place with shock, so she took the opportunity to slide her hands up the hot plane of his chest, circling around his neck, opening her mouth to his.

She'd had exactly one relationship in her life with a perfectly nice man who'd made for a perfectly serviceable boyfriend. She'd wanted normality, and so she'd found it with him. But he'd never made her heart beat fast like Flint. He'd never made her skin feel tight or her breasts feel sensitive, or made her ache right down between her thighs.

Sex had been fine. Workmanlike and practical and moderately satisfying.

But kissing Flint was none of those things. There was nothing workmanlike about the feel of his mouth against hers, and when he gripped her hips with his large hands, pulling her hard against him, she didn't feel moderate.

She felt as if she'd been set alight, exploding into flames like gas on a bonfire.

Leaning into him, she opened her mouth beneath his, totally forgetting about his hat and wiping that smile off his face. Forgetting about everything except getting more.

He must have been drinking Scotch, because she could taste the echo of it, dark and rich, along with something delicious that was all him. She couldn't get enough.

Yet just when she wanted him to kiss her even deeper, he lifted his head, looking down at her. There was no laughter in his eyes this time, only a hot green flame that made the ache inside her worse.

"What are you doing, Bree?" he asked roughly.

"You keep asking me that." Her voice was all breathless and husky after that kiss, but she couldn't make it sound any different. "I told you. I'm stealing—"

"My hat. Yeah, I got that. So what's that kiss got to do with anything?"

She could feel her face getting hot again, and instantly, her defensiveness kicked in. "If you don't want me to kiss you, just say so."

"Did I say that?" His hands were still on her hips, his grip firm. He wasn't letting her go. "No, I didn't. I asked what you were doing."

"I thought it was obvious what I was doing." She felt all exposed abruptly. Perhaps she'd been mistaken about the attraction between them. Perhaps that green flame was only anger. Perhaps he'd hated the kiss and he was offended and—

"Oh, no," he murmured. "Don't look like that." Then she was being pulled close again, and he fit her hips against his, making her aware of the hard length pressing against her. It was clear he was interested. Very interested.

"Flint," she began thickly.

"Why did you kiss me, Bree?" His voice had gotten

very deep. "Because you know you're playing with fire, don't you?"

She took a ragged breath, staring up into his eyes. "Am I?"

He gave a soft laugh. "You know you are, wildcat."

Somehow her hands were on his chest again, stroking his skin, all velvety and hot, and he didn't stop her. "So why did you stop? I thought…I thought maybe you wanted to…but if you're not—"

"Oh, I want to." He was fierce all of a sudden. "Believe me, I want to. You've been driving me crazy all goddamn week. But our past, Bree. I arrested you, for God's sake. It's not a good look for a sheriff."

Strangely, Bree felt something relax inside her. He hadn't pulled away because he didn't want her. The opposite, in fact. He *did* want her, and now that she looked at him, she could see the desire burning brightly in his eyes, all heat and wickedness.

It made her feel wicked too.

Because she wanted him back, she could admit that to herself now, and for years. Conscious of him whenever he was in her vicinity, of his height and his broad shoulders, and those wicked green eyes. And she'd ignored him because she thought if she did, then the feelings would go away.

But they hadn't gone away. And being near him here at camp, in his vicinity all the time… It was driving her as crazy as it was driving him.

Maybe stealing his hat had never been about actually stealing it. Maybe it had more to do with wanting to be caught.

"No one would know," she said slowly, trying the thought out for size and liking very much the fit. Of course, the other women might, but perhaps she could think of some handy lie. "I mean, if I stayed tonight. It might even clear the air between us. Get rid of the tension."

Flint's gaze became very intent, very focused. "Are you talking sex?"

She was blushing again, dammit. But she didn't look away. "Yes."

His gaze roved over her face. "You want me?"

"I…I—"

"Say it, wildcat. Say it out loud."

She didn't know why she was blushing. She didn't know why it was so hard to say. "I…want you, Flint."

The fire in his eyes leaped. "One night. That's all I can offer. And no one can know, understand? I want to keep this on the down-low."

"Okay," she said, her voice breathless. "One night. I won't tell a soul."

He didn't wait. He bent and took her mouth as soon as the words were out of it.

And Bree was lost.

His kiss was deep and desperate, his tongue exploring her mouth as if he couldn't get enough of her. And she couldn't get enough of him. She put her arms around his neck again, clinging to him, pressing her body against his, desperate for more.

He picked her up and put her on the bed, getting rid of his towel as he followed her down onto the mattress. Then there was nothing but heat and the delicious weight of his big, muscular body pinning her to the bed. She was still fully clothed, but then his hands were pulling at her T-shirt, easing it up and over her head, her bra following along behind. His mouth closed over the pulse at the base of her throat, tasting it, sucking gently at her skin as his fingers dealt with the fastening of her jeans. He stripped them off her, taking her underwear and everything else with them, so finally, she was gloriously naked beneath him.

His bare skin against hers was so hot and felt wonderful, and she gasped as he kissed his way down her body, his hands finding her breasts and stroking, his thumbs teasing her nipples, only to then be replaced by his hot mouth.

She groaned aloud as he licked and nipped at the sensitive peaks of her breasts, his large hands then spreading her thighs, giving him space to lie between them. There was a moment's pause as he leaned over the bed for his jeans, pulling out his wallet, finding a condom and putting it on. Then his hands were sliding beneath her hips and lifting her, positioning himself. And finally pushing into her, a hard, deep thrust that had her crying out, only for his mouth to cover hers, silencing her.

Bree put her arms around his neck, clinging to him, pleasure arcing through her as he began a slow, deep rhythm that brought a moan with every flex of his hips.

It was too good. It was wonderful. And it was not practical or workmanlike or moderate in any way.

It was fever and flame and fireworks exploding in the night sky. Heat and passion and desperation.

Bree dug her nails into his back as his movements got faster, and when he reached behind her knee and drew her leg higher around his waist, sinking deeper inside her, she moaned his name. Then his hand was between her thighs, finding the most sensitive part of her, helping her along, and there were fireworks for real, bursting behind her eyes as the orgasm rushed over her.

And his teeth closing on her neck and biting gently as he followed along after her.

CHAPTER EIGHT

FLINT HELD BREE'S trembling body against his, the effects of the orgasm still rolling through him. This sure as hell wasn't how he'd expected the evening to end, but he wasn't complaining.

Maybe it was a mistake, but if so, it was a glorious, beautiful mistake and he'd own it.

Finding Bree in his bedroom had been a shock, as was her suddenly going up on her toes to kiss him. She'd stolen his breath clean away.

He should have resisted her, should have pushed her away, but he hadn't. His thoughts had been full of her for days now, and her delicate touch on his bare skin, the feel of her soft mouth against his, had been too much. A line had been crossed. There was no going back and he knew it.

One night, he'd decided. One night and no one else would know. They could both deal with this insane sexual tension and then hopefully things would get back to normal between them.

Whatever normal was.

He got up to dispose of the condom, then came back to the bed, unzipping his sleeping bag all the way so he could open it like a blanket and pull it over the both of them. She lay against his chest, her soft, silky black hair spilling over his skin, and the feel of her warm body fitted to his was perfection itself.

Her breathing had slowed and he was very conscious of her thumb stroking back and forth over his skin. It felt good. Everything she did felt good.

"Have I really been driving you crazy this week?" she asked after a moment.

He grinned. "Yes. It's not entirely the fault of your shorts, though, believe me, they take some of the blame. It was also you being as nice as pie and not even having the decency to give me a cross word."

She laughed, the bright sound sending a thrill down his spine. He'd never heard her laugh before and, man, it was something. "Well, good. I was hoping it would annoy you. Plus, I thought it might distract you from what I was planning."

"Oh, the hat thing?" He let his fingers trail over her bare shoulder, loving the way she shivered beneath his touch. "Can take a girl out of the bad, but you can't take the bad out of the girl, hmm?"

Oddly, she stiffened. "That's not true," she said, defensiveness clear in her voice. "I'm not that girl anymore."

Ah, so that was the nerve he'd hit.

Flint took her chin in his hand and turned her head so he could look down into her dark eyes, see the expression on her face. Yes, there was defensiveness there too, echoes of that fourteen-year-old looking at him with suspicion and fury. "Why not?" he asked. "There was nothing wrong with that girl, Bree."

She stared at him for a long moment, then let out a breath. "I didn't ever want to go down the same road as my family. I'd always told myself I wouldn't be one of them. That I'd be better. That I wasn't going to end up as just another member of the White family in jail. But…"

"But what? Correct me if I'm wrong, but you're not in jail now."

"You don't understand. I broke my promise to myself. I wasn't going to be like Dad, who just took stuff that wasn't his because holding down an actual job was too hard. I wasn't going to take the easy way out. And yet what did I do?"

But Flint remembered that night and he knew her background. Her father had been in jail and her mother had spent all the family's money for the week trying to bail him out. There hadn't been anything left for food.

"You were hungry," he said. "You were fourteen and hungry. Which isn't a moral failing, I hate to tell you. Plus, it wasn't as if you'd held up a liquor store or anything."

Yet the expression on her lovely face remained serious. "It's the principle of the thing. I shouldn't have done it. I could have found food somewhere else. I didn't have to steal it."

He brushed a strand of hair off her forehead, settling her more comfortably against him. "You're very hard on yourself. Why is that?"

"Because…well…" She paused and bit her lip, a flush creeping into her cheeks. "Dad was mostly in jail and Mom didn't care, so who else was going to make sure I stayed on the straight and narrow? I only had myself."

Flint felt something in his chest ache. She'd been so furious that night, and he'd wondered if there had been more to it than simple anger at getting caught. He should have let her off with a warning, but he hadn't. He'd been too new and had wanted to do everything by the book. "You were so pissed when I put you in my patrol car," he said. "It wasn't at me, was it?"

She sighed. "No. I was angry at myself for making such a dumb mistake."

"Poor wildcat." He nuzzled against her hair. "I should have just let you go, but I was a rookie, and you know, protocol... Anyway, you should go easy on that poor girl. One little mistake wasn't going to send her into a life of crime."

"It might have. You don't know."

"Uh, I do know. I'm the sheriff, remember?" He touched her cheek because her skin was smooth and silky and he liked the feel of it. "I tried to find out what happened to you after you left camp. I wanted to talk to you while you were here back then, but I thought it best if I didn't. Anyway, I was worried about you. But funnily enough, no one would give me any information on where you'd gone. Apparently rookie cops looking up info on teenage girls wasn't allowed."

Her expression eased, her smile unexpectedly lighting up the dark space around them. "Really? Can't think why not." She ran her fingers over his chest again, sending sparks through him. "You didn't have to be worried about me. Taking me back to Sheriff McClain was the right thing to do, because then I got to go to camp. And camp helped me figure out what I needed to do to get on the right path and I did it. I worked hard at school, decided I'd try getting into real estate, moved to Jasper Creek and put my family firmly behind me. I still keep in touch with some of them, but I don't bother with Mom or Dad. They burned their bridges with me a long time ago."

There was a quiet pride in the way she said it that made the respect he already had for her grow. "You did good," he murmured. "You did really good."

She gave him such a sweet smile, it made his heart squeeze in his chest. "I know, real estate is not the world's most exciting job, but I like showing people around nice houses and maybe introducing them to what could be their new home."

"Hey, if you get something out of it, who cares whether it's exciting or not?"

"I guess." She wrinkled her nose and poked him in the chest. "What about you? Did you always want to be sheriff?"

He grabbed her poking finger and enclosed her hand in his. "No. First I wanted to be a pirate, then a garbage truck driver, then a fireman. Then I decided that stealing cars was way more fun."

Bree's eyes got very large. "You stole cars?"

He grinned. "What? You never heard about what a juvenile delinquent I was?"

"No, I did not." She tugged her hand from his, then folded both on his chest and propped her chin on them, gazing up at him. Her hair spilled over her shoulders in a black waterfall. She was so lovely, he ached. "Okay, you got me, Sheriff Dicker. I'm interested now. What did you do?"

"You're really still calling me Sheriff Dicker? After that?"

She flushed beautifully, but smiled. "I think most especially after that."

Flint wanted to pull her close, kiss her, take her beneath him again, and obviously his thoughts must have shown on his face, because she shook her head, grinning. "Oh, no, not yet. Tell me everything about your secret bad-boy past first."

"My secret bad-boy past is basically me being a typical sixteen-year-old boy and getting in with the wrong crowd. Drinking beer and drag racing, stealing cars, vandalizing property. All the exciting stuff."

"Wow." Her eyes were alight with interest. "Who knew?"

Strange. He hadn't told this story to anyone before, so why he was doing it now, he had no idea. But he didn't stop. "Yeah, my dad left when I was really young and he never kept in contact, so when I was around sixteen, I tried to track him down. I found his number and called him, but…he wasn't interested in having a relationship with me. I'd never liked hearing the word *no*, even back then, so I thought I'd visit him in person and talk to him." An old, remembered anger twisted in his gut. "Found out he was living in Portland, so I took the bus up there and visited his house. He was out in the yard, playing with a couple of boys, and I realized they were his sons. He was smiling at them, tossing them up in the air, the whole dad thing. He had another family, you see, and I guess he didn't want me being part of it."

There was sympathy in Bree's eyes, and her thumb resumed stroking his chest as if in comfort, and he knew he should shut himself up, but now that part was out, it seemed stupid to stop.

"I left," he went on. "Came back home to Jasper Creek. I was…angry. Angry because it was clear Dad thought his new family and his new sons were better than me. Otherwise why would he tell me not to contact him again? Anyway, I didn't tell Mom. I found a bunch of kids who were just as angry as I was and we got into a whole bunch of trouble, because why not? At the time, I thought that if that other family was more worthy than I was, then there was no point even trying."

"Oh, Flint," she said softly. "That's awful. And it's so not true."

He ran his fingers down her back, enjoying the simple delight of her silky skin. "Well, I know that now, but at the time it was…hard. The thing that saved me was Bill Mc-

Clain. He and Mom started dating, and he took an interest in me. I wasn't into it and basically told him where to go. But he persisted. And he got me to clean up my act, got me interested in police work, in how it can help people. He turned my life around."

"Is that why you're here?" Bree asked. "At Camp Phoenix, I mean? Helping out?"

"Yeah."

She smiled. "I remember you. Back from when I was at camp as a kid. I didn't want anything to do with you, though."

He grinned back. "Not surprised. That's why I kept my distance. I didn't want to get scratched again."

Bree rolled her eyes. "But you're here now because…?"

"Oh, yeah. Bill put a lot of faith in me and I want to repay that faith. Do something in his memory. Make him proud."

"You know," she said, very seriously, "I think he'd be very proud already. Not very many car-thief drag racers become sheriff."

Something odd shifted inside him at that, a strange tension he hadn't been aware of before. But since he didn't know what it was, he ignored it.

"Could say the same for you, wildcat." He bent and brushed his mouth over hers. "Now, I don't know about you, but I'm tired of talking. What say we do something else?"

"Good idea," she murmured and reached for him.

CHAPTER NINE

BREE WOKE IN the dark, immediately annoyed with herself for falling asleep in Flint's bed, which she hadn't planned on. Still, she felt amazing. Who knew sex with Flint would make her feel so good? She'd thought it probably would. She just hadn't thought it would be…well, *that* good.

A quick glance at the sky told her dawn wasn't far off, so she slipped out of bed, not wanting to wake him, and pulled on her clothes. His hat was on the floor beside the bed and she debated a moment, then reached for it, putting it on.

It was too big, but if she kept it on the back of her head, she could at least see.

She paused once more just before she left, to get a last eyeful of his hard, muscular body stretched out on the mattress. Had another debate with herself about whether to wake him up for a last round, but then reluctantly turned to the window and went out the way she came in.

Better not to stay. Better to leave it like this, without a goodbye. Mainly because if she stayed, she might end up asking for more than one night, and she couldn't do that. He'd been very clear that one night was all he could give her, and really, that suited her too. She wasn't looking for a relationship right now anyway.

Bree ignored the ache that told her she was a liar and walked back to the cabins through the darkness of the trees, enjoying the crispness of the air and smell of pine.

She did not think about what she'd told Flint the night before about her family and how angry she'd been at herself, or about what he'd told her. About how, despite his reputation for strict adherence to the law, he'd been a bit of a bad boy in his youth. Or how he'd told her about his father, and how she thought that maybe it was a story he didn't tell very often since he'd sounded so determinedly matter-of-fact about it. And she definitely didn't think about how curious it had made her and why he'd decided to tell her about it when they didn't know each other that well. Or about how he'd been at camp too and how similar their stories had been, both of them bad kids.

Also, there was absolutely, positively zero thoughts about the sex.

None at all.

Bree had just reached the cabin and was reaching for the door handle when it abruptly opened and Kinley came out.

Shock rippled through her and she stumbled back a couple of steps before catching herself, all the while cursing in her head.

Of course, Kinley would be up before the others. She had to be in order to get breakfast ready.

Kinley's eyes went very wide. "Bree? Where have you been?"

She tried a pleasant smile, attempting not to look like she'd come straight from Flint Decker's bed. "Oh, I…um…"

"We were worried," Kinley charged on over top of her. "You disappeared into the house and then you didn't come back and…" She stopped, her eyes getting even bigger as they zeroed in on Bree's neck. "Oh my God, is that a—"

"No." Bree slapped a hand over whatever was on her neck. "No, it absolutely is not."

But Kinley's gaze narrowed, her look of wide-eyed

worry turning deeply suspicious. "I see. You stayed the night, didn't you? You had sex with Flint Decker. You had sex with the *enemy*."

Having Kinley look at her with such disapproval was rather like getting a kitten scratch: unexpected and more discomforting than she thought it would be.

She had a brief moment when she considered lying about it because Flint had been very certain that he didn't want anyone to know. But then discarded the idea.

The others *would* have been worried about her, and she felt bad about it. Bad enough that she didn't want to lie to them. She didn't want to pretend it hadn't happened either, because that felt wrong too.

Bree lifted her hands placatingly. "Okay, look. I know. It was very bad of me to stay the night. But he caught me trying to steal his stupid hat, and then he started laughing, and I couldn't think of a good way to shut him up except to kiss him."

Kinley folded her arms, unimpressed. "Seriously?"

Bree felt herself blushing, which was ridiculous. It wasn't as if she'd never had sex before, after all. "All he was wearing was a towel. What else was I supposed to do? Say no?"

Kinley considered this, then wrinkled her nose. "Fine, I'll allow it." Her large eyes settled on the hat perched on Bree's head. "At least the operation was successful, I guess."

On many fronts, but Bree wasn't about to go into too many details. "It *was*. But you can't tell anyone, okay? Flint doesn't want anyone to—"

The door of the cabin opened suddenly, Violet's head craning around it. "Flint doesn't want anyone to what?" Then she took one look at Bree, the hat on her head and the bruise on her neck, and gave a slow smile. "I knew it. You've been up all night playing with Sheriff Dicker's d—"

"Hey," Clementine said primly from behind her. "That's my boss you're talking about."

Bree tried not to look too smug. "Why are you guys up so early?"

Violet came fully out of the cabin, followed by Clementine. "Because a couple of idiots decided it would be a great idea to have a loud conversation on the doorstep at five in the morning and woke me up." She fixed Bree with a direct stare. "Come on. Since you kept us up gossiping about where you might be, and then woke us up early, you can give us the details of your hot night with the sheriff."

"No details," Bree said firmly, deciding she needed to take charge of the conversation since it appeared to have gotten away from her. "Other than the sheriff has skills, and also, he doesn't want anyone to know that he and I slept together."

Clementine's eyes widened. "What skills?" she asked at the same time as Violet said, "Why doesn't he want anyone to know?"

None of the other women knew that Flint had been her arresting officer and she didn't particularly want to tell them. Then again…why not? Her night with him had been magical, special even, and she wanted to talk about him. Which was silly, considering it was a one-night hookup.

"Because," Bree said, "he was the cop who arrested me ten years ago and he thinks it's inappropriate."

Violet grinned. "I'm sorry, but that's hot. Please tell me handcuffs were involved. And no, not ten years ago—last night."

Kinley put her hands over her ears. "Don't tell me. I

don't want to know." She headed toward the mess hall. "Or at least wait till I'm gone."

"I also do not want to know," Clementine said.

"Good." Bree was blushing yet again. "Because I'm not going to tell you. Or anyone else." She gave Clementine a direct look. "Don't let him know you know."

Clementine raised a hand. "It's okay. Your secret's safe with me. I swear on the Camp Phoenix flag."

"Me too," Violet said, and her grin became approving. "Good going, Bree. Sex, and you got the hat too. Makes a nice change from stealing my sleeping bag."

She hadn't thought she'd needed approval from anyone for anything, still less from Queen Bee Violet, yet a small ripple of pleasure went through her. She grinned back at her. "I'm sorry about your sleeping bag," she said impulsively. "Also, your singing was pretty good. Flint was in the shower, so it didn't work on him, but you certainly got the others out of the house."

"I know." Violet looked smug. "Lincoln was very unhappy about it."

"At least there's that. Thanks anyway for helping out. And you too, Clementine."

Clementine flushed, a pleased expression on her face. "Oh, um, it was nothing." Then she looked concernedly at the sky. "We should start getting ready for wake-up. It'll be 6:00 a.m. soon."

The three of them went into the cabin, and as they got ready, Bree was aware that Clementine kept glancing her way, a slightly awed look on her face, while Violet kept throwing her a lot of conspiratorial grins.

It made her feel as if they shared some lovely, wicked secret and she liked that more than she thought she would.

Certainly, she'd never had that the first time round at camp, or at least, not initially.

As six o'clock arrived and reveille started playing, Bree was half tempted to come out wearing Flint's hat for the flag raising, but deciding it would prompt too many questions, she left it on her bed.

She felt both excited and strangely nervous as they all tramped up the hill for the flag raising, then gathered for the distribution of the day's chores. Her gaze immediately locked on to Flint's tall figure and, of course, he was bareheaded. It sent an illicit thrill down her spine knowing the reason for that was because his hat was currently sitting on her pillow. He looked nowhere but at her, a certain glitter in his eyes, one side of his mouth curving in that fascinating smile, and she wanted to stride up to him and kiss that smile straight off his face.

One and done, remember? He was clear.

Of course. They wouldn't be doing it again and she was fine with it. Perfectly fine. And that little drop she felt in the pit of her stomach at the thought, that little ache, was not in any way disappointment.

She'd push him to the back of her mind and not think of him, or at least not in that way, again. And as for his hat, that would be a nice souvenir and she might give it back eventually, if he was lucky.

He would be a…friend to her now. Only that. A friend.

Bree did not expect this to present any difficulties whatsoever.

Yet as the next few days passed, it seemed that there were, in fact, several difficulties.

Firstly, her heartbeat would accelerate every time Flint was in her vicinity, which seemed to be much more than she'd anticipated.

Since they'd finished visiting the town businesses, they were now having to manage and organize the materials that had been donated, and Flint always seemed to be somewhere she also was, helping unload books from Happy Ever After, or helping her and Clementine find bins for the craft kits from A Simple Thread. He'd be chatting to Kinley in the kitchens while she carried in bags of baking supplies from The Sugar Shack, or talking to Jackson in the admin cabin while she was filling in the donation spreadsheet on the computer there. Once, she and Violet were painting the walls in one of the cabins and she could hear him just outside, having a conversation with Duke, his deep voice sending little thrills through her, distracting her so much that she painted over her own hand, much to Violet's amusement.

Or maybe it wasn't him being in her vicinity. Maybe she was always in his. Or maybe it was only that she had become so sensitized to his presence, it didn't matter how far away he was from her; she'd always notice him.

What she did know was that whenever he was around, it didn't matter how many times she told herself she wouldn't look; she kept glancing his way. And every time his green eyes met hers, she'd feel the impact of it like a blow, sparks echoing through her.

It was really infuriating.

Then, a week later, she was walking innocently from the admin cabin to the dining hall when she caught a glimpse of him and Lincon unloading some of the plant supplies from the bed of his truck. It was an unseasonably hot day for May, the sun beating down. Flint had just grabbed a giant bag of soil and had hauled it from the truck to where the rest of the supplies had been neatly stacked. And she found herself coming to a dead stop, unable to take her gaze from the flex of his biceps, or the way his damp T-shirt stuck to every rock-hard muscle of his torso. Then he made matters worse by grabbing the hem of his T-shirt and using it to wipe his face, revealing his flat, muscled stomach.

Bree's mouth dried and she had to turn away, her heart beating way too fast. This was crazy. She couldn't be watching him this way. It made her feel like a creepy pervert. And why was she watching him anyway? They'd had their one night together and that was supposed to have gotten rid of these feelings.

She wasn't supposed to still want him.

"Bree?"

Bree froze at the sound of his deep voice from behind her. Oh, God, had he noticed her looking? How embarrassing.

"Did you want something?"

Argh. He *had* caught her looking. Sadly, running would only give herself away, so she dredged up her perfectly pleasant smile from somewhere, stuck it firmly to her face and turned around.

Flint, in all his glory, was standing not far away, black T-shirt sticking to his skin, his green eyes vivid against his tanned face.

"Uh, no," she said, forcing her brain to start working. "Not as such."

"You've been avoiding me," he said. "Again."

Avoiding him? No, it was the opposite, surely. She couldn't go two steps without him appearing from somewhere and being generally in her vicinity.

"I have not," she said, trying for cool. "Anyway, how can I avoid you when you're always around?"

"Am I?" He raised a black brow. "If I'm always around,

how come you've barely spoken three words to me since last week?"

Bree was aware of a certain shock. Had she really not spoken to him? It felt as if he was everywhere, his presence filling up the camp, or at least her part of it. And she must have said something to him. Surely, she had. And if not, she didn't know why she hadn't. She wasn't consciously avoiding him. It was just…

His presence makes you hot and you forget what you're saying and you don't know what to say to him anyway.

Sadly, that was all true.

"Well, I didn't mean to," she said, still trying for cool yet pleasant.

His gaze narrowed, and then he glanced behind him, as if checking to see where Lincoln was. Turning back, he took a step toward her and fixed her with those green eyes of his. "Where's my hat?"

She blinked. "Your hat?"

"Yeah, the thing that sits on my head. Shaped like a cowboy hat."

A little prickle of irritation crept through her. "So, that's all you want to know? Where your stupid hat is?"

The look in his eyes intensified all of a sudden. "Why? Did you want me to ask you about something else?"

"Like what?"

"You know what."

And there it was again, the tension between them, pulling tight, then getting even tighter.

She swallowed, feeling far too hot and far too sweaty. "Actually, I don't know—"

"Are you okay, Bree?" His gaze was fierce, hungry almost.

A rush of heat swept over her. "What do you mean 'okay'?"

"After last week—"

"I'm fine." She didn't want him to talk about last week. The only way she'd been able to get through this week was *not* to think about last week. "Really, really fine."

Yet he didn't look away. "So fine you're not speaking to me?"

She lifted her chin. "I don't have to speak to you every day, Flint."

He stared at her, and just like that, his gaze was full of those fascinating green sparks. "Don't get angry, wildcat." His voice had gotten very deep and slightly rough. "You're allowed to miss me."

Another wash of heat swept through her, along with a simmering anger that she very well knew was rooted in frustration and a desire she hadn't been able to put behind her no matter how she tried. And really, what she should have done was turn around and walk away, keep her temper leashed.

Yet she didn't. Instead, she took a couple of steps to where he stood and looked straight into his eyes. "I do not miss you, Sheriff Dicker."

She was expecting him to rise to the bait.

He didn't.

"That's a pity," he said instead. "Because I sure as hell am missing you."

Bree's anger drained away as quickly as it had come, leaving shock in its wake. "You miss me?"

Flint's mouth curved. "I told you that you drove me crazy, right? Well, you're still doing it, wildcat. I haven't been able to think straight for the past week." He took a step closer. "I want another night."

CHAPTER TEN

FLINT COULDN'T TAKE his eyes off her. Her hair was loose today and lying over her shoulders in a shining fall, and she was wearing those little shorts again, and all he wanted to do was rip them off her.

He hadn't been lying about the past week. It had been a nightmare. He'd had trouble concentrating, half his awareness constantly on his surroundings and whether she was there. And she always seemed to be. Every time her light, clear voice echoed, his body hardened and he turned in her direction.

It was insane. One night, that's all it was supposed to have been, and yet...he couldn't get her out of his head. None of his friends had suspected anything untoward had happened that night, though Lincoln had asked him the next day what happened to his hat. He'd muttered something about wanting a change, but no one else had commented on it.

Once or twice, though, he'd seen one of the other women glance at him appraisingly, even, much to his extreme annoyance, Clementine.

Women talked to each other, he knew that, and Bree's absence that night would have been noted. And he could probably take it that at least three other people knew Bree had spent the night with him, one of them being his deputy.

He supposed he should be grateful that none of them

had said anything to him, and luckily none of them had said anything to his friends. Not that he was actively trying to hide that he'd spent the night with Bree; it was more that there was no point telling them about something that wasn't going to happen again.

At least, he'd thought it wasn't going to happen again.

Until now.

Ridiculous. The whole point of sleeping with her had been to deal with their attraction once and for all, not make it more intense. Yet that's exactly what had happened. And it was *not* helped by the fact that he'd seen her watching him as he and Lincoln had unloaded the truck, quite blatantly checking him out.

Going after her had been another mistake, yet he had, and now he was here, looking into her dark eyes and seeing the same hunger in her that was gnawing at him.

He shouldn't have said anything. He should have stayed quiet. But he hadn't. There was only one way to handle this and that was another night.

She was blushing so prettily, that flash of anger having come and gone like summer lightning, leaving embers of something much hotter behind it. "I—" she began, then broke off, her gaze darting behind him. "Why, yes, Flint," she said a bit louder. "I did steal your hat. Shall I show you where it is?"

Flint didn't need to look behind him to know that Lincoln was around somewhere closer, so all he did was nod. "Sure."

Bree turned and walked quickly through the trees toward the cabin where she and the other women slept, and he followed. There was no one else around and thank God, because Flint felt himself get breathless, heat surging in his veins: there could be only one reason she wanted him to come to the cabin, and it wasn't simply to retrieve his hat.

Bree didn't look to see if he was behind her as she pushed open the cabin door and went in. He didn't hesitate, coming in right after her.

Only to have her palms land on his chest the moment the door shut behind him, and then he was being pushed very firmly up against the door, while she pressed her warm, sweet curves against him.

She stared fiercely up at him. "One night, you said. You were very clear."

"I know." He settled his hands on her hips, holding her even closer. "I thought one night would get rid of this attraction, but it hasn't. It's made it worse."

"Tell me about it." Her gaze dropped to his mouth. "So… another night?"

"Yes." He bent his head, brushing his lips over hers. "That okay with you?"

She shuddered, angling her head back farther. "Oh, yes… More than."

It was an invitation and he took it, kissing her hard and deep.

She gasped and then things got very desperate very quickly.

Flint turned them around, pushing her against the door. Then he pinned her there with his body, his kiss exploring deeper and more intensely.

Her hands crept under his T-shirt, her fingers on his skin, tracing and stroking and touching.

Hell, he'd said a night and a night did not mean sex up against a door in a cabin. Someone could come in at any moment and he still wanted to keep this on the down-low.

Flint reached down and grabbed her exploring hands.

"Wait," he murmured against her mouth. "I'm not doing this here. We need somewhere more private."

"Where?" She sounded delightfully breathless. "There's nowhere private here in camp."

It was true. There was the room he occasionally slept in at Jackson's place, but again, too risky.

He lifted her hands and kissed them, then let go and stood back. "Then let's go to my ranch. I can think of some excuse why you have to come with me."

She grinned. "That, Sheriff Decker, is a great idea."

He grinned back. "But first things first." Turning, he strode over to what must be her bunk because he'd seen a very familiar-looking hat sitting on the pillow when he'd first walked in.

"Hey," Bree said from behind him. "Finders keepers."

Flint picked the hat up, stuck it on his head, then turned back to her. "You didn't find it, wildcat. You stole it. So if you want it again, you're going to have to steal it again."

She smiled, the look on her face glowing, making something inside him twist, though that was surely desire, nothing more. "Don't get too comfortable, Sheriff. I might do just that."

Oh, he liked her like this. He liked her spitting and hissing, it was true, but this was good too. Her smiling at him, teasing him, and being sassy. Perhaps they could stay awhile at his ranch. Perhaps he'd even cook her dinner. He'd have to think of some excuse that would explain why she wouldn't be at camp tonight, but he was sure he could do that. Anything was possible.

Flint strode to the door and held it open for her, and she gave him a flirty glance from underneath her lashes as she went out.

Lincoln was still by the truck, having finished the last

of the unloading, and he gave Flint a narrow look as he and Bree approached.

"Got your hat back, I see," he observed dryly.

Flint feigned innocence. "What hat?"

Lincoln just looked at him. Then he glanced at Bree and back at Flint. "Going somewhere?"

"Yeah, there's another couple of people we have to talk to," Flint lied straight to his friend's face. "We'll be back later."

Lincoln's expression gave nothing away. "Uh-huh."

Five minutes later, as they pulled out of camp, Bree said, "I think he knows we're not going to 'talk to people.'"

She probably wasn't wrong. Lincoln might look like he couldn't be bothered 90 percent of the time, but in reality he was as sharp as a razor and never missed a thing.

Flint didn't know how he felt about that. The guys hadn't seemed worried about him and Bree potentially getting together that night at poker. In fact, none of them had a problem with it. So...did it really matter if people knew?

Then again, this might only be another one-off, and if it was, then making a big deal of the fact that they were sleeping together also seemed pointless.

Is it another one-off, though?

Flint pushed that thought away. It had to be. He wasn't up for anything more. The timing just wasn't right.

He glanced at her. "Does it bother you if he does?"

"Honestly? No." She bit her lip, then said after a moment, "The girls know too. Sorry. Kinley was up when I got back to the cabin and—"

"It's okay. I thought that might be the case." He gave her a narrow look. "You should have woken me up to escort you back to the cabin since it was dark."

"Well, they really would have seen you then. Besides,

I thought…" She let out a breath. "I thought it would be easier if I just left."

Flint shifted a little in his seat. When he'd woken up that morning and she was gone, he'd told himself he was fine with it, but… Well, he wouldn't have minded her lying in his arms for a bit longer. He certainly would have liked to have kissed her again. Not that it mattered.

"Don't worry about it," he said. "You're here now."

It wasn't far to his ranch, and soon they were driving down the long drive, and through the fields that surrounded it, before pulling up to the little red farmhouse that sat in the center.

The paint was peeling and the roof needed to be replaced, and there was quite a bit of work to be done in the interior, but the house had been sturdily made and it had a wide porch that ran the length of the building, which he loved. But most of all, it was his and it was a place where, conceivably, he'd have a family in, one day.

Not yet, of course, but one day.

He'd have a wife and children, a family. It was what he'd realized he'd wanted over the years. What he'd missed out on when he was young. Oh, his mom had been great and had done what she could for him. But he'd never told her about what had happened with his dad, because he hadn't wanted to worry her. And he'd never told Bill either. Mainly because there had been something uniquely humiliating about having your own father not even want to give you the time of day. Especially when it had been clear he'd found another family away from Flint. A better family, with better sons.

Well, he didn't need his father. He'd never needed him. He'd had Bill and, anyway, he was just fine. Now he had a house that was his, and one day, he'd be a dad and a much better father than his own ever had been.

Flint pulled the truck up in front of the house and got out. Bree got out too, and she stood there a moment, staring up at the house. And he was conscious of a strange tension inside him. He wanted her to like the house, he realized. Which was odd because why should he care about her opinion? Did it even matter when all she was going to see was the inside of his bedroom?

"Wow," she said as he came up next to her. "This is a great place. I can see why you bought it."

That weird tension released as abruptly as it had gathered, and he wished he didn't feel quite so pleased that she liked it, but he did. "Yeah. It needs a bit of work, admittedly, but I thought it had potential."

"Oh, it really does." Her dark eyes were alight as she studied the house. "It's got great bones. And that porch is fantastic." She glanced at him. "Why did you buy a ranch? Surely, you've got enough to do as sheriff already."

"It's true. But I don't like sitting around, and having a lot of outdoor physical work suits me. I find it satisfying. Police work can be thankless and sometimes you wonder if you ever truly make a difference. But here, you get out what you put in, and I like that. It gives me some balance."

She gave him a curious look. "Is that what you really want? To make a difference? And who to?"

He didn't need to think in order to answer her questions, mainly because there was only one answer. "Specifically? I want to make a difference to kids like I was once. Kids with no parental figures or no guidance in their lives, no support. Kids who are headed into lives of petty crime or worse. Kids who want to do better—and could—if only they had people who supported them."

Bree was silent a moment, watching him, her dark eyes full of something he couldn't quite pinpoint. Then she said, "You're a lot deeper than I thought you'd be."

He gazed back. "Is that a good thing?"

"Yes," she said slowly. "I think it is. You know..." She trailed off, looking slightly hesitant, then went on. "It probably doesn't matter now, but...you made a difference to me."

He tried to ignore the sudden warmth that settled in his chest. "I did? How?"

She'd gone pink, but she didn't stop. "Well, if you hadn't arrested me and taken me to Sheriff McClain, I wouldn't have gone to Camp Phoenix. And if I hadn't gone to Camp Phoenix, I wouldn't be in Jasper Creek, with a job I like and a house of my own." She put her hands in the pockets of her shorts and shifted a little awkwardly, but the look she gave him was direct. "Basically, if you hadn't put me in your patrol car, I'd have started down the path my family went down, and by now, I'd surely be in jail."

The warm thing inside him glowed and spread out. He hadn't been lying—police work *was* thankless sometimes, and sometimes it was hard to see how you helped people when all you saw was the worst in them. Certainly no one had ever thanked him for arresting them before.

He smiled. "Maybe I helped. But you'd already decided you weren't going down that path." She opened her mouth to protest, but he held up a hand. "And like I already told you, stealing food doesn't count as a major crime. No, the reason you're not in jail, wildcat, is you. You decided you weren't going to go down that path, and so you didn't." He reached out and drew her closer against him. "Don't short-change yourself, Bree White. You made a different choice and persisted with it. That's why you're standing here."

She gazed up at him, and this time, he couldn't tell what

she was thinking. But when she reached up and pulled his mouth down on hers, it soon became very, very clear.

And then he couldn't get her into the house fast enough.

CHAPTER ELEVEN

IT ENDED UP being more than one night. Then more than two. Then three, and after the fourth, they both stopped counting.

There was something illicit and exciting about sneaking around with Flint that made Bree breathless and almost fizzing with anticipation. They snatched a half hour here, an afternoon there, and a couple of overnighters that they were able to explain away perfectly rationally, in Bree's opinion.

She didn't think anyone else, apart from Violet, Kinley and Clementine, knew, and while the three other women were mostly understanding, there were times when she missed 6:00 a.m. wake-up because she'd slept too long at Flint's.

Whether the guys cared or even knew was starting to bother her less and less, mainly because spending time with Flint was rapidly becoming her favorite thing to do.

He was just…wonderful. Okay, so he was opinionated and bossy, but in the right context that was a turn-on for her. They certainly had a few spectacular arguments about small things that were soon followed up by some equally spectacular makeups.

And it wasn't just the sex, though that was admittedly amazing.

He had a wicked, sharp sense of humor that, combined

with his warmth and his unexpected kindness, his generosity and protectiveness, made him absolutely irresistible.

Plus, he'd told her that she was the reason she wasn't in jail like her family. That she shouldn't shortchange herself. And there was a small, secret part of her that had wondered if, over the years, she'd done just that. A tense, rigid part that kept whispering she'd never leave her past behind her, no matter how hard she tried. That, deep down, she'd always be a feral little criminal.

But that part was quiet when she was with him. In fact, it was almost as if she *could* be feral with him because he definitely seemed to like it.

A dangerous man and one she shouldn't allow herself to get closer to, especially when he kept on insisting this was a limited-time-only kind of deal, and that nothing lasting could come of it.

A few weeks later and they were at Flint's, the long shafts of late-afternoon sunlight shining through his bedroom windows making Bree feel warm and sleepy and sated.

They'd left camp earlier that afternoon on the flimsy pretext of "errands," only to head immediately to Flint's house, spending a blissful couple of hours in each other's arms. Now she didn't particularly want to do anything other than lie there naked on his bed, with his fingers stroking up and down her spine.

"You want dinner here?" he asked after a long, comfortable silence. "I can cook us a couple of steaks and there's salad. I can even hunt us out a bottle of wine."

That sounded great to Bree. More than great even. "I'd love that." She sighed. "Though, I haven't not turned up for a meal at camp before. And I think everyone might notice if we both weren't there."

"True. But we could say we got caught up in town and decided to grab dinner there."

Yes, they certainly could. Or…

Or you could stop sneaking around and have a conversation with him about where this affair is actually going.

Yes, she could. The real question was, did she want to? She'd been happy to let things go on as they had been for the past two weeks or so, but Flint's need for secrecy was starting to pall. As were his occasional reminders that their affair was just that—an affair.

Yet broaching the topic was going to end up popping this happy little bubble they were in, and she didn't want to do that. She wasn't ready for it to end.

Bree stared at the windows and the green fields visible beyond the glass, acutely aware of the man whose arms she lay in, the man who'd given her such intense pleasure. A man who wanted to help people and make a difference in his community, and who was always thinking of others.

A man who was everything she wanted.

That's the real issue, though, isn't it? You want him. You're falling for him.

She swallowed, her throat closing at the unexpected thought. No, she wasn't falling for him. She couldn't, not when he didn't want anything more than this.

Except…all she could think about was how much she wanted to be standing on that wonderful porch as his truck drove up so he didn't have to come home to an empty house. How much she wanted to cook dinner with him in the kitchen and chat about their days. How much she wanted to lie in his arms like she was doing right now, sharing their dreams and hopes for the future…

Yep, definitely not *falling for him.*

"Well?" Flint murmured in her ear. "Dinner? I could make it worth your while."

"In that case…" She forced those thoughts away and the aching feeling in her chest along with them. "Most definitely, I'll stay for dinner."

They got up after that, and she availed herself of Flint's shower, and she basked a little in it, determinedly not thinking about anything except how wonderful the pressure was and how good the hot water felt.

Flint had gone downstairs to start dinner while she dressed. One of Flint's T-shirts had been thrown over a chair by the window and, absently, she picked it up and put it on. It wasn't the first time she'd worn one of his T-shirts. The cotton was always soft and they smelled so deliciously of him that she couldn't resist. He seemed to like her wearing them too, since whenever she put one on, those fascinating green sparks of heat would glitter in his eyes and he got a little possessive.

She really liked that. She really liked everything about him.

You have to say something. You have to. You don't want to get your heart broken.

Bree tried not to think about that either as she came downstairs to the kitchen. Her heart was fine. At least, it was right now. She didn't have to say anything if she didn't want to and she didn't want to. What she wanted was to have dinner with him, that was all.

He was already fussing around, getting food out, looking absolutely delicious in worn jeans and a T-shirt, his feet bare. Then he did a double take, noticing the shirt she was wearing, a hot, possessive look in his eyes.

She gave him a mock stern glare. "No. I'm hungry."

His grin was wicked as he put down the saucepan he'd gotten out, coming over to her. "How can I help it when you look like that?" Taking her face between his hands, he kissed her soundly. "You should be wearing that and nothing else."

Bree's heart ached. She loved it when he couldn't resist her.

You love him, period.

No. No, she didn't. She wasn't falling for him, wasn't in love with him. She wasn't anything with him except maybe in lust.

"Maybe I'll change." She gave him a teasing look from beneath her lashes. "But after dinner."

He laughed, kissed her again, then let her go. "Fine. I guess food is important."

While Flint cooked the steaks, Bree sat at the scrubbed wooden table and helped chop some veggies for the salad, and they talked. And she couldn't help being aware that this was very like those little daydreams that she'd had upstairs, of them cooking together and chatting just like this.

This is what you want.

It was. She couldn't help it. And she couldn't ignore it either.

After the food had been prepared and they sat to eat, Flint began to talk about his ranch and what he wanted for it. Camp Phoenix was great, but he wanted to have something year-round for at-risk youth, and that's what he was hoping for the ranch. A place for young people to go and get a kind of reset on their lives, with boundaries and chores as a structure, but also a place to learn, such as how to care for animals and how to ride. It would give kids a taste of a different kind of life, especially city kids.

He was passionate as he talked about it and he made it sound so wonderful.

He was wonderful.

And she couldn't help thinking about her own life. About her job and her house, the life she'd always wanted, and yet…she hadn't thought about the future. She didn't want to be a Realtor forever, and she wanted a family at some point, but she hadn't thought about specifics. She hadn't thought about what else she wanted to do and who she wanted to do it with.

You do now, though. You want a life with him.

"You okay?" Flint asked.

They were sitting at the table, having finished eating, and Flint was leaning back in his chair, cradling a wineglass in his long fingers.

All she could hear was that thought echoing in her head, over and over again.

Yes. Yes, she did want a life with him. A life that was waking up in his arms every morning and eating breakfast together. Then helping him help those kids. Kids like him and kids like her, both of them making a difference to people. And then falling asleep in those same arms every night, his hands on her skin and his heart beating slow and steady beneath her ear…

You have *been shortchanging yourself. You have been for years, telling yourself that you're happy because you're not in jail, not a criminal. But that's not a future. You could want more. You could want better.*

"Bree?"

She'd been silent too long. She needed to say something and something that wasn't *Oh my God, I think I'm in love with you*. Because she couldn't say it, not when it would change everything. She'd thought she was happy and satisfied with her life, that she didn't want anything more than what she had.

But the fact was, she did want more. She just hadn't realized it until now.

"Oh," she said, hoping her voice sounded normal and not half-strangled with the intensity of her stupid emotions. "Listening to you talk about what you want to do with this place… It's really wonderful. Makes me feel like my own is a bit… I don't know. Small, maybe?"

"Why? You're enjoying what you're doing, right?"

She fought to get her heartbeat to slow down. "Yes, I do. But…I don't want to keep doing it forever. I want to do something else, something that makes a difference." She paused and looked at him, and then, risking it, said, "Something like what you're doing with the ranch."

Flint looked at her a minute, his expression unreadable. Then he put his wineglass down on the table. "You could help me, if you wanted. I mean, I'm not just thinking of having boys on the ranch. We could use a female role model." He gave a sudden, humorless laugh. "After all, I know what it's like not to have grown up with someone I could really relate to."

They hadn't talked about anything personal since that first night, when he'd told her about his father and how he hadn't wanted to see Flint, and she hadn't pushed. That wasn't what their affair was about.

It still wasn't. And if she had any sense, she'd let the remark pass without commenting. But the ache in her chest, the feeling in her heart, wouldn't let her. "You had Bill, though," she said. "Don't forget that."

Flint put his hands on the table, looking down at them as though they were the most fascinating things he'd ever seen. "It's true. I did. And he was more a father to me than my old man ever was."

Bitterness cut through the words like a knife, making her own heart feel as though someone was pinching it.

"You're angry with him," she said, then immediately felt like an idiot because any fool could see that.

Yet Flint only gave another of those laughs. "He didn't even want to talk to me, not one single word. So, yeah. I guess I am. Stupid after all these years."

"No, it's not stupid. He's your father and you were right to expect a certain level of acknowledgment from him." Bree reached over before she could stop herself and put one hand over his. "It's not your fault you didn't get it. You know that, right?"

Flint stared down at her hand over his, his mouth suddenly hard, and he didn't speak.

Her heart squeezed even tighter. Perhaps she was overstepping and pushing too much, getting too intimate. But she didn't want to stop. This was important. *He* was important.

"That's on him, not you," she went on, keeping her hand where it was. "Sheriff McClain saw you for who you were, Flint. He knew your worth. And it's not just Bill who saw it, but everyone in Jasper Creek. That's why you were elected sheriff. Because everyone knows that you're a good man. A caring, protective man, who looks out for his community and wants to help them."

Flint looked up, his green gaze locking with hers. "You really believe that?" He asked as if he didn't know, as if there was something inside of him that doubted.

"Yes," she said fiercely. "You didn't need your dad. You never did. All you needed was someone to believe in you, and you had that with Bill, and now you have it with the whole town." She took a breath, then added, "And me. I believe in you. And I love what you've got planned for this ranch. It sounds perfect."

His expression became suddenly intense. "Help me, Bree. Help me with the ranch."

This time, her heart didn't just squeeze—it twisted hard. With longing. Oh, she'd love to help him. She'd love it desperately. But she wanted more, she knew that now, so much more, and she wasn't sure if she was brave enough to ask for it. He'd been so insistent that this was temporary, after all.

She let go of his hand and sat back. "I...don't know what I'd have to offer."

"You have you. You're determined and brave. And you've got backbone enough to put me in my place, let alone a few ornery teenagers. You're good with people and you're smart." His eyes burned with something that made her ache and ache. "They'd love you. They'd look up to you. You'd be the most incredible asset."

Her throat felt tight. He always made her feel good, whatever they were doing, and not just physically. He made her feel as if she really was that determined, brave and smart woman, an inspiration, not a feral, furious teenager heading down the same road as her family.

She wanted to say yes and yet... And yet...

Being here on this ranch every day, being around *him* every day...

She stared down into her wineglass, at the red liquid in it. An asset. That's what she'd be, that's what he called her. An asset. She liked that, but she wanted more.

So tell him. You have to.

It was true. This ranch idea was important to him, and if she was going to refuse, she had to tell him why. She had to be brave. Because if she was ever going to have more, she had to ask for it.

Taking a breath, Bree lifted her gaze to his. "Is that all I am to you? An asset?"

He frowned. "No, of course you're not. You'd be an asset to the ranch is what I meant."

"I'm not talking about the ranch, Flint. I'm talking about you. I'm talking about us."

"Us?" His frown deepened. "What do you mean 'us'?"

"You know what I mean. This sleeping-together thing."

An odd expression rippled over his face, before it vanished, his features settling into determinedly neutral lines. "There is no us, Bree. We agreed on that."

And her heart, the stupid thing, dropped all the way down to the floor and straight through it, because that told her everything she needed to know about where she stood with him. Which was nowhere.

A deep, bitter disappointment settled inside her, made worse by the fact that she really only had herself to blame for it. She never should have kept on this affair with him, never indulged all those little fantasies. Never fallen in love.

Not when this was just another night and that was all.

He was just another mistake, like her shoplifting had been a mistake, and the only thing you could do with mistakes was pretend you hadn't made them.

"Sure," she said, her voice sounding strange even to her own ears. She looked back down at her wineglass. "Let me think about it, Flint."

A silence fell, awkward and full of sharp edges.

Then Flint cursed softly. "What is it? What did I say this time?"

"It's nothing." Bree lifted her wineglass and drained it, then put it back down on the table with a click. "I think I should go."

Flint stared at her. "You know I can't do more than this. You know that. I told you."

Of course he'd read her mind. He always seemed to be able to.

"Yes," she said shortly. "I know. You were very clear. You were clear the whole way through." She pushed her chair back and stood up, the urge to get out and get away from him suddenly overwhelming. "Can we go now?"

"What? Now?" Again, a flicker of some powerful emotion glittered briefly in his eyes. "I thought—"

"Look, you don't want more and I get that," she interrupted, deciding she needed to get this over and done with now, rip the Band-Aid off, so to speak. "So maybe we'd better end this whole sleeping-together thing. I don't see that there's much point drawing it out longer than we need to, and besides, someone might find out what we're doing, and we don't want that, do we?" She hadn't meant the words to sound so bitter, but they were all the same.

Flint's handsome features became curiously blank. He put his wineglass down and shoved his chair back, getting to his feet. "Okay," he said simply. "If that's how you want it."

No, that was not how she wanted it. That wasn't how she wanted it at all. But he wasn't protesting, wasn't fighting. He wasn't even rising to the slight snap in her voice at the mention of someone finding out.

He'd accepted that it was over, and so maybe she should too.

"Yes," she said. "Yes, that's exactly how I want it."

Flint turned to the door, his expression a mask. "Come on, then. Let's go." And he strode through it before she could say anything more.

CHAPTER TWELVE

FLINT WAS FURIOUS. In fact, he couldn't remember the last time he'd been so angry. And he wasn't sure whether it was at Bree or himself.

Bree made the most logical sense, since she'd randomly decided to end this perfectly amazing affair they were having, and for no apparent reason.

Then again, he wasn't a complete idiot. He'd been a total dick about the whole thing and he knew it. Insisting that this was never going to last and it was only a onetime, two-time, many-time thing. Meanwhile, he'd made love to her like he'd never made love to any woman, with excitement and passion and a raw desire he'd never experienced in his entire life. Talking to her about her terrible family and her job and the things she loved doing and the things she didn't. Loving being with her because she was warm and funny and smart as hell and, deep down, despite her early life, as idealistic as he was.

He should have called it off. He should have ended it at least a couple of weeks ago, but he hadn't. He hadn't been able to bear it.

Yeah, you're a coward.

Yeah, shit, he was. And now he'd done the worst possible thing: he'd hurt her.

She'd sat across from him at dinner, looking like all his dreams come at once in his T-shirt, and she'd put her hand on his, giving him comfort as he'd talked about his pathetic excuse for a father. He hadn't thought he'd needed it; all that comment had been was a moment of bitterness. Yet the second her hand had settled on his, he'd felt something ease in his chest, a tension in his shoulders lightening.

He hadn't ever had anyone offer him comfort in that way before. His mother hadn't been the most physical, and certainly Bill never had been. And now, as sheriff, the only thing resembling comfort he'd gotten was from the few and far between hookups he'd managed to arrange for himself.

But Bree's hand on his had made him yearn for something he hadn't even been aware he wanted.

You could offer her more, you dick. You know she wanted it.

He'd seen it in her eyes and he'd…well, he'd stopped her cold.

There is no us, he'd said. Like a goddamn fool.

He stared hard out the front windshield, trying his best to ignore the woman sitting in the passenger seat next to him. A woman he'd lied to, because of course there was an "us." It was just…he couldn't do it. He couldn't offer her anything more, because there *was* nothing more.

He had too many commitments and, anyway, the timing wasn't right, not when he had his sheriff's duties and then the ranch and his plans for it. There was no room in his life for a relationship. Maybe one day, but he couldn't ask her to wait for that day. Who knew how long it would be? It wouldn't be fair to her.

All totally reasonable excuses.

Flint almost growled and told his brain to shut the hell up. They weren't excuses. They were valid reasons. And at least he hadn't protested when she'd told him she wanted to end things, because that would have only compounded everything. He wouldn't lead her on, give her more nights of pleasure and more nights of sitting at his kitchen table, laughing and talking and enjoying each other's company. Making her want more and more, until…

Until what? She finds out that you're not worth the time after all?

The thought did not help his anger. No, it wasn't to do with him. It had nothing whatsoever to do with him. She was lovely and brave and stubborn and determined, and she deserved more than what he could give her, which was a few nights here and there and nothing more. Certainly nothing lasting.

That should have settled him, yet it didn't. The anger continued to sit there as he pulled into the camp and parked the truck.

Bree put her hand on the door handle and he thought she might get out without a word, and he wasn't sure what he'd do if that was the last thing she said to him, but then she paused. "Thanks for dinner," she said in a tight voice. "Thanks for the sex too. It was great."

Then she got out, shut the door and left him sitting alone in the darkness of the truck, their entire relationship encapsulated in three dry little sentences.

Dinner. Sex. It was great.

That was it, that's all it ever had been. And yes, it had been great. So why was he so pissed that it was over? Why did the sound of those three sentences make his chest ache? This was what he wanted—not to hurt her, of course, never that. But he didn't want more. He didn't. That's why he'd let her end it without even a protest.

Flint got out of the truck and slammed it shut, then headed over to Jackson's. He wasn't in the mood for company, but he didn't want to go back to his house, where the remains of his dinner with Bree were still on the table and his sheets still smelled of her. Back to his plans for the ranch that now suddenly seemed…pale and kind of lifeless.

He'd thought it was the best idea he'd ever had to have her be part of that. To have her there, helping him out with the kids. She had so much to offer and she'd be so good at it. She hadn't categorically said no, but that "I'll think about it" was pretty much a refusal, and hell, who was he to argue? If she didn't want to, then so be it.

You should have argued. You should have told her that you don't just want her help with the ranch—you want her living there with you. In your bed and in your life.

No, shit, that's exactly what he *didn't* want.

Ignoring the small voice inside him that whispered he was a goddamn liar, Flint went up the steps to Jackson's front door and pushed it open. Male voices drifted from the kitchen. It was poker night again.

As he entered, they all looked up with varying degrees of surprise.

"Where have you been?" Jackson asked, glaring at him.

Flint ignored him and pulled out a chair. "Deal me in."

There was a moment's silence. Then Jackson dealt out some more cards.

"So," Lincoln said as Flint picked up his hand. "I take it your evening with Bree went well?"

Asshole.

Flint debated scowling at him, then decided the best course of action was to act like nothing was wrong and he wasn't furious and didn't know what to do about the hollow ache in his chest that wouldn't go away.

"It went very well, thank you," Flint said roughly. "I presume you don't want a blow-by-blow."

"What are you doing with Bree, by the way?" Duke asked, his tone guileless. It didn't suit him.

"You know what he's doing with Bree," Jackson said, now glaring at his cards. "About damn time too, if you ask me."

Flint stared at him. "What do you mean 'about damn time'?"

Jackson didn't look up from his cards. "We know you've been hooking up, Flint. You've been doing it for weeks. Don't try to deny it."

In retrospect, he wasn't sure why he was so damn surprised that his friends knew. Trying to hide his affair with Bree—at least from his friends—had always been a futile exercise.

Flint glanced back down at his cards and grimaced. It was a shit hand. "Well, we're not hooking up anymore. It's over."

"Really?" Lincoln commented. "Didn't look like hooking up to me. Not with the way you've been staring at her."

Okay, that was enough.

He put his cards down on the table and looked up to find three sets of eyes looking back with not a little bit of judgment. Okay, maybe a *lot* of judgment.

"What?" he growled.

"What did you do, Flint?" Duke's bright blue eyes were very direct.

The simmering anger in his chest simmered a little more. "I did nothing." There wasn't any point in pretending it wasn't happening, not now. "I told her it was a limited-time-only deal and she was fine with it."

"Somehow I don't think she was fine with it," Lincoln murmured.

"Excuse me?" Flint demanded.

"You look like you want to break rocks with your teeth, Flint," Lincoln said patiently. "If she was so fine with it, why are you so angry?"

Chrissakes. There wasn't any point denying that either. "Because she wanted more," he snapped. "And I'm not in a space in my life to have a relationship—"

"A space in your life?" Jackson snapped back. "Would you listen to yourself?"

"It's true. I've got the ranch and the sheriff's department and—" He stopped, conscious of how empty all the words sounded all of a sudden. "I wanted her to come and help me with that idea I have for the ranch. She's just…she's just so…wonderful. She's got so much to offer and I…I wanted her to help me give those kids a chance and—"

"No, what you wanted was for her to give *you* a chance," Duke said unexpectedly. "That's right, isn't it?"

Duke knew. Hell, they all did. About what Bill had meant to them and how he'd dragged them all away from the paths they'd been on. The bad paths that led nowhere.

He'd thought he'd left that path behind him, thought he wasn't that person anymore, and yet…he could still feel it inside him, the echoes of his father's denial. Making him question his own self-worth. Making him question everything.

He carried it still, that kernel of doubt.

"What if she doesn't?" he heard himself say, even though he hadn't meant to. "What if, at the end, all she sees is…"

The boy your father never wanted?

He didn't need to finish the thought. They'd all heard the words he'd left unsaid.

"What?" Duke said dryly. "A sheriff who won a landslide victory? Who everyone in Jasper Creek thinks the sun shines out of his ass? A guy with big plans for that rundown ranch that could make a hell of a difference to a lot of young idiots? Yeah, what a comedown for her."

The ache in Flint's chest got worse.

You're afraid, that's what you are.

Was he? Was that all it was? His denial and insistence that he wasn't up for a relationship? Was it all just fear?

"She's a strong woman," Jackson offered gruffly. "She's got a good head on her shoulders. I think maybe you should be having this conversation with her."

"Definitely," Lincoln said. "Because you're talking relationship stuff and…well." He gave Flint his typical, lazy grin. "That's not my area of expertise."

But Duke's gaze was narrow and there was a warning in his eyes. "Don't hurt her, Flint," he said. "Don't make her be the problem. Especially when the problem is you."

Flint didn't like that. He didn't like that one bit. Mainly because he was afraid that Duke was right. The problem *was* him.

"I think there's a reason I heard the words *Sheriff Dicker* being bandied about," Lincoln said idly. "And it's not because you were being a good guy."

"Christ," Jackson growled. "I'm trying to play poker here, not solve Flint's relationship problems."

Flint's jaw ached. "I'm not having relationship problems, Jackson. I'm not actually in a relationship." Perhaps if he said it enough times, he'd believe it. Perhaps if he said it enough times, he'd even feel it.

"But you want to be," Jackson said. "So how about instead of delaying a perfectly good game with your bullshit, you go get the girl, take her home and make her happy. Or you can sit here stewing with a shit hand. Your choice."

Leave it to Jackson to make it sound that easy. Easy to ignore the echoes of his father's denial sitting inside him, that feeling of not being worth even one single word. Flint never knew why his father hadn't wanted to talk to him, had refused to see him, and he'd probably never know.

So now you're going to do the same thing to Bree? Because of fear?

Flint stared at the tabletop, his cards blurring, the thought lancing through him. Because it was kind of the same, wasn't it? He'd ignored the look of fearful hope in her eyes at the dinner table tonight, pretended he hadn't seen it. *I'm talking about us*, she'd said, and he'd said, *There is no us.* But he'd been a fucking liar.

Of course there had been an "us." Long afternoons in his bed, her stealing his hat, her arguing with him, her laughing with him. Her telling him he was a good man, that he had worth.

He wanted that. He wanted it desperately. But he'd refused her for a whole lot of dumb reasons that didn't make any sense. Because—yeah, he had to admit it—he was afraid. Afraid that, in the end, she'd see him like his father did. Not even worth the time to talk to...

Except, would she really be like his father? The Bree who'd squeezed his hand and stared at him with shining eyes as he'd talked about the ranch? The Bree who'd fought her way out of a shitty childhood and come out on top?

You know she wouldn't. So do as the man says. Go get the girl and make her happy, instead of sitting here stewing with your shit hand.

He didn't want a shit hand. He wanted Bree.

Flint shoved his chair back.

"You made a decision, then?" Jackson grunted, while Lincoln raised an eyebrow and Duke stared at him sternly.

"Yeah," Flint said. "I'm going to get the girl."

"Good," Jackson said. "And shut the damn door on your way out."

CHAPTER THIRTEEN

WHEN BREE STEPPED into the cabin, the others were already lying in their beds. Kinley gave her a curious look from her sleeping bag, while Clementine was obviously pretending to be asleep. Violet was reading by the glow of her fairy lights. She gave Bree a look from over the top of her book as she came in. "Where have you been?"

Bree's throat felt tight and fury burned like a fire in her gut. She didn't want to talk. She didn't want to do anything but go to sleep and pretend this whole crappy evening had never happened. Striding over to her bunk, she began angrily looking for her pajamas. "Out," she said shortly.

Violet's gaze narrowed. "Are you okay?"

Bree jerked her pajamas out of the bottom of her sleeping bag, where they'd gotten stuck and tangled. "I'm fine," she snapped. "I'm great. I'm the happiest girl in the entire world."

There was a silence and she realized she might have shouted that last part.

They were all staring at her. Even Clementine was peering at her from out of her sleeping bag.

Then, much to her horror, Bree burst into tears.

For a moment, no one moved, all of them staring, no one knowing what to do or what to say.

Bree wanted to stop crying, especially in front of the other three, because although they weren't enemies now, they weren't exactly friends. But there was an ache deep inside her, a pain in her heart that she didn't think was ever going to go away, and the tears just kept coming.

She put her hands over her face, not wanting anyone to see, though, really, it was far too late for that.

Then there was a rustle and someone was coming over to her and an arm went around her shoulders. "There, there," Kinley murmured comfortingly, giving her a squeeze. "Let it out. My therapist says crying is cathartic."

Moments after that, Violet and Clementine were there, both of them looking concerned. Violet had a handkerchief beautifully embroidered with flowers and thrust it at Bree wordlessly.

She took it, blowing her nose and wiping away her tears, all the while feeling like a complete idiot.

"Is it a man?" Violet asked. "I mean, of course it is. Only a man could cause this level of drama."

Clementine was scowling. "Is it Flint? What did he do?"

"If he hurt you, there will be blood," Violet vowed.

"Yes," Kinley said, giving Bree another squeeze. "We'll all help you kill him."

She hadn't been expecting such sympathy, not from these women who'd once been enemies and strangers, and for a second, she didn't know what to do with it. Then she heard herself say, "Yes, it's stupid Flint. Stupid Flint and his stupid hat. He cooked me such a nice dinner and he was so lovely. We had the greatest sex in the world and he wanted me to help him on his ranch, and he said I was an inspiration and that I had so much to offer." She stopped to take a ragged breath. "And then he said 'there is no us' and that he didn't want anything more, so I said it was over. And he said 'if that's what you want' and I said 'yes, that's exactly what I want.' But it isn't what I want. It's the last thing in the world that I want."

"Oh dear," Kinley murmured. "Should you have told him that?"

"I couldn't," Bree sobbed. "He's been telling me all this time he didn't want a relationship. It's not like I didn't know that."

"Sounds like that gives him a cast-iron excuse to be a complete asshole," Violet said, looking grim. "I think we need to pay Sheriff Dicker a little visit and show him the error of his ways."

"Yes," Clementine said with unexpected force. "I know he's my boss, but no one hurts my friends."

Bree swallowed, wiped her eyes again with the sodden handkerchief and stared at Clementine. "I'm your friend?"

Clementine blushed. "Oh, I—I mean, we don't have to be. I know I'm not one of you guys, but—"

"Yes," Bree interrupted, a sudden certainty settling down inside her. "Yes, you're my friend." She looked at Violet and Kinley. "You all are."

"Indeed." The light of battle had lit in Violet's eyes. "What's the point in being enemies with each other when the real enemy is men?"

"Agreed." Kinley gave Bree a last squeeze, then let go. "So, how are we going to do this? Shotgun? Knife? Hang, draw and quarter?"

As the warmth of their sympathy washed over her, Bree finally put down the handkerchief. She felt...steadier. It helped knowing she wasn't alone in this, that their first thoughts had been to defend her and support her. At least, if nothing else, she'd get some good friends out of this time at Camp Phoenix, and not just a broken heart.

"Guys, I appreciate the support," she said thickly. "But,

sadly, I can't let you kill him. I think...I think I love him, so his death would make me even sadder."

"Love?" Violet gave her a narrow look. "That's unfortunate."

"I know." Bree sighed, the acceptance of it settling in her heart, in her soul. "I'm in love with Sheriff Decker and it's the worst."

"Sheriff Dicker," Clementine corrected with some relish.

Violet glowered in the direction of the door, where presumably Flint was somewhere. "He needs that damn hat shoved up his ass. Alternatively, we could demand he apologize to you."

"Does he know how you feel?" Kinley asked. "I mean, maybe we should figure that out *before* we kill him."

"Well," Violet said, "as a lawyer, I'm all for innocent till proven guilty, but in this case—"

"He doesn't know how I feel," Bree interrupted, feeling the need to defend him because it wasn't entirely his fault. "I didn't tell him. I just...ended it instead."

"Oh." Kinley pushed her glasses back up her nose. "Perhaps you should have mentioned it to him? It's kind of important."

A little shiver went through Bree. She didn't want to admit the truth. That she hadn't fought, that she'd just let him go, because...well. She was afraid. Except these women were her friends, weren't they? That's what she'd called them herself.

"I should have," she admitted. "But I didn't because... I was too scared."

Violet's eyes went wide. "You? Bree White? The baddest girl in camp? Scared?"

"I don't believe it. Not you." Clementine shook her head. "What are you scared of?"

That you haven't left the past behind, that you're still that feral girl, heading down that dark path...

Bree sighed. "That he won't want me. That I'm not good enough somehow."

Violet snorted. "You? Not good enough? I wanted to be like you all those years ago, did you know that?"

"Me too," Clementine said. "You were so badass."

"You were," Kinley agreed. "And if Sheriff Dicker can't see that, then——"

There was a knock on the cabin door.

Bree, oddly buoyed by their unexpected praise, swallowed once more and wiped her eyes yet again with the sodden handkerchief. "I don't want to get it. Can someone——"

But Violet was already striding to the door. She pulled it open, but there was no one there. Then she looked down and picked up something that had been sitting on the step. "Is this an apology? A hint? What?"

It was Flint's hat.

He'd left his hat on her doorstep.

Bree's heart leaped and she crossed the room to where Violet stood, taking the hat from her before she could think better of it. "What is it doing here?"

"Perhaps he's giving it to you?" Kinley suggested.

Bree's heart began to race. "No, he said he didn't want more..."

Violet peered outside. "He's just over there. Do you want me to go deal with him? I'm quite happy to."

Bree's heart began to race even faster. They were right. They were *all* right. She *was* a badass. She'd once been the baddest girl in camp, and the baddest girl in camp didn't hide in her cabin, too afraid to tell the man she'd fallen head over heels for that she loved him. No freaking way.

"No, it's okay," she said, feeling suddenly fierce. "I'd better talk to him. Thanks, though."

Violet gave her an encouraging smile. "Go get 'em, tiger. If you need backup, just let us know."

"I will," Bree said, returning the smile. Then, feeling even more buoyant with the knowledge that these three women were in her corner, she stepped outside and walked over to where Flint's tall figure stood.

"Why did you leave this?" she asked. "I don't want your dumb hat. What I want is—"

"It's yours," he interrupted quietly. "You stole it from me, fair and square. Just like you stole my heart."

Everything Bree had been going to say vanished from her head. "I what?"

"I'm a liar, wildcat." His expression was lost in the darkness, but she could hear something fierce in his voice. "About not wanting more. About not wanting a relationship. I made up a whole pile of excuses to keep you at a distance and, well, they were just that—excuses."

Her chest was aching, a tremble starting deep inside. "Flint—"

"No. I need to say this. The truth is, I was afraid, Bree. My dad didn't even want to talk to me, and I think some part of me hasn't moved on from that. And that part is afraid that one day you'll look at me and see whatever it was that he saw in me. And I don't know what that was, but it wasn't enough to make him think I even deserved a conversation."

Bree's throat closed, the trembling getting stronger. She took a step toward him. "You know that's not what I see when I look at you, Flint."

"Yeah, I do know. But I didn't listen." He shook his head. "I didn't want to hurt you, Bree. I just…never imagined someone like you coming into my life and it's taken me some time to figure it out."

She swallowed. "Figure what out?"

Flint's eyes gleamed in the darkness. "Whether to go get the girl or sit there stewing with a shit poker hand."

"What? I'm better than a shit poker hand? Thanks for the—"

But she never got to finish, because Flint moved abruptly, closing the distance between them and pulling her into his arms. She resisted for all of two seconds, then melted against him, giving in to the tremble inside her, the hope she almost couldn't bear, her still-damp face pressed against his T-shirt.

"I'm sorry, wildcat," he said softly. "I'm sorry for hurting you. All that shit I said were excuses. I'm a coward. I should have said this earlier tonight, but..." His hands tangled in her hair, easing her head back so she was looking up into his beautiful face. "Bree White, I think I'm in love with you. I've been resisting it so hard, but I just can't do it anymore. I don't want us to keep going with our affair, because I don't want it to be an affair. I want more than that. I want a relationship. I want there to be an 'us.' I want people to know and I want you at my ranch and in my bed. I want you to share my life and—"

Abruptly, Bree couldn't stand it. She went up on her toes and kissed him to shut him up, then whispered against his mouth, "Damn you, Sheriff Decker. You stole my thunder. I was just coming out to tell you that I love you." Tears filled her eyes, but this time, they were tears of happiness. "But you got in first."

His hands tightened in her hair. "Well, don't let me stop you now, wildcat. Tell me again."

So she did, and when he kissed her again, it was with hunger and heat and the wild magic that they were so good at making together.

Then, finally, Flint murmured, "What say you we go home?"

"I thought you'd never ask," she murmured back. "Oh, and by the way, I'm keeping the hat."

* * * * *

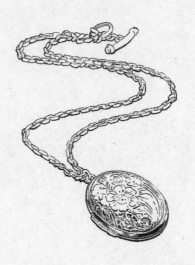

The One with the Locket

Caitlin Crews

CHAPTER ONE

LINCOLN TRAEGER WAS not easily riled.

Generally speaking, he was as quick to anger as the average vat of molasses, only slower, but Violet Cook was proving to be more of a challenge than he'd anticipated.

Truth was, he hadn't expected any challenges at all.

Much less one in tiny female form.

A thick skin had been required to survive his childhood. And an easygoing nature, at least on the surface, was an asset in his chosen career of hunting down all manner of assorted villains and ne'er-do-wells for the United States Marshals Service. He might have started out as an angry young man, like every other teen boy he'd ever met, but he'd grown. He'd *evolved*.

Lincoln considered himself downright laid-back these days.

He might have been quick on the draw when necessary, but he hadn't imagined that returning to the summer camp that had saved his life back when he was said angry kid—on a swift and terrible road to the kind of future he delivered to all kinds of criminals himself these days—would require any drawing of the weapon he never went anywhere without.

Figuratively or literally.

"You're not listening to me at all, are you?" she demanded, like she already knew all his weapons and might actually draw hers quicker.

This was highly unlikely.

But still, the notion smarted.

"I beg your pardon?" he drawled through the sweet, fresh air of this May morning, because in his experience, laying his Kentucky drawl on thick was an effective countermeasure all its own.

Especially here in Oregon, where the accents never ran like a good syrup, the ladies seemed to take a particular pride in their most serviceable shoes, and the locals moaned about hundred-degree weather when there was nary a speck of humidity to make the air dense enough to use as a pillow.

"I apologize," replied the object of his unusual ire. As ever, tiny Violet Cook wore a big smile. As usual, it did nothing to change the fact that she didn't sound the least bit apologetic. "Do you need me to talk slower?"

It took Lincoln a good, long moment to recognize the sensations he felt charging around inside him, so unusual were they.

But there was no getting around it.

Violet Cook, a little bit of a thing who was as pretty as she was decidedly unimpressed with him, had managed to lodge herself right up under his skin.

Lincoln had a mind to find that impressive. He was halfway there.

In the meantime, he rocked back on his heels and looked down at her. All the way down to where the top of her head barely made it to his shoulder, though he was fairly certain that she was marching around Camp Phoenix today the same way she did every day. In the same ridiculous wedge heels he'd heard her claim five or six times already, with a wave of a careless hand, were as comfortable as a pair of tennis shoes.

He didn't like the fact that he'd already spent entirely too much time imagining her out of those wedges that no one would ever call *serviceable*. And while he was at it, out of any one of the voluminous sack-like affairs she called dresses that should have made her look like a tent, but somehow drew attention to how slight she was, how delicate. She was otherwise all jet-black curly hair, flashing black eyes and the kind of eye makeup that should have looked out of place here in the woods. At a summer camp that wasn't even open yet.

But this was Violet.

So it only made her look all the more shockingly beautiful.

"That's mighty good of you, *Miz Cook*," Lincoln drawled, and he leaned into that drawl. The more hick he put into it, the more he could use it like another weapon. He relied on it as much as he did the lean athleticism he'd been born with and the trusty Glock sidearm he considered an extension of his body. Out here in Oregon, most offenders heard only the drawl and missed the fact that he was usually tying them up in knots they'd have trouble unwinding. Legally speaking. Lincoln enjoyed that. But he couldn't say he also enjoyed the patronizing sort of look Violet seemed to get whenever she heard him do it, not that it stopped him. "I reckon you'd better slow it right on down if you want me to understand you."

Violet sighed, and made a meal out of it. She looked all around, as if for deliverance, but there was no one else here outside the dining hall but the two of them. It had been a typical morning in any Camp Phoenix summer, even though it wasn't quite summer yet. Since there were no campers. Not yet. Lincoln and Violet had gone ahead and volunteered to help get the camp ready for its new season, after it had fallen into disrepair.

Lincoln, because the camp had changed his life, so much so that he'd bought in with his buddy Jackson, the camp's new owner and current commandant. Violet was here…for reasons that Lincoln couldn't make out. Particularly when her favorite pastime appeared to be glaring at him stonily from across rooms or from up close as if she'd seen more appealing specimens on the bottom of her shoe.

Not the reaction Lincoln was used to engendering in the fairer sex, he could admit.

While she put on her little performance of patience sorely tried, Lincoln tucked his hands into the pockets of his jeans and breathed in the sweet air. It smelled like the best days of his life here. It also smelled like a much-needed leave of absence—some folks called it vacation—from a job that ate up more of him all the time.

He was lucky enough to live down an hour or so south in the pretty Rogue Valley for the past few years. He'd grown to love that little slice of paradise, nestled between the Cascade Mountains to the east and the Coastal Range to the west. Though he spent too much time handling the seedier side of human nature, due in large part to the valley's location right there where the interstate came on in from California, he took care to find his way out of the mess of felonious behavior when he could. He loved the crystal clear rivers and lakes, the rolling pear orchards, and the vineyards that made a patchwork quilt of pretty fields and hillsides from gritty Grants Pass, to the north, all the way to the Shakespeare festival in the southernmost college town. He lived outside a Wild West monument of an even smaller town, in the foothills of the mountains, and considered himself just about satisfied.

But there was nothing like this place. Camp Phoenix, where Crow Lake—really more of a sprawling lake with the usual Western nonchalant naming conventions—gleamed through the trees and the sun seemed to shine even when rain threatened. Where everything smelled like sunshine and evergreens, and the spring wildflowers were enough to make a man come over all poetic.

Camp Phoenix was magical. Lincoln had known that from the start, when he'd gotten off the bus in Jasper Creek, surly and scared at thirteen—yet fully aware that this stupid camp that he hadn't wanted to go to in the first place was his only chance to get out from under the weight of his family's *freedom of expression*, as his granddaddy liked to call it, that had made all his relatives targets of various law enforcement agencies for as long as anyone could remember.

Lincoln had told himself he'd give it one night. One night, then he'd take off and find his own freedom somewhere, seeing as how he'd gotten out of Kentucky. No need to rush back. He'd had vague daydreams about big cities like Seattle.

But one night had turned into a whole summer. Then every summer after that, all the way through college, because he got the chance to be a counselor and give a little back. Something he tried to do whenever he encountered angry kids like the one he'd been, out there in his line of work. Just like the US marshal who had warned him about the life he had waiting for him and had told him about Camp Phoenix all those years ago.

Lincoln liked to pass it along.

Because this place still smelled the same today. All these years later, like nothing had changed, even though everything had. Now that he was the kind of man he'd been so sure he was genetically incapable of becoming. These were things he still couldn't quite believe and would never, ever take for granted.

It looked like Violet was finishing up the amateur dramatics, so he tuned back in to find she'd gone ahead and folded her arms, making her look even more unimpressed with him than usual. She wore dark, oversize sunglasses and she'd taken the time to push them to the top of her head, allowing him to enjoy the full force of her disapproval when she glared up at him.

The thing of it was, he really *did* enjoy it, when he'd have said he'd left the masochistic tendencies back home in Kentucky with all his locked-up kinfolk.

"It's really not that difficult," she said, and she was speaking very deliberately. Very slowly. Very much like she found him a bit simple—though he figured both of them knew that if she really did, she'd have been a whole lot kinder. "You and I have been tasked with getting the chapel ready. I hope you remember the chapel. Out in the woods. Open to one and all, but last I heard, the trail there hasn't been walked in some time and no one's seen the actual chapel itself for at least a few summers. That means we'll need to do a little bushwhacking. A lot of hiking. And a whole lot of brush removal. Do you think you can handle that?"

Lincoln blinked. "Can *you*?"

A slow head tilt. "Do you think that a woman is incapable of those tasks?"

"I think that you're dressed for a garden party, princess. Maybe a cotillion. Not so much with the bushwhacking when it looks like you have a full manicure."

"I have a manicure *and* a pedicure. And I was unaware

that there was a uniform for this kind of work. Someone should have told me that T-shirts and cowboy boots were what all the camp counselors here in Oregon were wearing. I would've stocked up."

"I like cowboy boots, not that you asked. It puts me in mind of my misspent youth. And a cowboy boot isn't most people's first choice for a hike through the woods, or any other forest-type activity, I grant you. But they are work boots all the same. Not sure your high heels count."

"I have an idea. Why don't you let me worry about what's on my feet? Seeing as how I'm a grown-ass woman and all."

"I can leave you to all the worry your little heart desires, Violet."

"That's a great comfort, Lincoln."

They were standing closer together, but he hadn't noticed making any such move himself. It would have been flattering to assume she'd done the moving, but he couldn't be sure. And that was the trouble he'd found in the weeks since he'd come back to Camp Phoenix and found Violet here, scowling at him as if he was responsible for the death of her family pet.

He couldn't remember.

He had no recollection of seeing her before, but she sure knew him. It made him uneasy. At the very least, it suggested the possibility of some distinctly ungentlemanly behavior, and while he'd certainly had his moments, he was pretty sure he remembered each and every time he failed to live up to his mama's "do as I say, not as I do" directives.

Lincoln aimed a smile her way. "I do have one question."

"Of course you do." Violet Cook, he'd learned, was a fancy lawyer off in Baltimore, where she had a passion for helping kids in trouble. This should have made them allies.

Yet, as far as he could tell, all it had really done was give her the kind of edge to her tongue that made every word she uttered a knife. He might've admired it if those knives were ever directed at someone other than him. She smiled with great forbearance. "I'm all ears. And when you're finished asking it, maybe we can actually do the job that we've been asked to do today and avoid incurring Jackson Hart's wrath. Just a thought. Seeing as how everyone else has been at work for half the morning already and I've already had to scrub latrines this month."

He could have taken exception to that characterization. He could have reminded her that cleaning latrines was no one's fault but her own.

But instead, he studied the woman before him. She was *so pretty*, and that was the problem. And, rack his brain as he might, Lincoln couldn't recall ever seeing her face before. He didn't understand how he could have missed her.

Because there were two things on this earth that Lincoln Traeger liked collecting. One of them was malefactors, garden-variety crooks and villains of all descriptions— especially if he happened to be related to them.

The more pleasurable collection was beautiful women, who he was happy enough to offer a drink and nothing more. Because pretty things were often better gazed upon than explored. That was a truth. Though it was also a truth that every time he indicated what might be his preference, the beautiful woman in question tended to take things in another direction.

And for all he liked to lounge around and pretend he was entirely too lazy to put the right number of consonants in a word or remember a name, Lincoln's memory was formidable. It served him well in his chosen profession. It had allowed him to rack up an impressive number of wins, tracking individuals who would prefer to disappear no matter how they tried to change their appearance.

He killed at *Jeopardy!*, too.

But he still couldn't remember Violet Cook.

"Well?" He reckoned she used that very voice in a courtroom while interrogating unforthcoming witnesses for the opposing side. "Will there be a question? Or will we just stand around staring at each other for the rest of the day, making it a certainty that Jackson will assign us unpleasant duties for our sins of sloth and laziness?"

She didn't have to make it clear that those were his sins, not hers.

It was less an implication than an undercurrent, and, really, more of a riptide at that.

"There are a lot of questions I could ask, now that you mention it," he told her, and she wasn't the only one who could put on a little show when she had a mind to. "But let's you and me focus on the most important one. I'm going to need you to help me out here, Violet."

"That is the least surprising thing you've ever said."

"Because here's the thing." And he hit her with the full force of his laziest smile. "I can't quite remember when exactly it was I got you pregnant and left you by the side of the road." He tipped his head to one side but kept his gaze trained on her. "You want to clue me in?"

CHAPTER TWO

VIOLET DID NOT want to clue him in.

She did not want to continue this conversation at all, and that was a hint that she was heading down a bad road. Given that she'd been born confrontational and had only gotten worse, according to her father, who could get in a brawl in an empty room and often did.

Violet had never been ashamed of her *argumentative style*, as an exasperated teacher had once dubbed it. She had always maintained that her entire personality was a natural consequence of being not only the youngest, but the only girl in a family of rough and rowdy men—each and every one of whom had been in trouble since kindergarten.

Drunken, violent louts, the lot of them.

She could even be affectionate about them, about what wastes of space they all were, as long as they quit asking her for money and stopped showing up on her doorstep, which, it had to be said, they had. Because the city of Baltimore was about two hours and whole worlds away from her hometown on Maryland's Eastern Shore on the banks of the Chesapeake, where Cooks had worked the water and the crab factories since they'd turned up on boats from England.

But she would have preferred a Cook family bar fight—otherwise known as a wedding—instead of this.

"Do you get a lot of women pregnant?" she asked hopefully, though it did nothing good inside of her to think about how a man might get a woman pregnant. About how *Lincoln Traeger* might get *her* pregnant, no less. That same bright, hot, messy fire that had first ignited inside her when she'd been too young to know better lit up again then, and she hated it. It *burned* and she *hated* it. "And having done so, do you normally choose abandonment as some kind of coping mechanism?"

"So I did do you wrong. Yet, oddly enough, I can't recall it."

"Yet you assume that the gaps in your memory are my fault somehow. Instead of the more likely explanation, which is the kind of behavior that likely brought you to Camp Phoenix in the first place."

"I wouldn't dream of making such a reckless accusation," came his slow reply in that impossible drawl of his that truly did sound and feel like a reckless slug of Kentucky bourbon, not that she'd experimented. Just to see. "But those memories do seem to be giving you some consternation here in the present. And I've always thought that it's better to pull back the curtain and put a little light on these things. Far better than letting them fester."

"I don't actually know what you're talking about."

But her heart was kicking at her, and there was that big old mess of fire inside, and this felt far out of her control. Like every other moment she'd ever spent near this man, and Violet *prized* control.

For all the usual reasons.

It wasn't fair. Lincoln Traeger—who, if there was a God, should have been pudgy and moonfaced and *significantly* shorter by now—should have been easily eviscerated with a single word. She'd assumed that was how it would go, now that she wasn't a lovesick teen girl.

Instead, he gazed down at her with unholy amusement. "Now, Violet. I think we both know you do know what I'm talking about."

And it was a humbling thing to discover, after all these years, that deep down she was just as much of a crook as any one of her brothers. She'd been heading that way when she was a teenager, sure. It had been a little too easy to get the dumb boys she knew to do her bidding, and she was ashamed to admit she'd explored her power in that arena. If a person could call her grubby little fishing town an *arena* for anything but collective downward spirals.

But then she'd come to camp, and that had changed everything. Her personal hero, Gale Lawson, had sat her down at the end of her first week that first year at camp, had looked Violet straight in the eye and had asked her if she ever considered using her ability to arrange things to suit herself to help others.

The answer, of course, had been no.

But she'd wanted so desperately to be the girl that Gale believed she could be. The girl Gale treated her as if she already was. She couldn't help but try—and it had completely changed the course of her life.

And in the intervening years, Violet had somehow forgotten that she'd ever been that heedless, feral creature in the first place. Her brothers still ran roughshod over Dorchester County back in Maryland. They were all watermen with wives and exes and too many kids who had no greater aspirations than to repeat all the same Cook family cycles. The drinking. The fighting. The genial desperation dressed up in stories of drunkenness, broken marriages, actual fistfights with the same old knuckleheads, and the same shenanigans they'd been getting into when they were fifteen. The biggest ambition any of her brothers had was running a scam that worked well enough to pay off their crappy mortgages.

She'd been so sure she'd broken that cycle. Smashed it, she would have said.

She *had* said that.

Except now she was staring up at Lincoln Traeger himself, who remained the single most beautiful man she'd ever laid eyes on. He was long and lean. She'd been sure that in the ten years since she'd last seen him, the eyes she remembered too well from her overwrought teenage years would turn out to be nothing more than a dull old brown, but no. They looked the way his voice sounded, like a long pull of bourbon, shot through with dancing summer light. Worse, for all those lazy smiles and the kind of drawl that could cure insomnia, there was a canniness about him. An intense focus he hid under all that Southern charm. She had no trouble at all imagining him rounding up criminals for the Marshals Service, which only felt like another betrayal.

But there was no betrayal so deep as the fact that she had literally tripped over her own two feet when she'd first laid eyes on him. She'd been a worldly fifteen, by her estimation, but he'd already been a counselor. Meaning he was fully reformed, widely lauded, and already off in college keeping squeaky clean and embodying all that Camp Phoenix had to offer. He'd lounged around camp in that way of his, his gaze so lazy, his drawl like butter and those low-slung jeans of his enough to make her teenage heart explode in her chest.

Not to mention all the other crazy sensations he aroused in her that, until that moment, she had assumed were lies that people put in foolish songs to make themselves feel better about acting like idiots.

She had tripped over her own two feet right in front of her favorite frenemy, Bree White.

Easy, Bree had murmured in that way she had, as if she knew everything and had done everything, and all of it was effortless. *He's not that cute.*

There's something about him, Violet had said with the deadly seriousness of a desperate teenage girl who intended to embody the lies she told even if it killed her. *He's not right. I think maybe he's evil.*

And she'd committed to that.

She'd made rituals, salting the earth every time he walked by. Pretending she needed to shower it off if ever he addressed her for some reason, usually while in one of the classes he taught, where she was quite sure she was indistinguishable from the rest of the girls.

Looking back, she could say with confidence that she'd done her best to create a relationship with this older boy who didn't know she existed, and to such an extent that every girl in her age group knew about it. Because that was the next best thing.

Especially because it turned out that Lincoln wasn't a dumb boy like all the idiots back home who she wrapped around her fingers without even trying.

Lincoln Traeger, regrettably, had been as smart back then as he'd been hot.

She had not been pleased to hear that he would be here this summer. But Violet was honest, as she did try to be if only in the privacy of her own head. She'd expected that while college-age Lincoln Traeger might have failed to notice her—as was probably only appropriate, given their age difference at the time, not that she'd cared about such things—it would be *highly unlikely* that his grown-up counterpart would do the same.

Men didn't fail to notice her, as a rule.

And nothing in her life had prepared her for being completely ignored by a man. Particularly a man she'd convinced herself had peaked at nineteen.

Fun fact: he had not.

"Cat got your tongue?" he asked, and it wasn't fair. It wasn't *fair* that a man could sound like that. It wasn't *fair* that his voice should shiver over her and through her, like a long, slow lick.

But nothing about the existence of Lincoln Traeger was fair.

Good thing, then, that Violet had never imagined that anything in life was fair. If it was, maybe her mother would have lived. Maybe her brothers would have behaved, even a little. Maybe she wouldn't be the only one in her family who'd gotten off the Eastern Shore.

"I can't say I've ever understood that expression." She realized as she said it that she was somehow entirely too close to him. Anyone looking from afar would be under the impression they were engaged in some kind of *intimate conversation*, when nothing could be further from the truth. She stepped back, with flourish, as if to indicate he was encroaching on her space, when it was patently clear that a man like Lincoln didn't have to waste his energy going around *encroaching* on anything. "I don't like cats, but even if I did, I can't imagine sticking out my tongue and letting them swipe at it."

"The thing about cats is that you don't *let* them do anything. They do what they want. That's their charm."

"It's funny what other people consider charming. Small mammals attacking you and relieving you of necessary organs, for example. Or, just to pull something out at random, a man so allergic to a little manual labor that he'll stand around and argue about anything and everything just to get out of a tiny bit of yard work."

She had heard Lincoln laugh. He did a lot of that with his buddies, former DEA agent Jackson Hart, local sheriff Flint Decker and local sheriff's sergeant Duke Cody. They were all great friends from way back, had returned to help save the camp just as she had, and expressed their devotion mostly through poker games on hastily erected card tables and snarky remarks.

But this was not that.

This was more dangerous. Lincoln's eyes lit up and his smile went lethal, but he didn't move. It was as if his intensity...sharpened, somehow.

The man was trouble. There was no getting around it.

Violet could have avoided this, she was all too aware, if she'd actually said something when the week's projects were handed out. But she'd been entirely too busy being passive-aggressively competitive with the other women she was forced to bunk with here in this adult version of summer camp. Far too committed to pretending to be completely unbothered by everything that was happening, the way she'd excelled at as a teenager—though the truth was, she liked her bunkmates a lot more now than she had then—that she'd sailed right in to a trap of her own making.

At least you got the eyeliner right, Kinley Parker had said in her usual, suspiciously flat way. She'd taken her time pushing her glasses up her nose as she'd handed out the breakfast trays, her gaze a little too direct. That should be a great comfort.

I'm sure you can ask Jackson to change projects, Clementine McClain had chimed in nervously, because Clementine was always nervous. That was what happened when you were the only nondelinquent in a camp filled with contenders for juvie from any number of different states. And when your father was the widely beloved Sheriff McClain. And you spent your childhood tattling to anyone and everyone. *I'm sure he's not completely unreasonable.*

They had all swiveled around on their bench to look over at Jackson, cane in one hand and bullhorn in the other, lecturing the table full of the tent campers. The poor fools had come back to help out but hadn't been quick enough to snag inside accommodation in the only decent cabin like Violet and her bunkmates had. He instructed the volunteers on their responsibilities to the grass on the bluff and how, exactly, he wanted them to seed any dead patches before the campers' arrival in June.

Yes, Bree had murmured, picking up her bug juice like it was a flute of champagne, *he seems eminently reasonable in all ways.*

That Violet had no one to blame but herself was galling. It made her think she needed to call each and every one of her obnoxious older brothers and apologize for all the times she'd told them that they made their own mistakes and could, at any point, choose not to do just that.

Only today did she understand—in full—the saltiness of their traditional replies to such commentary.

"If you want to hike through the woods and do a little hard labor just like you are, princess, who am I to argue about it?" Lincoln was asking, and that grin of his only widened. "If you think your ball gown is the appropriate attire for a questionable hike and some bushwhacking, hell. Have at."

And it was true that Violet liked a maxidress. Just like she liked a wedge heel, for while Camp Phoenix offered far more uneven ground than the streets of Baltimore—but not as much as some might think—she was a short woman who had trained herself to live in a wedge and really could do just about anything in them.

Maybe not hiking and hacking through the underbrush, at least not comfortably. But she didn't like the *sheer disbelief* that she could be anything but *in agony*. She had some jeans and a few pairs of shorts in her suitcase, but everyone kept commenting on the fact she'd turned up in a dress...

Violet was that contrary. She was that much of a Cook. She had already decided that she would literally break both of her ankles and smash her face open before she would admit that it might be comfortable to throw on a pair of shorts and flip-flops like everyone else. That was after two weeks of parading around in her usual outfits while everyone else trudged about looking grubby and hot. She had already decided that it was the *principle* of the thing.

And, sure, maybe she liked to pretend she'd grown out of some of those control issues.

But now that Lincoln had offered some commentary? Well.

She would head out right now and hike all nine-thousand-plus feet of Mount McLoughlin to the southeast and follow it up by summiting Shasta down in California in what she was wearing right now before she would ever admit to Lincoln Traeger that he might have a point.

The more he thought she was a princess out of her depth here, the better.

Because nothing pleased her more than being underestimated. She relied on it in court. Either opposing counsel found her bewilderingly pretty, so much so that they couldn't form a coherent sentence, or they acted like they were trying to beat the pretty out of her with their words and motions. Either way, she ended up with the advantage.

She'd be only too delighted to discover that after all these years, and all the shame of her teenage crush on him, Lincoln Traeger was just a man, after all.

Like any other.

Because she could feel that big, messy flaming thing inside of her, and she could admit that she really needed an advantage here. Any advantage.

So she smiled at him as if they'd reached a sweet agreement, then turned on her heel and started for the hiking trail.

Without so much as a glance back.

Because Lincoln still turned her head in ways she didn't like. He still got to her in a way no other man had since, and Lord knew Violet had done her best to get his face out of her head. He was still the only man she'd ever met who had looked at her, really seen her, then looked away.

But this was a different Camp Phoenix and they were different people. And she knew without having to look that he would follow. That gave her a technical advantage, anyway.

She told herself the little shiver she felt work through her at that notion was her gearing up for battle, nothing more. Because battle was the one thing Violet had always been good at. Maybe the only thing.

And she'd been waiting to have a real fight with Lincoln—not one in her head—since she was fifteen.

By her reckoning, they were way overdue.

CHAPTER THREE

LINCOLN HAD NEVER been much for church. But it was difficult not to feel a touch of the divine as he picked his way along the old trail, winding through the deep green woods with not a whole lot to look at besides the trees and the gentle sway of Violet's hips.

Lord have mercy.

The farther they walked, the more he found himself thinking about how this very same hike had seemed to him when he was a kid, all hormones and high hopes. If he wasn't mistaken, he had once taken Jamie Lee Adams by the hand and led her up along this very same hill, claiming he wanted nothing more than to let her teach him some of the Bible verses she liked to tattoo all over her body as if that made her less of a sinner.

The verses hadn't worked as intended, thank goodness.

It was enough to make a man consider taking up prayer—though he hadn't. He'd grown up too hard to believe in much of anything but what he could make of himself on his own. Some folks fought all their lives with their personal demons, but Lincoln hadn't spent too much time engaged in that kind of self-destruction, either. There was no need.

All of his personal demons were related to him by blood, and he'd spent the early part of his career helping put them away.

He didn't think much on sin these days, what with being

a grown man and all. And having left settled scores behind him in Kentucky years back now. So it felt like slipping back in time to find himself worked up over a silent walk through the woods with an impossibly pretty girl, catching glimpses of the lake through the trees as they went. It felt like magic again.

Like he'd lost his portion of it along the way.

In the quiet of it all, because Miz Violet Cook had made it clear she wasn't in a chatty sort of hiking mood, he could admit that this had been a tough couple of years.

If it hadn't been for his regular getaways with his friends, who had long since become the only family that mattered to him—whether it was a fishing trip or poker game or any old Sunday—he'd like as not be holed up in his little house perched on a hill down there in the Rogue Valley right now. Counting days until his leave was up and he could get back to work. So much a part of the job that he was useless as a man, like too many lawmen he knew. It was too easy to get lost in wrong versus right and all those slippery gray areas in between.

It was too easy to be nothing more than the collars he made and the mysteries he couldn't solve.

That wasn't who Lincoln wanted to be. It wasn't who he'd thought he'd be back here at camp, when he'd already changed his entire life and set himself off to college on a full ride because Lord knew not a single one of his kinfolk put any stock in an education. Or a single dollar, come to that. He remembered walking these same trails, sleeping in the same cabins, promising himself that, whatever else he was, he'd be *alive* in a way the Traegers back there in that holler never were. Not really.

But he wasn't sure he'd thought too much about what

that meant in practice until Jackson had told them his plans for the camp.

Since then, Lincoln was awake. He was *alive*. And he intended to enjoy every moment of his resurrection, when he hadn't even realized he'd gone and buried himself as surely in his job as all the rest of his family did in their various unlawful pursuits.

Including this moment. Finding himself alone in the woods with a remarkably pretty woman who seemed to hate him for no good reason.

Somehow, he reckoned, he'd muddle his way on through.

The fact of the matter was, for all that he'd called her *princess* and cast aspersions about her impractical shoes and the silly dress she wore, she moved nimbly enough up the trail. As she hiked, she sorted out the thick black curls that normally flowed down her back. She wrapped the hair in a kind of Rapunzel-like rope, around and around on the top of her skull, until it formed a thick ball that she tied on itself somehow. All while she carried on walking, charging up the trail as if she knew every step, despite the many places where nature had encroached on the path.

Meanwhile, if asked, Lincoln would have sworn that a bun like that was the kind of hairstyle that took a woman seventeen hours in a salon to achieve.

And yet, when he examined the reaction he could feel pumping around inside him, he realized that he wasn't at all surprised to discover that Violet Cook, who was, at a glance, the most high-maintenance female in the whole of Camp Phoenix's history—and certainly among its current residents—was secretly…not.

Or not entirely.

It was like a puzzle piece fell into place, somewhere deep inside him. Lincoln knew that feeling well. It was the marshal in him. It was like a new shaft of light, shining just right, illuminating something that had been hidden before.

Today, on this trail, it brought him straight to attention.

Because he had never felt something click into place like that about a woman before. Not one he didn't already find suspicious in a legal sense.

Lincoln didn't let himself think that through. He wasn't sure he'd like where he ended up. And what intrigued him was the difference between that high-maintenance mask she'd had on tight since day one…and the hint she'd just given him, without so much as a glance over her shoulder, that it really was a mask, after all.

And more, that there was a whole lot more beneath.

Once Lincoln started worrying over discrepancies, he knew, there was no telling where he might end up.

Just ask his kin.

He had to remind himself that Violet wasn't a suspect when she marched right up to a tree that had fallen before them, blocking the trail. Once again, she didn't bother to look back at him—and not because she was being coy. He could tell. She was used to being on her own. She was used to handling herself.

Lincoln could read it in the way she hoisted herself up and scrambled over the top of the tree trunk. A tad too nimbly for his peace of mind, as it happened.

And far too easily for a woman dressed in a flowy gown and high heels, whether with wedged soles or not.

He hopped the tree himself, half expecting to find her facedown on the other side, but instead, she was marching right along, bounding up the steepest part of the trail, which he knew from memory led straight into the chapel, like she really was in tennis shoes.

But she stopped there at the top of the trail. Her hands found her hips.

Lincoln caught up to her in a few steps and found his own hands in the vicinity of his hips as he followed her gaze and saw what she was looking at.

For a moment, it was like the past was superimposed over the present. For a moment, all he could see was what he expected to see. The pretty little chapel nestled on a hillside, surrounded by tall, stout evergreens, thick green undergrowth and no shortage of poison oak. There were no pews in the Phoenix Chapel, only logs cut and smoothed and laid sideways in the earth. The seating area was wide at the top, then narrowed down to the brace of madrones, the two trees with their stripped trunks gleaming that formed the forest altar.

You could sit anywhere, on any one of the seats, and stare straight on down to the clear water of the lake below. And on some summer nights there were sunset chapel services that had all of them staring, half blinded, as the sky turned red and the sun turned orange as it sank behind the hills across the lake. Then the whole of the camp went tripping back down the trail to their cabins, their way lit only by the stars above and the particular giddy freedom that came with being that young, safe and sound beneath the night sky while owls hooted and coyotes called in the distance.

But that chapel, the one he hadn't known claimed so much real estate in his memories, wasn't the sight that greeted them today. Everything was overgrown. Lincoln had figured Violet had talked about bushwhacking and whatnot to be ornery, but that was the correct term for what was going to have to happen up here. It looked to him like they were going to have to dig to find the old chapel, and maybe get a little creative while they were at it.

"Well," he said, drawing the word out into several syllables. "Shit."

Beside him, he could feel Violet bristle. "It's going to be a project, certainly. But this whole camp is a project right now. Jackson wants us to be ready to have a traditional sunset ceremony in two weeks. Do you think you can handle that, Lincoln?"

He took his time gazing down at her because, once again, she appeared to be talking to him like he was her no-account husband who'd cheated on her with her sister only to crawl on back to beg her for a little booze money. To pick a family story at random. "Do I look like I'm not handling something?"

Violet scowled at him. "I get that your whole thing is pretending to be too lazy to do anything, which is how you end up doing whatever it is you wanted to do in the first place, but this is the project that we were picked to do. This is a project that we will be doing. Do you understand me?"

"Violet," he said, because it turned out he liked her name. It sounded like laughter, and she made him want to laugh. When he was more about smirking than a good laugh, especially lately. "Princess."

"And, yes, the endearments are cute. Everyone likes an endearment. I love being called princess, actually. It feels like validation. So if you're trying to use that word to diminish me, I'm sorry to tell you that it's not going to work. What I need you to promise me is that I can count on you to make this chapel what it's supposed to be, and you can call me whatever you want while we do it. Can I count on you, Lincoln?"

"Violet," he said again, still working out that laugh thing.

"I have to ask. And I mean the question kindly, and with genuine interest in your answer. Who in the hell do you think I am? Because, and I'll apologize for any discourtesy here, you don't know me from a can of paint."

"I don't have to know you. I'm familiar with your type. Overly familiar."

"I appreciate you not denying the fact that you think you know me, as I think that's clear to you, me and the extended avian population of the Oregon woods. Not to mention the odd vole."

"Are voles *odd*, Lincoln? Really?"

"You'd have to ask them. But the fact remains, it's impolite, at the very least, to intimate that you have some insight into my nature. When, as best I can recall, you and I are barely acquainted."

"Wow." She didn't so much roll her eyes as make her tone do the work, scathing enough to burn down the hillside. "I apologize for hurting your man-feelings."

"Feelings are universal, princess."

She inclined her head, another little performance that managed to be even more scathing. "A thousand apologies. I had no idea you were so sensitive."

"I expect it's the Southerner in me." He smiled at her, a triumph of bland arrogance. Her dark eyes narrowed. "All that brash East Coast kind of talk makes me clutch my pearls, I'm afraid."

"Maryland considers itself part of the South."

"Only Maryland thinks it's Southern. Nobody Southern concurs. I expect you know that, too."

And once again, her arms were crossed. Once again, she had somehow closed the space between them. Or he had— but this time he was certain he'd remember that, because the fact was, he wanted to move closer to her. He would have known if he had.

A man tended to recall when he indulged a sweet tooth, after all.

"Let's circle back to who you think I am," he suggested.

"Oh dear. I can't promise I'll maintain the level of sweetness and light to keep you from a mint julep swoon."

He grinned his appreciation of that little swipe, and that felt like another puzzle piece. "I told you I can't remember you. You're too much younger than me for anything to have happened between us here at camp. Besides, any scandalous behavior on my part took place far away from Jasper Creek, Oregon. By design, you understand. I have a reputation to uphold out this way. All of that leads me to think that this spite and vitriol is coming to me courtesy of someone else. Do I remind you of a broken heart, Violet?"

She actually guffawed. "Certainly not."

Lincoln could admit he liked that answer, not caring much for the idea that when she looked at him she saw someone else. Not caring for that one little bit. "It has to be someone. Because I'm not afraid to draw fire, princess." And the fact she didn't mind he called her that meant he enjoyed saying it even more. Like a candy coating on something that was already sweet. "But I do like the gun aimed at me to be shooting at the correct target."

She glared at him. And yet it was as if the sun was setting already, even though he knew it was still morning. The air between them seemed to turn that kind of golden. Syrupy and bright, and shot through with almost too much heat to bear.

And there was far less space between them than there ought to have been.

Lincoln saw the unmistakable spark of heat in her gaze

and the way it tracked over her cheeks, too, so she was as flushed as a summer dusk.

And suddenly, all of this became incredibly clear.

It was almost a relief.

"It's funny you should say that," Violet was saying in that uppity voice of hers that he decided, then and there, he was deeply partial to. In the way a man was partial to a pretty woman, having nothing to do with *puzzles* or *light* or overgrown chapels. "I don't think I would have put my finger on it quite like that, but it's true. You do remind me of someone. A whole lot of someones, actually. I have four older brothers and guess what? They're all useless. Big, loud and undeniably charming, but absolutely useless all the same. Weird. It's like you're one of them."

"Darlin', please," Lincoln drawled. And this time he was the one who moved closer—definitively—so he could hook a hand behind her neck and commit to this. To this sweet, bright, wildfire moment, with her breath coming fast and her eyes hot and in every single part of him *alive* and here. Right here where he belonged. "I'm not your goddamned brother."

And then, just in case there was some lingering confusion on that score, he bent on down and kissed her.

CHAPTER FOUR

VIOLET HAD DREAMED of kissing Lincoln Traeger for most of her life. The part that she thought of as *her life*, that was, instead of the part before when she was nothing but another loser Cook kid on her long walk off a very short pier into the waiting Chesapeake Bay.

Since the moment she'd laid eyes on him and nearly landed on her face, she'd dreamed about kissing him. When kissing other men she'd happened upon along the way, she'd somehow found herself imagining that she was kissing Lincoln instead.

That sort of thing never ended well.

But now she understood that there was more than one reason for that.

The most important reason being the simple fact that nothing she'd imagined could have possibly prepared her for this.

For *him*.

The wild punch of it. How that lazy, endlessly amused mouth of his fit hers so perfectly, somehow hard and teasing at once, tasting a lot like his drawl sounded. How the *Lincoln* of it coaxed her into leaning forward with her hands on his chest, then surging up on her toes so she could get closer.

Then closer still.

So close that she could give herself fully into that kiss

that went on and on, like he'd taken everything he knew about making one word into a whole epic poem and doing it with the way he kissed her.

So hot and so needy that she couldn't tell if it was her greed or his.

Only that she wanted more. That she *needed* more.

All that messy wildfire inside of her that she'd nursed across whole years *blazed*. There were too many sensations battering her to make sense of any one of them. There was the kiss itself, but then the way it grew and changed, got deeper, then hotter.

So much hotter.

But there was also the fact that she was touching him.

Finally, she was *touching* him.

In one swift moment, at the top of the chapel trail, everything had changed.

And now, forevermore, she would have the hard planes of his chest imprinted on her palms. She would know, always, that he burned hot. So hot that she could feel the heat of his skin through his T-shirt, and she knew somehow that it wasn't from exerting himself by loping up the side of a mountain.

Right there on her heels, like she was Little Red Riding Hood in her bright red dress and he was a very big, very dangerous wolf.

Violet was distinctly aware of how much smaller she was than him. Especially now. He leaned down, cupping her face in his big hands, and he had to go a long way even though she wore her platform wedges. It made her feel shivery. It made her want to test their relative sizes by getting him to sweep her up in those arms of his, so she could wrap herself around him as if the two of them had been made to intertwine, to *fit* like they were two parts of a whole—

But this was sheer madness.

This was *Lincoln*.

And the truth of the matter was that Violet was already neck-deep in too many life changes to handle whatever *this* was, too.

So many life changes that she'd taken this opportunity to run away from her real life with an eagerness that might have been unseemly had there been anyone around to see it. But she didn't do other people. She didn't do friends. And she was nothing but an unwanted conscience to her family.

Her firm had offered her a partnership, the thing she'd always been certain she wanted, and it had made her... want to cry.

When Violet didn't do *tears*, either.

She didn't *want* her life to change. With that partnership or without it—which would probably mean leaving her current position. She didn't want to have to make the choice.

Violet *wanted* to carry on doing what she was doing, no matter that she could feel herself curdling inside from the relentless onslaught of the cases she handled and the politics in her firm. She *wanted* to keep a tight hold of the idealism that she'd learned right here in Camp Phoenix.

She suspected that would be the first thing she'd lose if she stayed at the firm. But she would launch herself into the Great Unknown if she left, when she'd been focused on getting a partnership just like this one since high school.

She *wanted* this decision to be a no-brainer and it wasn't, so she'd come back to camp instead.

And she *wanted* her favorite forever crush to remain just that—a *crush*.

Unattainable and unknowable, which was impossible if there was *kissing*.

That was what she told herself, anyway, as she pulled away.

Just like she told herself that she absolutely was not going to feel any kind of disappointment that he let her go so easily. Without even clinging to her, just a little bit, to make it clear that he *could have* held her in place.

If he'd wanted to.

She told herself she didn't *want* him to want to hold on, but she did. And she tucked that away to be ashamed about.

Later.

"What was that?" she demanded.

Because a good offense was sometimes the only thing a girl had.

Lincoln's gaze was about 100-proof just then. "I don't rightly know what they call it on the mean streets of Charm City, Violet, but where I'm from in those backward hollers out there in Kentucky, it's commonly referred to as a *kiss*."

"You kissed me." She tried to make that sound like an accusation. A judgment.

His gaze only got more intense. "I did. I did kiss you. You kissed me back, but we can put that aside for the sake of argument. I was the one who did the initial kissing, and I can own that. I sure hope I managed to banish any brotherly feelings you might've been harboring."

It was clear that Lincoln was not in any doubt that he had done exactly that.

Violet gritted her teeth. "I didn't say that I had brotherly feelings, did I? I said you *reminded* me of my brothers. A pack of charming dumbasses, one and all. Kissing me might not be brotherly, but it doesn't exactly mask the resemblance."

"You can just admit I'm charming, you know. I am."

She stepped back even farther because he was, especially when he looked at her like this. But then she was a little too close to toppling off the side of the trail and tumbling down the ravine. Something he noticed, too, clearly, because he hooked his hand around her elbow and tugged her back.

And Violet had to stand there and pretend she felt absolutely nothing. Not that punch of fire again. Not a sudden, concerning interest in the way each and every one of his calloused fingers felt against her skin.

The skin of her elbow and upper arm, that was. Not exactly an erogenous zone, last she'd checked.

This man was significantly more potent than she'd imagined, and she'd imagined him as a kind of conflagration.

God help her.

"This won't work," she told him sternly. "I hope you know that."

"I believe it did work. Or was that someone else kissing me the way you just did?"

She ignored that. Because she had no choice. "This isn't going to get you out of all the work we have to do."

"Darlin'," he drawled, and she hated how much she liked the way that word danced through her and deep into her, "I'm not a man who minds getting his hands dirty."

And then, to her astonishment—and deep annoyance— he proceeded to do nothing but *actually get his hands dirty*, working hard until it was time for dinner down in camp.

Worse, Lincoln proceeded to behave as if nothing had happened between them. Every day. For the next *week*.

It was the only thing worse than all the things Violet had imagined might happen if she'd kept on kissing him.

"Condolences," said Bree one evening in the cabin, as the four of them—an uneasy alliance if ever there was one, in Violet's opinion, not that anyone had solicited it— sat around as if they were practicing their congeniality. They did this every evening before Jackson's draconian lights-out policy kicked in at nine. And little as she might want to admit it, spending every day pretending to be utterly unbothered by Lincoln while in fact being bothered *unto her soul* did actually make the time she spent with her childhood rivals feel almost…relaxing. So relaxing she was tempted to imagine that they'd been friends all along.

Not that she knew what that meant for normal people.

Violet stretched out on her comfortable top bunk. The one she'd claimed just as ruthlessly when she'd arrived here as she'd claimed every top bunk she'd slept in the whole of her camping career. She basked in the lights she'd strung from the rafters, and delighted in the lovely linens she'd brought with her to make sure that, while she might be returning to camp, there was no need to return to full camper-like conditions.

After all, she wasn't fifteen any longer.

Something she would do well to remember.

"Oh," she murmured, with only slightly exaggerated innocence when she realized Bree's sharp gaze was on her. "Were you talking to me?"

"You *are* the one who went and scrubbed her entire body with sand that one summer to, quote, *rid yourself of the contagion*, unquote, that one time Lincoln's toe grazed your ankle during capture the flag," Bree pointed out.

It was true, however humiliating now. Why had Violet imagined no one else would remember these things?

"You hated him so much when we were sixteen that you claimed the sight of him made you physically ill and then spent two nights in the infirmary," added Kinley, eyeing Violet solemnly from her bunk below Bree's. "Have you been feeling sick?"

"I wanted to sleep in past reveille, actually," she replied, which was true. "That was the only way I could think to do it. Luckily, that was a long time ago. I don't know if it's better or worse to say that I've met so many horrible men both socially and professionally since, that some guy at a summer camp doesn't have the effect he once had."

"That makes sense," Clementine squeaked out from below.

But from the bunk bed across the cabin, both Bree and Kinley gazed back at Violet.

Bree looked amused. Kinley looked thoughtful.

Neither boded well.

"Anyway," Violet said grandly, and maybe a little desperately, "I forgot all about that silliness. I'm happy to report that while Lincoln Traeger is still as annoying as he ever was, I'm no longer susceptible. The joys of having grown up."

And then she made a great show of returning her attention to her book.

Later, as they all lay in bed after lights-out—though Violet refused to unplug her fairy lights on principle alone—she shut her eyes and pretended to sleep.

But that was about as effective as pretending she wasn't reacting to Lincoln in exactly the same overwrought teenage way she had back in the day. She had no idea how long she'd been lying there when she heard the faintest creak from the bedsprings from across the way. She opened her eyes, turned her head and caught Bree in the act of climbing down from her top bunk.

Not dressed for an evening jaunt out to the communal toilets, but very clearly dressed for an assignation. With Sheriff Flint Decker, who had gone from enemy to lover in a remarkably short time, to Violet's mind.

Not that Bree seemed to be suffering from any kind of whiplash.

"Are you sneaking out to meet a boy?" Violet whispered, in an exaggerated scandalized tone.

"Certainly not," Bree whispered back, as her toes touched the cabin floor. "Because I really am a grown-up, Violet. I'm off to do grown-up things. Not pretend teenage things, like some people."

And while that could have been the kind of harsh gibe like the kind they'd exchanged night and day when they were kids, it wasn't. Not tonight. There was a look on Bree's face that looked entirely too much like compassion.

Or worse, like she knew exactly what was happening inside Violet. Each and every one of the things that Violet kept telling herself couldn't possibly be real.

It was so bad that by the time she managed to pull herself together enough to respond, Bree was already gone. Leaving Violet to lie awake, fuming, until Bree reappeared in the cabin the next morning just in time to walk up Hollyhock Hill with the rest of them.

"I hope you enjoyed your adulthood last night," Violet said sweetly as, once again, she hiked beside the others in four-inch platform sandals. And the voluminous dress that made it look like she had a train.

"I can assure you," Bree said with a smug smile, "I did."

"Lucky you," Clementine said from Violet's other side. "Not everybody is allowed to act like an adult. Some people are treated like little girls forever."

"That's only to be expected, though," Violet replied. "Everyone here knew your father. Everyone in Oregon knew your father, as far as I can tell. You'll always be Bill McClain's little girl to them."

Clementine smiled, but she was looking away. "Lucky me."

Violet followed her gaze, right up to the top of the hill

where everyone was gathered around the flagpole already, and saw exactly who Clementine was looking at. Duke Cody, her fellow deputy.

But before she could focus on the implications of that, her gaze was inexorably drawn to Lincoln. Like he was a force of nature, there where he stood next to Duke. Just *existing* and creating all this *chaos* inside her.

And yet, though he appeared to be listening to whatever the other man was saying, those bourbon-colored eyes found Violet and held.

Hard.

Until she felt a little drunk as she walked the rest of the way. And here it was barely six thirty in the morning.

The flag was raised. The appropriate songs were sung. Jackson consulted his clipboard, handed out day assignments to those who needed them and indicated to those with longer-running assignments that he'd want updates by sundown.

Then, dutifully, they all turned and shuffled their way into the dining hall, where Kinley had breakfast waiting.

And all Violet could think about was that, somehow, she'd come careening back through time and was no better than the fifteen-year-old who'd turned up here that first summer, half-feral.

Maybe wholly feral, if she was ready to face herself with unflinching honesty.

She really didn't like the fact that she felt just as feral today.

And so, that night, after another long day of clearing brush and smiling blandly back at Lincoln while absolutely nothing happened between them, she found herself full of the kind of thrumming energy that had only ever gotten her into trouble. Right there in her cabin, where her bunkmates were turning in for the night. Or, in Bree's case, pretending to turn in.

She felt like she might explode.

Maybe the real truth was, she *wanted* to explode.

"I was watching you and Lincoln when you were updating Jackson on your chapel progress," Clementine said, her gaze on Violet as Violet paced the cabin floor. She didn't sound like little Clementine McClain, tattletale extraordinaire, who had been the bane of everyone's existence growing up. Tonight she sounded a whole lot more like the sheriff's deputy she was. She even looked at Violet in that cool, coppish sort of way.

"I hope you found it entertaining." Violet made herself shrug like it didn't matter to her either way. "That, obviously, is the goal."

"We were actually all watching," Bree chimed in from where she was lying in her bunk beneath her covers, pretending she wasn't fully dressed. And her dark eyes sparkling with what looked entirely too much like pure mischief. "Looking for all that notorious hatred."

"I don't think you hate him," Kinley said then, before Violet could respond to Bree the way she wanted to. With that breathtaking directness that Violet certainly didn't remember from their camper days. Kinley didn't even shove her glasses up her nose. She just watched Violet—as if she was as much of a detective as Clementine was a cop. "And he definitely doesn't hate you. He was looking at you the way I look at freshly baked snickerdoodles. So what I keep wondering, Violet, is if you ever actually hated him at all?"

CHAPTER FIVE

VIOLET STARED AROUND at her bunkmates, fighting her reaction. She didn't turn bright red. She didn't crumble. She
deserved a medal, frankly.

She looked at each of her cabinmates in turn. "Did I
miss where you guys all became so tight? Such that you're
actually ganging up on me?"

"No one is *ganging up* on anyone," Clementine said
hurriedly. And was back to Clementine the camper, not
Clementine the cop. A switch Violet wouldn't have liked
much if the cop hadn't been *at her.* "We aren't *actually*
teenage girls."

Though she looked less sure of that than maybe she
should.

"I think you know perfectly well that this cabin repre-
sents an alliance," Bree said serenely. Because they had
certainly formed one, hadn't they, to help Bree get together
with Flint. Even if that hadn't been the stated objective at
the time. "A friendly alliance, that's all."

"As your friendly ally," Kinley said, still looking at Violet much too closely, "I'll ask again. All that over-the-top
hating on Lincoln. Are you sure that's…the right word?"

Violet didn't break a sweat. She faced far worse things
than this every day of her life, simply walking to work.
To say nothing of what she did when she was actually in
court, defending her clients, all minors, from the terrible

things that the people who should have been protecting them did to them.

She didn't break a sweat, but she found herself going very, very still.

"I love an alliance." She waved her hand around the cabin. "But I was raised in a pack of wolves. By which I mean men. All grunting and beer, and certainly no conversations about *feelings*. I don't know how to do this."

"Do what?" Bree asked. So sweet. So serene. "Kinley asked you a question."

And to her surprise—and terror—Violet felt something open up wide inside her. It took her a long, panicked breath, then another, to realize that it wasn't the sudden onslaught of a new kind of stomach flu. It was perilously close to *longing*.

Because, little she might like to admit it, even to herself, these women had always been the only female influences she really knew. Her mother had died giving birth to her. Her entire life back in Maryland was men. Her whole family. All the so-called friends she'd had in school. Even in law school, the men had flocked around her and she'd never learned the tricks and mysteries of forming bonds with other women. They didn't trust her and never really liked her, and she'd always assumed that was their problem.

When deep down she'd nursed this endless ache that she didn't know how to do…*this*. That she didn't have whatever it took to figure out these girl things.

It wasn't that she was the kind of woman who liked to careen around telling anyone who would listen that she was only friends with men. She knew perfectly well those weren't friendships. Not really. She'd always known what men wanted from her.

And here, right now, in this beat-up old cabin in Oregon, she understood that she stood on a precipice. More, that all she needed to do was jump off it. And then maybe, just maybe, when she landed, she'd find all that girl stuff she'd always wanted so desperately.

Maybe that was all it took.

But even though she opened her mouth, she couldn't do it. She *couldn't*.

"It was hate at first sight," she said instead. She glared at Bree. "You were there. You saw it."

"I saw you nearly swoon at the sight of him, sure."

"It was a wave of hatred so intense it nearly knocked me from my feet." Violet stood a little taller now and she wasn't worrying about *precipices* any longer. "I wouldn't describe that as a *swoon*."

"It must be very hard to work with him, then," Clementine said, and she actually sounded consoling. "Though I have to say that I don't get all the intense hate. He's so... nice."

"Nice?" Bree hooted. "Lincoln Traeger is many things, Clem. Really, he is. But *nice* isn't the word I'd choose to describe him."

"Anyway," Violet said. Through her teeth. "I don't expect you to understand, Bree. Having decided to sleep with the enemy yourself while *some* of us maintain the purity of our initial convictions." She batted her eyes at her friend. Her ally. Her...whatever Bree was. "No pun intended."

She told herself she felt triumphant when Bree gazed back at her, the light of battle ignited in her dark eyes, the way it always had been when they were young. She told herself she didn't feel the slightest little inkling of regret.

"I stole Flint's hat for fun," Bree said, though that wasn't exactly how Violet recalled it. "A little prank like days of old."

"Is that what they call it now?" And Violet wanted to tell herself that they were fighting, but she could see perfectly well that she and Bree weren't engaged in the same battle here. Bree was extending a whole lot of rope Violet's way, clearly inviting her to go hang herself if that was what she wanted.

Violet was the one spoiling for a fight. And didn't she tell her lunkhead brothers—again and again—that they should try only fighting with the people they were actually mad at?

"If you hate Lincoln, then this is your chance to prove it," Bree was saying airily. "Don't steal something from him for fun. Take something that will hurt him. Since you hate him so much, it should be like child's play. Really stick it to him, with all that burning...*hate*."

Violet was aware of Kinley and Clementine looking back and forth between them. Clementine had a hand at her throat, her eyes wide. Kinley looked...thoughtful.

But Violet was contrary to her bones. Bullheaded by blood. "I can't think of anything I'd like to do more. With the hate and all, but there's one small problem. This is Lincoln Traeger we're talking about. He doesn't actually care about anything."

"Everybody cares about something." Kinley's voice was matter-of-fact. "It's just about finding what that is."

"Lincoln has a house down in the Rogue Valley, outside of Medford," Clementine said helpfully. So very helpfully. "That might be where he keeps the things he actually cares about. Not that I, as an officer of the law, can possibly support any breaking and entering or anything even slightly associated—"

"We know your objections and would never ask you to engage in such behavior," Bree said. Soothingly.

"I'm also an officer of the court and I could never countenance such an outrageous act." Violet waited a moment, then smiled. "Of course, I know where his truck is parked. And I don't think he locks it."

And that was how she found herself creeping through the night once again with her band of allies. *Not friends*, she reminded herself. Though, really, at this point, wasn't that splitting hairs? There was really only one term to describe the kind of relationship that led to skulking up Hollyhock Hill in the dark, no flashlights, stifling laughter while attempting to blend in with trees.

This was what it had been like when they were kids, too. Except for Clementine, who would have hung back to confess other campers' sins, camp nights had always been about breaking rules. Whenever necessary.

And because it was fun, it was usually necessary.

Maybe, came a voice from deep inside of her, *that word you keep looking for here has always been* friends, *dumbass*.

But something about that word made her heart hurt.

Almost as much as looking at Lincoln did.

And Violet wasn't out here tonight to examine that particular ache. She was out here for justice, she told herself. And to prove that she, by God, hated that man with every fiber of her being.

She led the way, moving sure-footedly over the pine-needled path that led up to the old house. Jackson had taken it over when he'd bought the camp and hadn't improved it in the slightest. The ramshackle old place, thrown together over time so it ran this way and that, looked as if the next big storm might knock it over. Maybe he liked it that way. Men, after all, could make themselves comfortable pretty much anywhere.

I'm not your goddamned brother, Lincoln had growled

at her, right before his mouth had come down on hers and wrecked every last bit of sense that had been in her head—

But she wasn't thinking about that. Not tonight.

Because there were lights on inside. Lincoln was staying here with Jackson, and Flint bunked here when he didn't feel like driving back down to Jasper Creek. Violet stood there for a moment, peering in the windows. She saw that the TV was on, playing some or other sporting event. There was the sound of water running in the kitchen, suggesting that someone knew to wash a dish.

This was not one of their cute little poker nights, and she thought that was a good thing. They were likely all concentrating on whatever it was they did with their evenings, possibly beating their chests and clubbing each other over the head like Neanderthals, who knew, and that meant the field was wide-open.

Violet glided over the yard, keeping to the shadows even though she thought it highly unlikely that anyone inside would be looking out. She'd worn her favorite black dress, just in case.

Lincoln parked his big old truck a ways down from the house, tucked up under some trees. He'd told her only yesterday that was deliberate, so he could back in and out without disturbing anyone in the house. That meant Violet wasn't likely to disturb anyone tonight, either.

"I don't know why you think there will be something in his car that would be meaningful to him when he could keep it in his house," Kinley said in an undertone as they all gathered near the hood of the truck.

"It wouldn't be hard to find his house," Clementine chimed in. "All I have to do is call a friend on the force down in the Rogue Valley."

"Maybe you haven't met Lincoln," Violet said, feeling

that same unfortunate wild current ramping up inside her again. "Does he strike you as a man who puts down roots? No. He wanders around, tracking fugitives. He's the very definition of a rolling stone."

"You know this from your extensive study of him, of course," Bree murmured. "A burning hate study, that is."

Violet slid her a glance. "I'm very observant, Bree."

"That's one word for it, sure."

Not choosing to dignify that with a reply, Violet tested the driver's door handle. She looked toward the house, but still saw nothing. Then she threw the door open, tossed herself inside and disabled the overhead light. As quick as she could.

It took maybe ten seconds, and then she was sitting in his seat, her feet dangling in front of her and nowhere near the pedals, because that was how tall he was. But she opted not to concentrate on *that*. Because they were all frozen in place, staring up at the house and waiting for the doors to explode open and all the men to come charging out, like the good lawmen they were.

But everything was quiet. One breath, then another. Violet started to feel just the tiniest bit full of herself.

"We had to move some brush out of the chapel the past few days," she told the others. "That's how I know that he likes to keep the things that are important to him close to him." She reached up and told herself her hand wasn't shaking at all as she unhooked the chain that hung down from the rearview mirror. She pulled it off, then held the locket attached to the chain in her palm. "Lincoln comes from a very long line of lifelong criminals. According to him, there's only one other person in his direct line who ever chose the path of righteousness."

She turned as she said it, sliding out of the truck to plant her feet back on the ground. As if sitting where Lincoln sat...did something to her. As if it was some kind of unearned intimacy, almost as impossible to catalog as that kiss.

Stop thinking about that kiss, she ordered herself.

"I can tell my own stories, darlin'," came an unmistakable drawl from the trees behind them.

And then everything seemed to happen both too fast and too slow. Yet all at once.

Her allies shrieked, then bolted, each in a different direction. Two of them laughing.

Violet herself stood still. And watched, as if she'd anticipated this very moment all along, as Lincoln emerged from the darkness to lean against that tree, those eyes of his glittering.

And fixed on her.

Not just on her, but on the locket she still held in one fist.

Yet Violet refused to back down and apologize like she surely would have, if she were smart. She was *supposed* to be smart. "Your great-grandmother succumbed to a touch of grift in her youth. Isn't that how you put it?"

"Some say it's a function of poverty. But as far as I'm concerned, it's just in the Traeger blood. Still, she thought better of her thieving ways. Tried her best to straighten out the rest of her kin, though that didn't take."

"And that's why you carry her picture in the locket." Violet's voice felt like a scrape against the dark. Or deep inside her own gut. "To remind yourself that she's your kin just the same as the rest and it's not blood that makes them do what they do. It's the choices they make."

"I'll confess that I'm touched." Lincoln sounded...hungry. Not touched. "I could have sworn you didn't pay the slightest bit of attention to that story. And there you were, gathering intel all the while."

"People think that being a good lawyer means knowing how to argue," Violet said, as if the darkness they stood in was some kind of confessional booth. As if she could say things to him here, beneath the stars and the high trees, that she resolutely avoided even thinking in his presence by day. "And, sure, I'm not afraid of confrontation. But the reason I'm good at my job is because I listen. I listen well and I know how to use what I hear to get results."

"And I imagine you're about to tell me what results you intend to achieve with my family heirloom?"

She looked at her hand as if it wasn't connected to her. Then back at him, and she didn't need daylight to make him out. His wide shoulders. That breathtaking height. That intensity that seemed to blaze at her, brighter than any of the stars above.

"This is proof," she told him. "Of how much I hate you."

He didn't laugh. Not quite. The sound he made was too dark, too targeted, to be a laugh. "You don't hate me, Violet."

That seemed to land in her like a punch. Like a deadly wallop. She thought she staggered back. She thought she tripped again and, this time, tumbled head over heels to the ground. She thought that, surely, one of those West Coast earthquakes had finally come and the earth itself was opening up beneath her feet.

When the truth was, neither one of them moved an inch.

Not one inch.

"I do," she whispered, in a scratchy voice that sounded nothing like her own.

"No," Lincoln said, and the look in his gaze was far more dangerous than any tectonic shift. "You don't."

And for a millennium or two, all of it hot and tight and breathless, they stood right where they were. Like they were planted there. Violet could hear that his breath was no smoother than hers, though that wasn't the comfort it ought to have been.

Not when she felt like nothing more than a panicked little vole, possibly terminally odd, facing down a giant hawk.

An image that did absolutely nothing to keep her calm.

"I'm going to need you to hand over that locket, princess."

Violet looked at the locket again. "And if I don't?"

"Then I'll have to take it from you, darlin'. One way or another."

And Violet had spent more than half her life tamping down all the things in her she considered unwelcome inheritances from her family. Yet, standing out here in the dark, with the stolen locket in her hand, she felt as wild and uncivilized as if she'd rolled out of the Chesapeake like a storm. As if she was as untamable.

"You can try," she whispered. "I hope you do."

And something in her, something far more dangerous than that wildfire mess she knew too well, began to hum.

Especially when Lincoln pushed away from the tree, suddenly looking like he'd never known a moment's laziness in all his life.

She knew, deep down, that this was the real Lincoln.

Which maybe meant that this was the real Violet looking right back at him.

But she didn't care about that. She couldn't. She kept her eyes on his and slowly, deliberately, stepped out of one high-heeled sandal, then the next. She lifted up his locket next. Held it up, then dropped the chain over her head so the locket slid between her breasts.

"I won't warn you again," Lincoln said, and his voice was so *low*. It moved over her like sex and silk, winding around and around, then sinking through her skin. Becoming part of her.

Changing her. Challenging her.

"I hate you, Lincoln Traeger, and I always will," she whispered, even though she knew as the words left her tongue that each one of them sounded like its own endearment. Like love poems, sighed out to the summer night.

But she didn't care.

Because it was time.

So she turned on her bare feet, gathered the skirt of her dress in one hand and ran.

And felt a deep kind of gladness roar open inside her when she heard him follow right behind her, like night followed day, deeper on into the woods.

CHAPTER SIX

LINCOLN LET HER RUN.

Hell, he encouraged it because there had always been a wildness in him. He'd been tamping it down for most of his life, pretending it wasn't there, pretending the simple fact he made different choices than the rest of his family meant he didn't have that same hectic call in his blood.

But something about Violet and the dark night all around them, that fire in her eyes and his great-grandma's locket around her neck, made it impossible to pretend.

He went after her, racing through the night, through these woods they both knew so well.

It felt elemental.

It felt *right*.

It felt like the natural culmination of everything that had happened between Violet and him, this dance they'd been doing since they'd arrived here and all the stories he'd heard about the lengths she'd gone to back in the day, determined to prove how much she hated him.

She didn't hate him.

Hate had nothing to do with this.

He could feel her all over him, like he'd already caught her. Like he'd already laid her out before him and drunk deep of her, the way he'd been imagining night and day since they'd started working on the chapel together.

Violet Cook was a major disruption. She woke him from

a sound sleep. She was every last one of his idle daydreams. She worked beside him all day long, never seeming to notice that she was fast becoming his primary, overwhelming obsession.

She might not notice. Sadly, his friends did.

And weren't the least bit shy about calling him out on his distraction, either.

But none of that mattered tonight.

Because despite all his fancy words and that call in his blood he'd learned to ignore before Violet had made it impossible, here in these dark woods, he felt like nothing at all but a man.

Flesh and blood and that pounding need within him.

She darted between the trees and he kept to her heels, everything inside him a kind of bright, molten heat and song.

He could have caught her at any time. But instead he drank his fill of Violet running, drenched in starlight, her black hair flowing behind her like she was some kind of ancient goddess. He basked in it as she shot down Hollyhock Hill, ran in a zigzag pattern through the cabins that were slowly being brought out of their dilapidated state, then out onto the bluff. She skirted the far edge of the tents set up there, a passing shadow in the dark, and he followed.

She could only be headed to the very trail that they'd spent the past week clearing and cleaning up. That was what waited in the woods on the far side of the bluff.

But then, something in him knew they'd been headed there all along.

He hung back just enough so she could keep her lead and that head of steam that had her vaulting over that old tree trunk, which they'd decided might as well remain across the trail, for a little rustic color.

Lincoln hopped the tree. Violet kept running up the trail until she finally reached the chapel. She didn't hesitate at the high end. She ran down the center aisle until she stood between the madrone trees with only the steep drop-off and the lake before her.

Only then did she stop.

And he was sure he could feel her heart going wild inside his chest as surely as he could feel his own.

Lincoln made himself stop at the edge, right there at the top of the aisle. He could feel the heat of the run in him. He could feel the night air against his face. And he could feel it like her hands all over his body when Violet turned to face him.

A dark, wild joy on her face.

He felt that beat in him, its own drum, as he slowly made his way down the aisle toward her.

And he expected her to taunt him, the way she did too well. To say something, anything, to change what was happening between them. To make it less than it was. To make it…digestible.

But she didn't.

Violet only waited there, barefoot and flushed and more beautiful to him in this moment than anything had ever been.

Ever.

And Lincoln thought, *This is alive. This.*

Violet.

As if it had all been worth it, these hard years, his even harder childhood, all of it leading him inexorably to this moment. To this woman.

It was more than puzzle pieces falling into place. He saw the whole pattern then. He knew the stories that he'd forgotten, of that angry girl years ago who muttered dark things under her breath every time he walked by. He'd thought it was funny then.

Tonight, it felt like a blessing.

"You don't hate me," he told her as he came closer. As he stepped between the trees, there on the wide stretch of grass and dirt they'd prettied up with their own hands. "Between you and me, Violet, I don't think you ever did."

"How would you know?" She laughed at him, but there was all that longing in her eyes, written all over her face. "You don't remember any of it."

"I don't have to remember. I hope I'm never too blind to see what's right in front of me."

"And what's that, Lincoln?"

It was a challenge.

But he was beyond that.

Because here they were, under the stars. And she was the one who'd wanted distance between them, a game he'd been more than happy to play, especially when he could see it annoyed her.

But he wasn't playing anymore.

Tonight she wore his great-grandma's locket around her neck. His history on a chain. She'd run through the camp, the woods, the night, like every last one of his fantasies.

And she looked a whole lot like his future.

Lincoln understood in that moment that the entire point of being alive was this. The right woman. A night sky thick with stars. These perfect woods, quiet all around them.

And this mad wonder between them, hot and bright, that he knew, without doubt, would burn on forever.

It already had.

This time when he kissed her, it was a claiming.

And tasting her, he was found.

He kissed her and he kissed her, and he indulged all the

fantasies that had been plaguing him since the first time he'd had that pleasure. And when he hit his limit, he picked her up and she wrapped herself around him with a greedy sort of joy that made everything in him catch fire.

She dug her hands into his hair. She wrapped her legs around his hips.

Lincoln could have stood like that forever, letting her climb all over him. It was much, much better than he'd imagined and he'd put some time and effort into the imagining.

But Violet pulled away again and fixed him with that imperious look from her black eyes, even darker and deeper now.

"For God's sake," she said in a voice of deep complaint. "What are you *waiting* for?"

Lincoln laughed, a long, hot round of sheer pleasure.

And then he took his time laying her down on the sweet little altar they'd built. He shrugged his way out of his T-shirt, kicked his way out of his boots and his jeans, then followed her down, where she, greedy and impatient in a way that suited her all too well and made him burn besides, had already stripped off that dress of hers.

He was glad that they'd taken it to the ground, because the sight of Violet Cook naked would have knocked him off his feet either way.

"I get it now," he managed to say with an approximation of his usual drawl as he stretched himself out beside her. "You wear those tents of yours as a public service."

"I wear them because they're comfortable," she whispered, but she was surging against him, moving her hands all over him as if she already couldn't get enough. As if she felt it, too, this ache. It was almost like panic.

Like there would never be enough of this perfect, unbearable heat and they'd barely even started.

"You wear them because if you didn't, I expect we'd all be following you around mindlessly, begging you for a single glance."

"Lincoln," she said against his mouth, her smile tasting as wicked as it looked. "You already do."

Everything flared between them then. A white-hot heat that should have melted them both away into nothing.

And it was hard to say whether he took her or she took him, swift and wild and hot.

Only when that was out of their systems did Lincoln stretch her out beneath him and recollect himself enough to take it slow like the Southern gentleman he was.

Or had always wanted to be, anyway. He'd wrapped it tight around the truth of himself, but he introduced her to that part of him, too. The part that had been an angry kid and was now a half-wild man, outside his own skin with the intensity of the things he felt for her.

He usually kept that part of him on a chain, but somehow, he knew Violet could handle him.

And she did.

That time, when he found his way inside her, it was shattering. He built her up and tore her apart again and again. Over and over, until there was nothing between them but starlight and wonder, and only then did he let himself go.

Holding her close, there in the night, so that fate could do the rest.

It was a whole lot later when he and Violet found themselves again, lying tangled up with each other after he'd handled their protection. Her head was on his arm, her dress pulled over the two of them like a blanket.

Lincoln lay with his other arm folded beneath his head.

He gazed up through the shelter of the madrone trees and allowed it didn't get a whole lot better than this.

But that was when Violet started singing.

Softly at first, but then the melody took hold. He had a stray memory of hearing her sing outside Jackson's house in the early days here this summer. Like then, he found himself caught in the sweetness of her voice. Angelic, he was tempted to say, as her song lilted out on the night breeze to dance across the lake.

They could probably hear it down in camp, and he'd bet that the folks in tents out on the bluff were either dreaming about supernatural creatures who sang like this—sirens and myths—or waking up right now, not sure if they were imagining it. That's how beautiful her voice was.

So beautiful, in fact, that it took him a whole lot longer than it should have to listen to the actual words she was singing.

Lincoln sat up slightly to look at her, finding her expression nothing short of holy—but the look in her dark eyes was purely devilish.

"Violet Cook," he said, drawing out the syllables of her name. "Those words are filthy."

She sang a few more of them, then shrugged as the last note faded away. "It's my favorite sea shanty. My brothers taught me all the most vile and offensive ones when I was little, because they thought it was funny when I'd sing them with my pretty little voice. Preferably to horrify the folks at church."

"Your brothers sound like terrible, reprehensible influences."

"They'd be delighted to hear you say that. They come from a long line of Chesapeake Bay watermen, but really, at heart, they'd prefer to be pirates. And I don't mean the cuddly kind. Not the Disney ride sort of pirates, if you know what I mean. Less *yo ho ho* and way more bottles of rum."

He wanted to sing his own song about her just…talking to him. Like they were friends.

Instead, he smiled. "I always wanted brothers but that didn't happen. My cousins are deplorable enough. Of the twenty-two cousins that make up my generation of the fine, upstanding Traeger family, I believe only two have avoided the pleasure of incarceration at one point or another. That being me and my cousin Nell, who's generally too busy having babies with an assortment of suitors to get involved in the usual family shenanigans." He shifted, pulling Violet close to him and then rolling her so she sprawled out over his chest. She rested her chin on her hands, looked down at him, and he thought he saw something solemn there in that gaze of hers. Something as big as the things he felt inside. "Of course, none of them got to come to Camp Phoenix."

"How did you find your way?"

"Pretty sure I talked about that all the time, back in the day. Stood up at sunset services and so on."

"Please, Lincoln. I was far too busy cursing your name."

"Because of that deep and abiding hatred we just experimented with here."

Her eyes sparkled. "The very same."

"It was the US marshal who arrested my father, at long last, who broke down some facts of life for me." Lincoln could remember that day vividly, even now, standing outside in the gloom of winter in the hills, where there was light but it was never really *bright*. "Pa had been on the run for quite some time at that point. That's what happens when you take it upon yourself to express your political opinions with C-4. He's just lucky there wasn't a higher body count. But the marshal who collared him took me aside and suggested I take a good, hard look at the man in handcuffs that afternoon. The man who'd spent the last eighteen months hiding under floorboards and slinking in and out of questionable hollers all over Appalachia. He asked if that was how I envisioned my future, because that's where I was heading, and did I want him to just take me in then and avoid the intervening years of bad choices? I declined the kind offer. So he suggested I look up Camp Phoenix and try to make something of myself instead of making myself a statistic like all the rest of my kin."

Against his chest, he could feel Violet's fingers tracing out a pattern. He couldn't have said why it comforted him, when he was certain he'd gotten over his family crap ages ago. But her touch comforted him all the same.

"For me it was the guidance counselor in high school," Violet said sometime later, when he'd almost forgotten there had ever been anything but the sound of the lake water against the shore. And her soft weight on him. "My favorite pastime was pitting various older boys against each other to see how much trouble it could cause, while I sat back and goaded them on."

"Shocking behavior."

He could feel her smile. "Mrs. Gunter's position was that I could be expelled for causing the problem. My position was that if I wasn't the one acting out, how could I be blamed for the stupid things boys did?"

"A lawyer even then."

"Always. She and I went around and around on that, but one time when I went into her office for more of that guidance nobody wanted, the Camp Phoenix brochure was on the desk. A picture of the lake and all those pretty trees, nothing like the dirty little fishing town I thought was the whole world." He studied her face as she talked, and brushed a tendril of her hair away so he could see her better. "To this day, I don't know if she was playing a little reverse psychology game with me or if she truly thought I was beyond help, but she snatched it right up and told me it was for kids who *wanted* to be good, not lost causes like me." Violet laughed. "I didn't like being told I was a lost cause, and certainly not by her. I applied for a scholarship that very same night."

"And look at us now," Lincoln drawled. "Such fine, upstanding citizens. Committed to law and order in all things, even if you are currently wearing a purloined locket."

He pulled on the chain around her neck, but made no move to take it back.

"Do you ever think...?" she began, but then stopped, sighing a little bit. When he only waited, she continued, but she wasn't looking up at him any longer. "Do you ever wonder what comes next?"

"I hope this isn't a discussion of the afterlife that will lead to you tossing me off the cliff, darlin'. That would just be cruel."

She wrinkled up her nose. "I'm a little more direct than that, I hope. I just mean... Lately I've been feeling like everything I've done since my first summer here has been about getting out. Leaving my hometown behind me, getting off the Eastern Shore, making sure I was nothing like anyone else in my family."

"I'm familiar with that particular model of existence."

"Can you live a whole life in opposition to the way you were born?" Violet asked quietly. "I mean, I'm sure you can. But *should* you?"

Sensation lit up inside of him. It was somehow more overwhelming than all those feelings he'd been having earlier about fate. And a future—with her, no less—when he knew he'd never had such notions with any other woman before.

But this was different. This felt like she really had gone ahead and shoved him off the side of this mountain. Like he was in free fall suddenly, and he didn't have the slightest idea how to reach out and grab hold of anything.

She sighed—when he didn't respond, when he couldn't—and laid her head on his chest. "Maybe it's just me." That beautiful voice of hers against the night again, though he knew she wasn't singing now. "It's just that sometimes I wonder if truly being a phoenix means constantly reinventing yourself. Not just the once. But again and again, like we're never done. Maybe we shouldn't *want* to be done."

And when Lincoln shifted her again so he could take her mouth hungrily, desperately, she met him the same way.

All that greed. All that glory.

As if, somehow, he could shake off the truth of what she'd said before it took hold.

CHAPTER SEVEN

"How," Clementine demanded in a low voice on the morning trudge up Hollyhock Hill, "do you still have *his locket*, Violet?"

Violet toyed with said locket as she walked, having worn a specific dress with a neckline that called attention to it, but said nothing. On her other side, Bree's eyebrows arched. "And you're wearing it, right out in the open. As if you don't care that he knows you stole it. How brazen."

"I've never really been known for my subtlety, Bree," Violet murmured, and Bree stifled a laugh.

"I can't believe he didn't catch you," Clementine was saying. "You must be ridiculously fast."

Violet bumped her shoulder against her bunkmate's. "I didn't say he didn't catch me, Clementine."

And found it far more entertaining than maybe she should have when Clementine's eyes widened. "Oh. *Oh.*"

"Yeah," Violet said as they got to the top of the hill and took their usual place. *"Oh."*

She stood with her hands folded demurely in front of her, fully aware of Lincoln's gaze all over her. And especially on her choice of necklace. She saw the others study it, too, clearly recognizing it for exactly what it was.

And no doubt knowing exactly how she'd gotten ahold of it.

Yet no matter how she dug down deep to find some old

shame to drag out, since so many people standing around the flagpole this morning likely knew how she'd spent her night, she couldn't.

She just couldn't.

"I kind of thought US Marshal Traeger would lock you up and throw away the key," Kinley said at breakfast, after she'd served the others and brought her plate over to their usual table. "But you really don't look like you spent the night in any kind of jail."

"He at no point mentioned involuntary confinement of any kind." Violet speared a chunk of her pancakes with a fork, flooding them with far more than the necessary amount of maple syrup. Which was the necessary amount of maple syrup, in her opinion. "Besides, I know an amazing lawyer."

"Sure you do."

Violet gazed back at Kinley, who seemed happy to get into a staring contest, shoving her glasses back into place in that extra-slow way she liked to do when she was being aggressive. Not that *she* ever thought *she* was being aggressive.

"I note that you're all very interested in helping this morning," Violet said, returning her attention to her pancakes because *she* chose to break eye contact as a power move. Not because Kinley won. "Unlike last night, when all I heard was a bunch of squawking hens before I was left on my own to fend for myself."

"I would've stayed to defend Clementine." Kinley was smirking like she didn't realize that she'd been outmaneuvered. "You've always seemed perfectly capable of defending yourself, Violet."

"Hey." Clementine frowned at them from across the table. "I can defend myself *and* all of you." When no one jumped in to agree with that statement, she frowned. "I'm literally a certified badass with a badge to prove it. A little respect, please."

And Violet found that despite being abandoned by her friends last night—had she really started just…using that word? Not even qualifying it?—she was in a good mood. A remarkably good mood. Much as she'd like to attribute that to the amount of sugar she was currently ingesting, she knew that the reality was one lanky, lazy cowboy who she could *feel* across the dining hall.

But it gave her pleasure not to catch his gaze, so she didn't.

"Did you hear that singing last night?" someone asked as everyone headed out of the dining hall a bit later to start the day's work. "I swear, I woke up in a panic and thought there were cats fighting. Until I realized fighting cats can't carry a melody."

"Who would sing like a catfight in the middle of the night?" Violet asked the man, who she vaguely remembered was named something like *Tim*. "You were probably dreaming. Unless, of course, it was one of the famous Camp Phoenix ghosts. If I were you, I'd keep my eyes closed and all my limbs safely inside my sleeping bag."

And the look on his face had her laughing the rest of the way outside, where Lincoln was waiting for her the way he always did. Leaning there against the nearest tree like he was too loose-limbed to stand up without assistance.

"Telling ghost stories at breakfast? That's hard-core."

"That's me. Hard-core all the way. Ask anyone in Baltimore."

"I don't need to ask anyone. I know from experience."

They stood there for a moment, just looking at each other. Violet waited for one of her usual reactions to men to roll through her. But none of them came. She wasn't swamped with boredom. She didn't feel annoyed. If anything, she liked the way the daylight played over his face, highlighting that sweet bourbon gaze of his. She liked the way the morning sun seemed to linger on all the parts of that body of his she knew so much better now.

She liked all of it, was the thing.

"You all right?" he asked.

"I believe I am," she replied.

And they both smiled. For a good while.

As the days rolled by, things just got better.

It was easier than it should have been to work with a man she'd slept with, when that had never been her experience before. It was Lincoln, she knew. He was different. Not because of that act he put on, drooping about like he was boneless and pretending he couldn't hurt a fly. She knew better than that.

The thing about Lincoln Traeger was that he was fascinating. And more, that he cared about Camp Phoenix every bit as much as she did.

Maybe she'd known that on some level. But watching it in action was something else. Lincoln showed her a spot she'd never found during her days here, a ways past the chapel into the woods, where there was a place to jump into the lake and an easy climb back up. So every day, they hiked out to the chapel and worked. Hard. Then, when they'd done enough work to have them both hot and sweaty, or frustrated because something wasn't going according to plan, one or the other of them would see to it that one thing led to another.

One thing always led to another. Gloriously.

And they'd end up on their own private little piece of paradise on the lake, in that tucked-away cove that was otherwise only accessible by the boats that weren't in the water yet. It was like they were the only people alive in Oregon. They explored each other in as many ways as they could come up with, and they both had vivid imaginations. Then they jumped into the lake to cool down.

With box lunches courtesy of Kinley, they could repeat that process the whole day long, until it was time to head back for dinner with the rest of camp.

To Violet, it felt like they were kids again. In the sense that every day seemed like a whole year, the way summer days always had when she was younger. Until she found herself almost as upset when it was finally time to unveil the new chapel—and therefore, the end of this perfect little world she and Lincoln had been living in for what felt like a lifetime—as she'd always been when camp ended in August.

Part of her thought of that chapel as hers and Lincoln's now—but that was silly. Even if it wasn't, what was she going to do? Tell Jackson that the chapel on the hill on the land he owned was off-limits to him?

She almost did it just to hear what he'd say.

Almost.

Instead, she gathered with everyone after dinner that night and took that same old traditional walk from the top of Hollyhock Hill, down to the bluff over Crow Lake, then up again into the woods so they could all gather in the chapel as the sun went down.

"This is wonderful," Bree sighed happily as they found their seats on the benches that Violet and Lincoln had cleaned up and made pretty and fought over placing *just so.* "Exactly how I remember it."

"Me too, but that's surprising, because I heard it was trashed," Kinley said from Bree's other side.

"Violet and Lincoln have spent all this time cleaning it up," Clementine reminded her.

Kinley's gaze found Violet's. "Apparently, they really have."

Violet tried to look as saintly as possible. "Your doubt in me is duly noted, Kinley."

"It's not so much doubt in you. It's more that I figured Lincoln would've handled the situation differently."

"Don't you worry," Violet said as Jackson made his way to stand between the madrone trees and faced the camp. Or the little group that made up the camp before opening day, anyway. "Lincoln handled himself just fine."

And that was what she found herself thinking about as Jackson began talking, delivering the kind of Sunday night talk that had always been a part of sunset evenings out here in the woods. Motivational, yet personal, and never religious—because the focus here was always on self-improvement. How can *you* fix *your* life? How can *you* sort *yourself* out?

Maybe it was only to be expected that she found herself thinking about Lincoln. About the variety of ways the man handled himself, and how he handled her, too. She thought about Camp Phoenix rising up again this summer, made new. She remembered what it had been like to be that teenage girl who'd applied to come here purely out of spite for Mrs. Gunter, who hadn't seemed to think that Violet was worthy of a second chance. She'd come here and tried her best to hold on to that spite, applying her bone-deep contrariness to everything, every day.

She thought about the wonderful Gale Lawson, who became, that first summer and all the summers after, a stand-in for the mother Violet had lost so young. And not the kind of cuddly kindergarten teacher mother figure, all pastels in a soft voice, that might have worked for kids less messed up.

Because Gale was about accountability, not pastels. Gale wasn't soft; she was about practical applications of talent and intelligence. She had high expectations for them all and yet encouraged falling short of those expectations, because that was an opportunity for growth.

And as she thought these things, out here in the woods staring at the setting sun, she knew. Deep down, Violet knew what she supposed she'd known since she'd left Baltimore.

She'd come here to change her life. And she could pretend she didn't know what that meant. She could pretend that because she didn't know how it would turn out, because it required a new and different dream than the one that had been fueling her all these years, that it was wrong.

But she knew better.

Violet wanted to pretend it had nothing to do with Lincoln, but she knew it did.

Because she'd never connected with a man the way she did with him. She hadn't known it was possible. Even though she'd come a long way from the teenage girl who liked to make boys do stupid things to win her favor, she couldn't say she really viewed men as much more than attractive ways to scratch a variety of itches.

Until Lincoln.

Lincoln told her that she was beautiful, but that wasn't the only thing he told her. He told her far more stories about his life. He didn't hide the darkness he saw in his chosen field, and he didn't try to convince her that she should shy away from the matching darkness in hers. He was the first man she'd ever met who seemed to find arguing with her—about things that didn't matter, like where to place benches in the chapel, and things that did, like different approaches to humanitarian crises—as much fun as getting naked with her. He never tried to shut her down. He wasn't like the partners in her law firm, who treated her like a loaded weapon and seemed to forever be looking for a decent gun safe to lock her up in when her forthrightness didn't suit them.

She felt a wave of something she told herself was joy, though it seemed to ache a bit more than joy usually did.

It was time to leave Baltimore. It was time to try something new. She watched the sun as it sank down into the hills across the lake, so that the water seemed to gleam like the paintings Gale had done in the arts and crafts cabin so long ago. Paintings Violet had always wished that she could replicate, because she loved painting. But the sad truth of the matter was that she had absolutely no talent where that was concerned.

Tonight it was almost like she could feel Gale sitting next to her. She could *hear* Gale telling her in her usual brisk way that a person's gifts came in two forms. One set to help others. Another to please oneself. *It's perfectly fine to love things that don't love you back*, Gale had told her matter-of-factly all those years ago. *Just don't lose yourself in loving them. Lose yourself in the things that do love you back, because that's just another way of getting found.*

And all these years, Violet had thought that meant the law. Her talents in that area, and all the ways she could help kids like her and kids who had it so much worse than she ever had. But tonight she thought about painting. Her eyes followed the colors in the sky back into the chapel, past Jackson, where he stood with his hand on his cane as he wrapped things up with an old camp song.

And then, inevitably, her gaze found its way to Lincoln.

He was standing on the end of one of the lower pews, and he wasn't watching Jackson. He'd angled his body so he could look back at her instead.

And Violet knew. That she could love this man as much and as deep as she liked, just so long as she didn't lose herself in it. That he was a gift of this summer. And at the end of it, who knew the things she would have learned about herself? That was what mattered.

She told herself she couldn't wait to find out.

When everyone turned and began making their way back down into camp, she smiled at her friends but didn't go with them. Instead, she waited for Lincoln to climb up the chapel hill and stand before her. She held out her hand and waited for him to take it. When he did, neither one of them spoke, though she knew they both felt the heat. That same old heat.

They didn't say a word. They just walked down the trail the way they had so many times already.

Up ahead, she could see flashlights bouncing off the trees. She could hear the laughter and conversation and snatches of old camp songs as everyone made their way back down into camp.

But she and Lincoln let the stars guide the way, the silence between them seeming thicker and sweeter than the night.

And she told herself, once again, that all of this was joy. The way she held his hand, memorizing his fingers in hers, as if she expected him to pull away any second. The way they moved together, side by side where the trail allowed it, as if they had always been perfectly in sync.

Violet thought of that fifteen-year-old she'd been, who'd tripped over her own feet at the sight of him.

Like that had been some kind of prophecy, all those years

ago. As if she'd known even then that she would have this time with him, all these years later. That he would teach her not that the world was different, but that *she* could be, if she wanted. That she could demand more, and ask for it. That she could take all the lessons she'd learned in this place and build herself a new future, if she dared.

She wanted all of those things. Violet knew that, deep inside, and no matter that the joy she kept telling herself she felt seemed a whole lot more like sorrow, just then.

When they got back down to the bluff, he walked her to her cabin. Every step felt fraught with meaning and peril, suddenly. Possibly because Violet knew that all the things she felt were too big, too much.

And he was Lincoln Traeger, who even ten years ago had been his own master class in lazy smiles that made the girls who followed around after him feel as if each and every one of them was special, when they weren't.

She told herself that was okay. He didn't owe her *special*.

If she'd learned anything at this place, and especially from Gale, it was that love was something you gave. It wasn't something you cataloged as you received it, trying to make it this thing or that. It was how she'd learned how to accept her family's limitations, something she was better at when she stayed away from her hometown. It was how she'd learned how to accept her own limitations, and all the many ways she wasn't good with other people.

All of that was *okay*. It was. Love was about the giving of it, and that was what mattered.

So she took his hand and brought it to her lips, brushing her mouth over his knuckles. "Thank you. For everything, Lincoln. And I loved putting the chapel together with you."

She expected a droll reply, but all he did was gaze down

at her in the light that spilled out from the cabin she shared with the others.

"I'll see you tomorrow," she said, and she was pleased at how calm she sounded. Because they'd never discussed what would happen when their project was over. They weren't like Bree and Flint, who were clearly seeing each other and liked to sneak around so they could spend their nights together. She had no reason to expect those things.

"Good night, Lincoln," she said softly, and she went to pull her hand away.

But he didn't let go.

Something in her flipped upside down.

"Violet," he drawled, in that particular way he had that made her name into poetry. "Darlin'. What do you think is going on here?"

She smiled. She made herself smile. "I have no expectations whatsoever. This is only the beginning of the summer. Anything can happen. I understand that. You have my blessing to be you."

He didn't smile. And his gaze, she couldn't help but notice, looked anything but lazy. And in fact, the longer she looked up at him, the more it looked as if he might be about to get a little US marshal on her.

That should have been less hot than it felt.

"I have your blessing," he repeated.

"We talked about this. I figure it's time for a second act. And you've been a part of my realizing that, certainly. But I'm not going to *cling* to you. I'm not going to make it weird. That's all."

"You're standing in front of me wearing my great-grandmother around your neck, Violet," Lincoln said, his voice low and dark. "You're wearing my past and you look a whole lot like my future. I don't need your blessing to be me, and heads-up, we're way past weird."

"This doesn't have to be anything," Violet insisted.

"Good," Lincoln retorted. "Because I don't want that. I want everything."

CHAPTER EIGHT

"YOU WANT...*WHAT*?"

She pretty much stuttered that out, her eyes wide and her face a little pale, which wasn't exactly the reaction Lincoln was going for.

"Are you letting me down easy?" he demanded. "You're going to have to spell that out for me, Violet. It's never happened before. So I'll need a bit of an explanation to get me up to speed."

"There's nothing to get up to speed," she all but *yelped*. "I've enjoyed what happened between us—"

"You've *enjoyed* it. That's the word you want to use. You *enjoyed* falling apart so many times you forgot your name?"

"—and all I'm saying now is that there's no need to make a big deal out of it."

"It is a big deal. It's a huge fucking deal. The biggest deal yet, darlin'."

She looked flushed, but also pissed, and there was so much happening inside him then that he couldn't really tell which he preferred. Because all he could focus on was the fact that, while he'd been out here thinking about *fate* and *forever*, she'd been figuring out how to bail.

"I have a lot of things to figure out, Lincoln," she told him, sounding faintly injured. "I thought I made that clear."

He folded his arms over his chest. "Let me help you out

with that, then. Quit your job. Move to Oregon. Give this thing between us a chance."

Violet laughed, but it was a sound of shock. "I can't… Nobody would… It's ridiculous. I'm not going to pick up and move across the country on the off chance that some hookup I had with a guy might turn into something!"

She said that as if it was self-evident. As if it was outrageous even to suggest something else. So he just studied her. He waited, letting the silence grow between them, especially now that the sound of chatter inside the cabin faded away, suggesting that her friends were probably listening.

The thing was, he didn't care.

"Why not?" he asked. "We can do a lot with an off chance, you and me. We already have."

She staggered back a step, then caught herself. "What do you mean, *why not?* Because that's not what a strong, independent woman does, Lincoln. Maybe you've never met any before, I grant you, but if I change my life—*when* I change my life—it will be for concrete, unassailable reasons. I will find a new job in an appropriate city. I'll sell my town house in Baltimore and carefully look for a house I can afford, in a neighborhood I like, that I can see growing in. That's how people move. That's how *grown-ups* move. They don't just…"

"Fall head over heels in love and think, what the hell, better to see what it's all about than spend the rest of your life regretting it?"

Lincoln could admit there was some satisfaction in the way her mouth dropped open at that. And later, maybe, he'd look back on this moment and feel some sense of triumph that he'd managed to render the famously mouthy Violet Cook entirely wordless. He was sure he would.

But he wasn't there yet.

"You can't... That's not how this works." She seemed to bristle at the way he looked at her. "Lincoln. It's *not*."

"You have a whole lot of rules for something that isn't about rules, darlin'." He moved a little closer, though she was skittish now. Jumpy. Those black eyes huge. "I don't know what this is between us, Violet. I just know I want to see where it goes. And I can't promise you that it will end well, but I know it won't go anywhere at all if we don't try."

"This is all moving too fast."

"Just fast enough to scare you, I reckon."

She stiffened as if he'd slapped her. "I'm not scared of anything."

"Just me, as far as I can tell. Pretty much from the moment you laid eyes on me all those years ago, isn't that right?"

"I hated you on sight. It happens. You have that effect on people, believe it or not."

"I've had that effect on you, Violet. Just you."

Her jaw went mulish. Why did he find even that cute? "It can't all be panties thrown at your head and sobbing women begging for a moment of your attention, Lincoln. Some of us are fully grown adult women with complicated lives that have nothing to do with you. And you're a marvelous distraction, but I never signed up for this...*derailment*."

A lesser man might have let that sting. Lincoln shook it off. "Violet. We just built a chapel with our bare hands, you and me. It was something messy, but we cleaned it up. We made it pretty. Peaceful. *Safe*. It took the both of us, but we did it. Hell, you did it in pretty dresses and ridiculous shoes. Why can't we build a life the same way?"

She shook her head. "You don't understand."

"You're not the only one who wants to make a change," he gritted out at her, and maybe he was a little more stung than he wanted to admit. "I do, too. And I know what I want."

"Lincoln."

But he didn't stop. "I love my job, but I'm tired of sitting alone in an empty house waiting for the darkness I deal with every day to take me over. I want to spend the time I'm not working really *living*. I want someone who doesn't resent what the job takes from me, but understands why I have to give it. I want all that good stuff, Violet, to balance out the bad. And I've never met a woman I thought could give me all of those things, until you."

She was still standing there too stiffly, with all that dark regret in her gaze. It made him want to break things, but he wasn't that messed-up kid any longer. For the first time in a long while, he regretted that.

"We haven't even made it through a month, and you want to talk about forever?" She shook her head. "That's not real. Real is time. A lot of time. Real is *hard*."

"Real is whatever we make it, darlin'. And I spent my entire life looking at examples of how I don't want my life to be. I know the difference. I'm not afraid of going after the things I do want, or the life I can see because of you."

She rubbed her hands over her face. She whispered his name.

He reached over and held her face between his hands, tipping her face to his.

"What happened to the girl who was so unafraid to hate me that she reacted to the news that I was in charge of Christmas in July one year by jumping off the dock into the freezing cold water of Crow Lake right after the flag went up, just to prove the point that she would rather risk drowning than succumb to my brand of evil?"

Something moved over her face. She swallowed, hard. "That's exactly what I'm doing right now."

"What you're doing tonight is drowning. What you did back then was swim, Violet. In your bright red flannel pajamas, like you didn't notice they were waterlogged."

"I thought you didn't remember any of that," she threw at him, but he could see that her eyes were getting too bright.

"The more time I spend with you, the more I remember everything," he replied.

"Then let me help you." She jerked her chin out of his grip and then she turned, stomping over to the cabin door and swinging it open. "This is me walking away from you, filled once again with burning hate."

And she slammed the cabin door behind her before he could tell her, once again, that she really didn't hate him.

He stood there, feeling something like *undone* in the dark, as he certainly hadn't expected that this would be a night of *declarations*. But he stood behind those declarations all the same.

And he did not intend to act like the kind of teenage boy he'd never been. He was not going to storm her cabin or howl at the moon. Nor was he about to indulge the inklings of the teenage boy he had been, and burn something down.

What amazed him was that he had to take a minute all the same.

He turned around and took himself back up the hill to Jackson's house, where he walked in a little mean, eyed his friends sitting around the makeshift table with the cards already out and helped himself to a big old bottle of whiskey on his way to taking his place.

"That looks healthy," Jackson commented. Happily without his trusty bullhorn.

"Things went well with Violet, then," Duke added, smirking. "You look great, buddy. Really."

"We can talk about Violet." Lincoln took a swig of the whiskey straight out of the bottle, classing up the place, but that was also better than burning shit down. These were his best friends, after all. Brothers by any measure. "And I can entertain myself in a time-honored fashion by beating the smirk off each and every one of your faces. You decide, assholes."

Next to him, Flint laughed, deep.

"Fantastic," he said, still laughing. He pounded Lincoln on the shoulder. "This should end well and I'm here for it."

And he dealt them all a hand and sat back, like he already knew how this would go.

Which made one of them, Lincoln thought darkly, and took another pull.

CHAPTER NINE

VIOLET SLAMMED HER way into the cabin and then stood there, frozen, as three pairs of eyes stared back at her. With what looked like pity from Bree, confusion from Clementine and a sort of curiosity from behind Kinley's glasses.

The urge to cry did not go away. It got worse. But she would rather die where she stood than cry, so Violet blinked it back and bit down on her tongue.

"That did not sound like it went well," Bree pointed out. Very mildly.

"Of course it didn't go well." Violet reminded herself that this wasn't her cabinmates' fault. And that no good would come from blaming them when it wasn't them she was mad at. She could save that for herself. "Lincoln Traeger has been the bane of my existence for more than half my life. Why would that stop now?"

"I don't think Lincoln is the problem." Kinley shrugged when Violet glared at her. "I think this is the kind of friendship where we tell the truth."

"It wasn't a friendship at all until about five seconds ago," Violet retorted. "I don't think you get to decide what kind of friendship it is."

This time there was no pretending Kinley didn't win the staring contest. "I just did."

"We could hear the whole thing," Clementine told her, and she was the only one who looked even slightly shame-faced. Or, to be more precise, she looked *a little bit* sorry that Violet was upset. Maybe. "And the only way not to hear it would have been to come outside and be *in* it, you see. So."

Violet started to say that they all knew how to climb out windows when necessary, but restrained herself. That was unduly argumentative and sounded a lot like she was trying to change the subject.

Was she trying to change the subject?

"What I want to know—" and Bree still wore that look that was a little too close to pity for Violet's taste "—is why you have to be so *sure* about everything."

"Like, in a general sense?" Violet bit out. "That would be because I have a distressing habit of being right. Even when I don't want to be."

"Why do you have to be so sure about what's going to happen with Lincoln?" Bree asked, her voice kind.

Kind.

It was like she knew.

Like she *knew.*

Violet opened her mouth to tell her it was none of her business, because it wasn't. And to suggest they all leave her alone, because she deeply wished that they would. But nothing came out. And Bree White was being *kind.*

And somehow, everything had changed.

Wasn't that what she'd been feeling up at the chapel?

She didn't know how to have friends, yet here three women stood, clearly indicating that they were willing to brave her greatest weapon—her mouth and her ability to wield it—to say so.

What more was she looking for? A lightning bolt from on high?

"I don't know how to do any of this," she burst out. "I don't know how to...*have friends*."

"No. Really?" But Kinley's mouth curved.

Violet rolled on, and not because she *wanted* to. She didn't *want* to. But because she couldn't stop. "The things that everyone else takes for granted have never made sense to me. Friendship, sure, but everything else, too. I have no trouble attracting men. I'm great for a night. A weekend. But start talking to me about anything more than that, and I ruin it. I always do. It's a gift I have."

Clementine frowned. "So they all talk about the *anything more* part...a lot? Is that actually a common thing for you?"

"I've had men spontaneously propose to me on the street," Violet said flatly. "But let's be clear about that. They're not actually talking to me. They want to collect a pretty little trophy to put on a shelf somewhere. It's not a compliment to hear from a stranger that you fit his decor. It's gross."

"Did Lincoln propose?" Bree asked, and she sounded almost idle. Violet doubted she was anything close to *idle*.

Yet she still answered. "He didn't...*not* propose. It was more like he proposed the possibility of..." But she couldn't say these things. It made her feel red and tight and *wrong*. "I thought you were listening."

"I was. I wanted to see if you were."

"The difference is, you're not a pretty little trophy on the street to him, are you?" Clementine chimed in then, sounding very reasonable. Violet blinked and wondered when she'd stopped thinking of Clementine as the tattletale of yore.

Kinley nodded. "He knows you."

Violet snorted. "Barely."

"The two of you have spent all day every day together for weeks now," Bree pointed out.

"That's not enough. You have to put in real time."

"Like how much?" Kinley folded her arms. "A month? Six months? Three years? What's enough time?"

"You don't understand." And Violet was horrified to find that her voice was thick. Then, she wasn't mistaken, she was perilously close to—

Then, horribly, she could feel tears splashing down her cheeks.

But she didn't die.

And her friends moved closer, like they were prepared to hold her up if she fell over. She believed they would.

"I'm only going to disappoint him," she heard herself croak out, as if the words were torn out of a deep, dark pit inside her. And they must have been, because she'd never said such things aloud. "I don't know how to *do* these things. That's what I'm trying to tell you. He shouldn't go saying the kind of things he's saying. It can only end badly. They all think I'm whatever it is they think I should be, but I'm not. And when he finally sees beyond all that…"

"Then what?" Bree asked softly. "He might find out you're a human being? A real person? Between you and me, I think he already knows that. He's spent his entire adult life ferreting out the truth about people, Violet. I don't think you're the mystery to him you think you are."

"He knows what all of us know, at the very least," Clementine said, her voice something like solemn. "We all share this place. This camp and what it means. No matter what kind of person you think you are, I know that who you really are is the person who moved everything in your life aside to come here for the summer. Just to make sure that Camp Phoenix can live up to its legend. That's no small thing to know about another person."

"And besides," Kinley said, "he *didn't* propose. This isn't all or nothing. All you have to do is give him a chance."

"If I do that," Violet whispered, "if I really do, then what will happen if…?"

But she couldn't finish. The tears welled up and streamed down her face, and she let them. Her three best friends in the whole world—her only real friends—moved in closer, each of them getting a hand on her, and she didn't just *allow* it.

She loved it.

Because she got it, finally.

What Gale had told her long ago. Violet had interpreted it to mean that you only went after the things that you knew you could win.

But maybe love was the risk, the reward.

Maybe it didn't matter if she knew what would happen next.

Maybe the *point* was that no one could know. Maybe that was the fun of it, too.

Because wasn't this supposed to be fun? Just like camp—even if everyone in this room had always taken camp *dead serious*, too?

Violet felt something move through her, like a wish coming true. She blew out a long, shaky breath.

And decided, then and there.

"I have to go," she announced.

"Are you going to break into Jackson's house?" Kinley asked, maybe a little too hopefully.

"Certainly not," Violet replied. She wiped at her face. "I'm an officer of the court, as I keep trying to tell you. I'm going to march right in the front door. Thank you, cabinmates and allies, for your support."

"Violet," Bree said gently. "I think it's time for an upgrade."

"We're friends," Kinley agreed. "Allies are for wars. Friends are for everything in between."

"The *life* part," Clementine agreed, closing their little circle right there in the middle of the cabin floor. All of them still holding on tight.

Violet couldn't help but grin around at her *friends*, happy that at least *this* was settled.

"Friends," she repeated, like a small vow. "I'll allow it."

"Damn right you will," Bree muttered. "Idiot."

She allowed that, too. Plus an extended rolled eye from Kinley and an awkward hug from Clementine.

And then, fortified at last, there was only one thing left to do.

CHAPTER TEN

THE FRONT DOOR of Jackson's house flew open, and Lincoln was immediately glad that he'd kept himself to the two slugs of whiskey.

Because he didn't need to be drunk, not when Violet came charging in with storms in her dark eyes and tears on her cheeks.

"Didn't realize we invited everyone over for our pickup poker night," Duke said from behind his cards.

Which was when Lincoln noticed that the rest of Violet's cabin had come in with her.

Flint lifted his chin in Bree's direction, and they grinned at each other. Clementine and Duke exchanged a look.

Jackson looked disapproving, but then, he always did. And he looked particularly disapproving of Kinley, Lincoln thought.

But Lincoln really only cared about the tiny one with curls and another sweeping dress. The one who was glaring right at him.

"Mighty nice of you to bring an entourage," he murmured, making sure to lounge disreputably, there with his whiskey and his cards.

And the heart she'd stepped on, no big deal.

"I'm in," she declared, like she was throwing down a challenge.

"Beg pardon?"

"I said I'm in, Lincoln." Violet's gorgeous, imperious gaze swept over his friends, then hers. "I didn't ask for an audience, but I'm delighted that one's here anyway. So we can be clear, once and for all, that I'm not afraid of anything. Not any of them. And certainly not you."

"If you say so, darlin'."

"I wasn't making assumptions," she snapped at him. "I was *trying* to give you the space I heard you ask at least ten different girls for when you were a college sophomore alone."

Lincoln stood from his chair, slowly. Very slowly, because his friends were all trying and failing to stifle their laughter, and hers weren't doing any better. "Violet. I'm not a college sophomore any longer, if you haven't noticed. Make a goddamned assumption."

"You better watch out, Marshal," she threw back at him, drawing herself up to her full height, which was still no bigger than a minute. "Or I really will move out to Oregon and right on into your house. And then what will you do?"

Lincoln smiled, and it took him a minute. And he watched as Violet softened, right there before him, until he could see it all over her, head to toe. Until she smiled back.

And that made everything else fall away.

Until as far as he could tell, it was just the two of them, standing here. They could be anywhere. She was starlight and sunshine at the same time. The whiskey hadn't done a damned thing except agitate him, but she was intoxicating.

And she was going to be his.

He knew it like he was a fortune teller. He knew it like he knew his own nature, and the beat of his heart.

He knew it like he knew that he would do whatever was necessary to make sure she never regretted this decision. And Lincoln Traeger had always been real good at bending the world to his way of thinking, or he'd still be stuck in a nowhere town in Kentucky, watching his life drain away before him.

But instead he was here, right where he belonged.

With all these fine people he'd made his family.

And Violet.

"I'll tell you what I'll do," he drawled, coming around the table. "If you take the trouble to come all the way out to Oregon for me, I'll keep you." He smiled at the shine in her eyes. "I promise."

"Sweet Lord," Duke muttered. "Just kiss the girl already."

Lincoln intended to. He ambled toward Violet, who was beginning to get that hot-eyed look he could feel inside him like the kind of rainstorm a smart man learned how to dance in.

"You don't know what to do with this, do you?" he asked as he came for her. "You've never known how to deal with it."

"I deal with this—with you—just fine," she whispered.

"I can handle you, Violet." He kept his gaze locked to hers. "Anything you throw at me, I can take it. You're not too much for me. I like you just the way you are. A little spicy, a whole lot sweet and, best of all, *mine*."

Forever, he thought. But he'd give her time on that.

At least part of the summer.

She tilted her head to the side as he stopped before her. "How many times must I tell you that I hate you? I always have, Lincoln. Everyone who's ever been to Camp Phoenix knows it. It's a legend."

"Baby," he said. "You've been in love with me your whole life. It's cute."

Violet was laughing as he swept her up into his arms. She was laughing as he kissed her, at last.

And both of them were laughing as he carried her straight out of that dilapidated old house, into the night and the future that was waiting for both of them, if only they dared.

Lincoln intended to dare, and dare big. He knew Violet would match him.

So the first thing he did was take her down to his cozy little house up high on a hill over the Rogue Valley, so she could see what she was in for.

"What do you think?" he asked her much, much later, after they'd found each other in his bed and enjoyed his shower. After he'd made them a meal and they'd talked about dreams and hopes and the future that felt like it was sitting there with them, making the night bright.

Violet turned to him, her back to the pretty valley laid out before them.

"I think," she said softly, "that I'm going to fall in love with you."

"I know you are." He inclined his head. "And, gentleman that I am, I expect I'll return the favor."

"I know you will."

They grinned at each other, out there on the deck he'd made with his hands. Where she would teach their babies to walk, and he would dance with her while they slept, around and around beneath the moon, until the only darkness here was the night.

Easily chased away by the stars.

"I think we're going to be happy, Lincoln," she whispered, like she could see it, too. "Wildly, madly, recklessly happy."

"Darlin'," he murmured, as she moved into his arms, "that's guaranteed. Just you wait."

And when Violet kissed him that time, and every time after, she tasted like forever.

Finally.

* * * * *

The One with the Bullhorn

Nicole Helm

CHAPTER ONE

KINLEY PARKER JERKED, upending half a bowl of pancake batter all over herself, when the piercing sound of the bull-horn echoed through the speaker in the kitchens, followed by the jaunty notes of reveille.

A full three minutes early.

Muttering to herself, she didn't even bother to clean up the mess. She dropped the bowl and whisk in the sink and then went to find the bullhorn's owner. Because she'd had enough.

Jackson Hart was a menace. He needed to be stopped.

She had thought *someone* would sort him out by now. One of his friends, or any of the women she was forced to share a bunk with—who had somehow become something like *friends* to her. They were all the type to take someone to task, or so it seemed to Kinley.

No one expected tiny, bespectacled, shy Kinley Parker to stop him. Sure, she'd once caused enough trouble to get herself sent to Camp Phoenix—skipping school, shoplifting, property damage, doing whatever she could to get attention from her parents—but she had never outwardly *defied* anyone. She was a sneaky delinquent.

And then she'd been sent to Camp Phoenix by parents who hadn't wanted to look at *why* she might engage in some attention-seeking behavior.

Lucky for her, because Camp Phoenix had been her salvation. A place of order. A place where she was a cog in a machine, instead of the afterthought problem to be scheduled and sent from house to house. Forever and always in the way.

She'd loved the camp so much, she'd stayed. The minute she could, she'd moved full-time to Jasper Creek, working at the Jasper Creek Diner during the camp off-season, and cooking in the Camp Phoenix kitchens every summer.

But for the past few years, since Camp Phoenix had last been in working order, her life had…stagnated. She'd stayed in Jasper Creek and kept her diner job. She'd rented a little apartment above the post office.

And she'd stalled out. She'd worked. She'd slept. And that was about it, aside from her monthly therapy session, which she never missed, always waiting for that magical piece of advice that might fix…everything.

Then Jackson Hart had sent out a message to former campers and staff. He was bringing Camp Phoenix back to life.

For the first time in so long, Kinley had felt the spark of interest. Jackson had remembered her, or claimed to. He'd checked in with her boss at the diner for a reference and done a background check.

Then she'd been rehired. This time as the head cook at Camp Phoenix. Which, truth be told, had been a lot more than she'd wanted. She would have been content to cook and be in charge of *nothing*.

But Jackson expected her to manage everything related to the kitchen and dining, and she hadn't been able to convince him otherwise.

Thinking of Jackson and his long list of crimes—insisting she take on responsibilities she didn't want, his abrasive demeanor and that damn bullhorn—she went to give him a piece of her mind.

She was not that kind of woman. She never had been, not even when she'd been causing trouble for her parents. But Jackson brought it out in her. People who thought they knew everything brought it out in her.

She marched out the back door into the still-dim light of morning to see Jackson standing there with his bullhorn in one hand, the cane he had to use when he planned on walking more than a few feet in the other.

Which he insisted they all do. Hike up Hollyhock Hill, fly the flag, then march back down. *If we behave as though Camp Phoenix has already reopened, then everything will run smoothly once it is.* According to Jackson, anyway.

She marched over to him. He looked her up and down with that cold, remote stare he'd no doubt learned doing whatever suitably terrifying things he'd done as a DEA agent, because as few run-ins as they'd had when they'd both been at Camp Phoenix, she didn't remember that remoteness about him.

"Problems in the kitchen?" he asked with that low, gravelly voice that matched this icier version of post-DEA Jackson Hart.

"Your stupid bullhorn went off three minutes early," Kinley said, glaring at him, even as her glasses slid down her nose.

Jackson looked down at the watch on his wrist. "Not according to my watch."

Kinley pulled the phone out of her back pocket and showed him the screen. "According to *mine*, which is from this century."

"Is that a pig in a cowboy hat?"

Kinley scowled and shoved her phone in her pocket. Because, yes, her lock screen was a picture of a mini pig in a cowboy hat. It made her smile.

Even if working for Jackson did not.

"We're the staff, *not* prisoners," she continued, though it was like hurling bouncy balls at a brick wall. "I know that's difficult for you to understand, but it's likely best if you do before any actual children arrive." She pushed her glasses back up her nose.

He watched the move with those steely gray eyes.

Then he looked past her. Because everyone was coming. All the staff Jackson had hired—in various states of disarray and ire—including the men Jackson called partners, even though everyone knew he was in charge.

At least of the camp, certainly not of the men themselves. None of the men who'd idolized Bill McClain and gone into law enforcement, then reconvened to help revive Camp Phoenix, seemed like the kind of men someone could be in *charge* of. Even if Bree had paired up with Sheriff Flint Decker, and Violet had swept US Marshal Lincoln Traeger clear off his feet.

Jackson said nothing once everyone was arranged, because what was there to be said? He expected everyone to follow the march up Hollyhock Hill.

Kinley did not follow as she usually did. She was *covered* in pancake batter. But before she could say anything, the infuriating Jackson was two steps ahead of her.

"Perhaps you'd like to use this time to clean yourself up, Kinley."

She glared at his back, fighting against the temper threatening to rise. Because Kinley was not a rash, belligerent person. She was shy. She liked to hide and be left to her own devices.

But when she was mad…well.

Jackson Hart better watch out.

JACKSON HART LEANED on his cane as he walked up the hill and ignored the looks from Lincoln and Duke, two of his oldest friends. He knew what he was about. He did not need any lectures on his treatment of Kinley Parker.

If he was hard on people, it would make the camp run efficiently. If the camp ran efficiently, that was all that mattered.

Because Camp Phoenix was his chance to straighten out his life now that the DEA was no longer an option. Without it…he had nothing.

It was his turn to raise the flag today, and he did so with all the gravity of a military funeral.

He didn't care that everyone was scowling at him, except Flint, who was perhaps the only one who fully approved of this part of the day. Though he likely would have made some adjustments.

But that was what being in charge was, and since Jackson owned the place now, he *was* in charge. He delegated when he saw fit, but the day-to-day running of the camp was his. And not one thing would go wrong.

He would make sure he didn't make any mistakes moving forward.

They marched back down the hill, where they would all gather in the dining hall and Kinley would serve breakfast, and he would conduct the morning meeting. Today, behind him, he heard more than the usual round of whispers and grumbles.

"I appreciate all the complaining," he said, pleasantly. "Really gets me ready for when the *kids* show up." He smiled, though he knew there was no warmth in it. All the warmth had been burned right out of him. "But ideally, when the kids show up, we could be the adults in the situation."

"Is there a Jackson Hart manual on how to 'be an adult in the situation'?" Violet asked.

He ignored her, as he found it in his best interest to ignore Violet Cook. She did not give in. She did not relent. She gave Jackson a headache.

When they returned to the bottom of the hill, Kinley was marching from the women's bunk in new clothes but the same scowl.

Jackson didn't know what Kinley had against him, but her irritation with him seemed far more pointed than everyone else's. *Personal* almost, which made no sense since they'd had very few meaningful, *personal* interactions.

Kinley seemed to find fault with everything he did. And unlike when she was a little mute creature scuttling around the kitchens helping Mrs. Zee back in the old days, she voiced these opinions now.

While scuttling around with her glasses constantly falling down her nose. Honestly, she was a grown woman. She should buy herself a better-fitting pair. Or go get them fixed. Whatever one did with corrective eyewear.

He considered *many* things his business in the running of the camp, but Kinley's eyewear probably didn't merit. Unless he considered it a safety issue, and since she did work in the kitchen with ovens and slippery substances and all manner of knives, perhaps he *should* say something.

But not today. Even he knew better than to broach the subject on a day when she blamed him for her own clumsy behavior.

Everyone filed into the dining hall. The coffeepot was already hot, the stacks of dishes and mugs ready. Everyone got their coffee, the women having their own conversation Jackson didn't pay attention to while he readied his clipboard.

He had every day planned down to the hour. Some people might call it *anal*, but some people didn't have twenty kids depending on him in the near future.

Him. To run the camp as his mentor had. To give these kids some stability, some sense of worth and purpose. So that instead of sinking into whatever bad situations they came from, they learned there was more out there.

And they could find it.

So, he'd be anal. He'd be tough. Hell, he'd be an asshole. He'd do whatever it took.

Because everything else in his life was over. He'd almost died. His partner *had.* He could no longer be a DEA agent unless he wanted to push paper and drown in bureaucratic red tape.

He didn't.

He wanted…to *do* something.

Pain be damned. Ghost of his partner be damned. Voice of his father be double damned.

Bill McClain had given him a purpose. So the only purpose Jackson could think to have left was to step into Bill's shoes.

Kinley walked out of the kitchen. She put pancakes and sausages out in warmers and uncovered a bowl of fruit salad with the help of Tim, who'd likely earned a role in the kitchen as he didn't seem to have much aptitude for anything else.

They didn't eat this well every morning. Sometimes it was reconstituted eggs or oatmeal with cold toast and some off-brand, off-color jelly. He trusted Kinley with those decisions because Bill McClain had once trusted Mrs. Zee with those decisions.

And on sunny days, Jackson had noticed, Kinley tended to pull out all the stops. Which always reminded him of the simple joy as a kid (who'd wanted to hate Camp Phoenix for *existing*) when he'd walk into the dining hall to find Mrs. Zee had also pulled out all the stops.

Something he'd never once experienced at home. Even when his father had been high or his mother had been manic, their elaborate or over-the-top gestures had been about money and excess.

Never anything as simple as a home-cooked meal.

Kinley looked up from her food, her eyes invariably locking with his.

He didn't often allow that to happen. There was something a little too perceptive about her dark brown eyes. Something unnerving about how unafraid she was to stare right at him these days.

And he was no coward, so he could hardly be the first one to break eye contact. So they just stood, half a dining hall away from each other, *staring*, while the rest of the staff commented on how good everything smelled while they helped themselves.

Eventually someone said something to Kinley and she had to look away, so he was free to get his own breakfast. He ate in the same methodical way he did every morning.

Head down. He did not engage in small talk. At seven fifteen on the dot, he pushed the little button on his bullhorn that let out a kind of beep—a softer version of the morning call, since they were all already gathered, but a quick, efficient noise that got everyone's attention.

He stood and began the meeting.

It didn't matter what he was discussing—every meeting went the same. He outlined the day's chores and who was responsible for what. He allowed anyone to voice concerns or suggestions, and, *oh*, were there concerns and suggestions.

But a team was only as good as its most underappreciated member, so he made sure that they all had a space to feel heard.

Even if he went ahead and did things the way he preferred nine times out of ten.

Okay, ten times out of ten. Just sometimes someone had a suggestion that matched what he was already thinking.

Today there were arguments, per usual. Whispers. A few giggles from the Kinley-Bree-Violet-Clementine contingent, which was an interesting development. The women had certainly not started the month quite so chummy.

Which was good, actually. Laughter was a sign of comradery. The staff didn't have to be the best of friends, but they had to be able to communicate. To be a united, stable, honorable force for kids who likely didn't have that kind of influence at home.

It would be his *good thing* for the day.

There were two things he'd never admit to another *soul*. First, that every day, without fail, he wrote one positive aspect of the day down in a notebook. Second, every morning he left the meeting—no matter how belligerent, argumentative or straight-out obnoxious everyone had been—with something he'd been missing for a very long time.

Hope.

CHAPTER TWO

"I'M GOING TO do it." Kinley stood in the middle of the cabin. She wasn't sure who exactly she was speaking to, just that after trying to wash the pancake batter out of her clothes in the communal bathroom with incredibly poor water pressure, she'd been angry all over again.

So she was going to do it.

"Do what?" Clementine asked, from where she sat cross-legged on her bottom bunk.

"I'm going to steal Jackson's bullhorn," Kinley announced. For all three women to hear. Because this had somehow become the thing they did. Bree had stolen Flint's hat. Violet had stolen Lincoln's family heirloom.

"I thoroughly support this decision," Bree said. "Please, destroy it while you're at it."

Kinley gave a little nod. She needed a plan, but it wouldn't be the first time she'd stolen. Besides, she knew Jackson's schedule almost better than anyone, since she had to be up earlier than most to make breakfast, and Jackson himself took turns with a few other staff members cleaning up the dining hall at the end of the night.

He rarely let the bullhorn out of his sight, but she just needed to think and she'd find a hole in his schedule. An opportunity.

She'd take it. Bury it. Set it on fire. *Something.*

"Bad precedent for that, you know," Violet said lazily

from her top bunk, where she was stretched out, flipping the pages of a book while fairy lights twinkled down on her.

Precedent? For a good ten seconds, Kinley could only stare at Violet, trying to make sense of what she was trying to say.

Precedent. Heat crept up her cheeks. "What?"

Violet shrugged, her dark eyes never leaving the page of her book. "I'm just saying there seems to be a theme." Finally she looked up, pointing at herself, and then at Bree.

Kinley's brain couldn't even *fathom*... "I can assure you no *themes* or *precedents* will be continued here." With *Jackson Hart*. "I'm stealing his bullhorn as *revenge*."

Violet and Bree exchanged a look that had Kinley even more irritated than she had been. Now, *that* was a dangerous precedent. She never behaved rationally when she was angry. And knowing it didn't change it, no matter what warnings she heard in her therapist's voice.

"Enter at your own risk," Bree muttered under her breath.

"It's *Jackson*," Kinley said firmly. "We all hate Jackson." Well, *hate* was probably a strong word, since he wasn't a bad person or anything. Just annoying as all get-out. And hate wasn't a very constructive emotion.

Though sometimes it felt great.

"What's the old saying? There's a thin line between love and hate?" Bree said. Sweetly. But Kinley had learned in the last few weeks, Bree was never really as *sweet* as she pretended.

Violet sighed and sat up in her bed. "However, Jackson *is* deserving of some punishment. And that bullhorn disappearing would be..." She mimed a little chef's kiss.

"He probably has six more hung up in his closet in a perfect, leveled line," Clementine offered.

When Violet and Bree laughed, Clementine preened.

Kinley just stood in the middle of it all, torn between her anger and...*precedents*.

Of course, she'd never have any romantic feelings for *Jackson Hart*. Besides, she'd sworn off men three years ago after her therapist pointed out she tended to get involved with men who vacillated between fully ignoring her, and then, just when she'd had about enough of it, love bombing her into sticking around for more bad behavior and indifference. And, in one very bad situation, violence.

In other words, daddy issues.

She shuddered at the memory, and at how obvious that pattern had been in retrospect. So obvious, and ending so badly, she had determined never to trust her judgment in men again.

Not that Jackson was anything like her father, or the man who'd set a fire in her bed to "teach her a lesson." The comparison made her laugh. Her father hadn't met a responsibility he was capable of keeping, and she didn't think Jackson was capable of stepping away from *any*, even ones that weren't his. The man who'd physically hurt her... Well, Jackson was cold and remote, but he was just...so honorable, it was ridiculous.

And why in the great wide world was she thinking about *any* of this? "I'm going," she announced. Because she had to do *something* with all the thoughts and feelings ricocheting inside of her.

"Without a plan?" Clementine asked, as if scandalized, when *she* had yet to steal anything. Likely ever, having been the sheriff's daughter and perpetual tattletale when Kinley had been a camper.

"Sometimes the best plan is none at all," Kinley said

loftily, pushing her glasses up. That wasn't true at all, of course. In fact, it was the recipe for all her worst decisions.

She knew this. Could feel old patterns emerging, could *hear* her therapist's voice in her head, telling her to take a breath. To count.

She ignored it all. Because irritation and anger *were* action. It wasn't wallowing, and wasn't she supposed to be acting?

Besides, her cabinmates, friends even, approved of this idea. Jackson deserved his comeuppance, and she would be the one to give it to him. Wouldn't that feel great?

It was hardly spray-painting every dirty word she could think of on her high school library's windows. *That* had been immature and pointless. Bullhorns disappearing had a very positive point.

She shoved out of the cabin, ignoring any reactions she might have garnered, and began a determined march toward… somewhere.

The night was cool and dark—she glanced up but didn't see any stars or moon. Clouds must have rolled in. Here, in the main part of the camp, there were lights—the little security light on the outside of the dining hall, and the larger one that shone down on the bathrooms.

It was Saturday, which meant Jackson was likely in the dining hall with Tim, doing the evening cleanup. She looked in the building's direction to confirm that, yes, lights still shone from inside.

She never saw Jackson with his bullhorn after the post-dinner flag retrieval, and she assumed that when he marched said flag back to his house, he left his bullhorn with it. He had to. Where else would he put it?

So, she had a window. She'd use it.

She walked toward his house. In all the years she'd been

a part of the camp, the layout hadn't changed, so she knew the way. Even in the dark, because outside the main part of the camp, it got *really* dark out here in the country.

She wasn't afraid of the dark. The dark had always been her companion. Where she had the courage to seek…some sense of power. Control. No one could see her, but she could do something…anything…to ease those whirling feelings inside of her. Whatever they happened to be at the time.

Tonight, it was irritation and determination.

The night rustled, animals and insects calling and buzzing to each other. The air cooled her heated cheeks and the exertion of the walk calmed her racing heart.

But nothing touched that anger she was acting on. Because she'd made a choice. She could hardly announce to Violet and Bree that she was going to do it and then go back on her announcement. It was asking for the kind of teasing usually relegated to Clementine.

Kinley wanted none of that kind of attention.

The house stood on a bit of a rise, just west enough of the entrance that Jackson no doubt always had a perfect view of anyone coming and going after hours. He probably had cameras set up or sat on his hill with binoculars and kept a log of every single entrance and exit.

She stopped for a moment and studied the shadowy house atop the hill. She knew for a fact no one had lived there in years, and yet Jackson had moved right in. When the accommodations weren't exactly *comfortable*.

She had the strangest image of him limping around that very not injury-friendly home and almost felt…sorry for him.

Which was *ridiculous*. A woman should not feel sorry for the man who treated everyone around him like children—at best. The criminals he'd chased at worst. And, sure, maybe they all had a little criminal in them, except Clementine, but Jackson did too. That was the worst part. He seemed to think that just because he'd straightened out—like they *all* had—that somehow made him emperor of the whole dang world.

She was about to start moving forward again, but something stopped her. She paused, listening to the dark. Had it been a rustle? Probably just a raccoon or something, but—

"Kinley?"

She yelped in surprise, whirling in the dark. She didn't see the owner of the voice, though she recognized the low rumble. She didn't know how he could not only see her, but know it *was* her.

"What the hell are you doing?" he demanded.

KINLEY SMELLED LIKE VANILLA. Always. This was a fact Jackson knew and yet had very carefully placed in the compartment where he held most uncomfortable knowledge he didn't want to face.

There was a list of things when it came to Kinley, and it wouldn't be smart to consider them here. Now.

Because, here in the dark, the vanilla scent was irrefutable. That's how he'd known the shadow of a person was her, not some crazed criminal like he'd originally thought when he'd begun creeping toward it, ready to fight it off.

"What are you doing?" he repeated when she said nothing. Unless a squeak counted, which to him it did not.

"Going for a walk," she said, sounding strangled. And very clearly lying.

"To my house? In the pitch black?" he asked casually.

"*You're* walking in the pitch black."

"Yes. On my property." He fished his phone out of his pocket and flipped on the flashlight. He pointed it at her.

She winced and threw up her hand to shade her eyes

from the direct light. "Are you going to interrogate me or something?"

"Are you doing something deserving of being interrogated?"

She dropped her hand and glared at him. "Stop pointing that at my *eyes*. I just…got turned around, I guess. Because I spent half my evening scrubbing pancake batter out of my clothes."

"And you're blaming me for this, I assume."

"Well," she replied, crossing her arms over her Jasper Creek Diner T-shirt. Her gaze was sharp, her scowl causing her glasses to begin their inevitable slide down her nose. "If you used that phone as a clock instead of an interrogation light, you would have sounded your bullhorn at the *correct* time and it would, therefore, not have scared the living daylights out of me."

"You know, I never understood that expression. What exactly are living daylights?"

She made a sound of outrage, and he noted the glasses slid another quarter inch or so. He gripped his cane tighter to resist the urge to reach out and push them up for her.

She would likely bite his hand off.

And there was something very strange twisting inside of him at *that* image, so he pushed it firmly away, into *the internal box*, and focused on the task at hand. "If you're planning some childish prank like your bunkmates' immature thieving attempts, understand that I was a DEA agent. I have dealt with some of the worst humanity has to offer. You will not be pulling one over on me."

"I suppose that keen nose for sniffing out trouble is how you ended up having to use that cane," she returned acidly. Then froze, eyes widening, as if she couldn't quite believe she'd said those words.

He'd frozen too. Because—well, hell—little Kinley Parker knew how to land a direct hit.

But he did not react in any way outwardly. After all, he'd spent a lifetime having insults hurled at him. From his parents to every lowlife he'd arrested. This was no different.

Except Kinley seemed sorry about it.

The silence stretched out, *throbbed*. While vanilla scented the air and her glasses slid farther down her nose.

"I shouldn't have said that," she whispered. And he could see the regret swimming in her eyes in the dim flashlight beam, but it wasn't the comment that bothered him. It was how *guilty* she looked. Worried that she'd hurt his feelings.

As if he had any feelings left to hurt.

"No, you shouldn't have, but it hardly matters. Unless you're planning on blowing up my house, that is."

She furiously shook her head back and forth. "Jackson…" But she didn't say anything else.

And he couldn't stand in the dark with that regret on her face, with the soft way she said his name, digging under how little he cared about her snippy little comment. It was true. He hadn't gotten himself out of that one unscathed and hadn't gotten Henderson out at all.

"Go back to the bunks, Kinley," he said, and he hardly recognized his own voice. It sounded so tired, and what did he have to be tired about? He walked past her, toward his house, waiting to say the last words until he was sure she thought he had nothing else to say. "You've broken curfew. So you'll need to be up even earlier than usual to scrub the toilets."

CHAPTER THREE

KINLEY STOOD IN the dark, utterly still. She was torn somewhere between total mortification over what she'd said, how awful it had been, and hating him.

Scrubbing toilets. Was he insane? She was a grown woman. He didn't get to impose a curfew on her just because he was the head of the camp. This wasn't ten years ago. She wasn't a scrappy teen needing to be taught a lesson.

She was the lesson-teacher this time around.

Yeah. *Yeah.*

She turned around and faced his house. There was a light shining through one window on the lower level. The bullhorn was in there.

Of course, so was he, but she could work around that. Maybe she hadn't stolen anything in a few years—going so far as to return a pen to the bank after she'd accidentally put it in her purse—but she had once been *quite* good.

All it really took was a little ingenuity and some flexible thinking. You couldn't go in with a plan. Not for something like this. You had to think on the fly.

So she took her time. She walked toward the house, not with the idea of stealth—Jackson being Jackson, he no doubt had some sort of door camera or security lights or *something*. Besides, who knew when Lincoln or Flint might come or go, particularly with all their *after curfew* liaisons with her bunkmates?

She walked right up the hill and onto the porch. Lights did flash on, and there was a doorbell camera affixed to the side of the door. She smiled at it as she pushed the button.

She expected him to answer it via voice, but instead the front door opened, though there was a screen between them.

He studied her, those gray eyes intense but opaque. Sometimes she found herself wondering what he thought about when he stared like that. Especially at *her*. What exactly was there to stare at? Or uncover? She was the same Kinley Parker she'd been ten years ago when they'd first met—perhaps a little more healed, a little less delinquent, but more or less *the same*.

He'd never stared at her like this before the past few weeks. And it wasn't a stare like… Well, she didn't know what it was like, except that he seemed to be *aware* of her, interested in figuring her out.

When she'd given him absolutely no reason to. Well, until maybe this moment. But she'd seen this stare before and it always made her feel a bit like she'd stepped into some kind of spotlight.

And instead of that being the nightmare she'd always figured it might be, it felt safe. There was no doubt in her mind that Jackson Hart was a safe space—no matter how obnoxious and type A he might be.

Why the hell was she thinking about this? Oh, right, because he hadn't spoken. He was just standing there, the screen between them, silent.

She smiled at him.

He said nothing.

"Can I come in?"

"Why would you come in?"

"I need to speak with you."

"I'm quite sure whatever it is can wait until tomorrow morning's meeting."

"It isn't about the camp, Jackson."

"Then what's it about?"

She heaved out a sigh. Honestly, he might be the most stubborn man alive. She went ahead and let herself in. Or tried. She pulled open the screen door. He did not move out of the way, however, so she was only faced with the wall of *him*.

He was very…large. Not the first time she'd noticed his size, especially compared to hers. It was just this was the first time they'd been quite this close when she had.

And alone.

After a moment that she might have called hesitation on any other man, he stepped aside and allowed her to move in.

She moved on sheer anger and bravado, or whatever one called this odd jangling feeling in her chest after being close to him, but she came to a short, unexpected stop not far from where he stood. "Well, this place is a disaster."

Jackson looked around as if he'd never once considered it. "Not so bad."

"Leave it to a man to think holes in the plaster, peeling paint and… Is that a leaky roof?" she said, pointing at the ceiling that—clearly—leaked when it rained. "To think a place is not so bad as long as he has *that*." She pointed at his television, which dominated one wall.

"What more do I need? Throw pillows?"

"It'd hardly be my first move, but they wouldn't hurt."

"Why are you here, Kinley?" he returned.

"I want to apologize." Which was not subterfuge. One of the things she'd learned in therapy was that when her anger did get the better of her, she tended to minimize the damage if she stopped, breathed and apologized.

But she was still going to find a way to get the damn bullhorn. Surreptitiously, she looked around the room. She didn't see it anywhere, because there wasn't much of anything in this room. Couch. TV. The end. When the men all got together to play poker, there was at least a card table and chairs, but they must get folded up and put away when there was no game to be had.

His mouth firmed. "For what?"

"You know for what. I said something awful, and the only way to deal with a bad decision is to deal with the consequences. To own up to it. I always do this sort of thing when I get angry, and I know it isn't healthy."

"People get angry, Kinley. It's the human condition."

"When *I* get angry, I get destructive." She walked around the room as she spoke, using the words to distract while she angled herself so she could see into the kitchen area. Also sparse, though there were kitchen utensils and a stack of papers on the counter—again, *men*—but no bullhorn. "Childhood trauma patterns are hard to identify and harder to break, but my parents didn't pay much attention to me, went on and had their *real* families, so I'd get angry and do something bad—it was the only way they'd remember I existed."

"So, you're saying you want my attention?" He said this with no inflection. Almost like a robot.

Her mouth dropped open and she turned to stare at him. *Want* his attention? "N-no, that isn't what I meant." But she *had* his attention in this moment and...

And what?

She didn't know.

"Then what did you mean, Kinley? Because I don't hear an apology. I hear a lot of excuses."

Shock and that unruly anger spurted through her. She was apologizing and he was finding flaw with it? "Excuse me?"

"I went to the same camp you went to. I've had my fair share of therapy. Not to mention psych evals to be where I was…and leave where I was with the DEA. I understand the function of these conversations. For this particular incident, you've blamed anger and childhood trauma and psychology, far as I can tell, but you did not actually apologize."

Her mouth hung open. She couldn't get it to do anything else.

"*I'm sorry.* That's all you had to say. All you had to mean."

She knew he was right. That she was used to…justifying her existence to anyone who found fault in her behavior. And maybe sometimes…using what she'd learned about her past to excuse behaviors she didn't exactly like about herself.

"But beyond all that," Jackson continued, more vehemently than she thought was necessary. "I don't need this. Your apology, your reasons. I don't care about what you said. I don't care why you said it. Maybe it was mean, but so what? Life is mean."

"Do you care about *anything*?" she demanded, bullhorn forgotten for the moment. Because he was being mean now, and he wasn't being wrong, so it hurt.

"I care about this camp."

"In order for this camp to be like it used to, you will have to care about the *people* in it."

Those words seemed to hang there, just like the ones before. Only she didn't feel bad this time because it was only the truth.

Sheriff McClain had cared about them. Gale Lawson, the social worker and art therapist they were planning on celebrating, had cared. Mrs. Zee and the counselors had made Camp Phoenix a success because they *cared*. It was why people had left lives behind to come here before opening to help Jackson rebuild.

They'd come from places where people didn't care, not on the regular, and Camp Phoenix had shown them they were worth something.

"As fun as this has been," Jackson said, in that stiff, detached manner he utilized so well, "and as noble a cause as *apologies for your trauma behavior* are, I've had quite enough for the evening."

"So have I," she returned, boiling with more anger than she had been initially. And she couldn't get the bullhorn right now, which only made her angrier. But that didn't mean she was going to leave empty-handed.

She whirled, using the quick move to hide what she was doing. Grabbing the nearest thing, blocking the move with her body, then holding it so he couldn't see what she had unless he came around to the front of her.

He didn't, so she marched out of his house and down the hill, and he was none the wiser.

Regret hit her about halfway down the hill.

JACKSON WAS NO IDIOT. He'd give Kinley credit. Her apology had seemed sincere, and she hadn't gone too full-blown obvious, but he was a trained law enforcement agent. He understood people. He knew what to look for.

She wanted his bullhorn. Maybe it was a dare or whatever the women considered their little rite of passage. Fundamentally, he wasn't even against it. He liked the fact they'd buried old hatchets and were working together to form bonds.

Bonds were why people were here. Why Flint, Lincoln and Duke had also bought into Camp Phoenix. The bond Sheriff McClain had given them all had changed them into men.

Friendships were important, fundamental even, when you came from a dysfunctional (at best) family.

He knew it would shock all four of the women to know he supported the reasons *behind* their actions, even if he couldn't support the actions themselves.

But it was best for them not to know. To consider him the lifeless automaton who was in charge. Who handled problems. The person who could tackle anything and everything and made zero mistakes.

Camp Phoenix needed that. Sheriff McClain had been that for all of them. In retrospect, Jackson and his buddies had seen the more…mortal side of the sheriff as they'd gotten older. He wasn't a perfect man, but he'd been a good one.

Still, the perfect paragon of their rose-colored hero worship had turned them into the men they were today. So it was good. To be that role model. To be the man on the fringes who people looked up to—maybe feared a bit.

But he couldn't quite dislodge Kinley's words. Because she'd talked about her childhood hardships. And he knew… well, something about neglect. About the ways it crawled inside you and made you someone else, even after years of rehabilitation, therapy and being a productive member of society.

He understood everything she'd said…and maybe that's why he'd been colder than he'd needed to be. To be certain she didn't *think* he understood. To be certain those very necessary lines between him and everyone else stayed uncrossed.

And maybe, if he was being completely honest with himself, because he didn't want to sit around and remember all the ways he'd felt that exact same anger inside of him and let it out in the exact same way Kinley had…until he'd learned to ice it all out.

Jackson sighed. He was tired. He needed to go to bed and— He hissed out a breath as a bolt of pain shot up his leg. He'd been weaning himself off the over-the-counter painkillers. A man who'd seen the ravaging toll of narcotics since he'd been a kid couldn't be comfortable when relying on medication of any kind.

But he'd overdone it today. Too long on his feet. Too much standing without the aid of his cane. Too much standing around talking to Kinley Parker about therapy and apologies. Neither of which mattered in the least.

He went to grab it, then stared at the empty space where he *always* put his cane when he walked in the door. It took him a minute to fully understand—not that he'd misplaced it, because he never misplaced things, but that she'd taken it.

He could only blink in surprise. The nasty comment had been one thing, but it was only fair and certainly good practice for when some mouthy, angry teenagers showed up. He wouldn't have been the least bit surprised if she'd found a way to take his bullhorn or abscond with his wallet or hat or just about anything.

But taking his cane was a low blow, and for some bizarre reason…it made him laugh. It was the funniest thing he could think of happening to him in a long time.

Little Kinley, with her falling-down glasses and her hiding in corners, had a sharp mouth, a nasty temper and a *mean* streak.

Probably wrong that it made him like her more.

He limped to the kitchen and took a few ibuprofen. Smiling. It didn't make a lick of sense. But when he got his good-things notebook out tonight, he'd write: "Kinley Parker stole my cane and it made me laugh."

Because this was a direct challenge and, well, Jackson lived for a challenge. He was here trying to revive this camp, wasn't he?

So, he had three options.

One, he could use one of his backup canes and pretend like nothing had ever happened. An intriguing option because it would no doubt confuse the hell out of her.

Two, he could get his back up and read her the riot act, give her every citation and nasty chore known to man. This, she would expect. And he might want to be the lifeless automaton to them, but he also wanted to keep them on their toes.

The third option was the worst. It was petty and childish, and while it might teach a lesson, it was hardly the behavior of a leader.

Two was a classic, and a quality choice for a reason. Even one had its merits. Three was irrational, irresponsible and totally out of character.

Which was why he'd chosen it. She'd expect one or two.

She'd never see three coming.

CHAPTER FOUR

KINLEY DID NOT waltz into the bunks and boldly declare she'd stolen Jackson's cane. By the time she got back to the cabin, the walk had taken care of the anger, and now, like usual, all she was left with was shame.

And Jackson's cane.

What kind of *monster* stole a person's walking aid? And why, even after years of therapy, couldn't she get it together enough to not let her anger lead her to all the same old ugly parts of herself?

She didn't want to celebrate victory. She wanted to *cry*.

So she tried to sneak into the bunk, and she was usually really good at sneaking in all the places she didn't want to be noticed.

But they were all waiting for her. When she slid in, cane hidden behind her back, they looked at her and frowned. In unison.

"No bullhorn?" Violet asked.

"Are you okay?" Clementine added.

Kinley shook her head. "I said something awful." She swallowed. "Then did something worse."

"Well. What was it?"

She repeated what she'd said, even though it was embarrassing. Because it felt like a kind of punishment, and didn't she deserve punishment? But she kept the cane behind her back.

Clementine's eyes were wide. Bree had her lips pressed together.

"Well, Jackson's not exactly undeserving of a nasty comment," Violet said philosophically. She did not seem in the least bit scandalized. Kinley knew that should make her feel better.

But she was still holding his cane.

"About his bullhorn, his schedule, his mean attitude? Yes. About his *limp*?" She brandished the cane. "And taking a man's *walking aid* is not…not good. It's horrible. It's sociopathic."

"I don't think you need to be quite *that* hard on yourself," Violet returned. "Sometimes a man makes a bed and a woman has to help him lie in it."

That brought…very different and strange images to Kinley's mind. And made her think about that moment in the doorway, noticing how *big* he was.

He'd *looked* at her. Not that she thought he saw anything particularly alluring or beautiful or bed related. Just that he had seen her. As a person. Not all the ways she hid in plain sight.

"He has others," Bree assured her. "You know a man like Jackson is endlessly prepared. You'll just…give it back tomorrow. It's no big deal."

It was nice of Bree to try to make her feel better. All of them, really. But she didn't feel better. Still, Bree was right. She'd give it back to him. Tomorrow. She'd…apologize again—because apologizing was healthy and nothing to be ashamed of. She'd give the cane back. Take whatever terrible chore punishments he felt like giving out and…

Maybe she'd offer to leave. She couldn't be any good to the kids if she was going to fall back into old patterns so hard, so quickly. How could anything she'd done tonight be considered acting like a good role model or setting a good example?

"Kinley." It was Violet's sharp voice that had her looking up rather than slinking away. "You're constantly spouting your therapist's words of wisdom, but they don't really matter if you don't apply them to yourself."

Unfortunately, that echoed what her therapist had often been telling her for the past few years. Learning was different from *implementing*.

She was very good at absorbing, understanding and even regurgitating...but actually putting the things she learned into practice? Well, that proved a bit more difficult.

She went to bed that night in the uncomfortable bottom bunk and tried to practice her apology, her resignation. She went back and forth between that being the right thing to do and the cowardly thing to do.

She didn't want to be a coward. She wanted to be a good person. She wanted to go...unnoticed.

So, you're saying you want my attention?

She kept hearing his careful question in her head. But she didn't. Wanting people's attention only led to bad places, and she wanted to walk to good places now. Stealing from Jackson, sparring with Jackson—it was bad. Getting his attention was *bad*.

And yet she kept marching right into the center of it, poking at him and stealing from him and being irritated by him. Kept thinking about steely gray eyes and an unsmiling mouth. The strength and resilience that must go into every single one of his days.

Because he hadn't spent the past year *wallowing*. He'd survived an explosion and then decided to make a difference. Maybe she was hopping on board with the difference, but no matter how much it had occurred to her to spur the camp back to life, she hadn't the funds nor the courage to make it happen.

She'd wallowed. He'd dug deep and acted.

She didn't belong here, it was clear. Everyone else was successful. A positive story of perseverance and all that Camp Phoenix had to offer.

She was pathetic.

When she finally fell asleep, exhausted from the mental gymnastics that went nowhere, she dreamed. Not of leaving. Not of being brave enough to stay. No, she dreamed of bed-related things.

And Jackson Hart.

JACKSON COULDN'T REMEMBER the last time he'd woken up in a good mood. Not just a determined mood or a hopeful mood, but a downright cheerful one.

He woke up even before his extra-early alarm. He was like a normal kid at Christmas—a normal kid, because he'd always dreaded Christmas. Didn't matter if it was a good one or a bad one, because one way or another, it always ended up bad.

No presents? Sucked. All the presents? Usually sucked more because he knew the fallout for what happened when his parents got an influx of cash.

So this wasn't that, because it would work out. Kinley would feel guilty for taking his cane, give one of her apologies that wasn't an apology, then maybe he'd rile her up some more so she gave him one of those impassioned lectures about care.

Her dark eyes got deeper when she did that. The same way they had when she'd spoken about the camp during her interview for the camp cook position. He'd seen potential there. A potential she seemed determined to hide.

Because, deep down, under all the ways she hid and scuttled, Kinley Parker had passion.

For the camp, of course. Not any other kind. Because he was resolutely not thinking about the way she'd stood at his door, ready to go toe-to-toe with him, and all he'd been able to look at—for a very brief moment he blamed on Flint and Lincoln sauntering around all paired up—was her mouth.

Shoving that thought aside, Jackson turned his mind to his revenge.

He grabbed one of his backup canes and, the pièce de résistance, a bandage he carefully placed over his forehead. Once satisfied, he headed downstairs. Lincoln was just slipping in the door—which meant he'd spent the night somewhere else. Jackson doubted it was in the women's cabin, so he narrowed his eyes.

"Do I even want to know?" Jackson greeted him.

Lincoln grinned. "Nope."

Jackson just hoped to God it wasn't his office.

"What happened to you?" Lincoln asked with a hint of skepticism as he tapped his forehead, where Jackson had affixed his bandage.

Jackson smiled on his way out the door. "Absolutely nothing." And he whistled the whole way down the gravel drive to camp headquarters. He stowed his backup cane in his office, then limped over to the dining hall.

His leg wasn't hurting him too badly this morning. He'd gotten a good night's sleep, which always helped. He'd learned how to go with the ebb and flow of pain, and it was improving. It'd never be back to normal, but his doctors assured him there was still room for improvement if he followed instructions, which he more or less did.

Kinley should already be in the kitchens prepping before the flag raising. He wanted to make a grand, surprise entrance, so he eased in through the front. He heard her before he saw her. She was singing along to some country music playing faintly.

Something about it made him stop. Almost...reconsider.

She had a pretty voice, and the song was low and mournful, and that loneliness in the song was echoed in the soft way Kinley sang the words to herself. Something compelled him to move forward—not to enact revenge, but to see her. What did her eyes do when she sang—deepen like they did when she was worked up about something, flash like when she was angry? Maybe they'd be downcast in that "don't look at me" way she hid behind way too often.

He stopped before he entered the kitchen because...well, why the hell did he know all the different ways her eyes could look? He shouldn't.

But if he was being brutally honest with himself, he tended to linger when it came to Kinley. Maybe, sometimes, he found himself staring and not quite sure why—except she seemed so determined to blend in and he wanted to... to...fix that for her. Protect her from the world that had made her afraid. Convince her to stop hiding everything she had to offer.

That was just...his job. His calling. Bring out the best in the people of Camp Phoenix. It didn't have anything to do with Kinley specifically.

Which was *not* brutal honesty. At all. Because a lot of people had pissed him off in the past few weeks, but he hadn't felt compelled to get revenge on any of them.

Still, that's all this was. A little revenge prank. Maybe Kinley specifically got under his skin, but that didn't have to mean anything if he didn't let it. So he stepped into the kitchen.

It was an oatmeal day. He tried not to wince.

He really hated oatmeal day.

Kinley turned, a faint blush creeping up her cheeks—he didn't know why though. Maybe she was worried he'd caught her singing.

But before she could say anything, or he could offer a greeting, she seemed to take in the bandage on his forehead.

She blanched. And because he'd been so...taken off guard, by her singing, by the journey of his thoughts, he forgot his plan and everything else. So they just stood there, staring at each other.

Her glasses slid down her nose as her eyes widened. And he had to shove his hands into his pockets because otherwise he'd reach out and push them right back up her nose.

It wasn't his job to fix her glasses. And he'd been a DEA agent for too long to allow himself prolonged distraction from his plan.

"Morning," he offered. "Oatmeal. My favorite."

She opened her mouth, but no sound came out. Then she pointed to his forehead. "Wh...at?"

"Oh, this? I just took a little tumble last night after you left." He lifted his hand and touched the edge of the bandage gingerly. "I guess I misplaced my cane and... Well, it's embarrassing, but what's an injured man to do?"

He was laying it on a little thick, but she swallowed. Hard. And said nothing.

"It's not that bad," he said, waving it away. "Do you want to take a look?"

Her eyes widened even more. "A look?" she squeaked.

"Sure." He moved forward, with an exaggerated limp, and started to peel back the bandage. He wasn't after *torturing* her. Just giving her a bit of a jolt.

He seemed to be succeeding.

Kinley seemed to be frozen by the offer, by him actually pulling the bandage away. She didn't move. He wasn't even sure she breathed.

Until he'd completely taken it off.

She blinked, then frowned, her eyebrows drawing closer together. "There isn't…" Her eyes narrowed and moved from his forehead to his eyes. "You didn't fall."

He flashed a grin at her—perhaps the first one he'd really felt in years. "No, I didn't fall, Kinley. But I *could* have."

"But you didn't! You didn't fall, and you wouldn't have because you're *you*. You probably have ten more canes just like it!"

He shrugged. "Only eight."

She made a sound of outrage, then moved forward and swatted him. A slap across the arm that was about as forceful as a feather.

He laughed. Not just a chuckle, or a little snort of amusement. He *laughed*. And it felt damn good. When was the last time he'd *really* laughed? Not just a chuckle at one of his friends' expenses, but an all-out *laugh*.

"That isn't funny!" she said, and she swatted at him again, but there was some sparkle of humor in her eyes. "What a terrible thing to do!"

He took her hand so she'd stop hitting him. Not that it hurt. Quite the opposite. Of course, then his fingers were curled around her slim wrist, and that certainly wasn't *better*. But he focused on the conversation at hand, not the feel of her warm, soft skin under his rough fingers.

"So was stealing my *cane*."

Her mouth firmed because she obviously couldn't argue with *that*. "So, are we terrible even?" she demanded, trying to tug her hand out of his grasp.

He should let go. He couldn't fathom why he didn't.

"Yes, terrible even. Let's go a step further. Truce?"

She looked at him skeptically, and her glasses slid down her nose until they were perched on the very tip.

Something about holding her wrist must have dulled his sense of preservation or short-circuited some part of his brain. Because he didn't resist this time. He reached out with his free hand and touched his index finger to the bridge of her glasses.

"You should get glasses that fit your face," he murmured. He didn't touch her. No matter how much his fingers wanted to take a detour, he carefully kept his finger affixed to the frame and nothing else.

"Glasses are expensive," she replied, her eyes never leaving his, her breathing seeming shaky.

"Shouldn't insurance pay for that?" He knew he was too close. Knew he should not be pushing her glasses up her nose, holding her wrist. Knew...a million things.

And ignored them all.

"The diner doesn't have a vision plan," she said, her voice quiet, her eyes large and directly on his.

"I'll look into it for the camp."

"Okay." Her pulse jumped, right there in her neck.

He should go, but he couldn't seem to pull his finger away from the bridge of her glasses, even though he'd finished pushing them up. Their breathing synced so it felt like they were in this very warm cocoon, drugged by the rhythm of it all.

But it was the idea that anything might be a *drug*, addiction, a *want* he couldn't control, that had him remembering himself.

"Oh, one more thing, Kinley?" Because if he didn't extricate himself, if he didn't leave with a parting shot, this became...

Complicated. *More* complicated, he admitted. So he

eased back—dropped her hand, pulled his finger off her glasses. Fixed that bland, cold smile on his face that had gotten him out of many a complicated situation.

"You will *never* get your hands on my bullhorn." Then he turned on a heel and left. Because he couldn't be late for the morning flag raising.

That was why he retreated, faster than he should.

He spent the rest of the day trying to convince himself of that.

CHAPTER FIVE

KINLEY RELAYED THE whole strange interlude to Violet, Bree and Clementine as they worked on the landscape around the front of the camp. She may have left out a few key details.

Like Jackson's laugh, which had been a jolt. More than a jolt. It had been like pulling a curtain away. His eyes crinkled when he laughed, and the sound was deep and pleasant. A completely different man appeared when he laughed.

And she'd…well, she might have been able to convince herself it was just the shock at him expressing any sort of mirth, but then he'd touched her. Pushed her glasses up and held her gaze and…

Lordy, what had *that* been?

She wasn't a stranger to attraction, or even desire. What she was a stranger to was having *any* of those feelings crop up with *Jackson Hart*. Or anyone like him. Honorable and dependable and…

She was, quite literally, losing her mind.

"Was he being literal or figurative?" Violet asked, bringing Kinley back to the current moment and not reliving all those morning moments.

"Huh?"

"When he said you'd never touch his bullhorn. Literal or figurative?"

Kinley stopped short. Her face heated. Oh, God. *Figurative?*

"I feel like bullhorn could be *very* double entendre here," Violet continued when Kinley said nothing.

"I don't see Jackson being quick with the double entendre," Bree returned. "Don't you have to have a sense of humor for that?"

Kinley opened her mouth to point out he did have a sense of humor. Maybe pretending to have injured himself because she stole his cane wasn't the height of joy and comedy, but he *had* laughed.

And it had taken away all that angst she'd felt about stealing it in the first place. About leaving or staying. She hadn't even thought of telling him she wanted to quit. Because if he could stoop to petty, then maybe what she'd done wasn't so bad.

Then he'd offered that parting comment and she'd been determined, all over again, to get his bullhorn.

The actual item. Not…

Lordy.

"Just remember, Jackson is the enemy," Violet said, pointing her trowel at Kinley. "I wouldn't think he had any charm to offer, but if he does, he'll use it against you. He clearly isn't above using anything if he's slapping on fake bandages."

Kinley kept trying to work up antagonism, but honestly, they *were* even. And even if they weren't, he'd *laughed*.

It was like catching a glimpse of someone else. Someone real. Someone she…

She closed her eyes and took a deep breath. She was off-kilter. Confused. She had to get her bearings with him again. Which meant she was damn well going to get that bullhorn. Truce or no truce. He'd laid down the challenge, hadn't he?

What happened to being good?

Well, if Jackson Hart could fake an injury in response to her stealing his cane, then wasn't she just following his example?

She let that thought drive her as she laid out a plan this time. A real break-into-his-house-and-abscond-with-the-stolen-item plan. And she took the offered help. She didn't need much. Just some lookouts to warn her if Jackson deviated from his routine—highly unlikely.

Bree and Violet had enough experience sneaking in and out of Jackson's house to know the security. They'd given Kinley the necessary intel, and then, in a surprising move, Clementine had offered up a key.

"It's not technically stealing. It was my dad's. And it's not exactly breaking and entering if you have a key."

"Aw, look at our little delinquent," Violet offered proudly.

Clementine appeared torn between beaming at the praise and guilt over her actions.

But it was six, and Kinley only had so much time. Jackson wasn't cleaning this evening. He was doing paperwork in his office as he always did on Sunday nights. Then he'd invariably walk up to the house at sunset.

"Everyone knows their lookout point?" Kinley asked one last time. Nerves fluttered in her belly, but she was determined. Driven not by anger this time, but by something else.

She wasn't sure what to call it, wasn't sure she wanted to examine it too closely. Because it tied in with Jackson and him pushing her glasses up her nose and his eyes haunting her dreams.

But she had to best him. She just *did*.

"Aye, aye, captain," Violet said with a salute, and then Kinley's three bunkmates—her three *friends*—slipped out of the bunk.

She gave them three minutes to get to their lookout points, watching each second go by on her watch, then slipped out herself.

Up the hill, a familiar path now. It was still daylight, so she had to use whatever cover she could find, but she was used to finding cover and hiding in plain sight.

She got to the back door—since Violet and Bree had both agreed that was the best access point. She used the key Clementine had given her and was gratified it fit into the keyhole.

So much for Mr. Security, huh?

Driven by excitement, she slid inside and took a moment to catch her breath. The consensus was that the bullhorns would be in his bedroom. Which was upstairs at the far end of the hall.

As she quietly climbed the stairs, she wondered why he put himself through not just this walk up the stairs, but the walk up and down Hollyhock Hill multiple times a day. Surely it was hell on his leg. Was he some kind of glutton for punishment?

She moved into his room and decided, yes. He was. The doors to the closet were missing. The window had a piece of masking tape over a spiderweb of cracks. The ceiling looked water damaged and his furniture matched the sorry state of the house.

What made a man do this to himself? she wondered. But compassion and empathy threatened, so she shoved it aside.

Because she was here for the bullhorn. And there it was. On top of his scarred dresser, which was missing half the drawers.

She crossed to it. *Success*. She held the bullhorn in her hand. It was only the one, but when she glanced at the clock on the nightstand, she knew she didn't have time to search for the others.

Everyone would have to be satisfied with one. Besides, it proved a point. All she wanted to do was prove a point.

For some reason the image of Jackson pushing her glasses up her nose popped into her head. And the heady desire to have him do it again.

Something slammed below and Kinley jumped a foot, though she managed to swallow down her shriek of surprise. It was the door. Followed by...footsteps.

She looked around wildly. There was nowhere to go. She could *hear* someone coming up the stairs. She had to hide.

There was nowhere. The closet didn't have a door; neither did the bathroom. There were only long curtains hanging from a crooked rod.

She scurried behind the curtain, heart kicking so hard against her chest it was a wonder he didn't hear it as he moved into the room.

There was a little gap between curtain and window, thanks to her body, that allowed her to see out into the dim room.

Jackson stood there. What the hell was he doing? Deviating from his schedule? And no one had warned her! She couldn't move to look at her phone, but someone should have seen. Should have texted.

Were they setting her up? She'd thought they were all friends and they'd just been messing with her all along.

Jackson yawned, loud and long, stretching his arms out wide. Then he slid his hat off his head and put it down on the scarred dresser. When he reached down to the hem of his T-shirt, Kinley's eyes widened so hard they hurt.

Surely he wasn't going to...

He took off his shirt. It fell with a little *plop* almost right next to her foot. She narrowly stopped herself from squeaking and jumping back from it. She blinked from the shirt to him standing just in her vision.

He started unbuttoning his pants. His *pants*. And *whoosh*. There they went. So Jackson Hart stood maybe ten feet away, wearing nothing but his boxers.

Oh, God, she had to get out of here. A Peeping Tom was worse than a thief. Or at least just as bad.

She closed her eyes and promised she would be good after this if she just somehow got out of it without embarrassment.

When she opened her eyes, she realized she had to move or her glasses were going to fall off. Plus, she wanted to see—

You do not want to see anything, Kinley Parker. But no matter how firm her inner voice was, it was absolutely a lie.

She wanted to see *everything*.

JACKSON HAD KNOWN Kinley was in his house the minute he'd seen Violet loitering outside his office. These women might have once been petty thieves, but he'd been in law enforcement too long not to know when he was being cased.

So, he'd snuck out. It had taken some doing and ducking behind what he could to avoid Clementine's careful patrol and, he assumed, Lincoln's clueless happen by on his way to find Violet.

Jackson was impressed. He hadn't expected Kinley to strike back quite so quickly. And she'd gotten past his security without him getting any alerts, which wasn't so much for safety as it was for making sure he caught any future campers trying to pull pranks.

He'd have to do some improving in that department.

The surreptitious walk up to his house gave him time

to plan. Much like this morning, he wasn't going with the obvious. He wanted to make her sweat a little.

You should not want that.

Okay, no. He should nip all this in the bud. He was the leader. He was supposed to be setting an example, keeping a firm line between him and everyone else. Not playing silly games of one-upmanship.

Maybe he'd just march in and tell her enough was enough. It was the responsible, necessary *Jackson Hart* thing to do.

Instead, when he stepped inside, he caught the faint whiff of vanilla that seemed to be Kinley's calling card, and he just...

Wanted to have fun with this whole ridiculous predicament. And not worry about what was *necessary*.

He let the door close with a little bit of a slam, so she knew someone was here. He heard the telltale creak of a floorboard above him. She was in his room.

He grinned.

He let his steps echo, his backup cane hitting hard with each move up the stairs. There wasn't any exit up here, so she'd just hear him coming and be caught. Red-handed.

He might have laughed again, but it would give him away. He took his time going up the stairs and down the hall to his room. When he stood in the doorway, absently remembering he needed to get doors one of these days, he surveyed the room.

There weren't very many places to hide, and she might have even caught him unaware for a second or two behind the curtain if he hadn't already known she was there.

But he knew.

He didn't grin, just walked in as if he was wholly unaware of her. His normal routine was to hit the showers, so he figured he might as well stick to it.

He set down his cane, then his hat. Pulled off his shirt and tossed it onto the ground closer to her—when he'd never actually toss his clothes on the ground. But it seemed to suit the situation.

She didn't move or make a sound, so he figured he had to double down and go with the pants.

He'd thought undressing would have her scurrying out and away, but clearly she was made of sterner stuff than he'd given her credit for.

He unbuttoned his pants, stepped out of them. He heard something then, followed by a weighty silence. Now, he wasn't about to go any further in the disrobing department, but...

Something clattered to the floor over by where she was. He looked over at it.

Her glasses.

It took a lot of willpower, but he didn't smile or laugh. He simply crossed over to the item, bent down and picked it up. He pretended to study them, then the curtain, before pulling it back.

She stood there, eyes wide, bullhorn clutched in her hands. He'd never seen her without her glasses, but they suited her. Something about her face without them was almost too...vulnerable. And this was about...fun.

Somehow.

Maybe he was warped. Maybe they both were.

"I believe these are yours."

She took the glasses from his outstretched hands and slid them back onto her face. She cleared her throat but offered no apologies. She straightened her spine.

Though her eyes wandered.

She held his bullhorn in her hands, and that was impressive. If he hadn't caught sight of Violet, she might have succeeded.

But she hadn't.

Before he could reach out and take it away from her, she pointed at his leg. Because somehow he'd thought it was a good idea to be in his bedroom in his boxers with Kinley?

"That's not a burn scar," she said, sounding faintly accusatory.

He looked down at his leg, and the angry marks from both a gunshot wound and the multiple surgeries he'd undergone after. No, not a burn scar, but very few people knew that, as everyone assumed he'd been *in* the explosion that had killed his partner. "How do you know it's not?"

She reached down and lifted her shirt. Something clutched in his chest, a kind of panic he hadn't felt since he'd tried to rush into a burning building.

This was getting out of hand, but any protests or changes in direction just became a blur as she exposed a soft swath of creamy skin…marred by the pink webbing of a burn scar, there on her side. It wasn't huge, but not small either. Maybe the size of his hand.

"Jesus, Kinley. How did you get that?"

She dropped her shirt and shook her head. "It doesn't matter. Point is—"

"It matters," he said darkly, because if someone had done that to her… If…

Her gaze came up and met his, a faint question in her expression. "It was a mistake," she said quietly. "I've made quite a few," she added, as if he couldn't possibly understand *mistakes*. As if he really was so different from her.

When he so often felt like he was made up of *only* mistakes.

Her past, her scars weren't any of his business, but he

had to know. He had to. "Your own mistake or someone else's?"

"It doesn't matter."

"And I'm telling you, it matters to me." Both just about killed him, but if someone else had done that to her—

"Someone else's." She sighed. "If it makes you feel any better, they're in jail."

It didn't. At all. Someone had…

"I thought you were in an explosion," she said, pointing to his leg again.

"I was shot trying to go into an explosion."

"Why would you go into…?" She trailed off, clearly putting the puzzle pieces together. He'd been shot when he'd attempted to go back in to get his partner out.

Instead, Henderson had died, backup had arrived and Jackson had been saved.

"Jackson…" He saw the pity in her eyes, and he wanted absolutely nothing to do with it.

"An impressive attempt, but you fail. Again." He plucked the bullhorn out of her hands. "And at some point, you're going to have to learn—you can't best me."

CHAPTER SIX

KINLEY SHOULD BE MAD. She wanted to be mad. She wanted to fight with him. Maybe she couldn't *best* him, but there had to be some way to win against him.

If he was clothed. Because right now all she could really think about was how her fingers itched to reach out and feel all that muscle. *How* did he look like that under his clothes? He looked like he could move actual mountains, even with the deep, angry scar on his leg.

He'd been *shot*. Trying to save someone. She'd known he was this sort of good, noble, *honorable* man, but it had been in a kind of misty, detached way. Like Sheriff McClain had been the sheriff and Clementine, Flint and Duke were police too. Yes, she knew they all did dangerous stuff, but she'd never really *thought* about it. The reality of it.

How much Jackson had faced, what he'd seen, what he'd survived and how that might have shaped some of his… harder choices.

"My eyes are up here, Kinley."

She jerked her head up, and all that embarrassment she'd wanted to avoid was right *here* because she was really, *really* having a hard time keeping her eyes up.

He had the bullhorn again. She was supposed to have escaped with it. Instead, she'd been let down by her lookouts. As if on cue, her phone buzzed in her pocket.

Jackson held out his hand. Like he expected her to hand

over her phone. She might have refused, she might have argued, she might have even scoffed.

But look at his *arm*. It was all muscle and more scars there, though clearly older. He was a voice of some kind of authority, and she wanted to place all her problems in his capable, *large* hands.

She pulled her phone out of her pocket and gave it to him.

He looked down at the screen, then read aloud. "From Violet. 'Target must have snuck out the back. ABORT.'" He looked down at her. "So everyone was in on it?"

"Well, if at first you don't succeed…make your friends accessories to the crime?"

His mouth quirked. Not a full-blown smile, but a hint of amusement in his expression. It was like his laugh this morning. She wanted more. She wanted to be the reason.

"Are you admitting to a crime, Ms. Parker?"

I will literally admit to anything at this moment. She swallowed, hoping to dislodge that errant thought and maybe calm all the ways nerves vibrated through her. And not the nerves she *should* be feeling. Like all the ways she didn't belong here—in Jackson's house, stealing bullhorns, in the camp at all.

"You're not actually in charge of me, Jackson," she managed, knowing she didn't sound outraged or forceful, but like she was suffering a hundred different earthquakes inside of her.

Because she was.

"No, I'm not," he agreed, but his voice had deepened. And he looked right at her. And it wasn't *cold*.

She should leave. She should…not be thinking about what it might feel like if he leaned down and put his mouth on hers. She should not…want that.

But she did. It was all she could think about. The possibility. She was far too short to close the distance between their mouths. Was she brave enough to?

She nearly laughed. This had to be so one-sided it wasn't even funny. But he was just *standing* there, and she was still tucked a little behind his curtain, so she had nowhere to go.

He didn't move, except to carefully turn and set the bullhorn and her phone down on the dresser next to him. But he did not give her room to scurry away.

Then he reached out, as he had this morning, and pushed her glasses up her nose. The traitorous glasses that had announced her presence, but she couldn't curse them as she sometimes did, because his finger grazed her cheek and her breath caught.

There was some little voice, her usual voice of doom and gloom, warning her not to fall for this. There was Violet's voice, telling her it was a trick.

But his eyes, all gray and silvery, gleamed like moons and she was tethered to the tide of them. Because she had never once been afraid of Jackson Hart, no matter how cold and detached he could be. He made her mad, he challenged her, but she was never…afraid.

When she was always afraid.

"I called about a vision plan this morning," he murmured, as one singular finger dragged down her cheek. She tried to make sense of his words rather than shiver all the way through at his touch.

He was *touching* her, *looking* at her. She could smell something piney in the air around them, and all those voices telling her this wasn't what she thought, warning her against subterfuge and charm like Violet had, just went…silent.

"Oh," she replied, breathlessly, never looking away from his steady gaze. And he didn't look away. Didn't falter.

"We should have something set up by the time the campers get here." His fingers trailed down her neck now, so that she was sure the only nerve endings she had were centered where he touched.

"That's...great."

"Kinley," he murmured, but he didn't say anything else. He just stared at her, his fingers still touching her. His eyes on hers like he was searching for something. Answers she couldn't begin to believe she had. Anywhere inside of her. How could she give answers to a man like Jackson Hart? Why would he want her to?

But his hand was on her neck, and he drew her closer somehow. So she could feel the heat of his body.

She knew she should stop this madness, break this moment. He was...having a stroke or something if he wanted to touch *her*, but his chest was right there and she wanted to know...

Warm. The skin itself soft, but hard underneath. All that muscle. Probably honed with sweat and motivation and everything that made him...him.

She let out a shuddery breath because he'd lowered his head. Closer to hers. And he was still touching her. Stuck here in this little curtain cocoon.

Except, she could run away. She realized this. He wasn't *actually* blocking her exit.

She just wanted him to.

Maybe it was that realization that allowed her to close that last whisper of a distance between their mouths. Or maybe she just wanted to chase this feeling where all those little voices in her head went completely silent, and there was only his steady gaze.

He pulled her closer, soft and slow. There was a gentleness here she hadn't expected. She couldn't have fathomed when he was so rigid and hard and *muscled*. But his hands were on her face, and he held her there, featherlight.

His mouth cruised over hers like he'd happily do just this forever. No rush. Just them.

Her blood swam. Some strange need throbbed inside of her that was…different. It was probably a mistake, but it wasn't the kind she'd made before. Because she felt safe here.

It wasn't a reaction to something else. Just him. Just them. She slid her arms around him, moved her hands up his back. And he kissed her deeper, but still with that gentleness that quieted all her usual self-recriminations.

No one had ever treated her like this. Like she might be precious, or someone to be careful with. She found herself wanting to cry and hold on to him forever.

Stupid girl.

He eased back, surely it was him and not her, and she blinked up at him, waiting for reality to crash back down. Because this was just another dream. It was too perfect not to be.

Kinley didn't believe in perfect. Not for her. So, she didn't cry. She didn't panic. She just waited.

He stepped back, giving her that avenue of escape she wouldn't have taken before, and she saw the regret. Of course he regretted it. It was *her*. Everyone always regretted her.

Maybe it hurt a little bit, but she wasn't stupid enough to have thought it would go any other way. She always knew reality was right there waiting.

"Kinley." His voice was hoarse, but she knew…

"Please don't apologize," she managed, hoping she sounded light and breezy instead of breathless and skewered through.

She tried to laugh, but the sound that came out was definitely *not* a laugh.

She scuttled past him, running away and not looking back.

THE LAST THING Jackson wanted to do tonight was deal with his friends, but they'd decided it should be a poker night and there'd be no way to explain why he didn't want to partake.

And he figured Kinley needed some time or she wouldn't have run away. Hell, he needed time.

What had he been thinking?

Well, other than the fact that he wanted her.

He was not a man who gave in to the whims of his wants.

Except when it came to her, apparently. She'd been bringing out a different side of him for weeks now. And he knew—he *knew*—he'd done the same for her. Because she'd stood up to him. Repeatedly. She hadn't run off and hidden.

Until he'd kissed her.

He hadn't been about to apologize. There wasn't anything to be sorry for.

He didn't think.

Maybe *she* was sorry. Maybe that was why she'd suggested it and run away. Maybe...

"Are you going to play or are you going to daydream?"

Jackson didn't bother to respond to Duke except to throw a chip into the pot.

"I don't suppose it has anything to do with Kinley?"

Jackson didn't flinch. He was too good for that. But he eyed Lincoln speculatively.

"And her scuttling out of here like a jumpy rabbit," he continued in his lazy way that was never really all that lazy.

"Is there any other kind of rabbit?" Jackson replied, not jumping to the bait.

He never jumped.

He also never broke the rules he'd set out for everyone's benefit. But kissing Kinley had broken quite a few. Not any rules that two of the men at this table hadn't broken, but he held himself to a higher standard.

Had to.

Didn't he?

"Are we avoiding the question?" Flint asked conversationally, studying his cards.

"She was trying to steal my bullhorn. Again."

"Is that a euphemism?"

He gave Duke a long, cold look and tried very hard not to think of the state of his *bullhorn* after he'd kissed her.

"I don't fool around." God knew that kiss didn't feel like any kind of *fooling*. If anything, it had felt as weighty as coming back here and buying the camp. Important. A choice that would change…everything.

He was a serious kind of man, but he'd never thought a kiss could mean enough to *change* things.

Until now.

"Maybe you should," Flint offered. "Not with Kinley or anything. But just in general. You know, unclench."

"Let the stick fall out of your ass," Lincoln added, oh so helpfully.

"Thank you for that pep talk."

He didn't plan on unclenching exactly, but if he'd enjoyed the past few weeks going toe-to-toe with her, while decidedly not toeing his normal, perhaps uptight lines, didn't that mean he might want to…relax?

He'd found hope here at camp, and in his one good thing a day, and something that had held tight since his childhood had eased. Returning to Camp Phoenix had finally given him the opportunity to choose light over dark. *That's* what he was doing here.

And Kinley was all light.

"Following suit?" Duke asked, dubiously enough that Jackson knew what he was asking.

But Flint and Lincoln had made their share of mistakes in tangling up with their women. Jackson knew he could not make mistakes with Kinley. "I'm not going to mess around, and I'm certainly not going to repeat the mistakes these two made."

"Of course not. Jackson Hart doesn't make mistakes."

Jackson scowled at that, even though it was just what he was always telling himself. Always ensuring he held himself to that higher standard.

In order for this camp to be like it used to, you will have to care about the people in it.

Kinley had said that to him, and he'd shrugged it off because of course he cared. But he realized that, sometimes, in being the untouchable automaton to *them*, he wasn't setting himself up as the leader.

But a man they couldn't trust. And that wouldn't do.

"I make mistakes," he said, shifting uncomfortably in his seat because those words were *painful*.

"If this is going to be another growl and grunt about your DEA days…"

"It isn't." Jackson shifted again. "I made Kinley think I'd fallen and given myself a head injury when she stole my cane. I knew she was trying to steal my bullhorn, and I let her sweat."

"Those don't sound like mistakes, bud. That sounds like having a little fun," Lincoln replied.

"Aren't those the same in Jackson's world?" Duke countered.

They had been. Without him fully realizing it until Duke said that. When had fun become a mistake? Or had he just always associated anything good with all the bad that could go wrong?

He didn't want to make any mistakes with Kinley—*wouldn't*. She was wounded too. He needed to tread carefully, but that didn't mean anything had to be a mistake.

"I kissed Kinley."

"You wild man, you," Lincoln drawled.

"It's against those rules I set out," Jackson insisted.

"Yeah, the ones we've all been ignoring?"

"Speak for yourselves," Duke replied.

"Point is, I'm not… I do the things I do for a reason, but maybe I could, indeed, unclench."

He was certain his friends had more things to say about *that*, but a knock at the door surprised them all. Jackson got up and grabbed his cane, but Flint beat him to the door.

Violet, Bree and Clementine all stood on the porch.

"Is Kinley here?" Violet demanded.

"No," Jackson replied. "She left a while ago."

"Well, she didn't come back to the bunk, and now it's late. We've texted her and called her and looked around. She doesn't have a car, and everyone's vehicle is here."

"We thought maybe she called a rideshare or something, but you would have seen her get picked up, right? Or your cameras."

And she'd need a phone, when hers was sitting upstairs with his bullhorn. "We were playing poker. I wasn't looking." He could tell the women were worried, and it made *him* worried. She had just run out of here and he'd assumed to go back to the bunk. To get a little space from something maybe she regretted.

But the look on the women's faces had an old memory

taking hold. The adults whispering. Mrs. Zee worried. They hadn't shared their concerns with any of the young counselors, but…

Kinley used to do this, he remembered suddenly. Not a lot, but every once in a while when she'd been a camper, particularly those first few summers, Kinley did a little run away. He was pretty sure only the main adults ever knew about it, but that one time he'd overheard.

And he'd been the one who'd found her, though he'd let Mrs. Zee take the lead and talk to her.

"I think I know where she is." He surveyed the worried expressions on everyone's faces. "You guys sit tight. I'll go look. If she's not there, I'll give you a call and we can do something a little bit more formal."

"Are you sure it should be *you*?" Flint asked, carefully.

Jackson thought about it, but then he nodded. "Yeah, I'm sure."

CHAPTER SEVEN

KINLEY DIDN'T CONSIDER it running away. She was still on the property after all, and she'd go back. Eventually.

She just hadn't been able to go back to the cabin and face her bunkmates in the moment.

She had failed. Hard-core. No bullhorn. He'd kissed her and Violet had warned her that he would distract her like that, hadn't she?

Obviously that was the only explanation that made sense.

So she needed some alone time. Some space. The stars and her own thoughts and to not feel the pressure of all those *eyes* on her.

She climbed, just as she had when she'd been thirteen and miserable in this new place.

She didn't know what anyone wanted from her—then or now. She didn't know how to mold herself into what she was supposed to be to be important here. She just wanted everyone to...

She just needed to be alone. She really should always be alone. She was a problem, everywhere she went.

Don't fall into those old self-loathing patterns.

But the problem with patterns was they felt familiar, no matter how gross, and that was a comfort. Nothing that had happened in Jackson's room felt familiar.

Except all that regret.

She scrambled out onto the rock where, if it had been

light, she could have seen the valley. At night, it was stars and moon and…she could feel like she didn't exist.

She let out a long breath, pressed her forehead to her drawn-up knees and tried to figure out what the hell she thought she was doing.

She'd thought coming back to the camp was proactive. A step in the right direction after years of stagnation. But she felt more miserable in this moment than she had before. She felt twisted up and confused and uncomfortable and…

She blew out a breath and tried very hard not to think about that kiss, because it had to be a lie. Nothing could feel that good. That right.

She squeezed her eyes shut and tried to sit very still while the night moved around her. While the air cooled and the insects whispered to each other, punctuated by the odd birdcall.

She'd watch the sunrise in a few hours. Then she'd face… Well, what had to be done. Leaving.

Because she wasn't good for anyone. She never was.

And she sat in that old, ugly thought for a very long time, while a gorgeous starscape moved around her.

"Breaking curfew?"

She jerked at the human interruption of all that wild nightlife noise, but somehow she wasn't surprised. Not enough to shriek or feel her heart beat hard against her ribs. It felt inevitable.

Like he'd always find her. Even when he shouldn't. Even when no one ever did.

She couldn't see Jackson in the dark, but she got to her feet and turned toward the shape of his shadow. "How did you find me?"

"Your friends came looking for you, and then I remembered this is where you used to go to hide."

"Remembered…but…"

"But what?"

"I didn't think you actually remembered me from camp." Why *would* he?

"I said I did."

"I know, but—"

"I don't say things I don't mean, Kinley."

No, he didn't, and it didn't really matter. They'd been at camp together a lot of different summers, as different versions of themselves. "Why did you remember me?"

"Why wouldn't I?"

"Is it one of those things where you remember everyone? Because you're Jackson Hart and it all just gets filed away? You could recite every cabin's tenants every year you were ever here."

"No."

"So why would you remember *me*? I am *not* memorable." And she knew she shouldn't want to be.

But she did.

"Probably lots of little reasons. That someone so shy and skittish might have done something bad enough to get sent to Camp Phoenix. That you were brave enough to run away, even if only for a few hours."

"Brave?" She laughed. "Ha. Ha."

"You think I'm joking?"

"Running away isn't brave, Jackson." He chased people who ran away. Arrested them or brought them here. While he always stood in place.

He moved closer, though none of this climbing could be good for his leg. And she didn't want him this close, precisely because she wanted him this close.

She stepped off the rock, but she could feel him watch her, even as he sat where she'd just been.

"I didn't know how to run away," he said, his voice soft but firm amid all this night. "I only knew how to break things, so I guess back then, running away seemed pretty brave to me."

She could not imagine him *breaking* anything. He was so careful. So perfect. But she supposed they'd all gotten sent here for *something*.

"I'm not really running away. I just needed to be alone. I'm just… It doesn't have to do with you, really. I am spiraling. I know that. I know all the signs, all the reasons, and I can't stop."

He didn't speak, and it was just too much. She couldn't stand the quiet, feeling his gaze on her even if she couldn't see it.

"You just can't understand. You guys can't understand. You went and did things, accomplished things. I'm in the same place, so behind."

"It's not a race, Kinley."

She shook her head because that proved he didn't understand. "It's not a race, but I'm in the *same* place. I keep waiting for something to break, to change, and it doesn't, so I just keep coasting, all tangled up and… I don't know what to *do*. It's been years and I'm in the *same place*."

There was a long silence. No doubt he was thinking of all the ways he'd made a mistake in kissing her.

But he didn't leave. He didn't give her those apologies she was so scared he wanted to give her. He patted the space on the rock next to him. "Come here."

She shook her head because…

"Sit down, Kinley," he said, firmer this time. Enough of an order that she felt compelled to listen. Gingerly she climbed back on the rock next to him.

Somewhere far off, a pack of coyotes barked and yipped, then trailed off.

Jackson handed her the phone she'd left on his dresser. If she'd had it, she probably would have texted her bunkmates. She would have texted them a lie, but she would have texted them. She supposed that was an improvement on *some* old patterns.

"Do you know why I became a DEA agent?"

She couldn't begin to understand why he was asking her that, but she figured the answer was easy enough. "To do something good, make a difference. Like Bill."

"No." In that same firm, no-nonsense, intractable way he'd told her to sit down. "I told myself that's what I was doing, but in the end, I started to realize I wasn't there to do good. I was there for revenge."

That did not compute with the man she knew he was, but he just kept talking. Explaining. Showing her pieces of himself.

"I got sent here because my way of dealing with my parents being drug addicts was to break things. Hurt people. I got in fights. I vandalized. I thought I was better than them because I didn't need drugs or alcohol to cause trouble. The trouble was all right there at the surface. Just me."

She understood, even if she hadn't gotten into fights, even if she hadn't set out to hurt people. She understood that driving need to prove something in some way. "I vandalized my school," she offered. "I spray-painted basically every swear word possible on the library windows."

He laughed. It wasn't joyful exactly, maybe more commiserating than anything, but it felt like when he'd laughed in the kitchen and she just wanted to give him that. Lean into it.

"And I used to be really good at stealing things."

"*Used* to be." He nudged her shoulder with his and she laughed and…

She didn't know how he made her feel better. It wasn't that she suddenly had solid ground or anything. She still didn't know what the hell she was doing.

But he was a shoulder to lean on—because he was quite literally pressing his shoulder to hers so she could lean.

So she did. She leaned and he put his arm around her, and she didn't think he should want to, but Jackson didn't say things he didn't mean, and he didn't do things he didn't want to or think were right.

"Bill and Camp Phoenix… I thought it changed me," he said quietly, gravely. "Gave me a purpose. Be like Bill. Get into law enforcement, and the outcome was more productive, sure, but it was the same purpose. I wanted to prove I was better than my parents. That I was the kind of man who would put people like them away. I wanted to hurt the kinds of people who'd hurt me. Maybe it was a constructive way of doing it, more or less, but it wasn't out of the goodness of my heart."

"But you did good things."

"Maybe. Do the ends justify the means? Maybe they do. But at the end of the day, I realized a few years in what I was doing, that maybe it wasn't the healthiest choice, but I didn't know how to step away from it. I needed that feeling of…power, revenge, whatever it was. So I get spiraling and coasting for a few years. It's what I did. They were the same old patterns, just on the right side of the law this time. Maybe all that up and down is part of the process."

Part of the process. Her therapist used that word a lot. *Process.* And Kinley had always thought of it as steps. Steps toward healing. You had to get better, closer with every step. And she didn't ever seem to accomplish that.

But Jackson made it sound like ups *and* downs. Like that was normal, not just…a failure.

"And I don't know if anything would have ever pulled me out of that," he continued. "Not something *I* did, because the thing that changed everything wasn't me. Wasn't a choice I made. It was a bullet and a choice made *for* me."

She flinched because the reality of it—she'd seen his scar, the pieces of what that bullet had done, and it hurt all the way through. To think he'd suffered that kind of physical pain on top of everything else.

"My partner died. He had a family. People who loved him. I didn't have anything."

I didn't have anything. It echoed in her soul. For the past few years, it had felt like she didn't have anything. And she knew that was partly her own doing. She didn't hold on to people. She didn't grow roots. Camp Phoenix was the only place where she'd ever tried to hold on and belong.

Then it had slipped away like everything else.

"I rode on that guilt for a while," he said, and she'd never heard him speak this much at once. He was spilling his guts and she wanted to hear it all. Partly because what he was saying made sense to her own situation in a way no one else ever fully had, and partly because…

She wanted to know him.

"It's kind of a martyrdom, I guess," he went on. "It's taken some time, some circles of those ups and down. God knows I'll probably fall back into old, bad patterns a time or two. That's life."

That's life. Simple as that. "Why are you telling me this?" she asked. He was a shadow, but she could picture him perfectly. Not because they'd spent a lot of the past few weeks together, but because he'd kissed her and she'd allowed herself to finally really *look*.

"I know I come off as a hard-ass. I've got lines and rules for a reason, and I don't see that changing. But ever since I bought this place, the course of my life changed. Because it wasn't about that revenge or power anymore. It was about doing good. Helping people. And somehow, all that good I'd lost has been coming back. However I'd spiraled, coasted, messed up, it brought me here. And here, right here, is pretty damn good."

Kinley let herself breathe for a few seconds. Was right here good? It was strange because it had been brought on by feeling *terrible*, but this, right here, was nice. Seeing this human side to him.

Having his arm around her.

Knowing he just...belonged here. Filling Bill's shoes.

"You're really good at this."

"I know you don't believe it, Kinley, but you are too. You listen, and you challenge. Any of the questioning I've done over the past few weeks has been because of you, because I know you don't... You're not trying to be antagonistic. For you to say something, you really have to feel it. Which means when you say it, it holds weight."

It stunned her. And a million old denials tried to break free, but there were so many she couldn't formulate words. And he was just here, with his arm around her, telling her all these things about himself.

"Here." He flipped on his phone's flashlight and handed her a little...book?

"What's this?" she asked, but she was looking at him in the glow of his light. He was all shadows and hard planes, but there was something different in his expression. A kind of vulnerability she'd only seen one other time.

Right before he'd kissed her.

"My 'good thing' notebook," he said, tapping the cover

of the notebook she now held. "Every night, I write down one good thing that happened. *My* therapist's suggestion after…everything." She felt him shrug. "I've never told anyone I have it, and I sure as hell have never shown it to anyone. But go on. Look through it."

"Isn't it personal?"

"Sure, but I don't mind being a little personal with you, Kinley."

Her entire being *fluttered*. She had to look at the book to keep from dealing with *that*.

She flipped through pages. Mostly the past several weeks had to do with the camp. *Signed the deed. Got our first camper. Kinley's chocolate chip cookies.*

She stopped at that one. Touched her finger to the ugly, masculine handwriting. Her cookies weren't anything special— *she* wasn't anything special—but as she flipped the pages and came to today's entry, she could only stare.

He'd written: *Kissed Kinley.*

She felt twin, competing, opposing feelings well up inside her. Something warm and wonderful and all that *new* he kept introducing. And the knee-jerk refusal that this could possibly be true.

And since that was familiar… She shoved the notebook back at him and looked away from him. "That's very sweet, but I don't think you need to placate—"

He cut her off, curt and sharp. "I don't know what the hell gives you the idea that I'm placating anything. Do you honestly think I'd break my own rules just to…pad your ego?"

He reached out, put his finger under her chin and applied gentle pressure until she looked up at him.

"I'm pretty good at pretending, but I'm not going to pretend I'm not attracted to you. Unless you want me to. Then we can forget any of this ever happened, but it will be because *you* chose it, Kinley. Not me."

She could have pulled her chin away from his finger, she could have refused to look at him in the dim light of his phone, but she didn't. She just stared, and somehow the truth came out.

"I don't know how to do this," she whispered.

"Okay."

"That's it? Just 'okay'?"

"Sometimes we wade into things we don't know how to do. I don't actually know how to run a camp. I'm following a lot of Bill's old notes, my own instincts, but I don't have a fucking clue. And I sure as hell don't know how to navigate this," he said, motioning between the two of them with his free hand. "It's against the rules."

It made her laugh, God knew why. Him and his rules.

"But it ties to this," he said, tapping the notebook. "And everything I told you tonight. I lived a long time in the dark, in the anger, and sometimes it still wins. But when I make a concentrated effort to choose the light, things change. *I* change. Not every second of every day, but more seconds than not."

It wasn't that anything he said was particularly groundbreaking. She'd heard a lot of it before. In generic terms. In terms about her own life.

But, fair or not, never from someone like Jackson, who seemed so perfectly with it and was sitting there admitting that it was a process, with ups and downs. And decidedly *not* perfect.

Saying her words had weight when he…he didn't lie. He didn't say things he didn't mean. He'd kissed her, written about it in his book as a *good thing* because…

He thought it was a good thing. He thought her words

had *weight*. He was touching her and all of this was new and different and scary.

Could that actually be…good?

She swallowed. "I don't want to pretend it didn't happen," she said, searching his face for something. Some sign that made sense, some familiarity that would remind her she was making a mistake, fooling herself. No one ever wanted her for long.

And they didn't, but maybe if he wanted her for a little bit, that could be okay.

"Good," he said firmly.

Good. He thought that was good. That there was something about her that was good. Good enough to be interested in, to kiss, to be a part of this camp. He'd probably change his mind, and she'd be ready for that, but in the meantime… She could pursue something with Jackson Hart.

Because she wanted him, and if he wanted her, she had to seize the moment while it lasted.

"I have some of those chocolate chip cookies in the freezer at the dining hall. We could go…have some."

His smile turned into a full-blown grin. "Now, that sounds like a plan."

CHAPTER EIGHT

JACKSON DIDN'T KNOW what to expect. He'd never really been that vulnerable with someone before, except maybe in his camper days here at Camp Phoenix.

And didn't that figure? Because those had been the best days of his life, here in this camp. He hadn't fully realized it at the time, because he'd been itching for independence and all that revenge he'd considered "justice."

Now he'd had all those things, and it didn't hold a candle to the teamwork and camaraderie and *dealing* with himself that he'd found here.

Kinley opened the freezer and pulled out a container of cookies. "Mrs. Zee used to make these special cookie sundaes. It was kind of like my special treat when I needed one."

"Sounds good."

He watched her move around the kitchen. She didn't look at him, kept her gaze on her tasks. She didn't try to make conversation, so he didn't either.

Once she'd defrosted the cookies in the microwave and added the ice cream and a dollop of whipped cream, she moved over to where he'd sat on a little stool. She put the bowl in front of him.

"They're not that special. I can't make them like she used to. It's just a basic cookie recipe from the bag and store-bought ice cream and—"

Her hands were fluttering around as she tried to somehow diminish the whole thing, so he took her hand and held it firmly in his until she looked at him.

"No one ever made me homemade chocolate chip cookies, so they're special by that fact alone."

Her eyes studied him, and maybe that was really what he remembered about her all those summers they worked together. She didn't say much. She hid in corners and shadows when she could. But she watched. She listened.

He knew she didn't want to be a counselor, but he also knew she'd be a great one for some of the kids they had coming.

They ate in silence for a few minutes, and she looked down at her ice cream and cookie, and he understood she was thinking. Considering everything that had happened in the past few hours, no doubt.

Then she abruptly set her bowl aside, stood and turned to him. She took a few steps over, so her thighs touched his knees, perched on the little stool. She put her hands on his shoulders, and they were about the same height this way. She leaned in and pressed her mouth to his.

He had promised himself he'd go hands off. Maybe not forever, but at least for tonight. He'd ease into it.

But he hadn't counted on her. Not Kinley Parker and all the incongruous pieces that made her fascinating and warm and perfect. Not the woman who hid in shadows, but then stepped forward and kissed him.

She always took the stand when it mattered, pointed out the flaws in his plans, argued with him—and somehow this kiss was all of those things.

Because he forgot about plans, and he'd agree to any flaws, kneel to any stand she ever made.

She was sweet and demanding, melted to him, but held him in her grip. Made all of his considerations of slowness and easing go up in smoke.

Because her hands, small and strong, slid up his neck, into his hair.

He held her by her hips, to anchor himself. To remind himself this could not be some wild grapple.

He wasn't a teenager. He was the leader. He was…

Lost. Found. Hers.

It was different from back in his room. Sharper. Needier. And he should maybe be above all that, but he wasn't. He stood, dimly thinking maybe the stool had toppled to the floor at his sudden movement.

Who cared? All he cared about was a better angle. Tasting her, deeper. Holding her, tighter. Getting his own hands tangled up in her.

He ran a hand down the length of her hair, wild and windswept, reveled in it. In her. "This is breaking so many rules," he murmured against her mouth, her jaw.

She laughed, tilting her head back as his mouth traveled down her neck. That faint scent of vanilla intoxicating right there, so he spent some time tasting the space between her collar and her jaw.

"And the ice cream is going to melt," he added, though she tasted better than any ice cream.

She didn't say anything—not agreement or denial, but with her head tilted back and her eyes closed, he didn't get the sense one was imminent.

"We should stop." But his hands hadn't gotten the message, because they slid under her shirt, felt the smooth, soft curve of her back. All the way up under her shirt, until he cupped the nape of her neck. Nudging her to look down at him.

When their eyes met, she shook her head. "Don't stop."

KINLEY KNEW IT was not the smartest thing she'd ever done, but she wanted to be a mistake he made. Wanted to be that important. He'd break his rules for *her*. Here. Now. In the dining hall, of all places.

She wanted that more than *anything* in this moment.

She could live with his regret more than she could live with him getting bored with her somewhere down the line. It could be a onetime thing. A mistake he wouldn't want to repeat.

She could handle that. She could handle anything, if he just didn't stop.

She tugged at his shirt, gratified when he immediately lifted his arms and helped her remove it. He was all *muscle*. Ridges and scars and a life stamped out across his skin.

She wanted to kiss away every hurt, but his mouth hadn't relinquished hers. He savored. Each kiss moving into the next like he could spend hours here. When she was all needy sensation, fidgeting desire.

She dragged her fingertips down his chest, to the waistband of his pants. He made a noise in the back of his throat, perilously close to a growl.

He peeled her shirt away, those big rough hands moving reverently over every inch of her, sparking some wildfire that was bigger and more dangerous than all that *reaction* whenever she got mad.

He unhooked her bra, and she shivered as the cool air blew across her exposed skin. And Jackson seemed to go about the whole business like he did everything. Seriously, thoroughly, expertly. He tasted, teased, his hand traveling a lazy trail under the waistband of her pants until he touched the aching core of her.

She gasped into his mouth, and that made his kiss wilder. His touch more electric, until she couldn't fight it or chase it—the shuddering climax simply swept over her.

Here in the middle of her kitchen.

She needed… She needed. *Oh, it is a dangerous thing to need*. But pleasure and desire drowned out reason and she reached out for more. He pulled off her pants, and his hand moved lightly, reverently, over the burn scar above her hip, the physical reminder of what happened when she let herself believe someone might actually love her.

She didn't want to think about those old mistakes, those old hurts. Not when Jackson touched her. Not when if she followed this wild, dazzling high, she was already prepared for the fallout on the other side.

She unzipped his jeans, never breaking eye contact. If it was wild and unplanned and fast, then it wouldn't matter so much. Or so she'd told herself. But it was already bigger, weightier. Something different…just like it had been before. Because he held her gaze. Even as she touched him, wrapped her hands around him, still watching those eyes. Always so hard, so sharp, turning to smoke.

She stroked, and he sucked in a breath, but he did not look away.

"Kinley, I don't have anything," he said through gritted teeth.

"I'm good on that end."

He didn't even spend any time considering that. Just moved again, lifting her, and if she'd had a second to think, she might have worried about his injury, but he had her perched on the counter and was inside her in a movement so fluid she'd never know exactly how it happened because he was *inside* her. Big and inexorable and perfect.

He didn't move at first, just held her there, close against him, deep inside her. It was too much and not enough. She tried to wriggle closer, watched his eyes get deeper, darker as he looked where they were joined.

She did it again, moving against him, until he gazed up at her, so fierce and uncompromising.

Just how she liked him.

They watched each other, as she moved against him, as he teased her. As their breathing got ragged, desperate.

It was too slow. It was too much eye contact. It was too big and *meaningful*, and she knew she should stop that right now.

But she couldn't look away. She could only be swept into the rhythm of tenderness. The rise of something more than pleasure swimming through her. He held on tighter and so did she, chasing that wild, weighty connection. Skin on skin, mouth on mouth. Holding on, needing, wanting, finding that pulsing, ragged release.

He pulled her close, their shattered breathing coming in the same pattern of staccato gasps.

"Spend the night with me," he murmured into the crook of her neck.

She swallowed at everything that clogged her throat even as her body swam with all that pleasure. She squeezed her eyes shut as she pressed her cheek to his shoulder. She should say no. Create some distance. Laugh this all off as that one-night thing.

She spent the night with him.

In his house, in his bed.

And in the morning, when she woke and he was still fast asleep, she opened her eyes and saw his bullhorn sitting on his dresser.

CHAPTER NINE

JACKSON FELT KINLEY slide out of his bed, no doubt thinking he was asleep. Jackson let her think that—she'd made it clear she'd get up before him to get to the kitchen, and she didn't want to wake him.

So he gave her that and listened to her move around his room, pause at the dresser.

He *knew* she was contemplating the bullhorn. He could have told her he was awake at that point. He could have stopped her. Talked her back into bed. Again.

Instead, he let her have her victory.

Sort of.

Once she'd snuck out, he got ready for the day, then brought her a clutch of wildflowers in the dining hall before anyone else woke up and watched her reaction. Pure joy, followed by a wariness he was determined to get rid of.

He didn't mention the bullhorn. When someone asked him about it at breakfast, he'd said he'd misplaced it. She'd smiled at him, and he would let her steal a hundred bullhorns for that smile alone.

The next night, he took her out to dinner, he held her in his bed, night after night, and he did everything he could think of to get that wariness to leave her expression, but no matter how many little pockets of enjoyment she showed, the waiting for something to go wrong crept right back in.

He warned himself to be patient. She was so certain

she was somehow behind, and maybe he didn't understand why she thought that. But he knew he could be good for her. Because he was steadfast. He wouldn't falter and he wouldn't make mistakes.

Not with her.

It was a few weeks later, at their morning hike to the flag-pole, when Jackson knew he had to address some things, with his backup bullhorn (because he hadn't asked about the one she'd stolen, and she hadn't offered), thanks to the sarcastic grumblings of Violet.

"You'd think getting laid would have chilled him out," Violet muttered.

Bree snorted, and Flint squinted at the sky, a surefire sign he was amused but wasn't going to show it. Duke and Lincoln grinned, while Clementine looked decidedly uncomfortable.

Jackson didn't look at Kinley. He just had a bad feeling he wouldn't like what he saw.

So he surveyed his staff and considered them. Their role here. His role here. What they would be to the campers who would arrive soon.

They needed to function as a well-oiled machine. So, he needed to clear the air, to refocus their attention on what mattered. Maybe he'd broken some of his own rules, and he didn't relish that.

But Kinley was worth it all.

Still, that simply meant a new series of rules needed to be enforced. Because there were a few relationships going on now, and that could be good. If handled right, if reg-ulated, it could offer campers what many of them likely didn't have at home: examples of different kinds of *func-tioning* relationships.

"This is how I plan on running the camp," he announced,

though he didn't use the bullhorn. He didn't need to. "Because the kids coming here need a hard-ass in their lives. Someone who cares about them turning it around and being the best version of themselves. This is who I am and this is how it's going to be—regardless of my personal life—unless something shows me I should change that viewpoint."

Violet didn't look away, but she didn't have a jaunty retort.

"Kinley once told me we need to care about the kids if the camp is going to be how it used to be, and she's right. But these kids don't need friends. They don't need enablers. They need people who see the best in them. And it won't be the same person for every kid, the same activity—it won't even be this camp for every kid, even if that's the goal. So, no, I won't be *chilling* out."

Everyone was quiet, which satisfied Jackson to his core.

"My personal life is not up for conversation or debate. Its effect on my mood or choices or rules is irrelevant. We are here for these kids, and that is it."

"I think that's something we all agree on," Lincoln said, in that lazy drawl that was all warning.

Jackson smiled coolly at him. "Good."

He raised the flag with all the reverence he usually did, but he didn't look at Kinley until they were walking back down the hill. Her eyes were downcast, and he couldn't get a read on her.

That frustrated him probably more than it should. As they reached the bottom of the hill, he took Kinley by the elbow. "I'd like to see you in my office."

She looked at him like she was steeling herself for the gallows but nodded and let him lead her to the administrative building. Something about the way she was acting, sort of closed off and blank, had him feeling oddly nervous.

He couldn't remember the last time he'd felt *nervous*. He shook it away and found himself behind his desk, where he felt more in charge. "I want to talk a little bit about what's going to change once campers get here."

She met his gaze, chin high. "You don't have to do this. I get it."

But that didn't make *any* sense. "You get what?"

"You don't have to, like, break it to me. I know what this is." She shook her head and muttered, "No one wants me for long, so—"

"What on earth are you talking about?" Not wanting her? "I want you. I want you for the long haul. That's why I want you to take a bigger role."

She blinked, her eyebrows coming together in confusion. "A bigger role?"

"A head counseling role. I think you could help a lot of our campers. I want you to be more partner in things."

She shook her head. "I don't...want that."

He shoved away his irritation. He knew she had issues, didn't they all, but her refusal to see all she *could* do made him feel like a failure. "Kinley, you would be amazing at it. And we need the variety of experiences—both for the campers and the younger counselors. You've got a ton of experience and a softer way of—"

She was backing away from him. Like he was asking her to commit murder or something. She shook her head. "No, thank you."

He understood life hadn't been fair—he understood more than most, probably, the way it could mess with you. But he was having a hard time understanding why he couldn't get through that protective wall she held around herself.

He left the safety of his desk and crossed to her. Took her hands in his and looked at those wild, panicked eyes. "Kinley. You can do this. I know you can. What's more, you should."

She tugged her hands away, and he was so surprised by the shocked and injured look on her face, he let them go. She whirled away from him.

"I don't *want* this, Jackson."

He couldn't understand her. Why he couldn't get through to her. Why she was so determined to just…run. When he'd made something here no one should want to run from. When if she was running, it meant at least partially *from* him. "You want to hide."

She turned back and glared at him. "Yeah, so what if I do?" she returned, clearly not offended by his accusation. "Hiding has served me well. Standing out never has."

"You know that speech I gave out there?"

He saw a flash of anger, which was much better than the defeat and panic whirling around her. "I'm not one of your campers, Jackson."

"No. But you're someone I care about, Kinley."

She shook her head. "It can't be both. It can't be all these blurred lines."

He would have said the same. A few weeks ago. But it wasn't a few weeks ago. "Why not?"

That seemed to stop her, but only for a moment. "Because… because of all that stuff you said out there. About hard-asses and…and… This was fun, but—"

"No."

She blinked at the hardness in his tone.

"It wasn't *fun*. It was real." He was frustrated with her response, but he also understood he'd gone about this all wrong. He'd started with the camp, but he should have started with the heart of it all. He'd been trying to protect himself a little, ease into this new…realization. Something he'd never dealt with before. Never really wanted to or chosen to.

But he'd chosen her. "Let's put the camp stuff aside. I shouldn't have started there. I should have started right here." His stomach had tied in knots. Like he was a kid again. That life of uncertainty, of never knowing what he was going to get.

But he wasn't a kid. He was a grown man who knew what was right. "Kinley, I am in love with you."

She started shaking her head again, and she looked *terrified*. Horrified maybe. "I don't want that," she said on a whisper. Then her expression hardened. "I don't want any of it!"

"Then what *do* you want?" he returned, trying to ice away that stab of pain. He'd once been good at *ice*.

She stilled, all that panic and frazzled motion coming to a stop. She stared at him and opened her mouth, but no sound came out.

And he didn't fully understand the fury inside of him beating all that cold he wanted to employ. Just that she wasn't…reacting the way he wanted her to—didn't see herself the way she *should*. She had so much more to give. Why did she always have to hide and run away?

Why wasn't his love enough?

"Because I hear a lot of things you aren't," he said, each word a volley. "Things you can't do. You don't want. But who are you? What do you want, Kinley?" *I would give it to you in a heartbeat.*

She sucked in a breath, like he'd stabbed her clean through. He didn't relish that, but he could hardly take it back.

He recognized something in her response. That desperate need to bury yourself in something else so you didn't have to face scary truths. So he softened. "I happen to find that scary myself, but it's true. It's what I feel. And if you need time to work this through, your feelings for me, what you want to do at the camp, I'll give it to you. But you have to understand nothing in your life changes if you refuse to let it. You think you're not, but you *are* brave." He took her by the arms, gave her a gentle squeeze, trying to will the words to seep into her. "When it matters. You just have to decide it matters. That *you* matter. And you do, Kinley. To me. To your friends. To this camp."

EVERYTHING WAS WRONG. His steely gray eyes. The firm pressure of his hands on her arms. His words. The feelings cartwheeling around inside of her that felt far too close to a hope that had only ever broken her heart.

She had been preparing herself for an *end*, ever since the beginning. Not...love. She was just getting her footing, finding a spark again. She couldn't fling herself into all...this.

He was too...

Too.

She pulled her arms out of his grasp. "I don't want any of this," she repeated, because she wanted it all so much she thought she might spontaneously combust. Because it was everything and she wasn't built for everything.

So, she turned and ran. Maybe not literally. Okay, a little literally. But he could have followed.

Thank God he didn't.

She went right for the cabin. Because the answer was clear now. Just another mistake in a long line of them. Thinking she deserved this camp or the people in it.

She pulled her bag from under the lower bunk and gathered all her things. She didn't have a car, but walking a few miles back into town might be good for her. She couldn't stay here. She couldn't *do* this. Jackson thought she could be brave.

But she wasn't. Never had been. She was a failure, and that only worked when nothing mattered.

So she'd go back to the life she'd had when nothing did.

"What are you doing?" It was Bree. Kinley hadn't even heard her come in and was so determined to finish her task, she didn't even flinch or stop.

"I'm leaving." Kinley hefted the bag on her shoulder. All that she'd left behind was Jackson's bullhorn. Sitting there on the center of her bed. She didn't know why she'd taken it, why they'd never discussed it.

Now it felt symbolic and…awful. "Can you give that back to Jackson?"

She pushed past Bree without waiting for a response. She walked right out the door, but Bree followed and waved Clementine and Violet over.

"What's going on?"

She didn't need to explain herself to them, but it was best if she made it clear this was necessary. They'd agree. Jackson had gotten the totally wrong idea about *everything*, but these women knew her.

"I've been thinking about leaving for weeks, but today really did it."

"I didn't think Jackson's speech was that bad," Clementine said, falling into step behind her. Why were they following her?

Kinley shook her head. "Not that." She'd agreed with everything Jackson had said at the flagpole this morning, and her heart had ached because she'd wanted to give some young woman what Mrs. Zee and Sheriff McClain and Gale Lawson had once given her.

But she wasn't *good* enough.

"Did you two have a fight?" Bree asked gently.

Kinley tightened the grasp on her bag strap and kept marching. "This isn't about me and Jackson."

"Isn't it?" Violet asked in that lawyer voice of hers, her pace never faltering as they trailed after her.

Why couldn't anyone just leave her alone? "No. It's about *me*. It's about…" She stopped walking for a moment, searching for the words. She turned to face them so they'd agree with her. Tell her she was right. She looked at all three of them, searching for something. But no words came.

When they'd been teenagers, they hadn't been friends at all. They'd even been antagonistic. But working together as adults had changed them into friends. People she cared about. People who cared about *her*.

Kinley, I am in love with you. He'd said that as seriously as he spoke about giving the campers what they needed. Like he meant it.

Her friends stood here now, clearly worried about her, wanting to talk her out of leaving, and she wanted…

To just *explode*.

Instead, she began to cry.

"Aw, Kinley." Bree stepped forward and put her hand on her shoulder. "What's wrong?"

Kinley shrugged it off and stumbled back, the bag falling off her shoulder. "Me! I am wrong. And everyone keeps acting like I'm not. Like I could fit in here. Like you're my friends and like he loves me."

She couldn't look at any of their faces, and she couldn't keep crying and falling apart like this. She had to get out.

"You're not *wrong*. The way other people have treated you, especially when you were a child, isn't on you, Kinley," Violet said quietly.

Kinley glared at her through the ever-flowing tears. "I know that!"

"You know it, but do you believe it?" Bree countered.

"I can't do this. That is what I know. I can't be…someone he loves. I can't love him. I can't. I can't. He doesn't… He's wrong anyway. He doesn't love me. He's just confused."

"I find many faults with Jackson Hart, but if he says he loves you, I'd be inclined to believe him. He's not one for *confusion*."

"You don't understand," Kinley said forcefully. "And I've decided to go. So I'm going."

She tried to move forward, to pick up her bag, but Violet had grabbed her arm. Kinley tried to jerk away, but Bree had taken her other one.

"I know what you need," Violet said, beginning to tug her forward.

So do I. To run away.

"Do you have your phone in your pocket?"

"What? No, it's in my bag, but—"

They dragged her forward, Clementine bringing up the rear. Kinley tried to fight off their grasps, but it was three against one. And she finally realized what they were doing.

"You can't! You wouldn't!"

"It isn't called the 'wake-up call' for nothing," Bree said as they approached the banks of Crow Lake.

It didn't matter how she fought them off. They worked together and tossed her right into the water. Only they didn't get a good enough swing in and she just landed with a thud in a few inches of water on the muddy bank. But enough cold water splashed up into her face and hair to get her wet.

Kinley sat there, the water seeping into her clothes, droplets falling from her hair. She looked at the three people standing on the bank, all with hands on their hips and fierce expressions that rivaled Jackson's on their faces.

"Wake up, Kinley," Violet said in her direct way. "You're the one who stuck around. The one who didn't feel the need to go off and prove anything else, because this was it for you. If anyone belongs here, it's *you*."

"Grown-ups don't get to run away. They deal with what's in front of them," Bree added.

"You threw me in the lake to make me grow up?"

"We threw you in the lake as a rite of passage," Bree replied. "So take the damn passage and meet us on the other side."

She expected them to turn and leave, because she had no desire to grow up or wake up or any of this. It was hard and scary and maybe the past few years had sucked, but she'd been in control. The *suck* was familiar.

This was new and scary and...wonderful.

They didn't leave her there. They didn't give up on her. Clementine held out a hand, and so did Bree. When they'd hauled her up and out, Violet fished a brush out of Kinley's bag and began to pull at the tangles.

"What are you doing?" Kinley whispered, new tears threatening.

Bree's and Violet's gazes met each other, then turned to Kinley. "We're being your friends, Kinley. And a camp friend is a friend for life. So you might as well get used to it."

Clementine nodded vehemently.

"We will be mad at Jackson on your behalf for a variety of reasons. I could start a list for you right now," Violet said. "But we can't be mad at him for loving you. We happen to think you're pretty lovable."

Kinley didn't know what to do with all this *support*. And she couldn't run away from it because Bree was holding her hand and Violet was brushing her hair and Clementine was trying to wipe the mud off her.

"And if you don't love him back, that's okay," Bree said reassuringly. "You only have to tell him. We'll support you. And if he's a jerk about it, we'll take him down."

He wouldn't be a jerk about it. He was too honorable. He, somehow, understood her too well. The reason he'd been mad was he'd seen through her. Running because she wasn't brave enough to stay.

And he'd loved her anyway. Her friends were taking care of her anyway. Something was crumbling inside of her and she was *terrified*, but she couldn't seem to rebuild all those things that were falling apart.

"So what am I supposed to do?" she asked, her voice raspy.

"If you love him, you tell him. If you don't, you tell him. You stay, because we all know you want to. And you carve out your own niche. Just like when we were kids. We find where we belong, and we plant ourselves there."

It wasn't any different from what Jackson had said, with all that carefully leashed anger she'd seen under the icy mask.

What do you want?

All she'd wanted when she'd first come here was a place to belong. And now... Now it was being offered to her, not just by Jackson but by all these women.

Who'd thrown her in a lake as a rite of passage. Who were all brave in their own ways—and seemed to think she could be too.

You are brave, Jackson had told her. But he'd asked her to be brave for herself, and she hadn't figured that out yet. Of course, if Jackson Hart thought she could... If these amazing, successful women thought she could...

Maybe it was time.

CHAPTER TEN

SOMEHOW IT GOT to be close to lunch and Jackson still hadn't left his office. Dimly, in the back of his mind, he knew he had things to do.

But he just kept replaying the whole thing in his head. He'd been so determined not to make any mistakes with her. So he couldn't comprehend how it hadn't gone according to plan.

That was for his old life. As a DEA agent, as the child of drug addicts. *This* new life, with a messed-up leg and bringing a camp back to life, was supposed to follow the plan.

He figured there was a lesson in there. He wasn't too keen on looking it in the eye though.

His office door opened.

"Here you are." Flint studied him. "Half expected to find you wrapped up in Kinley since, as far as I can see, that's the only reason you'd miss an inspection."

"No." Had he missed an inspection? Did he care?

The curt tone didn't deter Flint. He stepped inside, followed by Duke and Lincoln.

"My office is too small for you all to be crowding in here," he told them.

"You passed up an opportunity to nitpick our dirty work," Lincoln said, already lounging in the one available chair. "Clearly, you need an intervention."

"About what?"

Lincoln shrugged. "Take your pick."

"Should I give you a lecture about going and getting the girl?" Flint asked.

Jackson tried very hard not to growl. "I did, in fact, attempt that, because I'm not afraid of going and getting. *She* is." He shrugged, knew it was defensive and couldn't quite stop it. "I informed her I thought she should take a role as lead counselor. And that I loved her. She was less than enthusiastic."

"Maybe she doesn't want to be a lead counselor."

"Thank you for that brilliant insight," Jackson returned, stiffly. "Her telling me she, in fact, didn't want to was definitely not my first clue."

"You said it yourself. These campers are going to need different things, and we're going to be different things to different kids. Just because the way she does things doesn't fit into your little box doesn't mean she's wrong."

"It's not *my* box."

"Isn't it? Or maybe you want to give another speech about how you're not going to make mistakes like we did," Flint said, oh so calmly.

"It isn't my mistake," he said through gritted teeth. Because he knew, he *knew* she was capable of so much more than she believed herself to be. "She could do more. She *should* do more."

"You remember when Bill thought we should go into law enforcement?" Duke offered casually. Far too casually. "Did he lecture us, lay out the path for us and tell us how it's going to be?"

Jackson glared at Duke. "I didn't lecture anyone." Mostly.

"Or did he leave the applications out in the dining hall so we'd *happen* upon them?" Duke continued, undeterred.

"Did he answer our questions with honesty, letting *us* make the decisions? Because they had to be *our* decisions if they were going to matter."

Jackson couldn't deny Duke had a point.

Didn't mean he was going to admit it. Out loud.

"You might love her. She might even love you. But no one needs a boss in their personal life, Jackson."

"I wasn't trying to be anyone's boss," he muttered. Mostly, anyway. And it wasn't that he thought he *knew* better than her. Just that she needed a push. Or he'd just wanted her to want what he wanted. Maybe.

It didn't matter. She'd walked out, all panic and conviction and inability to tell him what she *did* want. So he could hardly chase her down and demand things from her. She had to figure it out. He was giving her the space to figure out what she wanted.

Because, like Duke had said, it didn't matter until she chose it.

"Well, this has been quite the constructive meeting I didn't call or ask for," Jackson said, trying on that icy mask that had served him well in the beginning. "But you all have work to do and so do I."

"You're used to being the expert, Jackson, but sad to say, Lincoln and I have you beat in this department."

"Feel free to beat me in this department," Duke said with a grin.

But Lincoln continued as if Duke hadn't gotten in his little joke. "Maybe, and this is just a crazy thought, you could talk about love without hinging it on her responsibilities at the camp."

"That isn't what I was doing."

"That is what you *do*. And it works in about every situation except this one."

"So what do you suggest?" he returned. Coldly. Sarcastically.

And he waited for an answer with something like fear jangling in his chest. A softer kind of fear than he'd ever felt as a law enforcement officer. Because this wasn't about life and death, danger and cruelty.

"Maybe make sure she knows the love isn't conditional."

"And she doesn't need to fit in your box of what you want to be worthy of it."

"That maybe, deep, deep, *deep* down, you're not the perfect ice robot."

"All right. All right. I get the damn picture," he grumbled, and he stalked out of his office. With no earthly clue what his plan was.

KINLEY DIDN'T WASH up or change. There was a certain time limit on her bravery, and if she gave her brain too much time to work, she'd lose this wave of courage.

So her hair was wet, but combed. Her clothes were damp and muddy, though not as muddy as they had been, thanks to Clementine. And her heart…

Jackson was right. She could be brave for other people, for right and wrong, but it was so much harder to be brave for herself. That hadn't ended well, not once in her life.

But nothing with Jackson was like anything else in her life, so maybe…maybe she had to believe this could be different too.

She figured he'd be in his office, and when she made it to the center of the camp, she heard a door slam open and watched as Jackson stormed out of it.

She stopped in her tracks. When he saw her, he did as well. They stood facing each other almost like an Old West duel. It should have been funny, but she wasn't ready to laugh. She was too busy trying to be brave enough not to run away.

He crossed the space between them. "What happened to you?" he demanded.

Only at that point did she remember the damp and the mud. "The girls threw me into the lake."

Outrage chased over his face. That formidable wave of a lawman wronged. "They're on latrine duty for a month. This is unacceptable. We cannot be engaging in these childish—"

"Jackson. Stop. It was a… Well, you wouldn't understand." She tilted her head and looked up at him. "Or maybe you would." She'd known he was friends with Lincoln, Flint and Duke, but he was so reserved she hadn't fully realized how deep that friendship went.

Now that she understood him, had seen the gentle man beneath all those hard edges, she realized those friends of his probably mattered more to him than she'd ever imagined.

Just like his outrage at her being wet and muddy came from a place of care. Jackson didn't say things he didn't mean and he'd said he loved her.

She still couldn't quite fathom it. Because she hadn't been trying to make him love her. She hadn't been desperate for his attention. It had just…happened.

So maybe it's true, and maybe, like this camp, it's the something you can believe in.

"I shouldn't have run away," she managed to say, holding his steady gray gaze. "I should have at least dealt with the topics at hand first."

There was a long pause as he seemed to digest those words. She expected him to smile or something, but there was only that cool gravity of his. "Maybe we should go somewhere more private," he said quietly.

She looked around. Her friends were standing behind her, though quite a few yards away. His were loitering around the porch of the admin building. And she and Jackson stood in the middle, like they were onstage.

Maybe this should be private, but standing here felt right somehow.

Bravery. She'd gotten her first taste of it by breaking rules. Her second here. Amid a group of people who'd worked to put together a camp where sad, angry and neglected children could come find some sense of…belonging. Peace. Hope. Strength.

"No. We should do this right here." In the center of the camp, the thing that had saved them both, the thing they both wanted to give their lives to. "I don't want to be a head counselor," she said. Firmly.

If she'd expected an argument, he didn't mount one. He nodded. "I'm sorry. I pushed it on you because it's what *I* want for you, but it's more important to me that you're happy. As long as you're *actually* happy, I'd—"

"But you weren't totally wrong about pushing me to do something more. I could take a small group of kids to work in the kitchen. Like Mrs. Zee did. I'm willing to start there."

He studied her face, looking for something, though she wasn't quite sure what. But he nodded. "Okay. That sounds good."

She knew she had to keep going, but she didn't know how to broach the topic. Not when he was standing there all tall and stiff and, if she wasn't fooling herself, with a strange glint of uncertainty in his eyes.

"Is that all?" he asked gently.

"No." She wiped her sweaty palms on her thighs. It felt a bit like she was performing for everyone, but no… It wasn't that. It was that the people around her had helped her realize she'd found her place.

And none more than the man in front of her with that very cool mask firmly in place. But she knew the man beneath the mask, the heart beneath all that armor.

"I've never been in love," she managed to say, though her voice shook. "Never believed in love." Did she not believe or was she just scared to? He'd accused her of hiding, and he wasn't wrong. She wanted to hide from the big and the complicated—because that had always been the *bad* in her life.

There was nothing bad about Jackson Hart. Except maybe his love of a bullhorn.

And wasn't the truth why she was so afraid—afraid enough to run away. It wasn't his feelings that scared her.

It was her own.

But there was no one in this world she trusted more than Jackson, so didn't he deserve the truth? The words? "But I believe in you. And...I love you."

She wasn't sure how she'd expected him to react, but the careful way he looked at her wasn't it. He leaned closer and lowered his voice so no one around them could hear.

"Kinley, I know I dropped a lot on you this morning, but it wasn't right. These are your decisions, not mine. You don't have to—"

"Love you?"

He opened his mouth, but in the end, it was like he couldn't come up with any words. Which she wasn't sure she'd ever really seen happen before. It almost made her smile.

"Loving you isn't really a decision I made. It's just something that happened. And it scares me because I want it so much and I've had bad luck in that area. But...you're different. This is different, and you seem to think I'm brave. So I guess I should start with being brave when it comes to you."

He inhaled sharply, then let it out. But he didn't say anything. She turned back to her bag and pulled out his bullhorn, which she'd retrieved, then held it out to him. "You're going to need this."

He looked at it dubiously. "Am I?"

"Oh, absolutely. I think I once heard Jackson Hart doesn't change. Because these kids need a pillar. Someone to depend on. And there's no one better."

He took the bullhorn. "And what do you need?"

"Someone to believe in me, even when I don't, maybe especially when I don't, believe in myself. What do you need?"

"You."

He made it sound simple, and she knew it wouldn't always be. But in this moment, it could be.

And then, to the cheers and whistles of their friends, Jackson dropped the bullhorn, pulled her close, and kissed her long and hard.

* * * * *

The One with the Trophy

Maisey Yates

To Nicole, Jackie and Megan (Caitlin).
You're just the best.

CHAPTER ONE

"WHEN ARE YOU going to lose your virginity?"

Clementine McClain was new to friendship. So she didn't really have an answer for this new situation, which seemed to fall under some advanced level of friendship to which she hadn't yet ascended.

She was *not* ready to graduate from remedial friendship to *this*.

The friendship curve had been steep. They'd all been stuck in the same cabin during the camp restoration—which had been perfect for Clementine, since it was an opportunity for her to have some renovation done on her dad's old place while she was out. But it had been difficult in terms of getting used to sharing her space.

Now, though, now that her friends sneaked out every night to be with the men in their lives, she sort of missed the togetherness.

She turned and looked up—way up—to the ladder her friend Bree was perched on, paintbrush in hand, from where she was sitting on the floor of one of the old Camp Phoenix cabins. They were rehabbing the last of the old buildings today, as June started to turn dry and hot, and the time the campers were arriving came closer.

Bree, Violet, Kinley and Clementine had been shipped off to cabin duty today with buckets of paint, varnish for the floors and mousetraps, which had made Kinley's eyes go round behind her overlarge glasses.

It's the country, Kinley. Mice abound. Violet had said this pragmatically.

Soon after, the mice will abound no more! Bree had said cheerfully, brandishing a paintbrush like a sword, in a display far more free and easy than any she would have made earlier in this endeavor. Before friendship and loving Flint Decker had changed her.

And off they'd gone to see to their duties. It had been a few hours of small talk. Some of it outside of Clementine's comfort zone; her three friends were now having "carnal relations," as her dad had called it, with three men that Clementine had known half her life, and it was a *bit much*. But some of the conversation had also been good camp memories from years past and plans for the soon-to-arrive campers.

So this felt out of left field.

"What?" She tried not to sound like she was choking, even though she was.

That was just a little bit overly personal. Plus, she hadn't actually told any of them that she was—

"Your *theft* virginity," Bree clarified.

"Oh," said Clementine, the word rushing out in a huff of relief. She could feel her face getting hot, which meant it was getting red, because the curse of being a ginger was fair, freckled skin that turned more strawberry than her hair ever could at the slightest provocation.

"I didn't mean… I mean…whatever the other situation is, is your business," Bree finished.

"I…I don't…" She really didn't want to be having this conversation.

"More importantly," Kinley said, "what are you going to steal, and from whom?"

Clementine was still getting used to this kind of thing. The way her friends just *said* things. And then of course there was the stealing thing, which was a whole thing in itself.

It made her scalp prickle.

Excitement. Terror. All of the above.

She didn't know.

Clementine liked to be *certain* about things. And ever since she had returned to Camp Phoenix for its grand re-opening, she had felt *uncertain*. From bunking with the girls—her former enemies, now turned friends—to just sort of being in a new daily schedule.

If you could call Jackson's schedule a "daily schedule" like that. It was more like an unreasonable dictatorship, but, whatever. From having to listen to reveille played over the loudspeakers at 6:00 a.m., to the long march up the hill to watch the flag get raised and on to their mess hall meetings, it was a lot like being in the army. Except she didn't get to carry a big gun.

And—with the exception of Violet, who was wedded to her personal style—wore Camp Phoenix T-shirts instead of neatly pressed uniforms.

And *also*, she had been challenged to steal something.

She had always been an outlier at Camp Phoenix. Mostly because she hadn't *actually* been a camper. She hadn't been a counselor either, and she was not one of the juvenile delinquents who had been brought in to learn to better themselves.

Her father had run the camp with a mixture of drill sergeant–level precision and nonjudgmental heart.

He'd been good at that.

Though he'd been especially good with troubled teenage boys.

And his motherless daughter…

Well.

Whatever. Clementine didn't need to get all weepy about her childhood. There wasn't anything she could do about it.

It was water under the bridge. You couldn't push it back and dam it up, couldn't live it again, change it or redeem it, no matter how much you wanted to.

Kinley was always talking about therapy. Her therapist said this, her therapist told her to do that.

Clementine didn't get the point of talking to a stranger about your feelings.

Violet was all about stating your case. In all venues, no matter what.

Clementine felt like there were times when an argument simply didn't serve.

Then there was Bree, who felt that anything tarnished could be made new. And that if it couldn't be polished into something shiny, a new perspective just might be the thing to brighten it up.

All fine. But Clementine figured burying the problem was even more effective.

That was also a new perspective, technically.

It was nice to have friends. Nice people she could talk to, even if it did make her feel like a teenager again.

Mostly because the peer pressure that she'd heard so much about back then was actually making an appearance now.

No one had ever tried to talk her into doing anything when she'd been younger.

You simply didn't go around trying to get the sheriff's daughter to engage in problematic behavior.

There were a lot of reasons that Clementine had spent her life in Jasper Creek as a bit of an outsider.

Her dad *tried*. It was just that he wasn't good at raising a daughter. He didn't know how to do it. He wasn't good with women. There was a reason he had cycled through many short-term girlfriends while Clementine was growing up, one of whom had been Flint Decker's mother, and a reason she had never actually had an actual stepmother.

There was also a reason he had thrived running the camp.

A reason it had called to him.

He had been great. A surrogate father to so many.

And an imperfect one to her.

But she had loved him. He'd been her only parent. She just acknowledged that it had left her at a little bit of a social disadvantage.

She'd always hovered around the edges of Camp Phoenix. Never a kid, a counselor or anything, really. She'd tried to be friends sometimes, but then if someone broke a rule, she'd felt obligated to tell.

She'd joined in for chapel in the woods, and making arts and crafts, and sing-alongs around the campfire, because she'd had to do something.

And when she'd been the right age, she'd even spent summers in the cabins with the girls. And everyone had hated her. For good reason, really.

She could see now she'd been an officious ferret. And nobody liked an officious ferret.

Everyone has their gifts, Clementine.

She could remember Gale Lawson, art teacher and the only maternal figure Clementine had ever had, putting an arm around her after Clementine had been trying to make

Popsicle-stick penguins with the others, and had ended up telling on Violet for making a penguin that was *anatomical*.

This had resulted in a fight that had made Clementine dig in and get mean, and then after, had made her cry alone in the arts and crafts hall.

She was always alone.

Maybe you have to figure out how to use your particular gift for justice and rules, add a bit of kindness to it, and see where it takes you.

The obvious destination had been law enforcement, like her dad. But in that moment, Gale had given her something to hold on to that had been her own. Justice, rules…but maybe some kindness too.

She'd taken that forward, to her career and back here to Camp Phoenix for this epic rebirth of the place that had changed so many lives.

And Clementine had finally made some friends here, but she still felt…outside.

It had come up that she was the only one of them who had never stolen anything. Because Bree, Violet and Kinley were genuinely former *hoodlums*.

Clementine wasn't even close to being a hoodlum.

The worst thing that Clementine had ever done was accidentally leave the gate open on her dad's property, which let all the cows out, who then filtered into downtown Jasper Creek, blocking all of Main Street.

Yes. That was the worst thing she'd ever done. And she hadn't even done it on purpose. She couldn't even claim it was a grand prank.

Violet was all about grand pranks. In a camp sense only. Violet was also a lawyer and had a very strong sense of legal technicalities.

"Oh, come on," said Violet. "We know exactly who Clementine is going to steal from. It's painfully obvious."

Oh, no. No no *no*.

"I could steal from Bert," said Clementine. "Is that what you mean?"

She mentioned the old groundskeeper because, well… She didn't want to mention the man she wanted to steal from.

She didn't want to talk about it. She didn't want to talk about *any of this*.

"You do not want to steal from Bert." Bree gave her a clear and piercing look. "Admit it."

"If this is an interrogation, I want my lawyer present." Violet grinned broadly. *"Present."*

Clementine narrowed her eyes. "I don't trust you to represent my best interests."

"You want to steal from Duke." It was Kinley who finally said it.

Her friends had all three stolen their items from men who had ended up, well, they were in love now. *Passionately.*

Clementine couldn't imagine passion on that level. Clementine was passionate about fishing, target practice, and deeply, *secretly* passionate about needlepoint, and no one needed to know about that, thank you.

But when it came to men…

She did her best not to picture *him*.

"Duke is practically a brother to me," she said. "A surrogate *uncle* almost, since the man is ten years older than me if he's a day. He—"

"You *like* him," said Kinley.

"You *really like* him," said Violet.

"I *don't*. I work with him. He was… I basically grew up with him. And I do not like him. I just…"

Couldn't fathom being with any other man, couldn't even go on a date with another man, couldn't think about kissing another man, because Duke Cody occupied her every dream and fantasy.

That was fine.

It was absolutely *fine*. And not *weird*.

As Violet would say, it was not an *action item*.

It was just a fact of her idiot, feminine body that had never had a damn lick of sense and could never quite be what she needed it to be.

But she was a professional at ignoring it.

"So how about it?" Bree asked. "What are you going to steal from him and when?"

"It doesn't have to be Duke," Clementine said.

"Well, who else do you know well enough to get something personal from?" Violet asked.

"Bert has a pair of hedge trimmers that he likes an awful lot."

"That isn't going to work," said Violet. "And I think you know that."

She narrowed her eyes. "You don't know what I know, Violet."

"No, I'm pretty sure I do."

Clementine fell back, exasperated. "If I were in my uniform—my real uniform—I don't think that we would be having this conversation."

"You aren't. You're in red short shorts and a T-shirt that says Happy Camper. I cannot take your rage seriously."

And this was where engaging in community service as part of her actual job—thanks a lot, *Flint*—was backfiring on her.

She was a deputy, and the problem was that Sheriff Flint Decker had known her for so long that he was overprotective, and liked to get her off the streets—the mean streets of Jasper Creek, where free-roaming cows were the biggest threat—whenever possible.

And then there was her partner.

The aforementioned man who had ruined her for all other men without even ever touching her once.

He also liked having her off the streets.

Because all of them treated her like she was a little kid.

Even Jackson, who was straight-up mean to pretty much everybody, crossed over into being...*paternally mean* to her.

It was terrible.

It was the cost of having so many men around her who had considered her father a parental figure to them.

"Fine," she relented, because the other thing she had no practice with was opposing her friends. "I'll steal from Duke. But not for the reasons that you think."

"We're friends, Clementine," said Bree. "You have watched us fall, one by one, to these men. Why can't you admit that you like him?"

Because she didn't know how to have these conversations. Because she was, in fact, a virgin, and not just in terms of stealing things.

Because she couldn't figure out how to do this female bonding thing while keeping hold of her pride.

She tended to put a bulletproof vest over all of her feelings. This made her feel vulnerable. And she didn't like feeling vulnerable. Her dad had never known what to do with vulnerable.

No one in her life ever had. So it was basically pull up your bootstraps and zip it. Don't cry about it.

She didn't like…having all these feelings.

The first time she'd realized that Duke Cody affected her, she'd wanted to fling herself out of her camp canoe and into Crow Lake, never to resurface again.

She had been seventeen.

And they had been working together to clean some things up about camp.

She had told him that she was going to go into the academy after she graduated.

"You sure about that, Clem?"

"Don't call me Clem." She reached into the water and picked up a plastic bag that had floated out there to the center. Sometimes the kids were so disrespectful of the environment. It made her mad.

"I'm just saying, do you really want to join up with the department?"

"Yes. I do. It's what I've always wanted to do."

"Why?"

"Because. Because it's what my dad does. Because I'm his daughter. And I want to carry on that legacy. And also because it's me. I care about…about justice and rules… and kindness."

And he'd smiled, sort of an indulgent smile, and it had lit up his blue eyes in just such a way. He'd been twenty-seven. A man already. Broad-shouldered and muscular.

He was wearing his deputy uniform that day. And she loved the way it fit over his body. She just thought he looked good. That he looked sharp.

"I worry about you."

That simple statement had ignited a sort of indignant fire in her belly.

He worried about her, and he shouldn't. He worried about her, and it made her feel special.

He worried about her, and she wished he wouldn't.

And she wished he would.

Forever.

"Anyway," she said. "I am much more focused on getting Gale back for the dedication of the art building. Which was an inspired idea," she said, directing that at Kinley.

"It wasn't really my— I'm sorry. I'm working on taking credit for my accomplishments." There was more of that therapist speak again.

Clementine would *like* to be annoyed by it, but mostly she was just *fascinated*.

What must it be like to have such insight into your own emotions, and to not want to run away and hide from them? She had a feeling she would never know.

"The biggest thing is finding her contact info. I assume you law enforcement people will be able to help with that?" Violet asked.

"Well, sure..." She gave the lawyer some cautious side-eye. "In theory, yes."

Flint could do it, of course, but so could Jackson or Lincoln or Duke. But it was supposed to be a surprise, their contribution to bringing Camp Phoenix back to its former glory.

So it would have to be her.

"I've got it," Clementine said. "I'll go down to the station and take a look as soon as possible. And then...I'm going to steal his football trophy."

"His football trophy?" Violet looked delighted and amused by this. "What football trophy?"

"Well, Duke was basically a juvenile delinquent until he was a sophomore in high school, which was when he got involved with the camp and with my dad, and after that, he became kind of a big football star at the high school. He was

MVP for the championship game one year. And he would never admit it out loud, but he is very proud of that trophy."

"I love it," said Bree.

"It's evil," said Violet.

"It's perfect," said Kinley. And right then and there, she decided that caving to peer pressure actually felt pretty good.

Resolved. Focused. She stood up and crossed her arms, determination and adrenaline coursing through her veins.

"So it's settled, then," she said. "Tonight, I'm going to lose my virginity."

CHAPTER TWO

DUKE CODY WANTED nothing more than to take a drill bit and push it through his ear and pretend that what he'd heard he had *not ever heard.*

He did not ever, ever, ever need to think *virginity* and *Clementine McClain* in the same sentence. And, God Almighty, he did not need to know she was planning on losing it tonight.

With *who*? He knew everything about Clem. He'd known her since she was knee-high to a prairie dog. Frankly, even now she was only about shoulder height to said varmint.

And how in the hell was he supposed to scrub that out of his head? There were things he just didn't need to know about his mentor's daughter, his deputy, his partner, his... his friend, really. Things he *sure as hell* didn't need to know. Whether or not she was a virgin being one of them.

Because—*regrettably*—he had begun to take note of her figure recently, and he was...

He was not on board with his own line of thinking.

The good news was, Duke Cody was comfortable being at odds with himself. He'd been a mess as a kid. He'd put it all away. He'd *reformed.*

So when he and Clementine had gone out to a ranch for a welfare check four months ago—he could remember the exact date—and he'd watched her sit and talk to the elderly

widower who lived there alone, make him a cup of tea…
then she'd smiled.

She'd turned to Duke and she'd smiled.

Right then, it was like the sun had come out from behind the clouds, and he'd realized she was twenty-four and
not fourteen, and that…

Well, that he wanted her to take care of him. It was a
weird, stupid passing thought. He'd always thought he needed
to take care of her. He'd sworn it to Bill on Bill's deathbed.
And he took that seriously.

But watching her sit there with that man, making him
tea…watching her handle that in a deeply empathetic way
he didn't think he ever could, he'd realized she knew more
about some things than him.

Except sex, apparently.

For. God's. Sake.

That she was going to lose her virginity in a time frame
he was now privy to was in no way okay with him. He did
not like it. *Not one bit.* If he hadn't been sent on this dumbass
busy errand by that asshole Jackson, it wouldn't have happened.

But he had been.

*Fuck Jackson. Honestly. Fuck him and his bullhorn
and…*

He walked into the room, holding the drill. "I heard you
might need this," he said.

The girls—all of whom were now shacked up with his
friends, except Clementine, of course—jumped.

"What? You're looking at me like I'm about to axe murder you all."

"Maybe *drill* murder," Kinley said, her tone dark.

"It's to aid in your project, you ungrateful wenches."

"Thank you, Sergeant Cody," said Violet, smiling sweetly.

But it was Bree who took the drill out of his hand and gave it a good buzz. With an easy smile on her face.

Clementine was beet red, and Kinley was looking at him from behind her glasses, her expression vaguely judgy, as if she had somehow sensed that he was wishing ill upon her significant other.

That was the problem, he suddenly realized. All of Clementine's friends were in relationships, and Clementine wasn't. So, she was feeling left out. Maybe she was making a hasty decision. In his mind, he scrolled through the Rolodex of fellow deputies she could be considering for the job.

He did not like it, not one bit. Didn't like a single one of those yahoos.

Clementine was too…*Clementine*.

She defied description. She was tough and sweet and good and could swear like a sailor. She was innocent but effective. There wasn't anyone he could think of who was special enough to be her first.

Except you.

No. Hell no.

"Thanks, Duke," Clementine said, looking almost combative now. "This is our job."

"Yeah, and I got sent to bring a power tool. Are you trying to get rid of me?"

"Yes, because Jackson assigned this to *us*. And we have to stick to the schedule."

He knew Clementine well enough to know that she got more officious when she was uncomfortable.

And she was clearly uncomfortable because of the conversation that had just been happening a few moments before.

"Clem," he said, "can I talk to you outside?"

Her face went through about three different expressions

in the space of a few moments. Her eyebrows shot up, then her mouth flatlined, and then her cheeks went red. "No."

Did she want to get back to getting hot tips on getting laid?

Well, hell and damn, don't think of that.

"Oh, stop it," he said. "You're being childish."

And suddenly, she looked...determined. And he didn't like that any better.

"Yes. I will go talk outside with you."

And then she marched through the cabin and out the front door.

She kicked up a cloud of dust when they got outside. It was dry. Warm. Getting to the middle of June and everything around them was baking. You could smell the bark, the pine. He loved this place. At least, he did *now*.

He could remember being a restless teenage boy couch surfing with his mother from honorary uncle to honorary uncle, never enough food, never any air-conditioning...

He'd hated the summer.

At least until Sheriff McClain had arrested him and, instead of sending him to juvie, had sent him to Camp Phoenix. Where from the time he was thirteen to when he was eighteen, he spent every summer there as a camper, and where thereafter he had spent his summers as a counselor, always making it contingent on whatever job he took that he would get that time. Of course, it was easy, since, at twenty-two, he had landed his job working for the sheriff's department.

Then Bill had died and the camp had fallen out of use and...

Now it was coming back.

And summer felt like it was full of promise again.

He looked down at Clementine, who was gazing up at

him with hazel eyes. Well, right about now, summer felt filled with something a bit scratchy.

"What are your plans for the night?" she asked.

Why the hell was she asking that?

"Poker game."

"Oh. So you'll be out."

"I expect so. We're playing at Jackson's place. You know, he lets us in that hovel and it isn't looking so bad. I think it's Kinley's influence."

"Kinley is still bunking with us."

"I think Kinley sneaks out more nights than she doesn't."

A strange expression washed over Clementine's face. A realization. "I bet no one but me is even spending every night in the cabin."

"That's rough. I thought it was supposed to be sisters before misters and all that."

Her eyebrows went flat. "Wouldn't know. This is kind of my first go-around with the sisters thing. If you can even call us that. I mean, two months ago we didn't even like each other and, well, now they're my best friends." She looked down. Then looked back up at him. "Well. They're great. They're really…they're really amazing. And they've inspired me to make some changes."

He narrowed his eyes. "Really?"

"Yes. I'm…going for things. New things. Adventurous… things."

"Really," he said, crossing his arms over his chest.

She looked up at him and took a step back. "Yes. What the hell is your problem?"

"I don't have a problem. I do not have a problem." And then he turned and left her standing there, and went to find Jackson, Lincoln and Flint.

"I have a problem," he said when he walked into the dining hall and found them all standing around.

"Okay," said Flint. "What's your issue?"

Lincoln leaned against the wall, treating him to a lazy gaze that managed to be questioning at the same time.

Jackson stood at attention, nothing relaxed about him ever.

"I just overheard something."

"Okay," Flint said, tilting his head to the side.

"Yeah."

Flint was technically his boss, but the thing was, Duke didn't really think of it that way, and he didn't think Flint did either. They were suited to two very different aspects of law enforcement. Flint was great at being the driving force in making changes. He was great at that political stuff. Duke had no interest in that. Public relations was not something he ever wanted to be responsible for; he preferred to stick to his beat. He preferred to be out there, physically keeping an eye on everything.

Including Clementine.

When she had joined up with the sheriff's department, her dad had been proud, but worried. And Duke had taken it upon himself to take care of her.

Maybe that was the problem. He still felt like he was trying to rescue her from the hail of bullets. Or in this case, a remedial dick.

Clementine McClain didn't deserve a remedial dick.

She deserved romance and...stuff. He didn't know anything about romance, but she ought to have it. And Jackson was the biggest meddler on earth and he should do something.

"I just overheard Clementine saying that she's planning on losing her virginity tonight," Duke said.

Jackson didn't get mad.

He didn't yell.

He didn't say he'd stop it right away.

Jackson *howled*. He slapped his bad leg and bent over laughing. And Duke could not remember the last time he had ever seen Jackson laugh, much less riotously.

He crossed his arms and glared at his supposed friend. "I'm sorry—this is funny how?"

Jackson straightened, the mirth on his face both evident and irritating. "That you think it's your business."

"You think *everything* is your business, Jackson. How are you laughing at me about this?"

Jackson said nothing. Absolutely nothing. He just chuckled and checked the time, moving his bullhorn into the ready position.

The man was getting laid. That was the problem. He'd been banged into submission.

"Since when is it your policy to not be in everyone's face?" Duke asked.

"Listen," Flint said, suddenly sounding high-handed and like his boss, which was not a thing they did, even though he was Duke's boss. "It isn't your business what she does. I know that you like to protect her because of Bill. And I don't blame you. Bill was a father figure to all of us. And Clementine was his only kid. It's natural that you feel a little bit—"

"She's like a *sister* to me," he said, but somehow, he pictured her face turned up to look at him, and then he thought of that moment four months ago when he'd felt like he'd seen her for the first time. *"Listen."* That was mostly directed at himself. "Because she is like a sister to me, I feel invested in making sure she's not making rash decisions. She's not even dating anybody."

"When was the last time *you* dated anyone?" Lincoln asked in that lazy way of his.

"Irrelevant."

"When was the last time you had sex?" Flint asked.

"Irrelevant."

"It isn't irrelevant," said Jackson. "You have double standards."

"It's not a double standard. If she genuinely hasn't ever— with *anybody*—then I get to be a little bit overprotective."

"No, you don't," said Jackson. "You are going to go and play poker tonight. And you are gonna put all of this out of your head. What she does or doesn't do is not your business."

He tried to internalize that. He tried to internalize it while he finished up at the camp, put his uniform on and did his reduced shift for the day.

He worked pretty much round-the-clock when he was doing the camp stuff. Helping with things at Camp Phoenix, and then always making sure to take some scattered patrols here and there.

He and Flint and Clementine were always on call, just in case. But there wasn't a whole lot of crime for them to worry about, to be honest. They hadn't been called away once all summer, in fact.

But yeah, he was worried about it. He kept imagining it. Some guy kissing her. Putting his hands on her.

It forced him to think of Clementine as a woman. Which she was. It was just that she was a woman he knew so well. Part younger sister, part friend. His partner on the job, but he felt protective of her. Because she was younger, because she had less experience. And yeah, because she was Bill's daughter. It was *complicated*.

He gritted his teeth and he ruminated on it for way the hell longer than he needed to.

And by the time the poker game rolled around, he accepted that he was probably too late to stop anything from happening. And so he was just going to play poker, and he was going to forget about it.

But he was pretty sure he was going to crack his jaw while he was at it.

CHAPTER THREE

SNEAKING OUT OF the camp was something that Clementine had never done before. But she couldn't draw attention; she was going to have to drive to get to Duke's house, and she had to do it while he was still at the poker game. She was going to have to count on him being distracted.

"I'll drive the getaway car," said Bree.

"I'll ride in the getaway car," said Violet.

"I'm also coming," said Kinley, pushing her glasses up her nose.

So that meant she had an entourage for her subterfuge. Their cars weren't parked by the cabin, but rather in a lot some ways away. Which saw them scuttling out of the cabin and down a dirt path that took them past the bathrooms, while they whispered and somehow managed to even shriek in a whisper the whole way.

"You guys are going to blow my cover," said Clementine, clutching the straps of the backpack she was wearing.

It was for the trophy.

Obviously.

"We are *not*. The guys are all busy doing their dumb poker game. This is the best time to do it. And good for you for finding out what his plans were tonight. That was pretty underhanded," said Bree.

"I honestly didn't think I had it in me," Clementine whispered, basking in Bree's approval.

Bree approached her car and tugged the handle, which unlocked it.

They all piled inside. Somehow Clementine ended up in the back seat with Kinley. Violet and Bree were in the front.

Top-bunk and bottom-bunk people. She supposed it was her own fault that she was a bottom-bunk person.

Well. She was *attempting* to be a top-bunk person. Via theft. Maybe that didn't make sense. Maybe it wouldn't make sense to almost anyone. But it made sense to her. Because she had been a good girl. A tattletale. A blank space for someone else's dreams for so long.

She buckled in and gritted her teeth as Bree drove slowly down the dirt road with her headlights off.

"Good thing electric cars are silent," she said. "And good thing I care about the environment. It's advantageous to my goals."

"You're assuming Jackson doesn't have an elaborate security system," said Kinley.

"Does he?" Violet asked.

"He's a man of many secrets," sniffed Kinley. "And talents."

"Jesus take the wheel," said Bree, dramatically removing her own hands from the wheel.

Kinley leaped forward from the back seat and stopped the wheel from turning. "We're going to get *caught*."

Bree put her hands back on the wheel and Kinley settled back by Clementine.

"You know we aren't actually at camp, right?" Violet asked. "It's just a game."

"Feels pretty real when you're hiking up Hollyhock Hill at six in the morning," Clementine grumbled.

And it brought up a whole lot of things that she would rather not deal with. So there was that.

She didn't realize she was holding her breath until they got by Jackson's house without anyone's phone ringing.

And then they were out on the main highway. Footloose and fancy-free.

They drove two minutes down the highway, to the little plot of land that Duke counted as his ranch. She wasn't sure exactly why it was a ranch, but he wore a cowboy hat. And on some level she…

All right. She found that to be compelling. Sexy, even.

That was not a word she would have ever used even to herself just a couple of months ago. But Bree and Violet used those sorts of words easily, and it made Clementine feel risqué and adult.

You are literally wearing a backpack, and shorts, and white tennis shoes with knee-high socks. You in no way look adult. Or risqué.

They pulled up to the house, and Clementine looked around nervously. "You can't park here. You need to drive over to the barn and park out back. I will signal you with my flashlight when I'm ready. If you see anybody pull up, you signal me."

"Orrrrrr," said Bree, "instead of being a good Girl Scout, you can just text, and we can text you."

Well, that seemed anticlimactic.

"Okay," Clementine agreed reluctantly. "Texting. I will try texting."

"You can do it," said Kinley.

There. Her fellow bottom bunker believed in her.

Though, Kinley wasn't even a bottom bunker anymore. In fact, Kinley had pretty successfully top-bunked from the bottom. She had tamed Jackson Hart. She had seen the man naked. Jackson Grumpy Asshole DEA Agent Hart. That was a superpower.

Clementine did not have any superpowers at all.

For a moment, she stared at Kinley, who looked enigmatic and owlish all at once behind her large glasses.

"You're a dark horse, Kinley Parker," Clementine said.

Kinley tilted her head to the side. "I am?"

"Yeah. You were like me. You were on the bottom bunk. And now you're sleeping with Jackson Hart…"

"I'm in love with him," said Kinley. "I'm not—"

"Are you going to tell us that you're not also fornicating with him?" Violet asked.

"Of course I'm not going to tell you that," Kinley said, wrinkling her nose so her glasses inched up slightly. "I'm not going to tell you anything."

Bree snickered.

"Okay," Clementine said. "I'm going."

She bailed out of the car and ran up to the front of the house.

"Please be a cliché, Sergeant," she muttered, as she bent down and lifted up his front mat. There was nothing under it. But he had a flowerpot. A flowerpot with nothing in it just to the right.

"And you call yourself a lawman," she muttered. She lifted up the pot and found a key underneath. She jammed it into the lock and unlocked the door. Then she slipped the key into her pocket as she went inside.

She was going to have to remember to put it back before she left, but she didn't want to leave it in the hole in case she had to bail.

She walked into the dark house and sneaked through the living room, and then back into…his bedroom. She pushed open the door and was assaulted by scents that were uniquely Duke. The detergent that he used, the soap. Probably deodorant. Spicy and utterly familiar to her because she often spent days riding around in the police cruiser with him.

She was so familiar with him, and yet she never got used to him.

And what the hell would he think if he had any idea that when she looked at him, she didn't just see her partner, or a surrogate brother. But…a man.

She was just gradually getting comfortable with the idea herself.

Maybe she should see a therapist. Maybe Kinley had a point there. She didn't like the idea of talking to a stranger, but there was definitely something a little bit wrong with her. Because she absolutely, 100 percent should be completely fine with the idea of wanting to be…*intimate* with someone.

She was twenty-four years old. She was so far past her prime as far as losing her… It was ridiculous. But her dad still lived in her head, and her deep desire to fit in with the boys and not be seen as less. And not being seen as less had somehow translated also into not being a whole being. Not being sexual. And not seeing them as sexual. And then when she was seventeen, Duke had ruined it. Just by existing. By breathing.

And she was standing in his room, pondering his scent, and she needed to get going.

She looked around.

There it was. The trophy. On the back shelf, right above his bed.

That wasn't safe. If Oregon ever had The Big One, the big earthquake that people always talked about, that was going to fall on his head and kill him. She was going to make sure to tell him that, after. After she paraded her spoils through camp. After she was finally initiated. One of the *girls*. Not one of the *boys*.

It felt like a big middle finger to her dad. She loved her dad. But she also felt like he kind of needed a middle finger on this one. She tried not to be angry. He had done the best he could.

But it had created some issues for her.

She moved quickly through the bedroom, not letting her gaze linger on the bed, and then she snagged the trophy.

And stopped. She remembered something. Wasn't that a camp thing? Running someone's underwear up the flagpole? Now, that would be something. She crossed the room to his dresser without even thinking, and then suddenly was confronted with Duke's boxers.

Her mouth went dry. Everything in her freezing up.

What the hell was she doing? She was simultaneously being the most childish she had ever been, while battling the most adult thoughts she'd ever had.

She couldn't handle this.

She picked a pair of plaid boxers up off the top and wrapped them around the trophy. Then she put both in her backpack. And it occurred to her as she went back out into the living room that she hadn't checked her texts, and maybe she should have. So while she walked out into the living room, she reached into her shorts pocket and grabbed her phone, and just as she was about to look at the screen, the front door swung open. And she found herself face-to-face with Duke Cody.

DUKE STOPPED IN the doorway and stared at Clementine. You could've hit him over the head with a shovel and he wouldn't have been any more stunned, because he couldn't be more stunned than he was now.

"What the hell are you doing here?" he asked.

And then he remembered. And then he realized. Fuck. Shit. *Shit*. Clementine had said that she was hell-bent on losing her virginity tonight. Clementine had asked what he was doing.

Clementine was *in his damn house*.

"What are you doing here?" he asked, lowering his voice.

"I... Nothing," she said.

"Nothing. You're in my house, when I'm not in my house..."

Her red hair was braided into pigtails, and she was wearing short red shorts and knee-high socks. And yet she did not look like a child. She looked like a woman. She was often padded out in her police gear, and it did a damn good job of hiding her figure. But the white cotton T-shirt she was wearing now made it very clear that she was a woman with curves. Petite, perfect curves.

He'd love to say this was the first time he'd noticed, but he'd be a liar.

He'd noticed.

Right now he was more than noticing.

Right now there was a wildfire in his living room.

"Clementine," he said. "Clem."

"Don't call me that," she said, that familiar angry expression on her face.

"Listen," he said. "I don't know what the hell— We need to talk."

"We don't. I was actually just leaving. It was stupid. It was really stupid, and you don't need to worry about it. You don't need to worry about me. I am... I was...I was looking for something," she said.

"Were you?" he asked.

"Yes," she squeaked. "I was looking for something of my dad's."

She winced. She was lying. She was a terrible liar. Clementine had never been anything but a goody-goody, and the fact that she was lying was so apparent, it was embarrassing.

"Just be straight with me."

"I can't do that."

"Clementine, I overheard you guys talking earlier today…"

"You know it's stupid. It's so stupid. It was…it was a dare. It was a really stupid dare, and I regret everything. I do. Regret it. I'm going to go."

"Hey," he said, reaching out and grabbing her arm when she tried to move past him.

She looked up at him, her hazel eyes bright, her lips parted. She was breathing heavily.

And something in him stirred.

Heat.

He jumped back like she was a whole bonfire and someone was aiming gasoline right at them. "We should talk," he said.

Because it seemed to be all he was capable of saying. In reality, he should let her run the hell out the door. Because he was being ridiculous. He hadn't had too much to drink. He never did. He was on the straight and narrow.

He was on the straight and narrow as he was supposed to be, and he was lusting after his mentor's daughter. The woman that he had sworn to protect even on the man's deathbed.

Shit.

She had come to him. They had dared her to do this? He was unclear on the details.

The details were probably not going to help.

Maybe not. Maybe not.

"I'm sorry," she whispered. "I was trying to be bold, and not myself."

"Clem," he said, "there is nothing wrong with yourself. And you sure as hell don't need to change to fit in with a group of people. Dammit all, you should know that."

"No, that isn't it. It's just… I have always been so good. I've always *been so good*, and not only that, I have never fit. I was never one of you guys. Not ever. And I was never one of them. I wasn't a camper. But I wasn't one of my dad's special boys either. I'm so glad that you had him. And I love him. I do. But I wasn't special in the same way. Not the way that you were. Not in the same way you *all* were. I was never one of the boys, I was never pretty, I was never—"

"The hell you're not pretty," he said. Because everything be damned. She was pretty. She was beautiful. He might've determinedly not noticed until the past few months, but it had always been true. And he didn't have it in him to hold it back. "You are beautiful, Clementine McClain. Don't ever say that about yourself."

Her eyes rounded, and she blinked. "You think so?"

"Yes."

"Duke…"

"I mean, hell, I'm glad that you had a change of heart. But honestly, if you came in guns blazing…you might've fulfilled your objective."

She frowned. "What?"

"Listen to me. I'm being an idiot. And you know, I didn't even drink at the poker game because I had to drive. I just didn't expect to be in this situation."

He was playing way too close to that bonfire now.

He realized his words had the potential to be the gasoline.

"What do you mean by that?" she whispered.

"I'm just saying, you're beautiful. I can see that you're uncomfortable. I'm not going to push anything. It's just that if you had kissed me…"

He was making a mess of this.

Unless you want to kiss her…

"If I *kissed* you?"

"Yes. I told you, I overheard what you said earlier. That you were planning to lose your virginity tonight."

Her face went white. And she took a step away from him. She looked down at her phone. "Oh, no," she said, seemingly to the screen. And then she looked back up at him. "Sorry. I'm— I have to go."

And then Clementine McClain ran away from him, and out into the dark of night. He stood there for a second, and then he went after her. "Clem!"

"I have to go," she shouted back. He growled and took off after her. But then a car came out from behind the barn, and Clementine jumped in, and off they all drove.

They were all together? What the hell had just happened?

He had no idea. And he didn't know how he was ever going to sort through this whole mess.

CHAPTER FOUR

"HE THOUGHT THAT I came to have sex with him," she screamed as soon as she was in the car.

"What?"

She was satisfied that she'd gotten a reaction out of her three friends. But only a little, because mostly she was horrified.

"He said that he overheard us. Heard me saying I was planning to lose my virginity tonight. And then he walked into his house, and I was there."

It was horrible. Awful. She *burned* with it.

Clementine McClain was the daughter of Jasper Creek's longest-running sheriff. She had never even glanced the edge of a shenanigan, and somehow, she was now positively *pickled* in shenanigans.

"Do you have the trophy?" asked Bree, ever goal oriented.

"Yes. I have his underwear too."

Kinley wrinkled her nose and shoved her glasses more firmly in place. "What's the underwear for?"

"To run up the flagpole, obviously," said Violet.

"Yes, Violet," Clementine said. "To run up the flagpole, of course. But I don't really want to have done any of this, because now I am *going to die*."

"Well, don't die," said Bree. "That would be completely impractical at this stage. Especially if...you are a virgin."

Clementine howled and covered her ears, folding over and putting her face in her lap. "I have never been so embarrassed in my entire life."

"You could just tell him that you don't *want* him to take your virginity," Violet said. "I mean, or you could just tell him he misunderstood and leave the status of your virginity out of the equation altogether. Men get very weird about that stuff."

Well, Violet was right about that. Because the whole conversation with Duke had been weird. Definite evidence of male weirdness surrounding things like virginity.

Except that wasn't fair.

It was a weird topic between *them*.

She and Duke didn't talk about stuff like that.

Mostly because she didn't talk to anyone about that stuff, but also, how could she with him? She remembered vividly the first sexual fantasy she'd ever had.

Her brain had taken that moment in the boat out in the lake and turned it hot and naked. Though, in a gauzy sense, because she had seen shirtless men, sure, but not totally nude men. It had taken her three days to be able to look Duke in the face again.

And now this.

She'd wanted him for seven years. Seven years. She was no closer to having him, or anyone else. She wasn't doing anything.

This was why she was a bottom-bunk person.

She didn't want to be a bottom-bunk person anymore.

"The *problem* is." And this was where she just had to admit it. This was where she just had to be honest. "Well, the problem *is*," she said. "*The problem is*, he said that if I wasn't so freaked out he might actually... He... Duke, who is the most handsome man I have ever seen, said that he would…not be opposed. And the thing is, I kind of wanted to do it."

"Oh," said Kinley.

"Clearly," said Violet.

"Yeah, that is pretty obvious," said Bree.

"So what am I going to do? I feel like I have inadvertently opened the door."

"Clementine's box, so to speak," said Violet.

"Yes. Do I want to close the box, or not?"

"Only you can answer that, C," said Violet.

"You don't think I should close it," she said.

"I'm not out here pressuring anyone into doing anything they don't want to do. However, if you need a little nudge to go do what you really want to do? That I'm here for."

She knew that. She did. They had never peer pressured her into doing anything she didn't secretly want. She wanted to have the rush of stealing the trophy. She wanted to be included.

This wasn't the same, though. This was about taking a long-buried desire and exposing it.

But isn't it the same? You have spent your whole life burying what you want. Trying to be good for your dad. Trying to make him proud.

She squeezed her eyes shut. "It'll make things weird."

"The weird cat is out of the weird bag," said Kinley. "You aren't going to get it stuffed back in."

Kinley had a point. This was why Kinley had graduated from the bottom bunk. Philosophically.

"This is insane," she said. "And I have no idea what I'm doing."

Kinley patted her shoulder. "You can't worry about that, Clementine. You have to worry about what you want and what you're going to get out of it."

What she would be getting out of it? She'd be getting Duke. The thought made her shiver.

Duke. Duke's hands on her body, Duke's lips on hers…

She fought against a feeling of shame as desire mounted inside of her.

She'd been taught to fear this. She'd been taught to suppress it.

Keep a cool head, Clementine. Don't get all female about men.

That had been her sex talk. She had constantly worried her head wasn't cool enough. And that she might be getting *female* about something or another.

And then she had. Gone and gotten female. Looking at Duke, of all people, which she knew would have made her father angry. If he had known…

He just wouldn't have approved. Not of any of it. And yeah, she'd had a complicated relationship with the man. He was the one who had raised her. He was the one who had been there for her in a practical sense. And he had been there for so many other people.

But he should have had a son. Bottom line. Clementine had not been a son. He had been saddled with her after her mother had run off, leaving him with Clementine Anne McClain. A redheaded little girl with a mouthful of a name.

He had never known what to do with her.

Consequently, she had never really known what to do with herself.

But Bree, Violet and Kinley weren't from easy backgrounds. In most cases, they hadn't even had *one* parent who cared about them.

At least Clementine had had that.

But above all else, she had watched these women fight for what they wanted. For what they deserved.

They were brave.

And that had been about deeper things. Love.

But they were fully self-actualized.

They accepted themselves. Violet had grown up in a family of men, and still, she had found a way to embrace her femininity—it was why Clementine had hated her on sight back when they had been teenagers. A woman that comfortable with her own beauty felt like a threat. And like salt in Clementine's wounds. A sign that there was definitely something wrong with her, since, in spite of it all, Violet had found a way when Clementine couldn't.

Then there was Bree, who had clawed her way up and become successful, fashioning something out of nothing, and then finding a way to fall in love with a man who was tangled in the more regrettable parts of her past. And was thriving.

And Kinley...

Kinley, who had not only felt invisible, but had decided to embrace it, had found a way to get the thing her heart desired. And to accept that she deserved it.

She had wrangled the most difficult man of all, and was happy now.

And Clementine didn't think she was standing on the precipice of true love or anything like that, but maybe she was standing on the precipice of a new part of her life.

Their friendship had taught her what was possible. What she wanted. What she could be.

Watching them work through their hardships...

It made her feel like she didn't have an excuse for sitting on her own.

And *there*. She had come to that realization *without* therapy.

"I want him," she said. "Simple as that. I have wanted him for years. I…have never had sex before."

That earned her pats all around. Because of her own behavior—she knew it was because of her own behavior—the girls hadn't liked her back in the day. They had taken her on this time and seemed to feel some form of pity for her, or see her as a mascot maybe. Or at least, that was how she felt. Right now, she felt like it was a little bit of genuine affection driving all of this.

"I'm not a sad dog," she grumped. "You don't need to pet me."

"You're so cute," said Violet.

"I'm *not* cute," she said. "I am an officer of the law. I carry a gun. I once tased a guy running a meth lab out in the mountains."

"So cute," said Bree. "A tiny little badass."

"Well, except in some ways," said Violet. "But you're on your way. You're going to become a sexual badass."

That was a heady thought indeed. But as likely as Clementine finding a unicorn in the woods and taming it, and using it in place of her patrol car. "I think that we are a long, long bridge away from me being a sexual badass."

"How much experience do you have?" Kinley asked.

"None," she said, because she was committed to this, she was in it. And, anyway, wasn't this part of friendship? Sharing all your stuff?

"Right." Kinley tried, and failed, to not look concerned by this. "You know that he isn't opposed to the idea."

"Right. But he's going to have to be into it after he realizes I stole his trophy."

"He's going to realize *that* as soon as he goes into the room. It'll take him longer to realize you stole a pair of boxers."

"Oh, right. I did that." It had only been a few minutes, but the conversation had moved so far downstream that she had kind of forgotten the original intent of the visit.

Not a shock, all things considered.

"I'm driving us over to Medford," said Bree decisively.

"Seriously?" Clementine asked. "It's, like, eleven o'clock at night. Why are we going over there? It's, like, an hour drive."

"Because we deserve milkshakes. And there is a twenty-four-hour fast-food drive-in, and we are going to get ice cream. Because you, Clementine McClain, have committed your first theft. And you are going to have sex. And that needs to be celebrated."

There was so much feminine energy all around her. And everybody was happy for her. Happy with this. No one was looking at her like there was something wrong with her. Like her needing a bra was embarrassing, or her needing pads required a phone call to one of her dad's ex-girlfriends, because it was just too much for him to bear.

She swallowed hard. "Thank you," she said, her throat tight. "I would love to celebrate that."

CHAPTER FIVE

WHEN HE WOKE up the next morning, he realized his trophy was gone.

And then he felt like an ass.

His trophy was gone because Clementine had taken it. And while he didn't know the finer points of everything that the girls got up to, he did know that Bree had stolen from Flint, Violet had stolen from Lincoln, and Kinley had stolen Jackson's bullhorn and cane, which had caused a full-scale riot. Which had been turned into something else.

Clementine had stolen his football trophy.

So was it some kind of bizarre mating ritual on their part, or was it just a thing they did, that had happened to become...?

Regardless. He had a feeling that was actually what she had been there for. And he needed to have a talk with her.

He wasn't embarrassed. He just felt like a dick. Because he had all but told her last night that if she wanted to go for it, he'd be all in. And what the hell was that? He checked out her rack one time and now suddenly he wanted to jump into bed with her?

He was better than that.

She was Clementine. She was...

You spend an awful lot of time telling yourself what you think she is, like that doesn't mean something.

He shoved that thought aside.

She was wonderful. He cared about her.

But that was it.

Duke's own family had been such a shit show. He had never seen a single example of functional love in his life. He didn't know who his father was; he didn't think his mother knew either.

One of those surfers was really tall, she had said once, casually. *Maybe you'll be tall*.

He *was* tall. So maybe the tall surfer was his dad. Or maybe the cowboy who reminded her of the Marlboro Man, who had picked her up from a truck stop when she was hitchhiking.

He had always sort of hoped it was him, just because he fancied himself a little bit of a cowboy, and he liked to think that maybe he had inherited something from the father he never knew. Why? Because at least he could pretend his dad had gone on to be somebody respectable.

He didn't know anything about his mother, and where she was now. It all felt like abandonment.

So it didn't really matter.

But yeah. When it came to functional families and finer feelings, he didn't know anything about that. He threw himself into what he did know. Into what Bill McClain had taught him about being a man.

Because that was what mattered. Being a good man. Taking care of those who needed taking care of. Being willing to put your life on the line for someone else. Devoting all that you were to service. That was what he had learned from Bill, and it resonated within him now.

Just take care of Clementine, he'd said, the last words that Bill had ever spoken to him. *She thinks you're something special*.

Yeah. Well, what did she think of him now?

He really needed to find her. Thankfully, it was five thirty in the morning, which meant he had to start heading over for the hike up Hollyhock Hill. He knew exactly where he would see her and when.

He put on jeans and a T-shirt, a cowboy hat, and got into his car, making the quick drive over to the camp.

By the time he got assembled at the bottom of the hill, Lincoln and Violet, Bree and Flint, and Kinley and Jackson were there, along with the staff and volunteers—who Jackson treated all the same. Jackson was looking at his watch, his bullhorn tightly gripped in his left hand.

Clementine was on notice.

But this was also the clearest indicator to Duke that none of the women had spent the night in the cabin they were supposed to be in last night.

And then Clementine came sprinting out from the trail that came from her cabin. "I'm not late!"

Her red hair was loose, which it really was, in a tangle around her. She was wearing a white T-shirt with the Camp Phoenix logo on it, and some blue short shorts this time.

She never wore shorts normally, because she was normally in uniform. And he had been getting quite an eyeful of her legs these last couple of months. Maybe that was half the problem.

Yeah. Her legs. That's the problem. Like you've never seen legs before.

They weren't just legs. They were *Clementine's* legs.

And suddenly, he imagined what it would be like to feel them wrapped around him…

He blinked. Hard. Like it might push the image from his head.

It didn't.

"No," said Jackson. "You weren't late."

And they all started the hike up the hill. It didn't escape Duke that this was twice as much work for Jackson as it was for anyone else. And that kind of summed him up in general. He was a hard-ass, but there wasn't a damn thing he asked of anybody that he wasn't doing himself even more.

It was what he had always respected about Jackson.

He moved himself over to where Clementine was, huffing and puffing up the hill more than she normally would be because she had gotten to the base of Hollyhock Hill on a dead sprint.

"Did you oversleep?"

"Yes," she said angrily.

He could see that she was carrying the same backpack she'd had on last night. His trophy was in there. He realized that now.

The trophy, which was what she'd come for.

Not his...

"Listen," he said. "I think I might've gotten it wrong last night."

She didn't say anything, and that made him question... everything.

"You were there to steal my trophy, weren't you?" he pressed.

She nodded once.

"I *heard* you say that you were going to lose your virginity."

She slowly turned from pale freckles, to pink freckles, to raspberry freckles before his very eyes.

"It was...my *theft* virginity," she said, as if that was perfectly reasonable.

"Oh."

He was grateful that everybody else had gotten several paces ahead of them, and were loudly talking about plans for the day, because, Lord Almighty, he didn't need an audience for this. He wasn't even sure *he* wanted to be an audience for this.

"So. Yes. You got it…wrong. I—"

"It's in your backpack, isn't it?"

She wrinkled her nose. "Yes."

"I can arrest you. Breaking and entering. Larceny—"

"Larceny," she said. "Over a trophy and a pair of underwear?"

"It wasn't grand larceny, but it was a small larceny." Suddenly he fully heard what she'd said. "You stole my underwear?"

The red in her cheeks deepened. "I… Well. Yes."

"Why?"

"To run up the flagpole. Which I was going to do this morning, but then I overslept."

He laughed. He couldn't help himself. "Why were you going to run my underwear up the flagpole?"

"Because it's embarrassing," said Clementine.

"Oh, Clem, that wouldn't have embarrassed me when I was fourteen, around the time it's intended to be embarrassing, and it certainly isn't going to embarrass me now."

"It would embarrass me," she mumbled.

He had never seen Clementine as a prude. She managed to keep up with the raucous conversation going on around her at all times.

But… He realized she was never sharing anything about herself.

"It would?" he asked.

"I'm just not… I don't know. Whatever. I don't want to talk about it. The whole thing was a misunderstanding?"

She looked at him, and there was a question in her eyes. Bright and intense, and he was afraid.

For one moment.

Afraid of what it meant.

Because, just like his whole reality had been turned upside down when he'd thought maybe he wanted something from her, rather than just standing guard over her, it felt flipped now.

"Why are you asking me like that?"

"Well, because you said…" She suddenly looked fiery, filled with determination, as if she was calling upon some kind of power inside of her. "You said that if I kissed you, you would be tempted to take me up on it. And I know why you thought I was there. So is that true?"

Straight fire lit through his veins, like he had taken a shot of whiskey. "Clementine…I went through all of yesterday thinking that you were going to go sleep with some random guy, and when you showed up at my house…I thought maybe you were there for me. And so…"

"Were you looking at it as a duty, or did you actually want to do it?"

"This is not something we should be talking about here."

"It's an easy question. I feel a little bit female over you. Do you feel male over me?"

"What the hell does that mean?"

"Something my dad said to me. He said don't go getting female over men. Here I am. I feel female about it."

"Fucking hell, Clem. I've known you since you were like three years old."

"And you've known me a lot of years when I wasn't three. I like to think that we're friends in our own right."

"We are." He nodded. "Partners."

"You know that I'm not weak. You saw me tase the meth lab guy."

"I did. And it scared years off my life when you went after him. I was afraid he was going to shoot you."

"But he didn't. Because I can take care of myself. Because I am an adult. Because I am a woman. And I am tired of pretending that I'm not."

"Have you been pretending that you're not?"

She closed her eyes and stopped walking. The breeze whipped up and fluttered through her hair, a golden, strawberry halo around her head.

"My dad didn't like to deal with that part of me. He was great. With you boys. But he wanted a son, Duke, and his relationship with all of you is evidence of that. He was fine with me. As long as I didn't remind him that I wasn't one of the guys. But I wasn't. I never have been. I've always been just a little outside of that group, and a little outside of, well, Bree and Violet and Kinley. I wasn't ever a camper, and I wasn't one of his special projects."

"You were his daughter," he said, momentarily forgetting the undertone of the conversation. "Nobody else belongs to him like you did. He loved you so much, Clem."

"Don't call me that. It's a boy's name, and I am not a boy, and it isn't my fault that my mother, who couldn't even bother to stick around, gave me a name with three syllables that nobody wants to say."

"Clementine," he said, starting again. "Your dad loved you."

"I know. That's what makes it worse. That's what makes it worse to be so mad at him. To want to just…rebel against him. But I grew up being embarrassed about needing a bra, and having a period, because my dad was embarrassed by it. And I grew up embarrassed to ever have a crush on any of the boys, because he made me feel like it was embarrassing. And so when I started to notice that you were handsome, I just thought I had to shut it down, and… If I had a chance to not do that, to not shove it down, well, then I want to do that. Because I was brave, and I stole the damn trophy from you. Because I'm trying to not be *that* Clementine. I want to be a brave Clementine."

He couldn't help it. He chuckled. "That makes it sound like you're trying to be a brave little orange."

She scowled. "I am not a little anything."

"You are, though. But that's all right. I know you're not a kid. I'm not blind to the fact that you're beautiful. Clementine…" He let out a long, hard sigh, a breath that felt like it had been lodged in his chest since last night. Or maybe for the last four months. "I'm attracted to you. But I also promised your father that I would protect you."

"Is sex going to *injure* me in some way?"

"Not the way you mean. But it's a *thing*, Clementine. And there are potentially heavy consequences that come with it. And it changes things."

"Has it ever changed anything for you before?"

"Look around us. Do you see all of our friends and how they paired off?"

"Yes," she said, and he could tell that her throat was dry.

"That won't happen. Because I can't…do that. It changed things for them, but you're right—it's never changed anything for me before. I've never been in a relationship. But I've had a lot of sex. So…it's pretty easy for me to separate the two."

"Maybe it is for me too. It is for some women. Besides, how many people get with the first partner they ever have? What I need is to deal with this. What I need is to get over this. And I trust you. So it seems to me like it's not a bad proposition."

"We'll meet tonight after the bonfire, okay?"

"Okay."

And he didn't know what the hell he was thinking, what the hell he was getting himself into; he didn't know where he was leading them.

Except, as he watched Clementine continue up the hill, he had the vague sensation that he wasn't leading them anywhere. It was her.

CHAPTER SIX

CLEMENTINE WAS BREATHLESS by the time they finished the hill climb, and she brandished his trophy for all to see. She kept the boxers in the bottom of her backpack. She decided to go ahead and *not* tell anybody about that.

But by the time she and Bree and Violet and Kinley were alone, headed to the now fully renovated art hall to take inventory and figure out what additional supplies they would need, and to discuss ways to include Gale in the re-dedication of the camp, she was nearly bursting with what had happened between her and Duke.

"He's attracted to me," she said as they looked around at all the storage and Bree made notes of where potential inventory could go.

They already had pottery wheels, a kiln, easels, bins and drawers, and were now figuring out how many beads, canvases, paints and other things they might want.

"He's attracted to you," Kinley said, smiling. "That's great news."

"Is it, Kinley? *Is it?*"

Kinley stared at her from behind her glasses. Which she supposed everyone who wore glasses did, but Kinley had a particular way of making it feel notable. As if the glasses magnified something you wished you could hide. "If you want to succeed at your gambit, yes."

"I don't *know* if I want to succeed in my gambit. I told

him that it was fine. That I just wanted…to rip the Band-Aid off, you know? And in some ways, that's true. In some ways, I just want to do it. Because I have been so disconnected from that part of myself. I have been so…"

She faced Bree and Violet head-on. "The reason that both of you rubbed me the wrong way back in the day was because you were both so…comfortable with yourselves. You're both so pretty, and you have no embarrassment about it, or concern. And it just—"

She stopped because Bree and Violet were laughing.

"Don't have *any concern*?" Bree shook her head. "Everybody, especially every teenager, is wildly insecure. The question is, which mask do you put over that insecurity? Is it invisibility?" She gestured toward Kinley. "Or is it being a little tattletale?" She looked at Clementine. "Or maybe it is trying to look as polished and pretty and okay as possible, so nobody knows what a mess you are inside. Or spending ten years ignoring the man who arrested you and internally calling him Sheriff Dicker, but the point is, everybody is insecure, Clementine. On some level. At some point in their life."

"Really?"

"Yes," said Violet. "Because life is hard. Because there is no handbook for it. Because when you grow up missing essential building blocks to make you into something less than a feral monster, you have some issues."

"I have issues," said Clementine. "I wanted to please my dad, and that's why I was a tattletale, and you all intimidated me—well, not you, Kinley, but I didn't like you either—and I just… It's because I wanted to be one of you."

"Did it ever occur to you that maybe we would've rather been you?" Kinley asked. "Your dad was always around."

"He was," she said. "Which makes me feel really guilty

about the fact that I've been feeling angry at him. Because part of this whole not understanding how to embrace being a woman, and having a sexuality, is about how he made me feel like it would intrude on his life if I did. It was very clear that he wanted to put a big old wall around it so that he never had to worry about it."

"Is that why you're a virgin?" Violet asked.

She would love to say yes. But it wasn't that simple. "Maybe partly. But Duke is another part of that. I think I sort of…imprinted on him? And because he's around me all the time, it's just… I can't think about sex without thinking about Duke. Apart from Aquaman. So, things are complicated."

"Look," said Violet. "Regardless of the outcome, an exorcism is clearly required."

"An *exorcism*. Well, that sounds intense."

"Sometimes it's intense, Clementine," Bree said, gently enough that it made Clementine nervous.

"I'm just saying. You need to do something about this. And you weren't ready, or you wouldn't be angry about being held up until now," Violet said. "Believe me. I'm very aware of how anger works."

And that was the truest thing. She wouldn't be angry if she didn't want this. If she didn't need it. She really felt like she needed it.

"He told me to meet him tonight."

"Well, meet him," said Bree. She looked around the space. "We need to get a sign made. The Gale Lawson Art Hall."

"Agreed." Clementine wrinkled her nose, and realized it was a mannerism she had picked up from Kinley. "I'll go to the station tomorrow and I'll look up the info. Then I'll get in touch with her."

"Perfect," said Violet, reaching out and hugging her. Clementine wasn't used to that kind of thing. Casual gestures of affection. But she liked it.

And it was okay that she liked it. It was okay if it made her soft.

It was okay to be soft.

It was okay to have desire.

It was okay that she wanted Duke.

And tonight, she was going to have him.

CHAPTER SEVEN

SHE DECIDED THAT she needed to go into the station that afternoon to get Gale's information. Because whatever was going to happen tonight...

Well. She might end up distracted.

The idea made her warm.

She hadn't put her uniform on to go in, which felt strange. But she had ditched the camp shorts and T-shirt, exchanging them for a pair of black skinny jeans and a plain white shirt. She felt a little bit hot, but wearing shorts just felt wrong.

And she hadn't gotten to the point where she felt comfortable in skirts or dresses yet. She was working on that.

But most especially, she would not be working on it in this context.

There was nobody around, which wasn't unusual. They were a small crew, and while this building served a few specific purposes, people didn't linger in it.

Especially not with how mobile all technology had become.

She decided to use the little cubby that served as Duke's office to do her search.

She pulled up the software required and got the contact info. Then she took a deep, shaking breath and took the landline out of the cradle. She dialed the number listed there for Gale.

"Hello?" An unfamiliar but pleasant-sounding voice answered the phone.

It wasn't Gale.

"Is Gale available?"

"Oh, yes. She's out in the back. Just a second." The other woman put Clementine on hold, and then returned just a second later. "Here she is."

And suddenly, Clementine felt...uncertain.

Gale was another person she had always wanted to be close to. But again, she hadn't been a camper. So while she had gone into the arts and crafts hall sometimes and put things together, she had always felt on the outskirts. But Gale had always been unfailingly kind and welcoming to her. It was one of those things that she would never forget.

"Hi. This is Clementine McClain, from Camp Phoenix."

"Clementine," she said. "Bill's daughter."

"Yes. Bill's daughter."

"I saw the news about your dad. I'm so sorry. He was a good man."

"Yes. He was."

Except it was just not enough words. And there wasn't enough time. There never would be. To say everything that he hadn't been to her. To get through all of it.

"We're reopening Camp Phoenix. Jackson Hart is spearheading it. I don't know if you remember him. He was one of the campers a long time ago..."

"I remember. Oh, Jackson, he was always..."

"A whole thing? He still is. But he brought some of us back together, and we are aiming to make the opening of the camp big. And we have a surprise for you, Gale. Because you mean so much to everyone. If you could make it out, we would be thrilled."

"I'd love to. The kids will be out of school then. If you

wouldn't mind if my whole family came. Candy and I adopted four teenagers a few years ago. It's been an interesting experience. But...our house is sort of the camp now."

"That's great. Really good."

"Just give me the details, and I'll be happy to arrange to come out."

"Thank you. Everyone's going to be thrilled."

"You know...if my family is up to it, and you don't have plans...I might be able to do more than just come for a visit."

Clementine listened to Gale's suggestion and was thrilled that the older woman was up for running the art program this summer. Otherwise, Bree and Violet would have been spearheading that, and Clementine had concerns about anatomical penguins.

There. She had done that. And she wrote down Gale's contact information so that she could send an official invitation, and get in touch with her again if she needed to.

She was so focused on what she was doing that she didn't hear the footsteps approach her. And when she finally had the sense that someone might be watching her, she looked up and saw Duke standing in the doorway.

"What are you doing here?" she asked.

"I might ask you the same thing. I came to pick up a couple of things."

"I was just..." She grabbed the notebook she had made notations on and pushed it underneath a stack of paper that was sitting there so that he wouldn't be able to see what she'd written down. They were committed to this being a surprise.

"What?"

"It's a surprise."

"A surprise?"

His lips turned up into a smile, his blue eyes twinkling dangerously.

"Let me see it."

"I will not," she said. "It'll compromise the surprise. Which, anyway, is not entirely mine, so I couldn't show you even if I wanted to."

"Come on now."

"No."

She stepped in front of the desk, just as he approached her, and suddenly, they both realized that they were breathing the same air. And everything seemed to stop.

His eyes went from twinkling to glittering, and there was a difference. There was something dangerous about this. Something foreign.

She couldn't recall him ever looking at her like this. But then, she couldn't recall anyone ever looking at her like this before.

"Duke…"

He kicked the door shut and moved closer to her, putting his hands on either side of her on the desk. He was so close, she could feel the heat radiating off his body.

She could smell him. His skin. Like the pines and sun-warmed park outside. Like the earth.

Duke.

There had never been another man who had meant quite so much to her, and she had spent so much time surrounded by men.

She had said to him that she was feeling female about it all. But that made it sound like it was generic. Like it could be anyone. Any man. And she knew that it couldn't be. Not ever.

It was Duke Cody for her, and that had been true since she was seventeen.

She didn't know what that meant in terms of emotional feelings. Love feelings. She cared a lot about Duke.

What she was absolutely clear on was that she was attracted to him.

And had never once been attracted to anyone else in the same way. Not even close.

In this moment, the second seemed to stretch on.

The glory of being near him. So close that she could see the beginnings of a five-o'clock shadow, so close she could study the blade-straight nose, sharp jawline and lips that curved when everything else was so uncompromising.

His face was so familiar, but not like this. Not set with intent so close to hers.

And she found herself lifting her hands, following some instinct that she didn't even know she possessed, pressing them against the hard wall of his chest, his muscles. She could feel his heartbeat raging there, and a surge of feminine power that she had never felt before in all her life went through her.

"Duke," she whispered.

And then he did something she'd never heard him do before. He growled. Full-on growled. He took his hands from the surface of the desk, wrapped his arms around her, pulling her against his body as he lowered his head and kissed her.

It was an inferno. The conflagration. The ignition of a deadly wildfire the likes of which she had never experienced before.

It was so hot. All-consuming. And her concerns about her inexperience were lost. Because Duke took a commanding lead, parting his lips and slipping his tongue into her mouth, sliding it against hers in a sensuous rhythm that sent a shiver of need all through her.

She followed his example. She met his every move with one of her own.

For all that Clementine often felt confused, she was never passive.

It was what had made her a horrendous tattletale. But also a hard worker. It was what had gotten her the job with the sheriff's department. It was what had brought her here.

She might not be certain about a whole lot of things, but she believed in action, and right now, she was exemplifying that.

They were supposed to meet at the bonfire tonight, but this felt right. Better. They would have to talk. She knew that they would.

But she didn't want their first time to be a summit. Didn't want it to be carefully planned.

This was happening, and it seemed to her that he was as lost in it as she was.

And later, much later, she would want to know all about that. When it had changed for him. She would have to return the favor and say when it had changed for her, she supposed. But that was fine. All right.

Her friendship with Bree and Violet and Kinley had taught her a little bit about sharing.

Had filled in some of the gaps inside of her.

She was a bit regretful that she was in skinny jeans.

But then, it didn't matter, because he pushed his hands up beneath her shirt, and his rough, hot palms skimmed over her back as he pushed the T-shirt up over her head, leaving her there in her rather serviceable white bra.

But she wasn't embarrassed, she couldn't be, because he looked at her like he was having a revelation. He didn't look at her like she was a project or a mousy virgin.

He didn't look at her like she was a pain in the butt.

Duke never had.

He was one of the few people who had never looked at her and made her feel like she didn't belong. Like he wished she would go away.

Duke was one of the few people who had always made her feel like she had a right to be exactly where she was, exactly how she was.

She wasn't comfortable with the idea of losing any more clothes before he lost some of his. So it was her turn to take off his T-shirt and give thanks he hadn't arrived in uniform. Just a white T-shirt of his own and some blue jeans. Looking sexy as hell, and she loved it.

She looked at his body, well muscled and covered with just the right amount of hair, and put her hands back on his chest, rubbing them over every inch of him.

She wanted him. And she wasn't ashamed of that.

He was making her melt. And she wasn't ashamed of that either.

She felt like a woman. And that didn't seem like a bad thing. Right now, it seemed strong. Right now, it seemed like the best thing.

He undid the snap on her jeans and lowered the zipper slowly, then pushed them down her hips.

She was in a pair of underwear as plain as the bra, and yet again, he looked at her like she might as well have been a scenic viewpoint off the Oregon coastal highway. Meaning that she was pretty damn amazing. And she had never felt quite so powerful while she trembled.

Had never felt so strong while she felt so weak.

Had never felt so fulfilled even while feeling lacking. Because her breasts felt heavy and they hurt, and her nipples were pulled into two tight points. Because she was wet and hollow between her thighs.

She was a woman well accustomed to taking care of her own needs.

She was twenty-four and eternally single. She'd figured out how to handle her own needs.

She knew what was happening to her. She was *aroused*. Beyond anything she had ever experienced.

But the difference between this and handling her own needs was that he was in control. It wasn't up to her to touch exactly where she wanted, when or how fast. It was up to him. And the idea of surrendering herself like that was… intoxicating. But terrifying.

And one thing she knew for certain—she couldn't have done it with someone else.

Maybe this was just a stepping stone. Maybe this was just flinging herself out into the sort of life where she could do this thing casually. But it couldn't be casual this time. Not this time.

He put his hands on her hips and pulled her forward, letting her feel the hardness of his arousal straining against the front of his jeans.

And it was her turn.

She undid his jeans and lowered the zipper. And she couldn't help herself. She put her hand inside, against the front of his boxers, feeling the shape of him there.

He was thick and hard.

And promised to be so much bigger than she had imagined. But in fairness, she hadn't really had an idea of *scale*.

She was *an innocent*, after all.

Yeah, a total innocent. She internally rolled her eyes at her own ridiculousness.

She swallowed hard.

"Okay," he said, his blue eyes on hers. And she knew

that it would be okay, because it was Duke, and Duke would never tell her anything that wasn't the God's honest truth.

Even now. Even in this.

"Just a second," he said through gritted teeth.

He locked the door, the shades to the office already drawn.

Then he crossed the room and opened up a cabinet. There was a blanket folded in there that they sometimes used when they had to bring victims in, and they needed something for comfort.

It was always freshly laundered and put back in between. And she was thankful that it was there.

He took it out and spread it on the floor, bringing her down with him, kissing her as they went.

She was grateful they weren't going to try to get acrobatic on the desk or with her against the wall. She might want to try that eventually, but it was beyond her right now. She felt *passionate* enough for that.

She did not feel like she possessed the skill for that.

He made quick work of her bra, and her underwear, and she was amazed at how *not* embarrassed she was. How right it felt.

For him to look at her like this. Because he was Duke, and she cared about him. Because she could see how much he cared about her when he took off his jeans and underwear. She gasped.

"I hope that's a good thing," he said.

"It is, but...I'm a bit concerned. About...fit."

"Trust me," he said, his grin turning wicked. He kissed her again, then down her neck, down to her breasts, where he circled one nipple with his tongue.

It was the most wicked, wonderful thing she could have ever imagined, and she felt transported. She moaned and arched up off the blanket, and he used his other hand to tease the nipple he wasn't paying attention to with his tongue.

She was on sensory overload, and then he moved away from her breasts, continued down her body. He grabbed hold of her hips and pulled them up toward his mouth, and that was when he pressed a kiss to the most intimate part of her. Before looking deep, devouring her.

She felt like she was coming out of her skin. This was so much more carnal. So much dirtier than she had ever imagined.

She had thought someday she would probably find somebody to have sex with, but she didn't think that it was going to be *this*. Uninhibited, incredible. Earthy and beyond thought.

But it was Duke. So it was good. So it felt right. And when he pushed a finger inside of her and began to work her gently with a steady rhythm that complemented what he was doing with his mouth, she began to lose sight of everything. Any embarrassment she might've felt. The earth. Everything.

He added another finger, stretching her, building the desire inside of her. He kept on teasing her, tormenting her.

And she pushed her fingers through his hair, holding him there. She said his name like a prayer. Maybe to remind herself that this wasn't a fantasy. That this was real. And it was him.

This was everything she had ever wanted all along.

And then she shattered. Because of Duke.

Everything felt hazy, and she wasn't entirely sure where he got the condom from, but thank God he had one. He opened it and rolled it over his length, and she felt a shiver of sensual desire watching him move his hand intimately over himself.

She was embarrassed just thinking of it, but someday, she'd like to ask him to touch himself in front of her. It seemed only fair since she had spent an inordinate number of years touching herself and thinking about him.

Then he came back over her, kissing her.

The head of his arousal pressed firmly against the entrance to her body.

She panted, trying to relax as he entered her. She was wet and slick, but he was big. And a lot to take in at once.

But she wanted to. Needed to. Because she needed this. When he was fully inside her, she gasped, gripping his shoulders and wrapping her legs around his waist.

He sank in just a bit deeper when she did that, and she let her head fall back as another release tore through her. He hadn't really even started to move yet. And then, when he did, everything in her fractured.

She didn't know if she was saying his name out loud or if it was simply echoing inside of her. She wasn't sure it mattered.

Because she had lost all inhibition. Because she had lost all embarrassment.

Because there was only this. Only need.

He moved in and out of her. Over and over again. And she felt pleasure impossibly building inside of her for the third time.

"Clementine," he said.

Clementine.

Not Clem.

Her whole name.

And this was all of her. Being tough and innocent and a woman—and his.

And that was when she shattered again, right with him, as he posted deep inside of her and said her name again.

She dug her fingernails into his skin, and the release seemed to go on and on for both of them.

And when it was over, she was acutely aware of the fact that they were lying naked on the floor of his office, of all places.

And it was the strangest thing, how she had managed not to have sex for twenty-four years, but the minute that door was open between her and Duke, she had sex in less than twenty-four hours.

Yeah. It was really something.

"Clementine…"

"I'm glad," she said. "I'm glad it happened like that. We can talk later. But I'm glad that… Anyway, I really do need to get dressed and get back, and let everybody know how my surprise is going."

Because suddenly, she did feel a little embarrassed. Suddenly, she did feel a little vulnerable.

Suddenly, she felt a little hedonistic, and a lot like maybe she had overplayed her hand or exposed herself, exposed just how much she felt for him. She had to think about that. Whether or not she cared. Whether or not it mattered to her if he knew how much she cared.

She never would have slept with him if she didn't care. She just wasn't like that. She couldn't have. And the truth was, she had never been with anybody in part because of the different issues that she had with her father, and with her femininity, and with everything, really. But the other piece was him. It simply always had been.

Right now, she didn't know how to say that. She wasn't even sure how to feel it.

Because right about now she felt stronger than she ever had, and a little bit like she was breaking apart inside.

And then he reached out and wrapped his arms around her, pulled her to him. "Are you gonna tell me what the secret is?" He had a dopey grin on his face that was sexier than it had a right to be. She just found that annoying.

She hit his arm. Which was solid as a rock. And sent a pulse of desire through her.

"No," she said. "Because it's not a secret. It's a surprise. That's different."

"How is it different?"

"A secret sounds sneaky. For the sake of sneakiness. A surprise is supposed to bring you joy."

"You have brought me joy already."

"Duke," she scolded.

"Clementine," he returned.

"Well, it's just… It is just that… It was just that…"

"What, Clementine?"

"I don't know. I can't think straight right now."

And that much was true. She wasn't sure that she had the brainpower to form even one coherent thought.

"You don't need to think," he said. "But you do need to get dressed. Because I don't relish the idea of being caught in here like this, and frankly, Flint would flip his wig."

"Oh, no," she said. "I couldn't handle being caught by Flint."

"You and me both. The last thing I need is him going high or heavy-handed on me. I don't like the guy enough to take that. And our relationship would erode."

She scoffed. "Well. That's a lie. You do like him."

"Sure. But not enough to take a lecture. Your dad was about the only person that I liked well enough to…" He stopped talking, as if he knew this was not a great time to bring up her dad. Or maybe it was. Maybe it was.

She slowly dressed, and then collected the notebook that she had slipped beneath the stack of paper on his desk. She shoved it into her pocket and shot him a warning glance.

He was also dressed, which was a real shame. Because she had liked the look of him.

"Well, I've got this. So…it's time for me to go."

"Clementine," he said. And then he crossed the room and wrapped his big hand around the back of her head, held her still while he leaned down to kiss her. But it wasn't an all-consuming sexy kiss. It was soft. Slow. It made her tremble. Took her breath away.

"We'll talk tonight."

"Yes, we will," she said.

Then she scurried to her truck before she melted on the floor.

That was perhaps the biggest feat of all.

Well. That and the fact that Clementine McClain was no longer a virgin.

CHAPTER EIGHT

WHEN FLINT WALKED into the department about a half hour after Duke had debauched Clementine *on the floor*, Duke did his best to keep any guilt off his face.

He didn't need to feel guilty about what had happened. He stood by it. He cared about Clementine, and if the care had taken the shape of sex, well, she had said it herself. It wasn't like he was going to injure her.

Of all the disingenuous bullshit.

Whatever. He was a man. Men were well-known for making excuses that allowed them to get laid.

Wow, try again, douchebag.

"Hey," said Flint, looking him over, something speculative in his eyes.

"Hey."

"Why do you look like you just got caught shoplifting by Sheriff McClain?"

Dammit. This was the problem with having family, even if it wasn't genetic family. The kind of family that you cobbled together through hardship and the good luck of having a mentor like Bill McClain.

They knew you. And when they knew you, they could see things about you. When they could see things about you... Well. Well.

"No reason at all. I just popped in to look at something on my computer really quick."

"Well, do be quick about it. Bonfire is not long from now. And you know how Jackson feels about people missing his scheduled events."

Duke shook his head. "I don't. Because I've never missed one, and I don't think anyone's ever seen a person who did. Jackson probably disappears them."

"Entirely possible. If I were you, I wouldn't go testing his humors."

"Absolutely not. So I'll just wrap up and head back that way."

He cleared his throat. "I saw Clementine leaving here about half an hour ago."

"What were you doing, loitering out in the parking lot for a half hour?"

"I wasn't. I drove into town and came back this way. Why are you defensive?"

"Are you digging for information? Do you actually want this information?"

"I don't know. I guess it depends on what's going on."

"Nothing. Nothing you want to know about. I just wanted my football trophy back."

"That's your official story?"

He looked his friend dead in the eye. "That is my official story, Flint."

"Well, as your boss, I must say that I'm pleased to hear that."

"You're not my boss."

"But I am."

"But we don't treat it that way."

"But *I* am," said Flint. "I am your boss. So, as your boss, I'm thankful that's the only story you have to tell me. As your friend, bullshit."

"Who said you were my friend? I don't have any need for friends."

Flint tilted his head back and rolled his eyes. "Oh, yes, there's the Duke Cody of old. No need for friends. No need for nothing. No creature comforts, no human connection…"

"Yeah, well, I know better than that now. Okay? I was just kidding. Obviously you guys are my friends. And Bill was like a father to me. And Clementine…"

"Is like a sister to you," said Flint, his face deadly serious. "Except she isn't, is she?"

He stood there for a long moment. He wasn't ready to divulge the details of what had happened between him and Clementine. It wouldn't be fair to her. Quite frankly, it would be distasteful. What had happened between them was between them. He wasn't about to tell Flint what they'd done on the floor of his office.

But the thing was, he wasn't the Duke Cody of old. He had been so closed off to people, to connection, to anything, when he had first come to Camp Phoenix. Opening him up had been like shucking an oyster. And it hadn't been pretty. He'd come a long way. When he had been thirteen years old, he'd have said that he hated people. That he didn't see any good in the world.

And sometimes it was easy for him to roll around playing the part of a cynical, world-weary man, but he wouldn't be in law enforcement if he didn't think, in some capacity, small changes could be made in the world. He knew they could. He knew because Sheriff Bill McClain had taken him in and made all the difference in the world in his life. Because he had watched himself, Flint, Jackson and Lincoln change. Because he had watched kids who had come through Camp Phoenix change. Violet and Bree and Kinley. He'd watched them change. Flint had arrested Bree when she was fourteen, and now they were in love, and Bree was a successful real estate agent.

Change could happen.

And it made him feel differently about the world and all the people in it. It just did. It made him feel like things could never actually be all that hopeless. All that set in stone.

It did indeed make him feel that way.

And so, he wasn't going to turn away from this connection, not entirely.

"Yeah. All right. It's not like that. But I do feel protective of her. I care about her."

"You love her?"

That stopped him cold. The words made his heart quit beating.

"No. Not the way you mean."

He had hope, thanks to his time here. But if there was one thing he couldn't do, one thing he would never do, it was make one person the center of his world.

He didn't believe in love like that. Not anymore.

He believed in friendship.

He believed in good. He believed in doing good. He wasn't cynical. But when he was a kid, his entire world had revolved around his mother. Her moods, her whims. He would never, ever enter into that kind of situation again as long as he lived. And people could sneer and talk about how Freudian it all was, but it didn't matter. It was what it was. He had been held hostage by his mother's moods. He had been held hostage by her instability. And then she had removed herself from his life completely. And frankly, it had been the only thing worse than having her in his life. Going from being wrapped in all that she was, wholly and completely, to having nothing to do with her at all.

It had been like the whole center of the world had collapsed. It was dysfunctional—he knew that now. The kind of thing people spent a long time in therapy trying to talk through. He just spent time in the woods trying to talk to himself about it. Maybe that wasn't the best solution, but he didn't have the easiest time sharing that sort of thing with anyone else.

"You sure about that?"

"I am absolutely sure that I am content with the structure of my life," he said. Because at least that was honest. He was on the precipice of something with Clementine—he could feel that. And he knew that he needed to keep his guard up. He wanted her. And the fact was, she was going to find someone to sleep with, whether it was him or not. So he'd wanted to make it good. And safe.

Bullshit. You just wanted her.

Maybe that was true. But did it matter if the side effect was a little bit noble? That was his whole life, after all.

He felt a bit that he was a cliché. He was like someone who had lost a bunch of weight becoming a personal trainer. He had gone from being a delinquent to being a cop. Turning himself into the antithesis of what he'd been.

Was it necessarily because he was noble? Or because he wanted to not be in prison? Because he didn't know a better way to keep himself on the straight and narrow? The side effect was that he did noble things.

So too with the situation with Clementine, he supposed.

He had wanted her.

And part of him ached for something deeper. And that was the thing that concerned him.

That feeling he'd had when they'd gone on that welfare check…

"Don't hurt her," said Flint. "Or I will be forced to do what Bill would've done."

"Which is what?"

"Take you out back and shoot you like you're Old Yeller. If you're rabid, you gotta be put down, son."

"Oh, shut up."

"Just saying."

"We have to get back for the bonfire."

"Yeah. We do."

And he had never been more grateful for a conversation with his friend to come to an end.

Yeah. This was complicated. The truth was, his life would've been simpler if he'd moved up to a mountain and not had connections with anyone. But he had a weakness. A hunger. To have people in his life. And having people in his life had proved to be good for him.

It was having a person… That was what made things impossible. That was what made them difficult. That was what made him the bad guy.

He would never be that.

CHAPTER NINE

THEY DIDN'T HAVE long before the bonfire, and Clementine was vibrating with energy. She'd had a crash right after, and when she'd been driving her truck back to the camp, she had nearly collapsed into a weeping fit. But then she had rebounded. She had overcome. She had triumphed. And now she was just elated. With sexual energy. Sexual satisfaction. Maybe Violet was right. Maybe she was a sexual badass.

Well. She wouldn't go that far. That was a bit much. That was probably just not quite the truth. But still. She had done it. And, whatever happened next, she had done this. She'd made a choice. Not for anyone else, but for herself. And she had to stand by that. She was happy to stand by it, in fact. And when she burst into the soon-to-be Gale Lawson Art Hall, she was feeling intense with her own triumph.

And then, as she looked around the room and saw Violet, Bree and Kinley, she realized there was another triumph that she hadn't fully taken on board. She had friends to share this with. To help her sort through her feelings. She didn't have a father who would disapprove of her, or the silence of the forest, or a passel of older surrogate brothers who would disapprove. She had friends. Who had been through this before. Who understood about sex and emotions. Who didn't seem to think that being female about a man was a bad thing at all, but rather that it was simply the way of things. A part of them that they were accepting of.

"I…"

And then something Clementine did not expect to happen happened. She started to cry. Tears slid down her cheeks, and she felt…ridiculous. Weak. She was supposed to be a deputy. She was supposed to be tough. She was the no-nonsense one. The rule-following one, the one who always knew what she was doing, when and how. She was… not the same person she had been a few hours ago, and not the same person she'd been ten years ago.

She was soft. And maybe that was why she had friends now. Maybe that was why she'd been able to be with Duke. Maybe it was okay to be a little bit soft. Maybe without the softness, you could never let anybody in. Like ground that hadn't had rain in too long. How could a seed ever take hold, take root?

"Clementine!" It was Violet who swept across the room and put her arm around her. "What happened? Did Duke do something to you?"

Kinley's eyes narrowed. "Did Jackson? I love him, but if he hurt your feelings—"

"No, it wasn't Jackson. It isn't Duke. I mean, it *is* Duke. But it's not. But it's… Oh, hell. I had sex with him."

She had expected a shriek, much like the one that had accompanied her statement about how he had thought she had come to lose her virginity with him—and not her theft virginity. But they didn't shriek. Instead, they looked at her with round concern.

"Are you okay?"

"Yes, I'm okay. Why is everyone acting like sex is going to cause me physical harm?"

"You're crying," Bree pointed out.

"I'm just overwhelmed. I'm overwhelmed and… It was amazing. He's amazing. I don't know what to do with all these feelings, though. I don't know what to do about anything. I don't... I can't believe that happened. I can't believe that I have people to tell. I'm just kind of overwhelmed with gratitude."

"Clementine," said Bree. "What do you mean?"

"I have felt really alone for a lot of my life. You know, my mom didn't stick around, and my dad made it clear that it was him. But also that it was her. That there was some kind of weak feminine thing in her that just couldn't handle him. So I spent so much of my life trying to prove that I could. And also...just not be her. Because she didn't love me. She couldn't have, or she would've stayed."

It was Kinley who looked at her with very serious eyes. "If there's one thing I spent a long time learning, it's that you can't take any responsibility for the actions of other people. And you can't live in response to them either. You get to be you, Clementine. And I'm not saying that's easy, or something that's just magically going to happen, but that is the journey, and you are allowed to let go of these ideas. Of these narratives."

All Clementine could do was sit there and try to untangle the way that wrapped itself around her soul.

But it was time for the bonfire, so there wasn't much time to sit around and ponder the particulars. They all trooped out of the art hall, and into the big firepit area that had wooden benches in a massive ring around it.

At least Jackson hadn't made them sing camp songs yet, but she knew it was coming, because they only had a few days left before the campers arrived, and they would need to have the songs refreshed in their memory.

Though, Clementine felt that she probably remembered all of them perfectly anyway. You didn't have that many years of camp songs drilled into your head only to have them desert you.

You could never escape the speckled frogs.

Or bear hunts.

This bonfire night was mostly just a way for Jackson to tell them all what would be happening tomorrow, and prepare them for what would be expected in the upcoming days as the campers arrived. There was going to be a big ceremony, which was where Clementine planned on presenting Gale.

They roasted marshmallows and, eventually, Duke did start to sing. And there was something about it that made her heart leap in her chest.

His smile, the way the flames lit up his face. Acting like things hadn't changed between them in front of everybody was almost impossible. And maybe kind of silly. Was there any chance Duke hadn't gone and immediately told everybody about it? She had.

Though, he had acted concerned about Flint catching them in the office. But then, being caught getting up to no good was different from casually talking about it later. After all, all the girls knew.

But still, Duke hadn't come to sit next to her, and he didn't touch her. So, she didn't make any move to do the same to him. But she joined him in singing about the little speckled frogs, which grew louder and more raucous, and Jackson might even have joined in, though his lips barely moved.

"All right," he said to finish it up. "Bottom of Hollyhock Hill, 6:00 a.m. I'll see you all there."

And Clementine noticed Kinley looking after him with a dreamy expression on her face. And Clementine had to marvel at the power of love.

Something that she had excluded herself from for all these years.

No. She hadn't. It was just that she had, well, she'd loved Duke all this time, and she hadn't known what to do with it. Any thought she'd had about doing this to simply get over her feelings for him immediately seemed silly.

As Kinley had said, she didn't need to live in response to the things other people had done to her. And this need to protect herself, to shield herself from the reality of what was happening between the two of them... That had to do with her dad. It had to do with her mom.

While Clementine herself had always had intense feelings for Duke, and she was utterly clear on them. Absolutely and completely.

So maybe she just needed to figure that out. Accept it. Ground herself, and not because she was sorry about what had happened between them. She wasn't embarrassed. She wasn't anything but happy that she had finally shifted her relationship with Duke.

And watching him now only made her more certain of that.

After the bonfire, he made his way to her. "Come back to my place for a bit?"

"Yes," she said, her breath coming out in a rush.

"I do want to talk, Clementine."

"Okay."

The drive back to his place was only a couple of minutes, but it did feel long as they drove through the warm night, the windows rolled down and the fragrant breeze enveloping her.

She had been to his house countless times. Had been to visit and even stay over if the occasion called for it, but not like this. Everything was different right now. Everything.

They felt the same and different. Just like his house. And as she walked inside, it was the familiarity that overwhelmed her. The familiarity layered with a sense of anticipation.

How strange it was. To have known someone all this time, to find his face so familiar, to find the fluttery feelings inside of her so familiar, but to find his kiss so new. To have seen him without his clothes for the very first time, and to understand, really understand, the fullness of what she felt for him when their eyes clashed.

"Duke—"

"I just wanted to tell you that I care about you. A whole lot. But I need to make it very clear that this can't go anywhere. By which I mean, we can be like we are, Clementine. What happened today, and what we've always been—together. But it can't be more than that. It just can't be. I can't love you or marry you or have kids with you. Nobody knows better than the two of us how important it is that a person not make promises they can't keep. I will never do that to you. But I need to be real clear—this isn't nothing. It's not just sex. It's all the friendship we've ever had, all the need that I've ever had to care for you. You mean more to me than any woman I've ever been with. But I know my limits. I will never be my mother, and I will never be my father. And part of that is knowing to never get myself into one of those situations that I can't handle. To never leave someone who was counting on me in the lurch."

Clementine felt so stunned by the speech, like she'd been stabbed through the heart. After all, she had just accepted that she loved him. That she wanted everything with him, and that she wasn't going to allow her parental hang-ups to determine what she could have with him.

And she felt…skewered. Honest to God, like someone had taken her heart and prepared it for roasting.

Over that campfire. To the tune of "Five Little Speckled Frogs."

She wanted him all the same. But her feelings had changed on that score. Yet she didn't want to leave. And she had no idea if this was an okay compromise to make. Or if this was the kind of thing that led you down a path of misery. She wanted him. She wanted his love. She wanted forever. And while she had never thought much about having children, if she did, she wanted them to be his. And somewhere in all of that, she could hear Bree pragmatically asking her if the real problem was that she had been a virgin and she couldn't imagine herself with another man.

No. Bree wouldn't say that. Bree was pragmatic, but Bree would tell her to trust herself.

And Violet would tell her that she was gaslighting herself.

Kinley would suggest therapy again.

And maybe Kinley was right.

Right in that moment, Clementine had no idea what to do. But she knew what she wanted. And on some level, she was bound and determined to have what she wanted after so many years of simply not having it. The truth was, whether she left Duke now or later, it wouldn't hurt her any more. She would be devastated not to be with him. She would never be able to be okay with him hooking up with other women again. She would never be able to sit with him in their cruiser and just think of him as Duke. He would always be Duke Cody, her lover. The man who had shown her what real pleasure was.

But most of all, the man she loved.

If it was as simple as not feeling that, she would've quit feeling it ages ago.

The risk had been set in stone when she was seventeen years old.

The question now was how much honesty to give him.

And she decided that, while she could deny herself what she really wanted, let herself have him while accepting half of what she really desired, she couldn't cut herself open for him. She couldn't reveal herself, not like that. Not now.

Or maybe the real issue was she was afraid that if she did, he would leave, or make her leave, and she just couldn't handle that. Because she wanted him. Because she loved him. Maybe that wasn't wrong. Maybe she needed to stop worrying so much about whether or not any of this was right or wrong and just accept that she was in it. For good or for bad.

She was making a decision. And it didn't matter what anyone else thought. All that mattered was what she wanted.

"I'm in for whatever," she said. "I always have been. I care about you, Duke. And it's always been like this for me. It always has."

And then he closed the distance between them and wrapped his arms around her. He looked at her for a long moment. "Clementine, I...I can't say it's always been this way for me. Hell, it's a good thing. But it has been. For a little while. And I've been trying not to—"

"When?"

Suddenly, it mattered. Suddenly, if she couldn't have his love, if she couldn't have everything, she just wanted to know this.

"Remember that welfare check we did about four months ago? I just watched the way you handled yourself, the way you took care of that man. I've never seen anything quite so beautiful. I just recognized then that you might be more grown than I'll ever be."

As declarations went, it wasn't the softest, but it meant something to her. Hit her straight in the heart and made her feel like she mattered. Like the thing she did meant something.

And so she kissed him. Closed her eyes tight and kissed him with everything she had.

The way his big hands enveloped her made her feel so delicate and cherished and wonderful that she didn't fight against it.

She had wanted to be tough all her life, and right then, she accepted that she was. And she could be soft along with it, and one didn't take away from the other. She could be both at the same time. Or she could just be soft. Vulnerable with him because he would keep her safe.

That felt like the greatest gift she could have ever received. To know that she was safe with him. Utterly and completely safe. She had always been on guard. Against disappointment, because her dad had made her feel like she needed to be.

Because he'd been hurt in love, she realized. And he didn't want that for her.

It cast his actions in a different light. But one thing Clementine knew for sure: hurt was out there, and it was inevitable, no matter what you did.

She hoped to avoid it with Duke, but the fact was, his little speech had hurt her already.

But she was choosing love anyway. Choosing softness anyway. Choosing vulnerability anyway.

Or maybe she was just choosing pleasure. Again. She was okay with it. Because she was suddenly completely okay with herself. So she kissed him, and when he started to take her clothes off, she felt powerful. Not exposed. She felt resolved.

She stripped his clothes from him and admired him. Every inch.

Familiar and unfamiliar all at once. A man.

Her man.

She had never thought it would be possible. But here she was. With him.

Clementine McClain had gotten her man. Maybe not perfectly, maybe not every which way she wanted, but this would do for now. It would do. And she would enjoy it. The whole outrageous, dangerous journey.

Because she wanted it. Needed it.

He lifted her up off the ground and carried her into his bedroom. His football trophy was there, back on the shelf.

"You know, if there's an earthquake, that's going to fall and kill you," she said.

He looked at her like she had grown another head. "What?"

"If you leave it there, and we have a big earthquake, it's going to fall on your head."

"I'm not worried about an earthquake," he said. "But I am a little worried that we might create our own, and I'm not about to go out like that. So, good point."

"You've never thought of that before?"

"I've never brought a woman back here before."

And suddenly, that he didn't bring other women back to this room, back to this bed, felt significant and real and wonderful. She would've been accepting of sharing this mattress with the women who had come before, but how glorious that she didn't have to.

And the truth was, he'd brought *her* back here. And there was a particular kind of glory in that. Yes. Indeed there was. He lay with her on the mattress, having already put protection on, his body pressed against hers, bare chest to bare chest, as he kissed her deeper and deeper. She got lost in the sensual haze of their need.

When he took her, she was ready, and she wasn't, all at once. When he took her, she cried out in pleasure, and also just a little bit in fear. The fear of how much this made her feel. But there was no turning back. She wanted him. More than anyone. More than anything. She wanted him, and she had him, for now. And it would have to be enough. When it was over, he held her, and she burrowed underneath the covers and against him. And when she woke up, it was 6:05, and both she and Duke were late.

CHAPTER TEN

IT WAS A MAD scramble to get out of the house, with Duke cursing a blue streak the whole way, and Clementine looking up at him with big worried eyes.

"What's so bad? Besides the two of us being late."

"The two of us being outed like this."

"Oh. I thought that you would've told them already."

He looked at her. "No, I didn't. Because it's between the two of us. I didn't see the need to go bringing those yahoos into it."

"You were planning on keeping it a secret forever?"

He lifted a shoulder, but the truth was, he hadn't thought about it all. "Probably not."

"Except, a little bit?" she asked.

"Yeah. Maybe a little bit. Just until it was established, I guess. Plus, I needed to talk to you last night, and I needed to make sure you were all right with all that."

"Yeah. Well, I am." She looked out the window, and judging by the vague look on her face, she wasn't entirely okay with it. But what the hell was he supposed to do about it? What he'd said was true. He wanted to give her honesty; he didn't want to build up her hopes and dreams into thinking that they could be...

He shut that down. They pulled onto the camp property, and the two of them jogged to the bottom of Hollyhock Hill, where everyone was already gone.

Great. Jackson hadn't even stayed to scold them. That meant they were in really big trouble.

They took off up the hill, and he admired Clementine's determination, and her commitment to stoicism—she refused to huff and puff. And by the time they reached the top of the hill, everyone was looking at them.

"You're late," said Jackson.

"No shit," said Duke.

"*Both* of you are late."

"Yep," said Clementine.

"Care to offer up an explanation?" asked Jackson.

And then Clementine did something completely unexpected. She pulled the bullhorn out of Jackson's hand and put it up to her mouth.

"We were having sex," she said into the bullhorn.

And that successfully silenced Jackson Hart. When nothing before ever had.

"Damn," said Flint.

"Oh my," said Kinley.

Lincoln let out a low whistle. Bree and Violet exchanged glances.

"Well," said Duke, "I was going to sugarcoat it a *little* bit, but yeah."

"Latrine duty," said Jackson. *"You,* not her."

Fair enough, he supposed. Though, seriously, Jackson just had to be a dick. Like he wasn't breaking all manner of his own fraternization rules with Kinley every night of the week. But then, he had a feeling that Jackson's response to him had to do with the fact that he also felt protective of Clementine.

Well. He didn't need to be. Wasn't his place.

After they dispersed, with their assignments given, Jackson pulled him aside. "Campers are coming in three days. You can't be running afoul of the schedule."

"Is that your only issue?"

Jackson looked at him, completely deadpan. "Yep."

"I don't believe you."

"Sounds like a you problem."

"I think you're punishing me because it's Clementine."

Jackson held up the bullhorn. "I'm not having this conversation with you. Or any conversation. You have latrines to clean."

And clean he did, until Flint came in to hear him muttering and cursing at the toilets.

"You know, you could tell him no," said Flint.

He looked up at Flint. "Sure. I could. But I'm here. The fact of the matter is, I've agreed to be part of the Jackson Hart circus. And that means if he wants me to be a dancing monkey, I have to be a dancing monkey. He does have a point. Campers are going to be here in just a few days."

"So. You and Clementine?"

"Yeah."

"Huh."

"Need I remind you, *you and Bree*?"

Flint nodded. "Yeah."

"After all your protesting. Six years younger than you, the girl you arrested. You're the sheriff. And need I remind you, Flint Decker, that I am not the sheriff for a very specific reason. I never wanted to take on that whole thing."

"Sure. Also, you wouldn't be able to beat me in an election. But tell yourself that. Also, I get it. Believe me. I get failing to keep your hands off a woman in spite of all your good intentions. But now you've gone and made you and Clementine camp business because you weren't careful."

"I'll be careful."

"See that you are. See that you are."

And that made him feel like he had done the right thing in making sure Clementine knew exactly what she was getting into. Because if even Flint didn't think he could handle it, then it had to be true. Truth be told, Clementine needed someone who could give her everything. And Duke just wasn't that man. He never could be. But she knew it. And still, last night, she had stayed with him. So that had to mean something.

CHAPTER ELEVEN

CLEMENTINE WAS VIBRATING with excitement by the time they went to pick up Gale at the airport.

They had driven to Medford together—and had stopped for ice cream again—and when they went into the small terminal area, and saw Gale coming through the revolving door, it was like the years melted away. Because there she was, short, silver hair neat and in order as always, her cheeks rosy, a genuine smile on her face.

"There are some familiar faces," she said.

And Violet didn't hesitate. She moved forward and caught Gale up in a hug. "Missed you," she said.

"You too, honey," said Gale.

A second later, a woman with long, curly hair and four teenagers came through the doors.

"This is Candy. And the kids. Michael, Alessia, Julio and Tasha."

Pretty soon, Violet was hugging them too, and Bree had leaned forward to give Gale a shy hug.

Kinley seemed to bolster herself into giving one, and Clementine hung back.

"No hug for me, Clementine?"

"I wasn't really a camper…"

"You were very much a girl who needed someone."

And that made Clementine want to cry. Because she had been a girl who needed someone. Desperately. And Gale had done her best to give it to her. And she found herself moving forward and giving her a hug.

"I hope that there are lots of crafts to do," Gale said.

That earned a groan from her kids.

"What?" Clementine asked the groaning group.

"Gale makes us do Popsicle-stick crafts all the time," said Tasha.

"And you like it," said Gale, treating her daughter to a smile.

"I guess."

They walked out to the camper van, and the family loaded up their carry-ons and Kinley got back behind the wheel.

Everyone else took their positions in different rows. The car was filled up with happy chatter. Catching up, and so many other things. It was wonderful.

It felt like family.

It really did.

And maybe it wasn't a traditional family—not the kind of family that you dreamed about when you were a kid—but Gale was family to her. Kinley, Violet and Bree were family to her.

Duke was family to her. Just like Jackson, Lincoln and Flint. "I'm so glad that you get to stay for a while. The cabins are all done, and they're gorgeous now. You wouldn't believe the difference."

"I've never been to camp," Alessia said softly.

"Me either," said Julio.

"Well, you're gonna love this camp," said Bree. "It's for everyone."

That was the thing that mattered the most about Camp Phoenix. It really was for everyone. Anyone who needed a chance to rise again.

Clementine had to wonder if that was part of the problem. She hadn't realized that she also needed to rise.

She had thought she wasn't one of them. But she was. She might not have shoplifted or anything like that, but she was wounded. There were things in her life that hurt her.

That held her back.

And she was fixing it. She was moving forward.

The repair of the camp felt like a metaphor. Having Gale back felt even more profound.

She felt full. Blessedly so. Wonderfully, perfectly full.

She had Duke, in the capacity she had him, whether it was the perfect promise of a lifetime love she would prefer or not.

She had him.

She had all this, and it wasn't going away.

She repeated that mantra all the way back to the camp, and when they arrived, Kinley and Violet secreted Gale and family to a cabin where they brought them snacks and other amenities to keep them busy until the arrival ceremony tonight.

The four of them were bustling around camp, moving up and down the trails with bedding and other supplies, in anticipation of the campers' arrival.

"Jackson is driving a whole busload of kids out tonight. With his bullhorn," Kinley said. "The man is living his best life."

"In no small part because of you," said Clementine. "You really have made that man over."

"What about Duke?"

Clementine hesitated. "I love him. But that's not something he feels like he can do. I'm trying to decide what that means to me."

"In what way?"

"I want to be with him. So do I leave him simply because he doesn't want to get married? Because he doesn't want kids? Because he can't promise me forever? Who can promise forever?"

"Some people can," said Kinley. "Jackson…" Kinley was private about her feelings. But she looked Clementine in the face when she said the next bit. "Jackson promised me forever. And I know that means that man will fight. Tooth and nail. I know that means forever. Because he doesn't give up. He got injured in the DEA for a reason. He's a stubborn cuss. And the thing is, all these men are."

Bree made a knowing sound. "Flint Decker would never promise anything less than forever."

"Well," Violet said, "in fairness, it isn't as though there weren't hiccups along the way."

"Yeah, but I have to accept that I might not be as lucky as all of you," Clementine said, thinking that she was about to get it all out bravely, but her voice trembled at the end.

"Oh, Clementine," Violet said. "I don't love that for you."

"It's giving sadness," said Bree.

"It's not. It's giving realism," said Clementine. "If a man tells you who he is, you ought to listen."

"Yeah. But Duke Cody has spent a lot of years showing you who he is. And men are liars. So I would go with what he showed, rather than what he told," Violet said sagely.

"Men are liars," Kinley agreed. "But I see what you're doing. You're trying to protect yourself."

"Yes," said Clementine. "I am."

"In my experience, love doesn't work when you're trying to protect yourself."

"I'll keep that in mind."

"We have another surprise," said Bree, grinning broadly.

"You do?" Clementine asked.

Violet looked askance at Bree. "You do?"

"I do," Bree confirmed. "Kinley is complicit."

Kinley looked back and forth. "Yes. I am," she said finally.

"Great." Violet narrowed her eyes. "I don't like being surprised."

"Weird. Because you were certainly gung ho about Gale being a surprise."

"For the guys. I like surprises when I am in control of them. I need to be able to turn the dial on how intense the feeling is."

"Oh, Violet," said Bree, putting her arm around her. "Me too. Which is why I came up with a surprise before you could."

"You're an evil bitch, Bree."

"You too, Violet." But they grinned at each other, and Clementine understood. Really understood.

The feud was over. They were different. They all were. But they had only gotten there with each other by not being so self-protective.

So Kinley maybe had a point.

"Am I going to like the surprise?" Clementine asked.

"That all depends." Then Bree smiled. "That all depends."

CHAPTER TWELVE

WHEN THE CAMPERS filed into the chapel, Clementine felt a well of emotion rising up inside of her. It was happening. The camp was here. And the emotion in her chest felt like it was going to burst on through. "Dad," she whispered, "you would've loved this."

And right then and there, she felt herself simply let go. Of her resentment. Of her anger.

Because this was her father's legacy. That and so many good things that he had instilled in her. Because Duke was right. He did love her.

But not only that, he had loved so many of the kids who came through here. He'd loved Duke. And Clementine could love Duke because of her father's intervention in Duke's life.

It made her father's shortcomings feel small in comparison to all the good he'd done.

The kids settled in, sitting on benches, their attention rapt on the stage...

Well. Some of the kids had their attention rapt on the stage. There were quite a few older teenagers who were rolling their eyes. Who weren't sure about any of this. Clementine had seen it so many times before. She looked toward the back of the room and saw a beautiful, sulky teen with blond hair and short shorts leaning against the wall. She glared at another teen girl with a halo of black curls, who returned the glare.

And she knew that she was looking at Bree and Violet 2.0. Who knew what journey they would go on this summer? Maybe they would be best friends by the end of it. Or maybe it would take ten years. But they were here.

She saw a girl who reminded her of Kinley, small and nervous looking amid the other kids. And then her heart hit hard against her ribs when she saw a little girl with carrot-colored braids, a skinned knee and downcast eyes. She might've been looking at herself.

She wanted to go over and tell that girl that she would be okay.

And she realized, her heart cracking, that she was going to be able to. At some point this summer. Because now they were here, making this difference, carrying on what Bill McClain had started. All together.

And then Jackson came up onto the stage, megaphone in hand.

"Hello, campers," he said. "Welcome to Camp Phoenix. I run a tight ship. Understand. We rise every morning at six o'clock and we march up Hollyhock Hill. After that, the real fun begins. Lateness will not be tolerated. And neither will attitude." He paused for a moment. "I expect you to give me attitude. And you need to expect that I will not tolerate it."

He went on to explain the camp rules, teams and point scoring. He talked about how they would each have cabin and counselor assignments listed for them after dinner.

He was getting ready to dismiss them when Violet stormed the stage. "Sorry, Jackson. But we have a surprise. Someone who is coming to help run the art program this summer. An expert in many mediums, and a fantastic mentor. Gale Lawson."

For the first time, maybe ever—well, certainly since

Kinley had stolen his bullhorn and cane—Jackson looked shocked.

She could see the faces of the other men as they took in what was happening. Gale was here. She came up onstage, and they all rallied around her. And then the men were hugging her, and that was a sight.

"There's more," Bree said, snagging the bullhorn. "We have decided to dedicate the art center to you, Gale. The Gale Lawson Art Hall will be open now and for many summers to come. Because you had such an impact on us, using your gifts. Because you taught us how to be strong. Because you taught us how to be brave. And most of all, you taught us to do something constructive with our hands."

That made Gale cry, and Clementine's eyes felt a little watery too.

"And while I have the bullhorn," said Bree. "Kinley and I have a little surprise, which we hope will help introduce all of our core staff to the campers, and also to honor all the hard work everyone did this summer."

Kinley scampered up to the stage, holding a giant bag.

Clementine could only stare. "Since you're here, Jackson," said Bree, "I will have Kinley present you with your award."

"My award?" he asked.

"Yes," said Kinley, reaching into the bag and pulling out a trophy. "Jackson Hart, congratulations. You win the award for Most Improved. You started out the summer as a grumpy, insufferable tyrant. And now you're just a tyrant."

He took the award, and he looked a little like he'd been slapped with a fish.

"Our next award goes to..." Bree fished the award out and looked at the carved plate on the trophy. "Lincoln Traeger.

Most Likely to Chase Down Runaway Children and Bring Them to Justice."

Lincoln slunk forward and grabbed the trophy, grinning. "Surprised they could fit all that on a trophy."

"They couldn't," said Bree, "but we trust you'll know the truth in your heart. And for Violet," she continued, "you win the award for Best Enemy Turned Friend."

Violet laughed and reached out to take her trophy. "If I was giving out the trophies, I would have given this one to you."

Bree smiled. "Thank you." Bree went back to her task. "I also have one in here for Kinley," said Bree. "You are The Bravest One. You know why."

She handed the trophy to Kinley, whose eyes looked a little misty behind her glasses.

"And here's one for Flint Decker. *Sheriff Decker*," Bree said, her face getting soft when she said his name. "You win the award of Top Pick. Because I would choose you every time."

He grinned, lopsided. "I don't know how that works," he said. "You know, since this is supposed to be an award ceremony, so someone else should have been in the running."

"But I made up the award," said Bree. "So it doesn't have to be fair."

"I guess," he said.

"And for Duke," said Bree, pulling another trophy out of the bag, "you win the Loyalty Award for your tireless work in carrying on Bill's legacy."

Clementine watched Duke closely as he went to collect his trophy, and she could see—clearly—that there was a mix of strange emotion on his face. Emotion she couldn't read.

I don't love that for you.

Violet's voice echoed in her head.

What was she doing letting Duke call the shots like that? Declaring he couldn't do love and marriage? It didn't seem right or fair to either of them.

Kinley wouldn't accept it. Bree wouldn't accept it. Violet wouldn't.

"And we have one more left," said Bree. She took a flower crown out of the bag, and Clementine's heart went tight. "Clementine McClain. You win a very special award." Kinley reached into the bag and took out a trophy. "You win One of Us."

Clementine walked slowly up to the stage, where Bree literally put the crown on her head like it was a coronation. And absurdly, when she took hold of the trophy, she wanted to cry. One of them.

One of them.

Not on the outside anymore. Not in between. She was one of them.

Bree and Violet and Kinley would never settle, and they would have never let their men settle either.

And Clementine was one of them.

So why was she doing it?

Clementine had a flower crown, so why was she just… accepting this?

"We actually do have one more," said Kinley. "It's for you, Bree." And it was Kinley who turned to Jackson, still standing at the back of the stage, and took another trophy he'd been hiding from his hands. "You win Most Likely to Succeed (it's just no one knew it yet). But we all know it now."

And Bree looked teary as she took her trophy. It was a good trophy, but she had to wonder if it was just because Kinley had thought of her.

They had all thought of each other. And she felt a lot more emotional about all of it than she would've guessed.

"All right," Jackson said. "Time to head on over to the dining hall. We've got pizza on the menu tonight, but I warn you all—if I catch any of you kids with your elbows on the table, there will be consequences."

And Jackson headed off the stage, out of the chapel and toward the dining hall. He held the bullhorn to his arm and carried the trophy with his free hand.

Clementine could only watch, the flower crown perched on her head, as all the kids filtered out of the room.

She looked down at her trophy. It was one of those generic trophies, with a gold person who had their arms stretched up high, and big wings spread out behind them. *One of us.*

And it felt especially symbolic that it had been given with the glorious flower crown. She looked up and saw that Duke was standing there.

"Nice award."

"You too."

"That was a hell of a surprise. You getting Gale to come back."

"Well, it wasn't hard. She was happy about it. Happy to do it."

"And she's staying?"

"Yes. For at least half the summer. With her wife and kids."

"Can't wait to catch up with her."

"Yeah. That will be good."

And there, right then and there, this just felt like the right thing to do. Because she was one of them.

Gale's words came back to her now too.

You were a girl who needed someone.

She was; she had been.

She'd had a lot, but she hadn't had everything. She'd needed more, and that was okay. It was okay that even though her dad had loved her, she'd felt like she was missing something.

And it was okay now that she wanted more, wanted to be more than he'd raised her to be.

She was more. She had found the way to be the things she needed to be.

She had found friends.

She was one of them.

She wasn't on the outside looking in, and she wouldn't be in this either.

"Duke, I love you."

Because she was one of them. Because she was standing here with him. Because she cared about him. Because he needed to know.

And most of all, because she really felt like, suddenly, everything had come together. Like she was all together.

"Clementine…"

"No. Don't use my name in that tone. I love you. I have for a long time. I love you, and it is… Whatever mistakes my dad made, he helped you find your way. He brought you to me. And Bree, Violet and Kinley brought me to this moment. You too, obviously. But the way that they…the way that they were brave. The way that they have changed and grown and the way that they've accepted me. That's changed everything. I don't care about following the rules anymore. I don't care about being perfect. And you know what? Yeah. I heard you when you said that marriage and all that kind of thing wasn't in the cards for you. But I want it. Dammit, Duke, I want it. I want to be with you. I want for us to have everything." She felt tears brewing, and she didn't even care. "Say something."

be focused on [...]... I was so focused on trying
not to lose everything. Maybe I lost her anyway, and
didn't realize it," she said finally.

CHAPTER THIRTEEN

DUKE FELT LIKE he'd been stabbed through the heart. She
was asking, demanding, to hear the one thing that he was
the most afraid to say.

Love.

He cared about her. Hell, there was nobody he cared
about more. But what she wanted was the one thing he had
sworn he would never give. Had sworn he couldn't give.

It's because it was...

Because he couldn't put the pieces of himself back together again. Because what she didn't realize was that even
though her dad had helped him, his mom had broken him
sometime after.

It was why he worked so hard to connect with people.
A lot of people. So that it could never be *one* person con-
suming everything. Never again.

"I can't."

"You're afraid," she said. Not angry. Just a statement
of fact.

"Some things in this life are worth being afraid of, Clementine. Dammit... You have no idea. My mother was a nar-
cissist. My whole life revolved around keeping her happy,
even after this camp. Even after everything. And then she
just... One day, I told her I couldn't have her always bor-
rowing money from me. She couldn't come to my house
at 2:00 a.m. completely stoned out of her mind anymore.

For God's sake, I'm a cop. I can't have my mom showing up with a crack pipe in her coat. But to her, that meant that I didn't love her anymore. That I didn't care about her. To her, that was a rejection. Of everything. Everything she was. And I…I was relieved, in a way, to have her gone. But I also felt like a terrible son, bad cop. What good was I if I could reform strangers, and not her? I couldn't fix her."

"You know that wasn't your responsibility." Her voice was low. Shaking with conviction. "We see it all the time as cops. We can't make people change when they don't want to change."

"Yeah," he said. "And we also see, all the time as cops, the way the family can't cope with that. The way people enable. I did that for years. And, in the end, I couldn't handle it. I fell apart. Losing her made me fall apart. And I swore to myself that I would never let another person matter that much to me."

And she didn't look angry. She just looked at him like he was sad.

Was he sad?

"Duke… I… That's terrible. I don't know what to say. I understand why you feel that way. I do. But the thing is, I spent all these years wondering where I fit. And now I'm… One of them. One of all of you. Not because I changed, but because I embraced all the parts of myself. I quit holding back because I was scared. So I'm going to fight. However I can. Whatever shape that takes. I'm going to fight."

"Please don't," he said. "Because I promised I'd protect you."

"The only thing you're doing right now is protecting yourself."

And with that, Clementine walked away. And just left him there. And he didn't know what the hell had happened, because he felt like a big piece of himself had been ripped straight through his chest, like he was lying there, bleeding out.

But he hadn't given her permission to mean that much to him. He hadn't. It wasn't supposed to be possible. Not without his say-so.

And he realized what an idiot he was. Because of course he didn't get a say. Of course. Of course his heart was involved, whether he wanted it to be or not. Lincoln appeared, pausing in the doorway. "Hey, there's a little bit of a dustup with a couple of the boys. Jackson wants you to come wrangle."

"Sure."

He had to remember why he was here.

But he stopped, midway to the mess hall. Why was he here?

Not just at this camp. But why had he survived his whole shitty childhood just to get to this moment when he couldn't...? When he couldn't have what he wanted most? He suspected he would be ruminating on that for a long damn time.

CLEMENTINE SWIPED TEARS off her cheeks as she sat by the fire.

"Oh, Clementine," Violet said, approaching her. "What happened?"

"I'll tell you what happened," Kinley said, sounding feral, sitting on a bench beside Clementine. "Duke dumped her. Jackson overheard it."

Clementine just about fell off the log. "*Jackson* heard that?"

"He *dumped* you?" Bree said.

"*Dumped* feels too high school for what just happened.

I was in high school and nothing like this ever happened to me then. It was… It's deeper than that. More than that."

"I thought you were okay with him not being able to do the love thing," Bree said gently.

"Well. I change my mind. Because you all gave me this flower crown. And this trophy. And the fact of the matter is, I have to act like I'm worthy of them. I told him that I wanted to be a brave Clementine. Not a scared one."

"That makes you sound like a brave little orange," Bree pointed out.

"Yeah. That's actually exactly what he said. But the thing is, I was just talking about sex. I was just talking about physical things. That's… I mean, now that I've had sex, I can confidently say that, while it is amazing, it's not the scariest thing out there. It's this. The love stuff. But I'm one of you. And one of you would never take less. He would never take half."

"No," said Violet. "But we all spent a lot of years taking just that. We aren't exactly the poster children for perfect, well-adjusted lives. We weren't."

"No. But the fact that you all are now gives me hope. Because all I can hope is that he comes to his senses. That's why I told him. I didn't think that he would want me. Want this. Not yet. But I'm hoping that he'll get there. That's what I hope."

"I hope you're right too," said Bree, sitting on the other side of her. "Because I would hate to have to kill him."

"We'd be in competition for that job," said Violet.

"I'll gut him first," added Kinley, her tone vicious. "He'd never know what hit him."

Her money was on Kinley.

"Well, don't kill him. Because I would like to… I'd like to see if there's any possibility that it could work out."

"Fair enough. He's got forty-eight hours." The fire reflected off Kinley's glasses and made her look slightly menacing.

Clementine laughed, but inside, she thought she wasn't going to last forty-eight hours. So, he really needed to have a revelation, and fast.

"THE FUCK."

And that was how Duke found himself getting slapped on the back of the head by Flint, in a move that was not a boss move, but a pissed-off friend move. "You *dumped* her?"

Duke edged away from Flint. "It wasn't really a dumping."

"You fucking tool," said Flint.

"Dick," said Lincoln.

Jackson just grunted.

"Listen, I am not… I'm…I'm freaking out, okay? I don't want to do this. I really don't want to do it with her. Because she is… She's everything. She's everything and I just about died when she walked away from me. How the hell could I ever survive losing her?"

"You lost her," Jackson said, looking incredulous.

"He has a point. You already did lose her," Flint said.

"It's different. It's…"

"No, idiot," said Lincoln. "You are lying to yourself. You think that you can get out ahead of the heartbreak. That somehow you're not already wrapped all the way around her. But I assure you, dumbass, you are entwined. There is no getting away from that woman without losing half yourself. Don't you think that if it was that easy to walk away from love, we all would've just done it? Of course we would have. But we had to dig deep and fucking change. And that sucks. No one would do it if they didn't have to."

"I don't know how to change. I don't know how to not… walk around with all this weighing on me. I don't know how to be normal."

"None of this is normal," said Flint. "We just do our best. Look at Bill. He wasn't normal. He gave Clementine a passel of issues. But that didn't mean he wasn't a good man. We're not going to be perfect. Our relationships aren't going to be perfect. But you know full well Clementine isn't your mother. You're just scared. And there's only one thing a man can do when he's scared, Duke."

He thought of Bill McClain, looking at him. Those steely eyes staring straight into his soul. *Bravery is being scared and saddling up anyway.*

And he knew that they had all heard the same quote in the same voice, right at that same time.

"Saddle up," said Lincoln.

"I…"

"Yes?" Jackson asked.

"I love her. I love her. It's the, well, all the everything else I don't know what to do with."

"That's just it, idiot. You just love her."

"I do know how to do that."

Except…he could see her. At seventeen. Looking at him from across the other end of the fishing boat. He could see her. Taking care of that old man at the welfare check. He could see her, lying in his bed, naked and perfect. He could see her looking up at him in wonder as he sank inside of her.

He could see her. Loving him. All that time. And what terrified him the most was the deep need that rose up in him. The thing he'd been trying to deny. It was easy for him to offer to take care of her. What he was afraid of was asking for her to take care of him. Because no one ever really had. Not his whole life. He wanted something that maybe he couldn't have.

But she'd said she loved him.

He'd never loved anyone before.

But he did now. He really did. And it was worth whatever risk was out there.

"I guess there's only one thing to do," he said slowly. "I've got to go lose my virginity."

CLEMENTINE WAS SLEEPING—well, she wasn't sleeping, but she was curled up on the bottom bunk when they all heard the sound of a pebble hit the window.

Violet shrieked dramatically, jostling the fairy lights around her bed.

Kinley snorted and seemed to simply sink deeper into her sleeping bag. Bree hopped out of bed and was in some sort of fighting pose. Clementine just lay there and stared at the bottom of the top bunk. They had all stayed with her tonight. Sisters before misters, they had said.

Then a rock hit the window again.

"I swear to God," Bree said. "That's that raccoon…"

"I don't think raccoons have fashioned tools to try and signal the occupants of our cabin, Bree," said Violet.

Kinley snorted softly.

Another rock hit the window, and Clementine got up. "I'll check."

"Thank you," said Bree and Violet at the same time.

"You're the cop," said Violet. "It seems sporting that you be the one to check out the odd noise."

"I've got it."

She went to the door of the cabin, opened it and saw him standing there. "I need to talk to you," he said.

"Oh."

And then Bree, Violet and Kinley—still in her sleeping bag—appeared behind her.

"She doesn't have permission to break curfew," Violet said icily.

"It's okay," said Clementine, her heart warming over their display of protectiveness. "I'll talk to him."

She went outside. The night was cold, and she was wearing flannel pajama bottoms that did little to block the chill. "What do you want, Duke?"

"I came to lose my virginity."

It was so shocking, she nearly choked. "What?"

"My *love* virginity. I love you, Clementine. And I think the moment that I fell in love with you was four months ago. I watched you take care of that man, and I thought, *I want that*. Because you know what? I was headed toward a life of being him. Alone. In a house all by myself. I don't want that. I want you. I want you to wrap a blanket around me and give me some tea. I mean, not necessarily literally, but I want that. And it was easy for me to take care of you. But it's the hardest damn thing in the world to admit that I want some softness. That I want you there for me. That I want you to love me."

"Duke," she said, her heart pounding so hard she thought it was going to claw its way out of her chest. "I already do."

"Really?"

"I told you I did. I meant it. I get why you're scared. Life has given us a million reasons to be scared of this. But life also brought us together. And, in the end…we have to trust in something, right? So why don't we trust in that?"

He couldn't argue. She loved that he couldn't argue.

"Okay," he said, his voice rough. "I trust you. I trust this. I trust us. I love you, and I want everything. Everything I've never had. I want my world to revolve around you. It's a risk I want to take. Because when you walked out of that chapel, I asked myself what the hell the point of life was if you weren't there with me. If I made it all this way, and then stumbled right when it mattered the most, what else matters?"

"Duke," she said, stepping forward and wrapping her arms around his neck, kissing him. He put his hand down on her rear, and she moaned.

"Damn raccoons," Violet shouted from inside the cabin.

"Oh. Well. We have an audience."

"Let's go back to my place. Where we won't have an audience."

She took his hand and let him lead her down the path. Toward his place. Toward their future.

And suddenly, her whole heart lifted. It was just the beginning of the summer. This was just the beginning. Of this year. Of their life.

And suddenly, she got goose bumps all over her arm. "We did it," she said.

"We did what?"

"It took us all this time, but we really did rise from the ashes. Brand-new."

They just stood there for a second in the dark, letting that wash over them.

"Well, hell," he said. "So we did. It's amazing what love can do for you."

She smiled and looked up at the full moon and the stars. "Yeah," she said. "It really is."

EPILOGUE

THE UNOFFICIAL DEDICATION to the new Camp Phoenix happened late the second night. The kids had been run ragged all day, and it was clear factions were forming. Some friendships were developing, some rivalries. As they always had, through the years, every camp cycle, every different group of kids.

People were like seasons. Even in all their beauty and differences, they were the same.

Bree, Flint, Violet, Lincoln, Kinley, Jackson, Duke and Clementine filed into the chapel at 11:00 p.m., exhausted from the day, their arms around their significant others as they entered the hushed space.

"Here we all are, Bill," Jackson said. "Because of you."

"And all these kids are here too," said Lincoln. "Because you decided to make a place where we could come and imagine a new life for ourselves."

"And what a life," said Flint, pulling Bree close.

"You changed us, and every other kid that came through this place," said Duke. "You gave us a chance."

"We have an award for you," said Clementine, a tear glittering on her cheek.

She held a trophy out and set it on the stage. "Camp Dad. If you hadn't been a father to all of us, we wouldn't be here."

And it didn't matter that he hadn't been perfect.

He had shown up.

When many others had given up, he had tried.

There might have been mistakes along the way, but all of those could be covered by love. By the fact he had treated every kid who he'd encountered like someone with a future. Which made the past matter not quite so much.

It was the ethos of Camp Phoenix, after all.

There might be ashes, but you could always rise.

"Thanks, Bill," said Jackson.

It was Kinley who began to sing. "Five little speckled frogs…"

Everyone else joined in. "Sitting on a speckled log."

As hymns went, it was a strange one. But in this chapel, in this moment, it was perfect.

When it was through, they all might have been a bit misty-eyed, even though some of them would never admit it.

As they turned to leave, they shut the lights off, but by some mistake or miracle, one stayed on. And shone bright down on the trophy.

The eight of them went back to their respective cabins, not as couples since they were in charge of minding the children now—though they found their ways to make time together.

Because, in the end, that was the lesson of camp. Love always found a way.

A beacon that shone through the darkness.

Or maybe just a single light that shone down on a trophy in a chapel in the woods.

The love one man had poured into the place, spilled over and made more, never ending.

Love had brought them here. And love would lead them on.

* * * * *